THE LOST SOUL

When a mysterious fire kills her adoptive parents, Madeleine's most dreaded fear comes true – she and her beloved brother Oliver are separated. Worse still, Maddie is suspected of starting the fire, and she is sent to a children's home. Far from idyllic, she is subjected to a harsh regime of abuse and degradation. Maddie makes a brave attempt to escape. But her brief weeks of freedom soon end when she is caught and taken back to River House. Maddie clings to her determination one day to be reunited with Oli, giving her strength to endure what lies ahead.

THE LOST SOUL

THE LOST SOUL

by

Rosie Goodwin

Magna Large Print Books
Long Preston, North Yorkshire,
BD23 4ND, England.

British Library Cataloguing in Publication Data.

Goodwin, Rosie
    The lost soul.

    A catalogue record of this book is
    available from the British Library

    ISBN   978-0-7505-3488-8

First published in Great Britain in 2010 by
Headline Publishing Group

Copyright © 2010 Rosemarie Yates

Cover illustration © Ilona Wellmann by arrangement with
Arcangel Images

Published in Large Print 2011 by arrangement with
Headline Publishing Group Ltd.

Magna Large Print is an imprint of Library Magna Books Ltd.

Printed and bound in Great Britain by
T.J. (International) Ltd., Cornwall, PL28 8RW

To the staff at Golden Sands with all my love.

To the staff in Cardiac Radiology with all my love

Prologue

'Come away – you'll get burned.' The girl snatched her younger brother away from the blazing chip pan.

The child stared up at her blankly as she hauled him across the kitchen floor away from the fire. They were right next to the back door, but she saw at a glance that the key was not in the lock. There would be no escape that way, and the flames were now travelling along the worktops, dangerously close to the door leading into the hallway, which was the only exit left open to them.

Panic made her feel faint but she knew that she must stay calm. Perhaps one of the neighbours would spot the fire through the window and call the fire brigade.

'Oliver, listen to me.' She shook him urgently to drag his attention away from the flames. 'We have to get into the hall and make for the front door. Try not to look at the fire, just hold my hand and come with me.'

She began to move forward but the child dug his heels in, too frightened to move. It was then that the hungry flames snatched at a pile of clean tea towels, and before she could blink, the curtains flared up and thick black smoke began to fill the kitchen. Oliver started to cough as Madeleine tightened her grip on his hand. He was only nine years old but he was a sturdy little chap for his age and she knew that if he fought her she would have no chance of getting him out of there. They would both be killed; burned to a crisp by the flames or asphyxiated by the smoke. It wasn't much of a choice.

'*Please,* Olly! Do as I say.' She deliberately kept her voice calm so as not to panic him further, but she too began to cough now as she watched the smart wooden doors of the kitchen units fall prey to the hungry fire.

'Get down onto the floor. We'll be out of the smoke that way,' she urged, and crying softly, he dropped to his knees. 'That's it ... now follow me, there's a good lad.'

Side by side, the children crawled across the floor as the cut-glass goblets in the fancy display cupboard cracked like gunshots in the heat. Inch by inch they went, with Madeleine encouraging her little brother all the way. They had almost reached the door when the pile of blazing tea towels toppled onto the floor, and instantly the door they were heading for began to smoke.

'*Damn and blast!*' Tears of frustration stung at Madeleine's eyes. They had literally seconds left to get out of there now before the whole place went up and that way out was blocked off too. With every ounce of strength she possessed, she yanked Oliver along behind her, stumbling to her feet as she reached the door. The handle was red hot and she felt the skin on her hand scorch as she grasped it.

But she didn't stop to think or feel – she just tugged at it, crying with relief when it opened. The cold air entering the room seemed to incense the flames behind her, for suddenly there was a loud explosion as the gas oven blew up.

The force of it flung them forward, and she saw that Oliver's nose was bleeding. He must have banged it when he fell on the parquet floor. Now the flames seemed to be chasing them and within seconds, the carpet that ran the length of the hallway was alight as she tried to lift him. He was sobbing so hard that he was incoherent, but she closed her ears to the sound as she focused on the front door ahead of them. She felt the heat behind them singe the hairs on the back of her legs and pushed her brother ahead of her.

When they reached the front door she cried out in frustration, as she saw that the key was missing from that lock too. In the time it took her to feel along the windowsill where she knew her mother kept the key, the flames were licking greedily at the hall curtains on either side of her. Oliver was clinging to her tightly, his body racked by sobs. He was partially sighted and she could only begin to imagine how terrified he must be. But there was no time for sympathy. That would come when she had got them both out of the house to safety.

At last her fingers closed around the key and she nearly sobbed with relief as she tried to fit it into the lock with shaking fingers. And then the door was open and she shoved Oliver out into the cold night air. They collapsed onto the immaculate lawn in front of the large detached house and watched in horrified fascination as the flames took hold of the staircase.

There was another loud explosion from the kitchen and Madeleine saw the lights in the next-door houses click on. Within seconds the neighbours had spewed out of their homes to join them, knuckling the sleep from their eyes.

'Good Lord above!' Mrs Wickett from next door exclaimed as she tightened the belt on her dressing-gown. 'Whatever has happened? Where are your parents – and have you phoned the fire brigade?'

'Th ... there was no time,' Madeleine stuttered as she held her brother's trembling frame close to her.

The woman turned and addressing her husband, who had come to stand beside her, she cried, 'Richard, go and phone for the fire brigade immediately.'

The man turned without a word and hurried away to do as he was told.

Lights were snapping on in the houses up and down the street now, and soon a small crowd had assembled on the grass.

Windows were blowing out in the heat and the whole place was ablaze. It had been such a beautiful house – now with the smoke belching from every opening it was almost unrecognisable. As the spectators stood there in silence, a face suddenly appeared at the front bedroom window. It was Michelle, the children's adoptive mother. She began to bang on the glass as people looked on in horrified fascination and just for a moment her petrified eyes fastened on Madeleine. The room behind her was alight with flames and they watched her struggling with the window catch, but then suddenly she disappeared from sight as the sound of sirens screamed on the cold night air.

Minutes later, the fire engine ground to a halt on the road and firemen were rushing everywhere. Madeleine and Oliver were hustled off the lawn and within minutes a fire hose was trained at the heart of the blaze. But even so, everyone there knew it was useless. The place was like an inferno. There was no way anyone was going to come out of there alive.

'Who's in there?' a fireman asked, and before Madeleine could answer, Mrs Wickett told him, 'The children's parents, God help them.'

Mrs Wickett had her arm tight about Madeleine's shoulder now and was softly crying. Madeleine supposed that she should be crying too, but she was too numb with shock for now to feel anything. Another fireman had placed a ladder against the bedroom window where the woman had briefly appeared minutes earlier, but it was soon apparent that there would be no chance of him getting into the bedroom. The window had cracked and the flames that licked through it were forcing him back.

And so they all stood and watched helplessly as the house slowly burned to a shell.

Chapter One

September 1990

'Madeleine, are you feeling well enough to speak to me?' The policewoman spoke softly as she addressed the girl in the hospital bed.

Maddy, as she preferred to be known, stared back at her without replying. She had been in Derriford Hospital in Plymouth for two days now and had barely uttered a word to anyone, apart from to ask after her brother, who was in the next ward.

She had escaped the fire remarkably well, considering the ferocity of the flames. Apart from burns to her hands and the back of her legs and smoke inhalation, she was unmarked.

The second police officer glanced at his colleague and now she tried again.

'Madeleine ... Maddy, I know this can't be easy for you, but we have to try and get to the bottom of this. It seems that the fire was caused by a chip pan bursting into flames. It was almost midnight, love. What on earth were you doing in the kitchen at that time of night?'

Maddy chewed on her lip for a moment and then muttered, 'I was going to make my brother Oliver some chips.'

Again the two police officers exchanged a bemused glance. 'But wasn't it rather late to be thinking of cooking?'

Maddy shrugged her slight shoulders and clamped her mouth shut, but minutes later she suddenly asked, 'What about Mum and Dad? Are they OK?'

This was the part that the policewoman had been dreading, and she gulped deep in her throat before saying gently, 'I'm afraid the firemen couldn't get them out in time.'

'They're both dead then?'

'Yes, dear. I'm afraid they are.' The woman had expected the child to break down but she just lay there, her face as white as the sheets, staring straight ahead. The girl didn't seem to be showing any distress whatsoever, but then the young officer supposed that she might be in shock.

'Look, perhaps it might be best if I gave you a little time to come to terms with what's happened, love,' she said tactfully, as she rose from her seat. 'I'll come and see you again tomorrow, Maddy.'

The girl barely noticed as they left the room, and raised a heavily bandaged hand to stroke away a tear. What was going to happen to her and Oliver now, she wondered. Only minutes later, her question was answered when the door opened once again and a young fair-haired woman in a smart grey trouser suit appeared with a folder beneath her arm.

'Hello, Maddy.' She flashed the girl a friendly smile as she drew the chair up to the bed and sat down. 'I'm Sue Maddox, and I was the social worker who took you to your new mum and dad when they adopted you and Oliver five years ago. I did visit you a few times after that, but I doubt you would remember it. I'm so sorry to hear about what's happened. How are you bearing up?'

Maddy sniffed, and without answering the question she asked bluntly, 'What's going to happen to me and Oliver now?'

'Well, to be honest, no one is quite sure yet,' Sue answered truthfully as she flicked a lock of hair across her shoulder. 'Later today, your adoptive grandparents are coming in to visit you and we shall be approaching them to see if they might be able to take on guardianship of you.'

'Huh! There's fat chance of *that* happening,' Maddy retorted scornfully. 'Neither of them ever liked me. They didn't think I was good enough for their precious daughter.'

'Oh, I'm sure that isn't true.' Sue's face was sad as she looked at the sullen child in front of her. She could still remember the day that she had taken Maddy and her brother to live with the Donovans and the terrible tantrum Maddy had thrown.

As the girl gazed out of the window, Sue watched her closely. She certainly didn't behave like a child who had just been told that her parents were dead.

At twelve years old Maddy was quite small for her age. She was slight of build, totally opposite to her brother who was quite tall and sturdy. Oliver had been just four years old when he was placed, and had few memories of his birth family. His birth father had left them when Oliver was just a baby and from then on his mother had sunk into a depression, which had resulted in her turning into an alcoholic. Numerous one-night

18

stands had resulted in two more children, but as the Social Services Department had tried to help her, things had gone from bad to worse until they had been forced to take all four siblings into care. She wondered how the other two children were faring. Molly and Ryan would be six and seven years old now and had been placed with two other adoptive families in different parts of the country. Until the day the Department had taken them away, Maddy had been like a little mother to her siblings and Sue knew that she must still miss them dreadfully. She was very protective of Oliver and seemed more concerned about him right now than the fact that her new parents had died in the fire.

She sighed. Maddy was bordering on being plain, and it was only her wonderful big brown eyes and her shock of thick wavy brunette hair that saved her from being so. Sue imagined that she could actually be attractive, if she smiled more. Her thoughts were stopped from going any further when a large lady accompanied by a tall gentleman entered the room. The woman's eyes were red-rimmed from weeping, and as she approached the bed she stabbed a finger towards Maddy.

'I *knew* our Michelle should never have taken you on,' she said accusingly, her beautifully modulated voice belying the cruel words.

Sue realised that this must be Michelle's mother, the adoptive grandmother. The woman was shaking and Sue's spirits sank into her shoes. If her greeting was anything to go by, there would be little chance of her taking on the care of the children.

Rising from her seat, Sue faced the woman, who ignored her as if she didn't exist. Her focus was firmly fixed on the child lying in the bed.

'I hope you'll be able to live with yourself,' the woman spat. 'You've killed my daughter and my son-in-law – and after all they've done for you too!'

'Now please,' Sue tried to intervene. 'I suggest you calm down. What happened was obviously nothing more than a terrible accident.'

'And what do *you* know about it?' The woman rounded on her. 'You haven't seen the way she treated the poor souls. She's never had a decent word for them since the day they took her in out of the kindness of their hearts. She was nothing but trouble to them from the very beginning!' She was openly sobbing now, and the man at her side was trying to ease her out of the room.

'Come on, love,' he said softly. 'There's nothing to be gained by this. Let's go.'

After glaring at Maddy for one last time she then followed him from the room, with Sue in hot pursuit.

In the corridor she blew her nose noisily on a handkerchief that her husband kindly provided her with and Sue remained silent, giving her time to compose herself. She was a large, well-built woman, immaculately dressed in a smart navy-blue suit, with tightly curled blonde hair that looked as if it wouldn't budge even in a gale. Her husband had kind eyes, which Sue saw were full of pain. The couple had just lost their only daughter, so she was prepared to make allowances for the woman's outburst. After all, it couldn't be easy for her.

After a few minutes, Sue dared to say, 'I'm so sorry for your loss. What's happened is absolutely dreadful.'

The woman eyed her warily. 'And just who might you be?' she asked.

'I was the children's social worker and I handled the adoption when they came to live with Michelle and Peter.'

'Oh.' The woman scowled before bursting into a fresh torrent of tears.

Her husband looked at Sue apologetically. 'I'm afraid this is a very difficult time for us.'

'Of course, I do understand – but actually I was hoping to speak to you both.'

'Then let's go into the day room,' he suggested. 'I spotted it as we came in, further down the ward.' He took his wife's elbow and Sue followed them to a small room full of easy chairs with a television set in the corner.

Once they were all seated she began tentatively, 'The reason I wished to speak to you was about the children's future. Obviously they have no one now, and in circumstances like this the Department always tries to place them with the extended family whenever possible.'

The woman seemed to swell to double her size as she stared at Sue indignantly. 'You can't be asking if *we* would be prepared to have them, surely?'

Sue felt her cheeks flame. 'Er ... that's exactly what I was going to ask you, actually, Mrs Green. The alternative is that the children will have to go back into care.'

21

'Then so be it!' The woman faced Sue squarely. 'I don't care if I never set eyes on either of those two again. You can have *no* idea how difficult they have been – well, Madeleine at least. And what's more – I don't believe that the fire started accidentally. I think that nasty girl started it deliberately – and I shall be telling the police a thing or two, you can be sure of it!'

'Very well. I apologise for asking, but you must understand I had to.'

The woman stamped past her and after flashing Sue a timid smile her husband followed, closing the door quietly behind him.

Sagging down onto the nearest seat, Sue sighed. Well, that went down about as well as a lead balloon, she thought. It seemed that the only option for the children now was for them to go back into care, and that would mean yet another major upheaval in their young lives – but what alternative was there?

She knew that she should go back in to Maddy but she just couldn't face it. I'll come back tomorrow, she promised herself, and quietly slipped away to tackle the teetering pile of paperwork that was waiting for her on her desk back at the office.

Chapter Two

'When can I see my brother?' Maddy asked for at least the tenth time the next morning. The nurse who had just changed the bandages on her hands kept her eyes averted as she replied, 'Sister will tell you when he's well enough to have visitors.'

Maddy's heart sank. Whenever she asked to see Oliver, the reply was always the same and now she was seriously worried. Perhaps he was desperately ill? Or perhaps the burns he had sustained were worse than she had thought. It was obvious that something was wrong, otherwise they would have let her see him.

She watched quietly as the nurse collected the soiled dressings and left the room, then swinging her legs to the edge of the bed she slipped off it and padded to the door. She had been put in a small room next to the nurses' desk, but one glance into the corridor assured her that all the nurses were busy down at the other end of the ward. Barefooted, she tugged the hospital gown they had supplied her with more tightly about her and stepped out into the corridor, then with her heart thudding she set off towards the doors at a trot.

Once through them, she stood and looked about as she tried to get her bearings. They had told her that Oliver was in the next ward and she went in that direction, hoping that no one would intercept her. On the way she got a few curious glances, but thankfully no one challenged her and soon she was at the next set of double swing doors. Peeping through the glass in the top half, she waited until a nurse carrying a bedpan stepped into a sluice room and then she hastily slipped through them. She began to move along as quickly as she could, glancing into each room as she went. She prayed that Oliver wasn't in the main ward and her prayers were answered when she passed the third door and spotted him inside. The room was colourful, with Disney characters painted on the wall behind his bed. Oliver didn't even look round when she closed the door and she hurried across to him.

He was lying very still with his eyes staring sightlessly up at the ceiling above him.

'Olly,' she hissed, as she took his hand. 'It's me, Maddy. Can you hear me?'

When he showed no sign of having heard her, she began to cry softly. What was wrong with him? He seemed to be locked in a world of his own. She had just opened her mouth to speak to him again when a nurse suddenly entered.

'Who are you?' Her eyes raked up and down Maddy's slight figure as she took in her dishevelled appearance and the hospital gown she was wearing, and then she suddenly smiled. 'You must be Madeleine, Oliver's sister,' she said. 'I was told you were in the next ward. But what are you doing here, dear? Did somebody bring you to see your brother?'

Madeleine glared at her defiantly. 'No, they didn't. They wouldn't, so I came on me own.'

'Oh, I see.' For a moment the nurse seemed lost for words but then she pulled a chair closer to the bed and told Maddy kindly, 'Well, now that you are here, you may as well sit down, pet. I'll just go and let the ward next door know where you are, so that they don't worry about you, and then I'll be back.' She swung about without another word, and the instant she had left the room, Maddy turned her attention back to the figure on the bed.

'Oliver, what's wrong?' she whispered as tears clogged in her throat, but once again he showed no signs of having heard her or of even being aware that she was there. By the time the nurse returned, Maddy was really crying.

'Why won't he answer me?' she asked with a catch in her voice.

'I'm afraid your brother has been like this since he was brought in.' The nurse saw no reason to lie. 'Oliver is in deep shock.'

'And how long will he be like this?'

The nurse shook her head. 'It's hard to say, to be honest. Physically there isn't a lot wrong with him, but his mind has shut down. Hopefully when he comes out of it he'll be fine.'

Maddy dragged her eyes away from the girl to stare down at Oliver again, and at that moment another nurse pushing a wheelchair joined them. Maddy recognised her as a nurse from the ward she was in.

'Here you are,' she said with a smile. 'We were just about to get a search-party out for you. What are you doing wandering about like this?'

'You wouldn't bring me to see me brother. I was

25

worried about him so I decided to find him on me own,' she muttered.

Sympathy flared in the woman's eyes. 'Well, you have seen him now, so how about I get you back to your own bed, eh? I'm sure you'll be allowed to visit him again very soon.'

It was on the tip of Maddy's tongue to refuse to leave, but knowing she was beaten she slowly crossed the room and dropped into the wheelchair. At least she knew exactly where Oliver was now, and if the nurse didn't keep her promise she would come and see him on her own again.

As the nurse steered the wheelchair back into her own room, the girl saw that the police officers who had visited her the day before had turned up again. She sighed resignedly. She was feeling strangely tired and would have liked to rest, but she supposed that now that they were here, she might as well listen to them. She didn't really have much choice in the matter.

'Hello, Madeleine,' PC Roberts smiled stiffly as the nurse helped her back into bed and straightened the blankets. 'I think we ought to have that talk now, don't you?'

There was something about the way she spoke that made Maddy flinch inwardly; the friendly note that had been in her voice the day before had gone.

'There are a few things about the fire that don't quite add up,' the woman went on, 'and we need to discuss them.'

'Such as what?' Maddy shot back before she could stop herself.

'Such as the fact that you chose a very strange

26

time to start cooking supper for your brother.'

Maddy clamped her lips together and fixed her eyes on a point above the woman's head.

The silence seemed to stretch on and on, until the woman said quite unexpectedly, 'From what we've been hearing, you never really got on with your adopted mum, did you?'

Maddy gulped but remained quiet.

'We've spoken to the teachers at your school and they told us that your mother was repeatedly being called in because of your bad behaviour. Is that true, Maddy?' Without waiting for an answer, the officer plunged on, 'We've also spoken to your adoptive grandparents and your neighbours, and they all told us much the same – that you and your mum were constantly arguing. They said you even got violent with her on occasions. Did you hate her, Maddy?'

'Yes, I *did!*' Maddy said hotly. 'She never wanted a daughter, she just wanted someone to clean and fetch and carry for her. The only one either of them cared about was Oliver. They never wanted *me.*'

The two police officers exchanged a meaningful glance and now the policeman took out a notebook and hastily began to scribble in it.

'Maddy, did you set light to the kitchen deliberately?' he said. The question was such a shock that colour flooded into the girl's cheeks and her mouth gaped open.

'I ... I ...' She suddenly became silent again. There didn't seem any point in saying anything and she didn't much care what happened to herself now anyway, so let them think what they liked.

'I think you *did* set light to the kitchen on purpose,' the officer went on. 'You wanted to get back at your mum, didn't you? Are you glad that she and your dad are dead?'

'Yes!' Maddy looked towards the window, her face expressionless, and now the policewoman rose from her seat and looked down at her.

'We shall be back she said quietly, and then she turned and left the room with her colleague.

Once she was alone, a silent tear slid down Maddy's pale cheek. She knew that she should be feeling sad about the fact that her adoptive parents were dead, but what she had told the policewoman was true: all she could feel was relief. Michelle Donovan had been a bully. Oh, in public she had always appeared to be a doting mother, but in the privacy of her home it had been a different act altogether. From the second Maddy got home from school each day until she dropped exhausted into bed each night, Michelle had worked her into the ground. At just eight years old, Maddy had been able to clean and cook as well as a grown woman, but she knew that she could have put up with that if she had received just one kind word – but all her new mum had ever shown her was scorn. 'We took you from the gutter,' she would tell the girl scornfully, and, 'You should be grateful for all we do for you.'

Well, Maddy wasn't grateful, and she realised with a little shock that she really *was* glad that her adoptive parents were dead. No matter where she and Oliver were placed now, no way could it be as bad as living with the Donovans. Turning onto her side, she burrowed beneath the blanket and

28

sobbed broken-heartedly.

Later that night, when the ward was in semi-darkness, she once again sneaked out of bed. At the bottom of the ward she could see a nurse bent over some paperwork at a desk, working by the light of a lamp. Keeping to the shadows, she crept towards the double doors and silently slipped through them. A quick glance either way assured her that the hospital was deserted, and so once more she made her way to the next ward. She just wanted to check that Oliver was all right before she settled down to rest.

His room was in darkness. Tiptoeing in, she flicked on the lamp at the side of the bed and gasped when she saw that it was empty. The bed was freshly made up, and there was no sign that he had ever been there.

Her heart began to hammer in her chest. Running back into the corridor with her dressing gown flapping loosely about her, she looked for a sign of a nurse, and when she saw one she raced down the long ward towards her.

The nurse caught her arm and said, 'Please don't run. What is the matter?'

'My brother – Oliver Donovan – where is he?' Maddy said hoarsely, and all around them, patients began to stir in their beds.

'Come with me.' The nurse guided her into a small dimly lit office and demanded, 'Now, who are you? And what are you doing here?'

Tears were streaking down Maddy's cheeks now as panic gripped her, and she waved a trembling finger in the general direction of the room that Oliver had occupied.

'M ... my brother was in one of those side wards earlier today. Where is he now?'

'Ah.' As the nurse suddenly realised who the girl was, the harsh expression slipped from her face and she looked at Maddy sympathetically. 'Your brother has been transferred to another hospital.'

'But why?' Maddy's lip quivered.

The nurse strummed her fingers on the edge of the desk as she thought how best to explain. 'Well, the thing is, Oliver was in deep shock, as you'll know if you saw him this morning. There was nothing really physically wrong with him, so the specialist decided to send him to another hospital that deals with patients who are suffering from trauma.'

'What ... you mean like a mental hospital?' Maddy asked fearfully, remembering back to the awful place her real mum had ended up in.

'Oh, no, no, nowhere like that,' the nurse assured her. She had a daughter who would be about Maddy's age and her heart was aching for the girl. If the rumours that were circulating the hospital were true, the poor kid had just lost her mum and dad in a fire and now she was terrified because her brother had disappeared too. Why the hell hadn't someone explained to her about where Oliver had gone, she wondered, and cursed softly under her breath. No wonder the poor girl was so distraught. That little lad was probably all she had left now.

'Look, why don't you sit down and I'll make you a nice cup of tea, eh?' The nurse knew that she should really be getting Maddy back to her

30

own ward before the staff there missed her. But the girl looked sadly in need of a bit of tender loving care – she was going to supply it, and sod the consequences. The girl looked, in fact, as if the bottom had dropped out of her world. Gently pressing her onto a hard-backed chair, she made her way to the ward kitchen to put the kettle on.

When she returned only minutes later, Maddy was gone. The nurse frowned as she placed the cup and saucer on the desk, wondering what she should do next. It was as she was standing there that someone in the ward rang their bell. The lass had probably gone back to her own ward, she assured herself and, straightening her apron, she hurried away to see what the patient wanted.

Chapter Three

Outside the hospital, Maddy wandered along the deserted streets. A bitterly cold wind whipped the cotton gown about her thin legs and her bare feet soon turned blue, but she didn't feel anything. She had no idea at all where she was. She had lived some way away from the hospital and so everywhere was unfamiliar to her. She didn't much care. The way she saw it, now that Oliver was gone she had nothing left to live for. She had already lost her two younger siblings when she came to live with the Donovans and now she had lost Oliver too.

Up ahead, a broken bottle on the pavement

glistened in the light but she walked straight across it, cutting her foot in the process. She winced with pain. Now she was leaving a trail of blood in her wake but even that didn't slow her steps and she limped on, blinded by tears. A slow drizzle quickly turned into a downpour, and soon her gown was clinging wetly to her and her hair was plastered to her head.

Eventually she came to a crossroads where a sign pointed towards the city centre. It was seven miles away – an awfully long walk. But then, where else did she have to go? She had no home now and the city centre seemed as good a place as any to head for. Occasionally, cars drove past her and each time she heard one coming she quickly moved into the shadows of the buildings until they had gone. After a time her footsteps slowed as a wave of fatigue washed over her. She had the urge to just lie down and sleep but was too afraid to, so she carried on, forcing one foot in front of the other with her head bent against the pouring rain.

After a while she became aware of a very old man on a bicycle splashing towards her through the puddles in the road. She blinked in surprise, wondering what he might be doing out so late at night. Most of the houses she passed were in darkness and she guessed that it must be very late indeed now.

When the man drew abreast of her he stopped and gazed at her through the rain. She too stopped and they eyed each other warily. He was dressed in an old mac that had clearly seen better days, and a cap was pulled down low over his eyes.

'So what's a little 'un like you doin' out all alone at this time o' night then, eh?' he asked.

Maddy glared at him. 'That's none of your business,' she informed him imperiously.

He chuckled, a throaty sound that echoed along the quiet street. 'Run away from home, 'ave you?'

'No, I have *not*,' Maddy retorted, and began to limp on. He rode slowly along at the side of her, taking in her bare feet and the strange gown she was wearing. 'Got anywhere to sleep?' he asked now, and despite her misgivings, Maddy halted again and slowly shook her head.

'Hm!' He climbed off his bike and to her surprise, he then peeled off his coat and draped it around her shoulders. 'It'll keep a bit o' the rain off,' he told her, then climbing back onto the bike he pointed towards the crossbar. 'Get on 'ere,' he ordered. 'Yer can kip at my place tonight if you've a mind to. It ain't posh, but it'll be better than bein' out in this.'

Maddy hesitated. She had always been warned never to go off with strangers, but what alternative was there? She supposed anywhere out of the rain was better than nowhere. Eventually she approached him and after hoisting her up to sit side-saddle on the crossbar, he placed his arms either side of her, gripped the bike handles and wobbled off. Maddy could feel her head sinking forward with tiredness. They seemed to go for a very long way but eventually he drew the bike to a halt outside a small terraced house.

'This is it,' he told her, as he helped her down. Crossing to the front door, he quickly unlocked it before pushing his bike inside. Maddy timidly followed him. Seconds later, he clicked a switch and the room was illuminated by a bare light bulb that swung from a cracked ceiling. She looked around in amazement. The room was so cluttered there was barely a square foot of floor showing. Old newspapers and magazines were piled everywhere, along with all manner of other things. He leaned his bike up against the wall, oblivious to the water running off it all across the bare wooden floorboards. Then, nodding towards a door, he set off in that direction and she reluctantly followed him, wondering if it had been such a good idea to come here after all.

She found herself in yet another room almost as cluttered as the one she had just walked through, but at least there were odd pieces of mismatched furniture in this one and a low fire was burning in the grate. The kitchen next door to it was absolutely filthy, with every single surface covered in dirty pots and pans. There was a musty smell in the air and she wrinkled her nose in distaste.

'Help yerself to anythin' yer fancy,' he told her, peeling his wet cap off and tossing it onto a pile of dirty pots. He then turned about and headed for a door that she guessed must lead upstairs, as if he had already forgotten that she was even there.

'Er ... excuse me. Where shall I sleep?' Maddy asked nervously.

Pausing to look back at her, he cocked his thumb towards the ceiling. 'Straight along the landin', second door on the right. G'night.'

'Good night.' Maddy watched him disappear

before looking around bemused. Her adoptive mum had always wanted everything just so, and Maddy wondered what Michelle Donovan would have thought if she could have seen this place. She would probably have had a fit. Still, the girl consoled herself, even if it wasn't very clean at least it was dry in here, and up to now the old man had appeared to be quite harmless. She briefly considered trying to find the things to make herself a cup of tea, but soon decided against it. All she wanted to do right now was sleep, but first she knew she should deal with her injured foot, which was throbbing painfully. When she crouched down and examined it, she could see a sliver of glass in the wound. Gritting her teeth, she pulled it out, making the wound bleed even more profusely. As she looked around, she saw an old tea towel thrown haphazardly onto the worktop and she hastily bandaged her foot with it. The cloth was little more than a rag and she dreaded to think of the germs that must be on it, but she wasn't in a position to be fussy and at least it should stem the bleeding.

When she was certain that she could do no more, she approached the door leading to the upstairs and paused to listen. Everywhere was as silent as the grave so she limped up the stairs, being careful to make as little noise as possible. At the end of the long landing was the bathroom, which she soon discovered was just as filthy as the kitchen.

After drying herself off as best she could on the cleanest towel she could find, Maddy approached the room the old man had told her to use, dreading what she might find. She opened the door, and after fumbling along the wall, found a light switch and snapped it on. What she saw made her gasp with surprise. She was looking at a very pretty, clean little room. The mahogany furniture was dated, as were the flowered curtains and the matching bedspread, but even so she was thrilled. No one would ever have believed that they could find such a room in this house; it was a total contrast to the rest of the place. Sighing with relief, she approached the wardrobe. Perhaps there would be something in there that she could borrow to sleep in. She was shivering with cold now and the hospital gown was still clinging to her.

After opening the door she was again surprised to find herself confronted with a number of girls' clothes all neatly hung on wooden coat hangers. Once again they were very out-of-date, but at least they were clean and dry. Next she tried the chest-of-drawers and came upon a small pile of fresh clean nightdresses. Taking one out, she saw that it was made of broderie-anglaise. It was ankle-length and came right up to her neck with long sleeves that ended in filled cuffs, but even so it was a welcome change from the garment she was wearing.

Dry again, she padded back to the door, and was relieved when she saw that there was a lock on it. After turning the key she clambered into the bed, shivering as the starched white sheets settled over her. It was remarkably comfortable, although she was sure she was far too nervous to sleep. That was her last thought as exhaustion claimed her.

She woke late the next morning to the sound of someone shuffling about in the kitchen down below. She yawned and stretched, then panicked as the events of the night came back to her. Where was she? She hopped down out of bed onto the pretty flowered carpet and crossed quietly to the window, where she peeped out into the street below. The row of terraced houses opposite looked much the same as one another. They all opened directly onto the pavement and only the colours of the front doors and the curtains hanging at the windows distinguished one from another. Now, turning back to the room she had slept in, she studied it more closely. The main colour scheme was pink so she assumed that at some time it had been the old man's daughter's room, but where was she now? And why were all her clothes still hanging in the wardrobe? It seemed very strange.

She opened the door and glanced cautiously up and down the landing. The smell of frying bacon wafted up to her and tempted her from the room as her stomach growled in anticipation. In no time at all she was back downstairs, where she saw the old man standing at an ancient gas stove expertly flicking bacon in an enormous blackened frying pan.

She saw now that he was even older than she had first taken him for, and wondered what could have made him go out riding the streets so late at night and in the blistering rain. His hair was snow-white and in desperate need of a good cut, and grey whiskers sprouted from his chin. He

37

was painfully thin and his back was hunched, making him appear even smaller than he actually was. His dirty clothes hung loosely off him, and even from the open doorway she could smell the ripe scent of him. She wondered how long it had been since he had last had a bath or a shave. His hands were gnarled and his face had so many wrinkles that one seemed to run into another.

Sensing her presence, he looked towards her as if it was the most natural thing in the world that she should be there.

'Grab yerself a plate an' get some o' this down yer,' he invited, and now Maddy's eyes flew around the room as she tried to spot a clean plate. Eventually she gave up and taking a dirty one from the sink she hastily washed it as best she could beneath the tap before handing it to him. He flipped some bacon on to it, along with a couple of slices of fried bread, and after thanking him she carried it back into the middle room and devoured the meal in seconds. Minutes later he joined her, handing her a mug of tea, and she waited for him to start asking questions. She had discovered that grown-ups were good at that, but instead he stared into the low-burning fire in the grate, apparently perfectly content to do without conversation.

'Er, thanks for letting me stay last night,' she ventured.

Glancing towards her, he shrugged. 'Stay as long as yer like,' he muttered, and then resumed staring into the fire.

She sat quietly for a time, reluctant to disturb him, before asking hesitantly, 'I was wondering, would you mind very much if I borrowed some of the clothes out of the wardrobe in the room I slept in?'

'Help yerself,' he told her through a mouthful of bacon. 'Just so long as they're washed an' ironed an' put back fer when my Gwenny comes 'ome.'

'Who is Gwenny?' Maddy dared to ask but he ignored her, and so after a time she carried her plate into the kitchen and went back upstairs.

As she rifled through the clothes in the wardrobe she found that they were even more old-fashioned than she had first thought, but seeing as she had nothing to wear apart from the hospital gown she had arrived in, she supposed that they would be better than nothing. She chose a tartan kilt that fastened at the side with a large safety pin and then found a green roll-neck jumper in one of the drawers to go with it. There were various items of underwear in the drawers which were at least two sizes too large for her, but it was good to be warm again, and her foot wasn't hurting so much this morning either. On the dressing-table was a silver-backed hairbrush, and after brushing her hair, Maddy felt slightly better. She straightened her bed and made her way back downstairs again, only to discover that the old man had disappeared. It was then that she realised she hadn't even thought to ask his name. His bicycle was missing from the front room and now she stood, hand on hips, surveying the chaos that surrounded her.

Deciding that it would do her good to keep busy, she began to collect armfuls of old newspapers and carried them through to the kitchen where she deposited them in a pile by the back door. She couldn't take them outside as the door was locked. This operation took her at least an hour, and by the time they had all been removed, she could finally see the floor again – although the room was far from being really tidy.

Next she gathered up the dirty cups and plates that were strewn here and there, and they too soon disappeared into the kitchen. Three large fat cats watched her impassively as she worked, miaowing with disgust when she had cause to disturb them. Within an hour the room was cleared, revealing the ill-matched furniture that had been buried beneath the rubbish.

As she drew aside the curtains, which had been tightly closed, thick dust flew into the air, making her cough. The windows behind them were so grimy that she could barely see through them, so she went into the kitchen and after finding a bowl, she filled it with warm soapy water and set to cleaning them.

The next job was the floor. She searched high and low for a mop but when she couldn't find one, she got down on her hands and knees and scrubbed every inch of it with a rag. Next she dusted the mantelpiece and finally she stood back to survey her handiwork. The room was still a long way from being presentable, but at least it was much better than before.

Deciding that she deserved a break, Maddy went into the kitchen then, and after rummaging about in the cupboards, found some tea and sugar. There was only a drop of milk in the bottle in the ancient refrigerator so she washed a mug and drank the tea without it. It was as she was standing there that she heard a key in the front door and seconds later the old man reappeared with a large carrier bag dangling from the handle-bars of his bicycle. After propping it against the wall he scratched his head in bewilderment as he looked around the room, but he said nothing as he carried the bag through to the kitchen and dumped it on the draining board.

He gave Maddy no more than a cursory glance before throwing his old mac over the back of a chair and sinking into it, burying his head in a newspaper.

'Would you like a cup of tea?' she asked nervously.

'Argh, if yer like,' he grunted. 'There's some milk in that bag I just brought in.'

She rushed away to put the kettle on again. It was when she carried the drink through to him that he stabbed his finger at a piece in the paper. 'Is this you?' he asked, as he peered at her more closely. 'It says 'ere that a twelve-year-old girl left Derriford Hospital last night an' the police are lookin' for her.'

Maddy gulped, but decided to tell him the truth. There didn't seem to be any point in lying. 'Yes, it is,' she admitted, then: 'Are you going to tell them that I'm here?'

He shrugged his shoulders. 'Well, seems to me if yer ran away yer had good cause to, an' it ain't no business o' mine. They're sayin' as you're suspected of startin' a fire in your home an' that you managed to get your younger brother out o' there. Did yer?'

'Did I what?' Maddy demanded. 'Start the fire

41

or get my brother out?'

When she was not forthcoming with any more information, he sniffed and didn't pursue it and she sighed with relief. Then after a few moments she dared to ask, 'What's your name?'

'Why do yer want to know that?'

'Well, if I'm going to be staying here for a while I have to call you something, don't I? My name is Maddy, but then you already know that if you've just read about me in the paper.'

For a moment she thought that he wasn't going to answer her, but then he muttered, 'You can call me Whizzer, everybody else does.' He then ignored her as he slurped at his tea and suddenly feeling in the way, Maddy slipped into the kitchen and began to fill the bowl with hot water. If she was going to be staying here for the time being, which it appeared she was, it would be nice to have some clean pots and pans to use.

Sighing, she began on the mountains of washing up, wondering where Oliver was right now and if he was all right.

Chapter Four

Maddy had now been staying with old Whizzer for over a week, and during that time she had become accustomed to his eccentric ways. He came and went on his bicycle as he pleased, sometimes disappearing for hours. When he was in the house he ignored her for most of the time as if she

42

wasn't there, but that suited Maddy. She had needed a quiet place to lick her wounds, and Whizzer had provided it for her without asking for a single thing in return.

During the time she had stayed there she had worked tirelessly, seeing it as a way of repaying him for his kindness, and now the house was almost unrecognisable from when she had first arrived – not that Whizzer ever commented on the fact. She knew that he could see the difference in the place by the way his eyes flickered over it, but he never offered any praise, nor did she expect any. She was actually glad to scrub and clean; it gave her less time to worry about Oliver and what might be happening to him.

Since Whizzer had brought her there she had not ventured from the house. She knew from the local newspapers that he brought home each day that the police were still looking for her, and was terrified about what would happen should they find her. PC Roberts had made it more than clear that she believed Maddy had set the fire deliberately, and the girl wondered if she would be sent to prison. It was a daunting thought. Even so, she knew that she couldn't stay here for ever. At some stage she would have to go and find out what had become of Olly. There would be no peace until she knew where he was. But she decided that could wait until the fuss had died down a little.

Each day, Whizzer would return home with a carrier bag full of shopping and Maddy would cook him a meal. He would eat it without a word, and then she would clear away the dirty pots while he settled down to read his paper.

This evening looked set to be no different, until he suddenly glanced up and said quietly, 'It says here that your parents are to be buried tomorrow.'

'Oh!' Maddy stopped in her tracks on the way to the kitchen as shock coursed through her. She had tried not to think about Peter and Michelle Donovan, but now she was forced to. *Buried.* It seemed so final – although she still couldn't pretend that she really missed them, especially Michelle. Peter she had hardly known, as he'd been out at work most of the time, and under Michelle's thumb, the rest.

'Were you wantin' to go to their funerals?' Whizzer asked.

She hastily shook her head.

'Fair enough.' Whizzer turned away again as Maddy moved on to the kitchen. There she leaned heavily on the edge of the old porcelain sink as her thoughts ran riot. Up until now she had been lucky, but the police were bound to find her eventually – and then what would become of her? If they locked her away, who would look out for Oliver? They had no one but each other now.

Her thoughts went back in time to when she had been a part of a *real* family. Her dad had loved them then, and things had only started to go wrong after he left. Heartbroken, their mother had slipped further and further into a world that was ruled by alcohol and one-night affairs. As the eldest, Maddy had done her best for the younger siblings who had been conceived after her own father Tom had gone. Molly and Ryan had never even had the privilege of knowing who their fathers were. And then had come the day when she arrived home from school to find two social workers waiting for her. They told her that the youngest two had already been taken into care and now she and Oliver would be joining them, with the same foster-carers. When Maddy asked where Anna Barnes their mother was, she was told that she had gone to a special sort of hospital where she could get the help she needed.

In fairness, the carers that the children had lived with had been kind, but Maddy was not prepared to trust anyone and had not formed any kind of a relationship with them, no matter what they tried to do for her. There had been numerous court appearances to discuss the children's futures, which Sue Maddox told her about but the girl was never allowed to attend. She just waited for the day when her mum would come home to them all. But she never had, and eventually Molly and Ryan were taken in by two separate families and she and Oliver were adopted by the Donovans. From that day on she had never been happy until...

Stopping her thoughts from going any further, Maddy slowly washed and dried the pots and then after a mumbled good night to Whizzer she climbed the stairs to her room feeling utterly depressed. She was just twelve years old and yet she felt as if she had the weight of the world on her young shoulders. She couldn't ever remember a time since her father had left them when she had felt safe and loved. Since his departure, everything seemed to have gone downhill at the speed of a rollercoaster. For a long time she had hoped that he would come home, but now all she felt for him was hatred. To her mind he was the cause of the family being torn apart and she hoped that she would never have to set eyes on him again.

Her throat clogged with tears as she thought again of her true mother and her siblings. They would be growing up now, just as she and Oliver were, but one day, she vowed to herself, she would find them again. *All of them.* Now the tears began to fall. Was her mother still in the awful home they had sent her to after her breakdown, when drink got the better of her? Maddy could still remember Sue Maddox taking her to see her mum there. The mental hospital on the outskirts of the town had been a dark, forbidding place, and Maddy had thought even then at the tender age of seven that no sane person who went there would remain so for long.

She and her three siblings had stayed with their foster-carers for a time after that, until the day that Sue had come and taken Molly and Ryan away. Molly would be six now and Ryan would be seven. Time was slipping by. All Maddy knew was that Molly had gone to live in Nuneaton in the Midlands where they originated from, and Ryan was somewhere in Birmingham.

Sighing, she crossed to the chest-of-drawers that she had been tidying that morning. Beneath the underwear that was stored there she had come across three photo albums and now she started to look through them as she tried to take her mind off her predicament.

The first one she opened was full of photos of a family consisting of a mother and father and a baby girl. They all looked very happy and as Maddy stared at them she realised with a little shock that the man in the pictures was a much younger Whizzer. This must be his wife and daughter. She flicked through the pages, wondering where they were now.

The second album contained pictures of a toddler, happy and giggling in most of them. The third and final album made Maddy shudder as she saw a young girl, possibly just a little older than she herself was now, wearing the kilt and jumper that she had borrowed from the wardrobe. The book was only half-full – and after that there was nothing. The pictures just stopped abruptly. Maddy frowned as she placed the albums back where she had found them. Perhaps the girl in the picture was the Gwenny that Whizzer had referred to? But where was she now?

Deciding it was really none of her business, she lay down on the bed. Just before she drifted off to sleep she heard Whizzer slam the front door as he left the house. Used to his nocturnal bicycle rides by now, she yawned and thought nothing of it.

The next day began much as all the others. She woke to the smell of bacon frying and hurried down to join Whizzer for breakfast. It was the only meal he ever cooked and she wondered how he had managed before she went to stay there. The cats were also eating, all in a line on the kitchen floor. She stifled a smile. Some of her hygiene habits must be rubbing off on him, after all, since he had used to feed them amongst the rubbish that had littered the worktops – but she wisely didn't make any comment.

After breakfast, Whizzer disappeared off on his bicycle and Maddy tried to think of something to do to occupy herself. I know, she thought, I'll tackle some of the dirty washing. There were piles of it in the bathroom and she guessed that Whizzer hadn't done any for ages.

She briefly thought of asking Whizzer for some money and to point her in the direction of the nearest launderette, but her fear of being found by the police quashed that idea almost immediately. Instead she began to fill the bath with hot water. Underneath the sink she found a packet of washing powder that had obviously been there for a long time, and after adding a liberal amount to the water she shoved a pile of clothes in to soak and began the unenviable job of washing them all by hand. An hour later the first lot were rinsed but now she wondered how she was going to dry them. Through the bathroom window she could see a clothes-line strung the length of the yard Whizzer shared with his neighbour so she heaved the heavy washing into a basket and carted it downstairs. She had found the back-door key some days ago whilst cleaning the kitchen and now she placed the basket down while she un-locked it. Luckily it was a cold breezy day so she hoped she might be able to dry the things if she hung them out to blow.

She stepped cautiously out into the yard, keeping a wary eye on the neighbour's back door, hoping that no one would see her. But she had pegged no more than a few dripping items onto the line when the door opened and a plump middle-aged woman appeared.

'Oh, hello.' She smiled pleasantly. 'I thought Whizzer must have someone staying with him again. I haven't seen his windows look so clean for years. Why don't you let me put those through my spin-dryer for you, love? They'll take forever to dry like that.'

'It's all right, thank you,' Maddy told her self-consciously, wondering what the woman had meant when she had said Whizzer had someone staying with him 'again'.

The woman wasn't going to take no for an answer. 'Don't be so silly, it won't take no more than a minute or two,' she insisted. 'Come on, give them here. We'll have a cup of tea while they're spinning. And I'm Mrs Pike, by the way.' And so saying she crossed the yard, grabbed the washing basket and disappeared back into her kitchen as Maddy stood there nervously wringing her hands. Seconds later, the woman's head popped out of the door again. 'Well, come on then,' she urged. 'Don't stand there like the cat's got your tongue. The kettle's on, so come and have a break with me.'

Feeling that she didn't have much choice, Maddy reluctantly crossed the yard and entered the woman's house. Her kitchen was a world apart from Whizzer's, boasting every labour-saving device that was on the market from what Maddy could see of it. It was also scrupulously clean and comfortable.

'Sit yourself down there, love.' The woman

waved towards a chair and Maddy perched on the edge of it, feeling more uncomfortable by the second. Why couldn't this Mrs Pike have just left her alone and minded her own business? She saw that she had already put the clothes in a spin-dryer that stood next to the sink, and the machine was shaking as if it had the ague as water poured out of a pipe that was attached to it before gurgling away down the sink.

'There, get that down you. I reckon you've earned it if you've done all that lot by hand.' As Mrs Pike pressed a china mug into Maddy's hand, the girl summoned up a weak smile.

'So...' The neighbour, who was dressed in trousers and a smart blue blouse, plonked down into a chair at the side of her, patting her short brown curly hair into place. Maddy thought that she must be quite old – forty at least.

'How long did you say you'd been staying with Whizzer then?'

'Er ... about a week or so now,' Maddy muttered ungraciously.

'Really? And how do you know him then?' There was a Bruce Springsteen record blaring out of the radio on a small table and that, combined with the sound of the spin-dryer, which was now dancing as if in time to the music, meant Maddy could barely hear her.

'I... Whizzer is my uncle,' she lied, saying the first thing that sprang to mind.

'*Really?* Well, blow me! I didn't even know Whizzer had any relatives left, poor soul. Losing his wife and then Gwenny so soon after one another was awful, wasn't it? But then you wouldn't have been born then.' She shook her head as her mind drifted back into the past. 'It was a tragic time for him,' she confided. 'His wife died suddenly. Massive heart-attack, by all accounts, and then poor Gwenny was found dead in a back alley down by the docks only months later. She'd been raped and stabbed to death. She was only fourteen. I thought it would kill the poor bloke at the time. Him and his missus had lived for that girl. But his way o' dealing with it was to pretend it had never happened. He still thinks she's going to come home. If you were to ask me, I'd have to say your uncle's gone a bit doolally since then.' She tapped her head with her forefinger and became silent for a minute as she observed Maddy over the rim of her mug. Then, leaning slightly forward in her chair, she said, 'So you're his niece, are you? Funny he never mentioned one before. But then Whizzer is off with the fairies half the time now. And the lodgers he takes in ... huh! He's like a home for waifs and strays, he is. He's had everybody, from single young mums-to-be, to drug addicts, staying there since Gwenny died. I've warned him, "One of 'em will do for you one of these days", but will he listen? Will he hell as like. Not that it's any o' my business who he has in his house, o' course. But then you'd know all that, if you're his niece.'

'I ... er ... actually didn't get told much about him at all,' Maddy muttered guiltily.

The woman raised her eyebrows. The girl was a surly little thing and she couldn't really say that she'd taken to her. Anyone might have thought that Manda Pike was doing her a disservice by

51

spinning her clothes, rather than a favour.

Much to Maddy's relief the woman then placed her mug down and hurried over to the spin-dryer. After opening the lid she loaded everything back into the basket again and Maddy quickly drained her mug and went to take it off her.

'Thanks,' she mumbled, as she headed towards the back door. It was as if she couldn't get away quickly enough.

'Aw, won't you stay for another? An' perhaps I could tempt you to a biscuit?'

Maddy shook her head as she sidled past her. 'No, thank you. I really ought to get on.'

As the girl made a quick escape, Manda Pike bit on her lip. She was an ungrateful little madam from what she could see of her, and seemed to have a right chip on her shoulder. The girl's face seemed familiar too – but for the life of her, Manda couldn't think where she had seen her before. It'll come to me, she told herself, and collecting the dirty mugs up she went about her business. One thing was for sure, she wouldn't be offering to help *her* again.

Once the clothes were all pegged securely on the line, Maddy shot back to the sanctuary of Whizzer's kitchen, heaving a huge sigh of relief. It hadn't been such a good idea to venture out into the yard, after all, but at least no harm had been done. The woman had seemed to swallow the lie about her being Whizzer's niece. She decided she'd wait until it was dark before she hung the rest of the clothes out. That way there would be less chance of her being waylaid.

Now that she was alone again she began to

ponder on what Mrs Pike had told her. Poor Whizzer, losing his family like that. No wonder he was so quiet. She decided she would make him an extra-special meal that night as a way of showing her appreciation for all he had done for her, and with that thought in mind she began to scrabble about in the fridge, which was now scrupulously clean and shiny, to see what food was available.

Next door, Mrs Pike hummed along to the Michael Jackson song on Radio One as she squirted a liberal amount of polish onto her dining table. Her mind was working overtime. If Maddy really was Whizzer's niece, she had waited an awfully long time to crawl out of the woodwork; and wasn't it a rather funny time for a girl her age to be visiting? It wasn't half-term, was it? She didn't look any older than twelve or thirteen at most; shouldn't she have been at school? And come to think of it, she was dressed very oddly, too.

A picture of the girl's face flashed in front of her eyes and she frowned. She was sure she had seen her somewhere, and recently – but where the hell was it? Once the table was gleaming she glanced at the clock on the wall. Colin would be home for his lunch soon so she ought to get a shufty on. Her husband was a great one for routine and liked his food to be on the table ready with his newspaper when he stepped through the door.

It was as she was laying the paper at the side of his cutlery that her eyes were drawn to the headlines, and sinking onto the seat she began to read of the poor couple who had perished in a house fire. They were being buried together today, poor sods. And as if that wasn't bad enough, their daughter had gone missing too. There was a picture of her with her younger brother and the police were appealing for anyone who might have seen her to come forward.

As she stared at the girl's face, Manda Pike's heart did a somersault in her chest. *Now* she knew where she had seen Whizzer's so-called niece before – and if what the papers were saying was true, that girl next door might have been responsible for their deaths.

Whizzer lifted his knife and fork and began to eat his midday meal. Maddy had made him a steak and kidney pie and a pile of fluffy mashed potatoes just as she knew he liked them. As usual he said not a word so it was something of a surprise when he suddenly laid down his fork and started fumbling about in his trouser pocket. He then placed a Mars bar on the table and pushed it across to Maddy.

'Wh ... what's this for?' she asked, as colour burned into her cheeks.

'It's for bein' a good gel.' Whizzer then went back to eating his meal as Maddy felt a little glow start up inside her. She truly couldn't remember a time in recent years when anyone had been kind to her.

The pair of them went on with their meal and were almost halfway through it when someone suddenly knocked loudly on the front door. It would have been hard to say which one of them jumped the most. Whizzer never had visitors and Maddy wondered who it might be and if she should make herself scarce.

'I'll get it.' Looking none too pleased at the disturbance, the old man slouched away from the table as Maddy picked at her food. If it was a friend of his come to call unexpectedly, she would go to her room to give them some privacy. She heard a muttered conversation and then the sounds of footsteps on the bare wooden floorboards in the front room.

She started to rise from the table but then froze as she found herself staring into the face of PC Roberts, the policewoman who had questioned her at the hospital.

'Hello, Madeleine.' The woman's eyes were as cold as marble chips. 'I wondered how long it would be before we found you. I think you'd better get your things together and come with me, don't you?'

'I ... I don't have any things,' Maddy shot back, as her frightened eyes sought Whizzer's. He moved past her and started to eat his dinner again as if there was no one else in the room.

Maddy felt tears sting at the back of her eyes, but she held on to them and stuck her chin out defiantly. This was it, the end of freedom. She briefly thought of trying to make a run for it out the back way, but knew it would be futile. Pulling herself up to her full height, she walked towards them, pausing to tell Whizzer, 'Thanks for helping me out.'

He glanced at her, and just for a second she could have sworn she saw tears glistening in his eyes as the policewoman took her by the elbow and led her away.

Chapter Five

Maddy had been at the police station for two hours, but it felt more like two days. She had been interviewed yet again about the fire and how it had started, but throughout the questioning she had remained stubbornly silent. The young male PC who had also been present during the interview had been kind, bringing her cold drinks and biscuits, but the policewoman had looked at her for most of the time as if there was a dirty smell under her nose. Maddy was aware that she must look odd in Whizzer's daughter's ill-fitting, old-fashioned clothes, but she'd gone past caring. She didn't care about anything any more. The only time she had cried was when they had informed her that they would be bringing Whizzer in to interview him too. It seemed a shame for him to have to become involved, when all he had done was take her in out of the goodness of his heart.

'Did he touch you while you were staying with him?' PC Roberts had asked at one point.

Maddy had stared blankly back at her. '*Touch me?*' When she realised what the policewoman was implying, she was appalled. 'Of course he didn't *touch* me! Whizzer is just a harmless old man, who gives a home to people who need it. He's *good!*' she had snapped. And now here they still were and Maddy had no idea what was going to happen to her next. She supposed they were going to lock her away in prison, now that they were certain that the fire hadn't been an accident.

It was as they were sitting there that the door opened and Sue Maddox appeared. Maddy felt strangely pleased to see her. She was about the only ally she had left now.

'Are you all right, Maddy?' the young woman asked as she sat down next to her.

The girl nodded miserably. 'I'm fine. But they won't tell me where Oliver is or if he's all right. All they want to talk about is the fire.'

Sue glared at the police officers before touching Maddy's arm gently. 'Let's try and forget about that for now, shall we? I think you've had enough for one day.' As she spoke she looked pointedly at PC Roberts before spitting out, 'You shouldn't even have questioned her until I got here. Maddy is a minor, as you well know.'

The woman glanced away, looking vaguely guilty.

'Right, I've found somewhere for you to go temporarily, so shall we go and get you settled in?' Seeing the look of fear that flared in Maddy's eyes, Sue smiled at her kindly. 'It's all right, love. There's nothing to be frightened about, I promise you. You're going to stay with some foster-carers. And while we're on the way to them I'll tell you all about where Oliver is and how he's doing.'

Maddy rose from her seat, glad that she was finally going to be let out of the depressing little room at the police station. She followed Sue to the door, where Sue paused to tell the police-woman, 'I've left the address of where Maddy will be staying with the Desk Sergeant, but I suggest if you wish to speak to her again, you inform me. I *insist* on being present at any future interviews. Do you understand?'

The officer nodded as Sue guided Maddy out of the room. Soon they were outside and heading towards Sue's car, which was parked just around the corner from the station.

Maddy settled into the passenger seat beside her as the social worker steered the car away from the kerb.

'We haven't got far to go,' Sue assured her. 'And I'm sure you'll like it at the Tranters'. They're a lovely couple.'

'And what about Oliver?'

'He's absolutely fine, I promise you. He's been transferred to a hospital where they can help him. As you know, he was deeply shocked after the fire – which is quite understandable, of course. When he's a little better he'll be able to have proper counselling and then hopefully you will be able to see him again.'

Maddy felt as if a great weight had been lifted off her shoulders. It was good to know that he was safe at least.

'Actually,' Sue went on as she looked at Maddy, 'I'm quite glad of this chance to have a little time alone with you. I thought perhaps there might be something you'd like to tell me?'

'Like what?' Maddy said as she crossed her arms protectively across her chest.

'Like what *really* happened on the night of the fire. I'm sure you are aware that everyone thinks you did it, Maddy. Was everything all right between you and your parents? I mean – to all intents and purposes they appeared to be the perfect doting couple, but *you* lived with them, so you know the real story. Were they good to you? Did you get on with them?'

When it became obvious that Maddy wasn't going to say another word, Sue let the subject drop. But something wasn't right here; she would have staked her life on it. If – and of course it was a big *if* – Maddy *had* started the fire, why had she done it if she was happily settled? Had her adoptive parents been as kind and loving as they had appeared to be, or was there something that Maddy wasn't telling her? Things just didn't add up.

While all these thoughts were racing through Sue's mind, Maddy stared glumly from the car window as they drove through Plymouth city centre. It was now late September and a bitterly cold wind was blowing. Her adoptive mum and dad had taken both her and Oliver to the centre on rare occasions as a treat. Once they had visited the Elizabethan House and the Merchant's House and then they had gone on to McDonald's for tea. It was one of the rare happy memories she had of living with them.

Soon they had left the busy streets behind and after a time Sue pulled up in front of a small detached house. It was nowhere near as big as the house she had lived in, but it looked neat and tidy all the same.

Sue came round and opened the door for her, and just for an instant, Maddy had the urge to run away again.

Taking her arm as if she could sense her indecision, Sue smiled reassuringly at her. 'You're going to be just fine,' she told her soothingly. 'Now come on, Kirsty and Andy are waiting for you and I don't mind betting they'll have something nice ready for your lunch.'

They walked up a path that led to a small, double-glazed porch and Sue rang the doorbell. She could only begin to imagine how awful the poor kid must be feeling at present. Her whole world had fallen apart yet again – and now here she was about to be dumped with strangers.

A blonde-haired woman who looked to be in her mid-twenties appeared in the porch and smiled at them through the glass in the door as she fiddled with the key on the inside of the lock.

'Hello there and welcome,' she greeted them once the door was open. After ushering them both past her into a small hallway, she nodded towards a door that led off it, telling them pleasantly, 'Go on in and make yourselves at home. I'll be with you in a jiffy. I've got the kettle on and everything all ready for a cuppa. I dare say you'll be ready for one, won't you, Maddy?'

Maddy nodded cautiously. Kirsty wasn't quite what she'd expected. Her last foster-mum had been much older, and so she had assumed that Kirsty would be too. Maddy thought that she was actually quite pretty. She had shoulder-length blonde hair and blue eyes, and she was dressed in jeans and a brightly coloured T-shirt.

Glancing around the lounge Maddy decided that it looked quite cosy – homely, sort of. There were magazines spread out on a coffee-table and a comfortable leather three-piece suite was positioned around a television set that was placed in one corner of the room. As she stood there she heard barking and the next minute two little gold and white dogs hurtled into the lounge and began to jump up at her.

'That's Lilibet and Talullah,' Kirsty grinned as she followed them with a tray of tea in her hands. 'Don't be frightened of them – they're only puppies and very playful. This breed is well-known for being yappy, but they're very friendly. They're shih-tzus, and Andy and I spoil them dreadfully. They have the run of the house. You do like dogs, don't you?'

Maddy shrugged. In actual fact she had always longed to have a dog but she didn't want to commit herself to anything at the moment. She had suggested it once to her adoptive mum, and Michelle Donovan had nearly had a fit. 'A *dog!*' she had gasped, as if Maddy had asked her to adopt a wild tiger. 'Why, I wouldn't even entertain the idea. Just imagine all the exercise they would need – and think of all those dog hairs all over the carpet – *ugh!*' And so Maddy had never been allowed to have one, but now here were two that were desperate to be friends. Perhaps it wasn't going to be so bad here after all?

As Sue and Kirsty completed the necessary paperwork, a man appeared in the doorway holding a paintbrush in his hand.

'Hello there, you must be Maddy,' he said with a friendly wink. 'I won't shake hands, love. Kirsty here has got me busy painting in the spare room as you can see. No peace for the wicked, eh?

61

We've got the mother-in-law visiting at the weekend, so her indoors is cracking the whip.'

'Oh, stop moaning you,' Kirsty scolded, but her eyes were twinkling as she told Maddy, 'This is Andy, my other half. You'd think I'd asked him to paint the Severn Bridge the amount of grumbling he's done about one little bedroom. He never seems to mind when I have his mum and dad to dinner, though. I've no doubt you'll meet them all soon. Andy's parents only live around the corner, so we get to see quite a lot of them.'

Andy took a mug of tea from the tray and helped himself to a ginger nut biscuit as he asked Maddy, 'Has Kirsty shown you your room yet?'

Solemn-faced, she shook her head.

'Then we'll take you up to have a peep in a minute,' he promised. 'You're the only one here at present apart from us, so I've no doubt Kirsty will spoil you rotten.'

Maddy decided that she liked Andy too. He was very tall with wavy fair hair and smiling blue eyes.

Leaning towards her he confided, 'Kirsty says she's taking you on a shopping spree this afternoon. Huh! I've no doubt she'll be in seventh heaven. Kirsty can shop for England, so be warned.'

Kirsty slapped playfully at his arm. 'Why don't you just shut up and get back to work? You should know by now that we women *need* to have a good shopping trip now and again. It's what they call retail therapy, isn't it, Maddy?'

Not quite sure how she should answer, Maddy stayed tight-lipped. When Sue finally left half an hour later, Kirsty and Andy took Maddy upstairs to see her room. Like the downstairs, her room was clean and reasonably tidy, but nothing at all like the clinically pristine house she had lived in with the Donovans. There was a single bed against one wall with a cream bedspread and some pretty lace-trimmed cushions thrown on it. The dogs were bounding around her feet, furiously wagging their tails. It seemed that not even the bedrooms were out of bounds to them. Maddy struggled to keep her face straight as she imagined what her adoptive mum would have thought of it. In Michelle's house everything had had to be just so; even the cushions on the settee had to be exactly in place – and woe betide Maddy if they weren't. The ornaments on the shelf, all made of very expensive china, were thoroughly dusted each day and then washed each week before being put back within a quarter of an inch of where they had come from.

Maddy glanced around at the rest of the room. There was a pine wardrobe and matching chest-of-drawers, and pale lilac curtains hung at the window. Posters of pop stars had been pinned to the walls and Maddy suddenly felt as if she had entered another world. Never in a million years would she have dared to pin anything on her walls at home.

'Do you think you'll be comfy in here?'

As Kirsty's voice pulled her thoughts back to the present, she nodded.

'Good. Well, let's go and have some lunch and then we can get off shopping, eh?'

Maddy followed her back downstairs and soon

after found herself sitting at a table in the kitchen with a big plate of fish fingers, peas and crusty bread and butter set in front of her.

'Want some tomato ketchup or salad cream to go with that? I'm afraid I'm not the best cook in the world,' Kirsty admitted, then throwing her head back she laughed aloud. 'To tell you the truth I *hate* cooking, but I promise you won't starve and if there's anything you don't like, just tell me.'

As Maddy picked nervously at her meal, washing it down with a glass of apple juice, she wondered why Kirsty and Andy didn't have any children of their own. There were three bedrooms upstairs from what she had seen of the house: one of them was theirs, there was one for her and a spare one. She was tempted to ask, but thought better of it. She felt awkward enough as it was without them thinking she was a nosy parker.

After lunch, Kirsty dumped the pots in the sink to soak and hurried off to get her bag and her coat.

'Don't you have a coat?' she asked, as she eyed Maddy's strange outfit.

When Maddy shook her head, Kirsty said easily, 'Well, we'll put that on the top of the list this afternoon then. Meanwhile, you can borrow one of my short jackets. It will probably bury you, but we can turn the sleeves up and it will be better than being cold.' So saying, she hurried away to return a short time later with a denim jacket that she threw towards her. 'There you go, love. Now let's get off. We're wasting valuable shopping time.'

Andy winked at Maddy as she passed him in the

hall. 'It's all right for some,' he groaned. 'Here are you two off to enjoy yourselves while I'm left wielding a paintbrush.'

'Just as it should be.' There was a teasing note in Kirsty's voice. 'Now get back to work. I shall expect that room to be finished by the time I get home.'

'Yes, ma'am.' Andy pretended to doff an imaginary cap and bowed as she swept past him, leaving a waft of her Charlie perfume in her wake.

She and Maddy took the bus into the town centre and for the first part of the journey Kirsty kept up a constant stream of cheerful chatter. Unable to respond, and feeling overwhelmed, Maddy clamped her mouth shut as she gazed vacantly from the window. Beside her, Kirsty sighed, and the rest of the bus ride took place in silence.

Much later that evening, when Kirsty and Andy were curled up on the sofa enjoying a cup of cocoa before retiring to bed, Andy asked, 'So how did the afternoon go then? I don't mean the shopping. I could see by the number of bags you came home with that you'd bought Maddy enough clothes to last her for a year. I mean, how was she?'

Kirsty absently wiped away a lock of blonde hair from her forehead as she sighed, 'Not brill, Andy, if I'm to be honest. In fact, it was hard work just to try and get a word out of her.'

'Mm ... I think I know what you mean. She's a sullen little thing, isn't she?'

'Well, from what Sue told us she's been through, she's had enough to make her be sullen,' Kirsty replied. 'She could be quite pretty if she smiled, I'm sure of it. She's a bit on the scrawny side but she's got a nice face. And her hair and her eyes are lovely.'

Andy stared into his cocoa musingly. When Sue Maddox had first approached them and asked them to take Maddy, they had been forced to think hard about it. Sue had told them that the police suspected Maddy might have set light to her adoptive parents' home, and it was daunting to think that she could possibly do the same to theirs. But then both he and Kirsty were firm believers that everyone was innocent until proven guilty, and so they had made the decision to give her a chance. Whether they had made the right decision or not, only time would tell.

'How much longer do you think it might be now?' Kirsty suddenly asked, and he knew instantly what she was talking about.

'How long is a piece of string?' he said soberly. 'Social Services told us that babies don't become available for adoption very often, love, so we just have to be patient.'

'Yes, I know you're right.'

As Andy planted a kiss on the top of her head, his heart ached. The couple had discovered two years before, following numerous tests, that Kirsty could not have a baby and shortly after they had put their names down on the adoption register. They had also become approved as foster-carers and both of them loved having young people and children in the house. But still Kirsty longed for the day when they would be able to have a child of their very own. One that they could keep for ever, who would not be moved on. But babies and toddlers were in great demand by prospective adopters now. Gone were the days when a stigma had been attached to unmarried single mothers. Most of them were keeping their babies nowadays, which meant that he and Kirsty might have a very long wait ahead of them.

During that wait, they were determined to do their best for the children who came to stay with them, and Sue had assured them that they had done a grand job with the kids they had cared for so far. He just hoped that they would be able to do the same for Maddy; he somehow sensed that the poor kid was something of a lost soul.

The following day, Maddy met Andy's parents for the first time and she thought what a mismatched couple they were. Andy's mother was a mousy little woman who wouldn't say boo to a goose, whilst her husband was very extrovert and loud.

'So you're the latest addition to the household are you, sweetheart?' he bawled as he slapped Maddy soundly on the backside. The girl flushed although Kirsty laughed. Maddy noticed that he was flirting quite shamelessly with Kirsty but she saw that Andy seemed quite amused by the fact.

'Leave her alone, Bill,' Kirsty urged. 'You're embarrassing the poor girl.'

'Aw, she'll soon get used to me,' he grinned cheekily as he eyed Maddy up and down. She felt her skin crawl. Bill Tranter obviously thought he was God's gift to women, which probably explained why his long-suffering wife seemed to pale into insignificance in his presence. He was like an older version of Andy to look at and Maddy supposed that he was quite good-looking for his age, but all the same her dislike of him began there and then and she hoped that she wouldn't be forced to see too much of him.

Chapter Six

'So how are things going?' Sue asked Kirsty as they settled down to enjoy a cup of tea together in the young woman's lounge.

Kirsty frowned as she thought how best to reply. 'Well ... all right, I suppose. I won't pretend that Maddy is an easy kid to get on with. She still tends to speak only when spoken to and she spends an awful lot of time in her room. Too much time if you were to ask me, but there's not much we can do about it. And she obviously hasn't taken to Andy's parents. Or Andy's dad at least. She's off like a shot the second he sets foot through the door, although I can't think why. Bill is always the life and soul of the party and he goes out of his way to make her feel welcome.'

'Hm. And how is she doing at her new school?'

'It's much the same there, to be honest. Her teacher says she's quite bright but isn't good at mixing with the others in her class. She's very withdrawn and won't join in, by all accounts. During the half-term holiday, Andy and I tried to encourage her to come out with us, but she wasn't having it. She just wanted to stay in her room, although she did come with us to a bonfire display on November the fifth. When it was her birthday last week I asked if there was anyone she would like to invite over from school, but she just shook her head. I mean, she was thirteen, a teenager, and to most girls that's a big deal. Andy and I got her a cake but she didn't show much interest in it, and as soon as she'd opened her presents and had a slice, she shot off to her room again. We bought her some Michael Jackson tapes too, but I haven't even heard her play them yet. She seems more interested in spending time with the dogs than us. They've even taken to sleeping in her room with her now, not that we mind, of course.'

Sue sighed as she placed her cup down.

'Have you had any luck finding her a longer-term placement yet?' Kirsty asked as she offered Sue a biscuit.

Sue helped herself to a custard cream. 'We haven't even started looking yet,' she said. 'There's no point until we know what the police are intending to do. As you know, they seem to think that Maddy set fire to her parents' home deliberately, although there's no concrete evidence to substantiate that, and Maddy hasn't admitted to anything. She just said she'd put the chip pan on to make her younger brother some supper.'

'And do *you* think she did it deliberately?'

Sue sniffed. 'It does sound a bit fishy, doesn't it? Starting to cook chips at gone midnight, I mean. What's more, Maddy hasn't shed a single tear over her parents' death as far as I know, and she made no secret of the fact that she had never been happy with them – although I find it hard to believe that she would be capable of doing something quite so drastic deliberately. If she was behind it, I reckon it was a cry for help, nothing else. That lass is no more a murderer than I am.'

'She really misses her brother,' Kirsty told her sadly. 'Is there no chance of her going to see him?'

'Yes, there is, actually – which is one of the reasons I've called in today. Oliver is out of hospital now and with carers. I was wondering if perhaps I could take Maddy to visit him after school on Friday?'

'Of course you can. That might be just what she needs to cheer her up,' Kirsty told her enthusiastically. 'But how is he now?'

'Not good really,' Sue told her. 'The poor little soul can't seem to recall a thing of what happened that night. It's just as if his mind has shut it out, and according to the doctors he might never remember, which I suppose wouldn't be a bad thing. It must have been a terrifying experience, watching his home burn down with his mum and dad inside it. If it hadn't been for Maddy managing to get him out, he could have died too.'

'And what will happen to him now?'

'I think he'll go for adoption again,' Sue said. 'Oliver is only nine years old so he's still just about young enough to settle into another new family.'

'But what about Maddy? Won't they be placed together?'

'There's very little chance of that. Most people don't want to adopt a girl her age. And besides, as I said, it will all depend on what the police decide. If they can't prove beyond a shadow of a doubt that Maddy burned the house down, she'll probably get sent to a home somewhere.'

'Oh no!' Kirsty was horrified. 'What – you mean somewhere like Borstal?'

Sue grinned. 'Borstal was a place for rebellious juvenile delinquents. I hardly think that Maddy quite falls into that category, do you?'

'No, I don't,' Kirsty retorted hotly. 'I'll admit Maddy isn't the easiest kid in the world to get along with, but I'm sure there's a heart in there somewhere. She must have asked at least a dozen times about that old man who took her in when she ran away from the hospital. She's been terrified that he would have got into trouble for helping her. And yet I do find it strange that she never cries for her mum and dad. From what you've told me, Maddy appears to have had a happy settled five years with a good family, but if that's the case why is there a question mark over whether she tried to burn them to death? Are you *quite* sure that she was as happy as it appeared?'

'I really can't answer that,' Sue acknowledged. 'But where are we going to find these wonderful people who would offer a home to a girl with Maddy's track record? It's hardly exemplary, is it? And as soon as we tell them that there is even the *remotest* possibility that she might have burned her parents' home down with them inside it, who is going to be willing to take her?'

'Andy and I did,' Kirsty pointed out.

'Yes, you did, but you and Andy are a rarity and it was only for a short time.'

Kirsty leaned forward and hugged her knees as sympathy flooded through her. She just knew that the girl could be happy if she could only find the right home. Sometimes she watched her when she was petting the dogs and saw the gentleness inside her. More than anything, she needed someone she could trust now.

The two women lapsed into silence for a time but then after glancing at her watch, Sue rose reluctantly. 'I'm afraid I shall have to be making tracks. I'm due in court with another of my cases in half an hour. *Bless him.*' Her voice was laced with sarcasm. 'I've been there three times with him already. It's car theft this time. The trouble is, because he's only thirteen he knows the worst he'll probably get is a slap on the wrist. There's no hope for some of the kids on our books, believe me. They're already destined to become tomorrow's criminals and the worst of it is, it's mostly because of what they've gone through before they come into care. Some parents have an awful lot to answer for.'

Kirsty nodded in agreement as she followed Sue to the door. The kindly social worker had given her a lot to think about, and that's exactly what she did for the rest of the afternoon – until Bill Tranter dropped by.

When Maddy got home from school that afternoon she had a glass of milk and then disappeared to her room to do her homework. Kirsty sighed as she watched her going upstairs. Maddy had been attending her new school for four weeks and Kirsty had hoped that by now the girl would have made some friends, but as yet there was no sign of a single one.

Andy breezed in from work some time later like a breath of fresh air and kissed his wife as he slung his coat over the back of a kitchen chair.

'Something smells nice.' He sniffed at the air appreciatively. 'What's for dinner then, love? An' where's the little 'un?'

'We've got shepherd's pie. It's a recipe from that Delia Smith cookbook you got me for my birthday, and Maddy is upstairs in her room, as usual. Your dad popped by and, as soon as she saw him, she shot off upstairs like a bolt of lightning.'

'I don't think she's clocked on to the fact that Dad is a bit of a charmer yet,' Andy chuckled. 'Dad will flirt with anything in a skirt, but I doubt Maddy has met anyone like him before.'

Andy thought his wife seemed a little quiet but decided not to comment on the fact. If something was wrong, she would tell him in her own good time.

'Right – well, I'll lay the table and then I'll nip up and get changed before we eat.'

Kirsty nodded absently and once again he wondered what might be wrong. She was usually very chatty when he first got in from work.

'It was flippin' cold out today,' he commented, as he collected the knives and forks from the kitchen drawer. He was hoping to get some response but Kirsty remained musingly quiet. 'Harry Barlow had to go to hospital this afternoon an' all,' he went on. Andy was a builder and winter wasn't the best time of year for his job. It could be bitterly cold working on the building sites, and sometimes when he got home, his hands and feet had lost all feeling. When Kirsty didn't even bother to ask what sort of accident Harry had had, Andy gave up and hurried upstairs to wash and get changed out of his work clothes.

Half an hour later they all sat at the kitchen table tucking into the delicious meal Kirsty had prepared for them. As usual, Maddy was quiet but tonight Kirsty was too and Andy was almost glad when the meal was over. Maddy went off into the lounge to watch *Dallas* with the dogs close behind her, and Andy stayed in the kitchen to help Kirsty with the washing up.

'Is something wrong, love?'

'Sorry?' Kirsty blinked. She had been so lost in thought that her husband's words had gone over her head.

'Sorry, I was miles away,' she muttered. 'And no, there's nothing wrong exactly, but I do need to talk to you later when we're on our own.' She cocked her head towards the lounge door and he nodded, understanding what she was saying. Whatever she needed to talk to him about, it obviously concerned Maddy.

An hour later, Maddy stood up from the settee and headed for the door, telling Andy on the way, 'I'm off to get a bath and then I'm going to bed. Good night, Andy.'

'Good night, love,' he answered.

Andy waited until he heard the bathroom door shut upstairs and then hurried into the kitchen to Kirsty, who was uncorking a bottle of wine. He was unable to control his curiosity a second longer.

'So come on then, put me out of my misery,' he

74

said teasingly as he took a seat at the kitchen table. Kirsty joined him with two glasses and poured them both a drink before beginning. 'Sue came to see me today. She'd come to ask if she could take Maddy to see her brother after school on Friday.' In her mind she saw the radiant smile that had lit the girl's face when she'd learned the news. She had looked totally transformed, even quite pretty.

'Yes – *and?*'

'Well, the thing is, we got to talking. Sue told me that they would probably be looking for new adoptive parents for Oliver. But Maddy ... she said that they might decide a residential unit is the best place for her.' Her eyes were full of pain as she raised them to her husband's. 'Can you even begin to imagine how awful that would be for her? I mean, I know Maddy isn't the easiest girl in the world to get along with, but surely she deserves another chance? The poor little sod.'

Andy sighed. 'I hear what you're saying, love. But what can we do about it?'

Kirsty took a deep breath before blurting out, 'We could agree to keep her long-term. Or we could even adopt her ourselves.'

'You *what?*' Andy almost choked on the wine he had just tasted. '*Us* adopt her? But I thought we'd agreed we'd wait until a baby or a toddler came along!'

'We did,' Kirsty admitted guiltily. 'But we could still have our baby later on, Andy. Just think of it – when it came along, it would have a built-in big sister. I'm sure Maddy would love it, if the way she talks about her little brother is anything to go

75

by. She's so alone, Andy. From what I can see of it, she's got no one in the world who gives a cuss about her – and I'm sure she'd settle, given time.'

Andy was amazed, but he supposed that what Kirsty said was true. They could still have their baby when the time was right and people did have more than one child.

'It would be a big commitment,' he said cautiously, hoping that Kirsty was suggesting this for the right reasons. Was she so desperate to have a child that she was even considering taking older ones now? 'Especially if the police's suspicions are true and Maddy *did* set light to her parents' home.'

'I know that.' Kirsty looked at him imploringly. 'But please don't dismiss the idea out of hand. Promise me that you'll at least think about it.'

He nodded as he tried to take in what she had suggested. Yes, he would think about it, but it would have to be long and hard.

Upstairs in the bathroom, Maddy lay in the bath with tears streaming down her cheeks. Unbeknownst to the couple downstairs, she had heard every word that had been said. The kitchen was directly beneath the bathroom and sound travelled. It was unbelievable that Kirsty was actually considering letting her stay there, and it made a warm glow start in the pit of her stomach. But what about the residential home she had mentioned. Would it be like a prison? She shivered at the thought. It would be terrifying to be locked away. Her worst nightmare come true. As memories flooded back, she shuddered uncontrollably despite the warmth of the water. Michelle had been very good at shutting her away – although no one else but herself and Oliver was aware of the fact. There had been a cupboard under the stairs and once, Kirsty had been forced to spend the whole night locked in there because she hadn't cleaned the kitchen floor properly. It had been cold and dark, and Maddy could remember crying herself to sleep, terrified of what Michelle might do if she banged on the door and asked to be let out. And then people wondered why she wasn't grieving for her. Oh, she could have told them a tale or two if she'd had a mind to. But what would be the point? Michelle and Peter had been well-respected in the community. Who would take her word against theirs? No one had ever seen the bruises that Michelle had inflicted on her. She had always made sure they were in places that couldn't be seen.

And now this latest bombshell. Kirsty was really considering keeping her! Maddy tried to picture what her life would be like if Andy agreed to it. The Tranters were the kindest people she had ever known apart from Whizzer, and they asked nothing of her. In fact, when she tried to cook or clean, Kirsty would stop her, telling her, 'That's woman's work. You just enjoy being a kid while you can, eh?' Up to now, Maddy had kept them at a distance, but she determined that from now on, she would try harder.

St John's School which she attended now wasn't bad either. There was a girl there called Tamara who had been trying to befriend her. Maddy had kept her distance from the girl, but now she decided it would be nice to have a friend, and some-one to come home to each night who cared. She thought of the two little dogs that had become her constant companions and the cosy bedroom she slept in. Kirsty didn't mind if it didn't always look like something out of a magazine, and she was always trying to talk to her. *Really* talk to her, as if she was a real person who mattered, not someone who should be seen and not heard. If she stayed here she might get to see Oliver regularly too. It would be like a fairy story with a happy ending.

On that thought, Maddy clambered out of the bath and dried herself on a big fluffy towel, a broad smile now on her face. She wouldn't think about the other option that Kirsty had men-tioned. The residential unit. It sounded horrible and her luck had to change some time, didn't it?

Chapter Seven

'Are you all ready then, Maddy?'

'She's been ready for the last half an hour and hovering by the window,' Kirsty answered for the girl with a smile.

Maddy flushed with embarrassment. It was late Friday afternoon and she had run all the way home from school and could hardly wait to see her brother now.

'Right, we'll get off then. Goodbye, Kirsty, we shouldn't be gone for more than a couple of hours. Oliver's carers live in Tamerton Foliot which is only a few miles away as the crow flies. Trouble is, we're going to hit the Friday rush-hour traffic now. Everyone will be on their way home from work.'

Sue led Maddy to the front door and once they had gone Kirsty stood staring out of the window. Andy seemed to be warming to the idea of offering to keep Maddy, although he hadn't given her a definite answer as yet. Over the last few days she had detected a softening in the girl's attitude towards them and was sure she could make it work if she was given the chance. She hadn't mentioned anything to Sue or Maddy yet. The way she saw it, it wouldn't have been fair to anyone to even suggest offering Maddy a long-term home until she and Andy were 100 per cent sure that it was right for them. And even then a lot would depend on what Maddy thought of the idea; she might not want to stay with them.

Sighing, she bent to stroke the dogs that were skittering around her feet before heading for the kitchen to start the evening meal of baked potatoes and gammon steaks. Andy would be home from work soon and no doubt he would be starving as usual.

Once they were on the way, Sue took her eyes from the road for a second to look at Maddy. The girl was obviously nervous, but then that was to be expected. She had gone through an awful lot in the last few weeks and had been worrying about her brother constantly.

Hoping to distract her, Sue remarked, 'You'll like Tamerton Foliot. It used to be a lovely little village nestling in a valley but now it's more of a

79

dense suburb of Plymouth. It's actually got a lot of history attached to it. There's a very old church there that dates back right to the twelfth century and just outside its boundaries is a very old hollow tree called "The Copleston Oak". Legend has it that it's named after the Lord of the Manor at the time, Sir Christopher Copleston. He murdered his godson with a dagger beneath it in 1562.'

Maddy folded her arms as she continued to gaze from the window. She wasn't really interested in a history lesson, however grisly, at the moment. All she really wanted was to see Oliver again, although she sensed that Sue was only trying to take her mind off things.

Sue meantime clamped her mouth shut as she noted Maddy's trembling jaw. Remaining silent for the time being she negotiated the busy rush-hour traffic in the centre of Plymouth and left the young girl to her thoughts.

Some time later, they came to the road that led downhill to Tamerton Foliot, and despite herself, Maddy stared ahead with interest. It was a pretty place, and in the distance she could see where the River Tamar and the River Tavy merged before broadening out into a large estuarine creek. The village was situated at the edge of a heavily wooded nature reserve and Maddy felt sure that Oliver would like living here. When they passed the small picturesque church of St Mary's, Maddy correctly guessed that this must be the one that Sue had told her about. A few streets further on, they drove past a more modern Methodist church, and then before she knew it, Sue was turning into a driveway that led to a pretty thatched cottage.

'This is it,' she told Maddy cheerily as she drew the car to a halt, but then lowering her voice, she told her passenger, 'Maddy, dear, don't be too concerned if Oliver seems a little quiet. He's doing really well, I promise you, but he suffered a serious shock on the night of the fire and he still isn't quite himself again yet.'

With her mouth set in a grim line, Maddy nodded as she got out of the car. Before they reached the door it opened and a plump middle-aged lady, who looked very elegant in a string of flawless pearls and a smart red jumper and pair of black slacks, hurried out to meet them. Her hair was streaked with grey above the temples but she had a kind smile which she directed at Maddy as she advanced on her with her hand outstretched.

'Hello, my dear. You must be Madeleine,' she gushed. 'I'm sure Oliver is going to be delighted to see you. He's such a *lovely* child. You must be very proud of him.'

Without waiting for an answer, the woman began to usher Maddy and Sue inside as Sue told her, 'Maddy, this is Mrs Simpson.'

Maddy took a deep breath as she was shown into a little hallway that had parquet tiles on the floor. They were so highly polished that she could see her reflection in them, and she was reminded of the home she had lived in with her adoptive parents. It was just a little too spick and span, more of a show house than a home. The woman paused at one of the doors leading off the hallway to tell her, 'Oliver is in here, my dear. I'll let you go in and spend some time with him, whilst Sue

81

and I go off to the kitchen for a cup of tea, shall I?'

Maddy nodded numbly. Her mouth was dry as she watched Sue and Mrs Simpson head off towards the back of the property. Then, once they had gone from sight, she put her shoulders back, pushed the door open and stepped into the room. It was surprisingly spacious, with a low beamed ceiling and an enormous inglenook fireplace where a roaring log fire was burning brightly. Chintz curtains hung at the numerous small leaded windows and comfortable chairs were dotted here and there around the fireplace.

Oliver was sitting on one with a storybook open on his lap, but his eyes were staring sightlessly off into space.

'Oliver ... it's me, Maddy.' She quickly crossed to him, and after kneeling beside him, she took his hands in hers and gently shook them up and down. For a moment, Oliver did not react, but then his head slowly turned in her direction and a little smile twitched at the corners of his mouth.

Maddy caught him to her in a bear hug. 'How are you?' she asked, but he merely stared vacantly back at her, the brief flash of recognition she had seen in his eyes gone as if it had never been. He was looking well and was smartly dressed in black trousers and a blue jumper that exactly matched the colour of his eyes. One day he would be blind. Doctors had told his adoptive parents some years ago there was no cure for his eye condition, and Maddy found herself wondering how he would cope with it. Particularly if she wasn't there to give him support. She knew only too well that if Oliver were to go for adoption she might never be allowed to see him again. Most new adoptive parents wanted their children to have a fresh start, and frowned on them having contact with their siblings.

Deciding to act as naturally as possible, Maddy began to chatter away as she hitched herself onto the seat next to him.

'It's gone really cold this last few days, don't you think? I walk to school from Kirsty and Andy's house and by the time I get there I'm frozen through. Andy reckons we're going to have a bad winter. He says he can't ever remember it being so cold in November. Do you get out much, Oliver?'

She waited for a response and when none was forthcoming she rambled on, 'Andy and Kirsty who I'm staying with are really nice. Mrs Simpson seems nice too. Do you like her?'

Again there was nothing. Not even a sign that he had heard her, and now her shoulders sagged and she became silent as she cuddled her little brother to her and wondered what was going to become of them both.

Sue and Mrs Simpson found her in the same position half an hour later.

'I did warn you that he was a little quiet, didn't I, dear?' Mrs Simpson said sympathetically. 'But I assure you he's doing just fine. He's eating and sleeping really well; we just need to get him talking again now.'

As Sue looked at Maddy's dejected face, a lump swelled in her throat. Poor soul, she found herself thinking. 'I ... er ... suppose we should be thinking of getting back, Maddy,' she suggested quietly. There didn't seem to be any point in staying any longer. Oliver was quite clearly locked in a world of his own and didn't even seem to be aware that his sister was there.

Maddy nodded, all the misery she felt showing clearly on her face. She kissed Oliver soundly on the cheek and then stared at him as if she was locking the sight of him away in her memory before following Sue from the room. Oliver didn't even blink or look in her direction.

'Don't worry, dear. I'll take good care of him,' Mrs Simpson assured her as Maddy climbed into the car. Maddy nodded and looked away as Sue reversed the car off the drive and started on the journey home.

Kirsty was waiting for her when they got back. She looked at Maddy anxiously.

'How did it go, love?' she asked.

Maddy shrugged. 'All right, I suppose.' And then she was haring up the stairs as Sue and Kirsty watched her helplessly. They both sensed that there was nothing they could say that would make her feel better.

'Poor little mite,' Kirsty said.

Sue nodded in agreement. 'Still, at least she's seen him again,' she pointed out. 'She might stop worrying about him now that she knows he's being looked after.'

The two women said their goodbyes and once Sue had gone, Kirsty paused at the bottom of the stairs wondering if she should go up to Maddy. She decided against it. The girl might need some quiet time to herself, and Kirsty didn't want to intrude. The dogs had followed Maddy as usual, so now Kirsty went to read the newspaper until Andy got in from work.

It was over dinner that evening that Andy suggested, 'How about we get the foot ferry over to Mount Edgcumbe tomorrow, eh? I heard the weather forecast earlier on and it's going to be cold but dry. It might be nice to wander round the gardens if we wrap up warmly.'

'That sounds nice,' Kirsty chipped in tactfully. Maddy had scarcely said two words all through the meal and Kirsty guessed that she was upset after seeing Oliver. 'If the weather was better we could have had a walk along the beach to Jennycliff or Mothecombe, but it's a little cold for that.'

'We could visit Buckland Abbey if you don't fancy the ferry,' Andy said. 'You never know, we just might get to see the ghost of Sir Francis Drake floating along the corridors.'

Kirsty shuddered. 'Oh no, thank you very much. I think we'll stick to the first option. What do you think, Maddy?'

Maddy simply shrugged and after exchanging a glance, the couple lapsed into silence.

The trip the following day turned out to be a surprising success, and Maddy actually came out of her shell a little as Andy pointed out places of interest at Mount Edgcumbe. After catching the ferry back to Plymouth they wandered around the little cobbled streets surrounding the harbour and Andy took them for tea in a pretty little café before they set off for home.

As usual, Maddy shot off to her room when they got back, and Andy opened a bottle of wine and poured himself and Kirsty a glass. 'Come on, let's curl up on the sofa and see what's on the telly, eh? It looks like her ladyship has battened down the hatches for the night. I doubt we'll see her again unless she pops down for a drink.'

'You're probably right, but wasn't it nice to see her smiling today? I think she really enjoyed herself, even if she can't bring herself to tell us.' Kirsty snuggled up to Andy on the settee contentedly.

It was almost half an hour later when he suddenly said out of the blue, 'You know what you suggested – about us keeping Maddy? Well, I've had time to think about it now and if you still feel the same I think we should do it.'

'*Really?*' Kirsty was absolutely thrilled with his decision. She was sure that they could help Maddy to become a happier child, if they were given the chance.

'In that case, I shall ring Sue Maddox and put the idea to her first thing on Monday morning. This could be a new start for Maddy,' she said. And then she settled down, wondering how she was going to keep this to herself all weekend without blurting it out to Maddy. She really would have to speak to Sue first and see how she reacted to the idea, but oh, it was going to be so hard – and Monday morning suddenly seemed a lifetime away.

Chapter Eight

First thing on Monday morning when Kirsty had seen Maddy off to school she rang the Social Services offices, only to be told that Sue Maddox was already in a meeting. Kirsty groaned with impatience and left an urgent message asking Sue to call her back as soon as was possible.

She then watched the clock as she tackled the housework. Sometimes it was like getting through to God when you needed a social worker, as Kirsty had discovered very early on in her fostering career. It was almost one o'clock when the phone finally rang and snatching it up, Kirsty beamed when she heard Sue's voice.

'I need to see you as soon as possible. I have something to tell you,' she bubbled excitedly.

'Funnily enough, that's exactly what I was going to say to you,' Sue told her, sounding very down in the dumps. 'Could I come round in, say, an hour?'

'Of course, I'll put the kettle on,' Kirsty trilled and then she waited, constantly glancing out of the window for a sign of Sue's car.

When Sue arrived she followed Kirsty into the kitchen and threw her bag onto the table despondently. Kirsty was so full of the suggestion she was about to put to her that she didn't even notice.

'Andy and I have been talking a lot over the

weekend,' she chattered cheerfully as she turned the kettle on. 'And we've reached a decision. The thing is, we want to offer Maddy a long-term home – with us.'

Glancing at Sue, she was surprised to see that there was a deep frown on her forehead. 'I thought you'd be pleased,' she went on hesitantly. 'You said yourself that kids of Maddy's age are hard to place long-term, and I'm sure we could help her.'

'I'm sure you could too,' Sue told her regretfully, 'but sadly, it isn't going to happen.'

'Why not?' Kirsty was bemused.

'Because the meeting I've been in all morning concerned Maddy, and a decision has been made. She's to be put into a residential unit until she's at least eighteen. They're not even willing to consider placing her in another family environment.'

'But *why?* That's bloody ludicrous,' Kirsty objected hotly. 'You know as well as I do how difficult things have been for Maddy. She doesn't mix well, and if you stick her in one of those godforsaken places she'll just get lost in the system.'

'I couldn't agree more.' Sue dragged her hand through her hair. 'But it's not down to me. The powers-that-be have decided that's where she should go, following the fire at her parents' home, and there isn't a thing I can do about it. I really wish there was, especially now that you've made this wonderful offer. I will put it to my boss, of course, but I truly don't think there's much chance of them changing their minds. I'm so sorry, Kirsty.'

Kirsty sank down at the kitchen table as the

colour drained from her face. It seemed so unfair. Maddy deserved to be within the bosom of a real family, not locked away somewhere.

'When is this going to happen?' she choked out.

'As soon as possible, I'm afraid. Possibly even by the end of this week. They already have somewhere in mind for her in Gloucestershire, and if there's a place available it will be all over bar the shouting.'

'Poor Maddy,' Kirsty whispered.

Sue hung her head. She was no more pleased with the decision that the Department had reached than Kirsty was, but she was powerless to alter it.

'Why has she got to stay there until she's eighteen?' Kirsty asked eventually. 'That's five years away – a lifetime to a young girl like her. She'll be institutionalised by the time she comes out.'

'Because the police report stated that if she *did* start the fire, she could do it again and put more people at risk. They have no evidence whatsoever to suggest that she was responsible, and because she's a minor they can't take matters any further, but they're not prepared to risk another incident.'

'Oh.' Kirsty felt numb as she tried to anticipate how Maddy would react to this latest development. 'When will you tell her?'

'Well, we should know if there's a place available by tomorrow lunchtime, so I thought I'd come round and break the news to her after school, if that's all right with you. I'm afraid you're going to have to keep a very vigilant eye on her once I have told her, though. We don't want her running away again.'

'Huh! I wouldn't blame her in the least if she did,' Kirsty retorted as anger replaced her disappointment. 'We were willing to love her for who she is, and now she's having that snatched away from her. Could you really blame her if she did run away? I know I certainly would, if I was in her shoes.'

Hoping to avoid a scene, Sue rose hastily from the kitchen table. It seemed to her that Kirsty needed some time to herself to come to terms with what she had just heard.

'Look, I think it might be best if I made tracks,' she said tactfully, and without waiting for a reply she slung her bag across her shoulder and headed for the door where she paused to add, 'I'm so sorry, Kirsty. For what my opinion is worth, I think you and Andy would have made Maddy wonderful parents.'

And then she was gone, and as Kirsty listened to the sound of her car drawing away, the tears she had so valiantly held back now coursed down her cheeks and all she could think was, *Poor Maddy.*

'Right, I think that's everything then,' Sue muttered as she re-entered the house after placing the last of Maddy's possessions in the boot of her car. It was Friday morning and she now had a three-hour drive ahead of her to Gloucestershire. Andy had stayed at home to see Maddy off and he looked almost as upset as Kirsty, who was clearly struggling to hold back her tears.

'I'll write to you,' she promised as she faced Maddy, who looked deathly pale. Maddy glared scornfully back at her. She had been happier living with Andy and Kirsty than she had ever been in the whole of her life. She had lain in the bath listening to them talking about letting her stay with them for always, and had waited with anticipation for them to ask her how she felt about the idea. But they never had and now she was about to be shipped off again. Their good intentions certainly hadn't lasted for long, the way she saw it. When Sue had come to see her on Tuesday to tell her of the proposed move, Maddy had felt utterly betrayed. She had trusted Andy and Kirsty, wrongly it seemed now, and the hurt went deep.

'Take care of yourself, won't you, love,' Andy said, but she ignored him as she bent to stroke Lilibet and Talullah for one last time. She would miss them, that was a fact.

Without a word she ignored Kirsty's outstretched arms and stormed from the house.

'I'm so sorry,' Sue told the distressed couple. 'I did try to explain to Maddy that none of this is your fault, but I'm afraid she isn't in the mood to listen at the moment. I'm sure she'll write to you and keep in touch once she's had time to calm down.'

'She won't.' Kirsty shook her head. She already knew Maddy well enough to know that the girl would simply write off the time she had spent with them as a sad experience. In her mind they would be just people who hadn't cared enough to give her the stable home-life she craved. And now Kirsty could only stand and watch as Sue drove Maddy away and hope that things would work out in the end for her.

As they left the city of Plymouth behind them, Sue tried to start a conversation but soon realised that she was wasting her breath. The girl sat slumped in her seat, her arms folded across her chest and a scowl on her face.

Maddy knew that under other circumstances she could have enjoyed living in Plymouth. She had loved the little cobbled streets in the older part of the city and the harbour had always held a great fascination for her. It was just the parents she had been placed with that had been the problem. Resentment bubbled inside her. Whizzer had been nice though, and she had thought that Andy and Kirsty were lovely. Until they'd changed their minds about keeping her, that was. Oh, Sue had tried to tell her that the decision for her to be moved to a residential unit had been taken without their knowledge, but Maddy didn't believe a word of it. The way she saw it, the long and the short of it was that no one had ever *really* wanted her, which was why she was now being carted off to the back of beyond somewhere.

Sue had lapsed into silence and that suited Maddy just fine, so she closed her eyes against all the painful thoughts that were racing through her mind as they eventually came to the M5 motorway and cruised along it.

Some time later they left the motorway, and when they came to Cirencester, Sue pulled into a service station. 'I think it's about time we had a break, don't you?' She forced herself to sound cheerful. 'My mouth is as dry as the bottom of a birdcage. Come on.'

Maddy reluctantly followed her into the café and slipped into a seat by the window while Sue hurried to the counter to get them both a drink. She returned a few minutes later with hot burger batches and two steaming mugs of tea.

'This should keep us going.' She pushed Maddy's food across the table to her, but the girl continued to stare out at the car park. 'Try and eat at least a little bit,' Sue urged. 'I know this isn't exactly the Ritz, but the burgers are actually quite nice.' Again Maddy simply ignored her and Sue's appetite suddenly died too. She could only begin to imagine how miserable Maddy must be feeling and wished there was something she could say to make her feel better.

'Will I ever get to see Oliver again?' Maddy suddenly asked out of the blue. With every mile they had driven she had been aware of the distance stretching between them, and now she had the urge to escape and run back to him.

'I don't know, Maddy,' Sue answered truthfully. 'That will all depend on whether the new parents we find for him will allow it.' She had never willingly lied to the girl before and had no intentions of starting now, even if the truth was painful to hear. She expected tears and tantrums but Maddy remained remarkably calm, although Sue could clearly see the pain in her eyes.

'I need the toilet,' Maddy announced, and as she scraped her chair back from the table, Sue rose with her.

'It's over there – look.' Pointing towards a door in the back of the café she lowered her voice and said, 'You won't go doing anything silly, will you?

Like trying to run away, I mean?'

Maddy merely gazed at her scornfully before barging away through the tables in the direction Sue had pointed. She had in fact thought of doing just that, but somehow she knew that she would only be caught as she had been when she ran away from the hospital.

When she returned to the table minutes later, Sue was standing waiting for her.

'We may as well get off again then,' she told her, and Maddy obediently followed her out to the car.

The silence was deafening again now as they drove along, and when she couldn't stand it any longer Sue said brightly, 'It's a lovely part of the country where you'll be staying, Maddy. River House is in the Cotswolds.'

Soon they were passing through picturesque little villages where traditional mellow stone cottages nestled in old-fashioned gardens. The last remaining leaves that were clinging to the branches of the trees were russet and gold. It must be breathtaking here in the summer, Sue thought as she imagined the gardens full of hollyhocks and roses and sweet-scented stocks. Even now in the late autumn the places they passed were breathtakingly pretty. A world apart from the bustling city of Plymouth they had left so far behind. They passed barns and churches with massive buttresses and stone-tiled roofs, but Maddy didn't even glance at them. At last Sue saw the sign for Stow-on-the-Wold. River House was situated halfway between there and Longborough, and she steered the car in that direction.

She would be glad when this day was over now. It was proving to be even more depressing than she had anticipated.

They continued to drive along country lanes bordered on either side by fields that seemed to stretch away for ever until at last Sue pointed upwards.

'That's River House up there – look.'

Maddy followed her finger but all she could see was a high stone wall above them on the hillside. When they finally pulled up outside the enormous wooden gates, Sue left the engine running while she got out of the car and rang a large bell set into the high stone wall. A small slot in one of the gates opened and an elderly man peered out at her.

'Hello.' Sue tried to sound as cheerful as she could. 'I'm Sue Maddox, a social worker. I have Madeleine Donovan with me. I believe you're expecting us?'

The man grunted something inaudible as the slot in the gate slammed shut again and Sue hurried back to the car. Seconds later, one of the gates began to slowly swing open and Sue drove through it. Curious, Maddy glanced back across her shoulder to see the man shutting the gate again before securely bolting it. She shuddered involuntarily. It was like entering a prison. Perhaps that's what it really was and Sue hadn't dared to tell her? She focused on the road ahead now. They were going along a very narrow, tree-lined drive. The trees met overhead in places and it was suddenly very dark and dismal. After a few minutes they rounded a bend and River House came into view ahead of them. Maddy supposed that at some time it must have been a very imposing house, but now it looked sadly in need of repair. It was an enormous building, with turrets and endless chimneys stretching upwards into the leaden grey sky. The paint on the many windows was flaking off and the front door looked as if it hadn't been stained in years. Three deep stone steps, worn in the middle where numerous feet had trodden them across the centuries, led up to it.

Sue drew the car to a halt and smiled at her encouragingly. 'Here we are then,' she announced, as if she was delivering Maddy to a holiday camp. 'It's a lovely place, isn't it?'

Maddy glared at her as if she thought Sue had lost her marbles. There was nothing lovely about it from what she could see of it. Sue hopped out of the car and began to unload Maddy's things from the boot. Then, smiling brightly, she gathered the bags and the cases together and climbed the steps. She rang a bell at the side of the door and seconds later they heard the sound of a key in the lock and a tall lady confronted them.

'Ah, you must be Miss Maddox. We've been expecting you. Do come in.'

The woman barely looked in Maddy's direction and the girl began to think that she must be invisible as she helped Sue struggle into an enormous hallway with her luggage. After dumping it down on the tiled floor she glanced around apprehensively as the woman finally turned her attention towards her.

'And you must be Madeleine.' Her eyes were

cold as she eyed her up and down.

'It's Maddy,' the girl muttered ungraciously, thinking how ugly the woman was. She had a pronounced Adam's apple, which wobbled when she spoke, and her hands were so large that they looked out of proportion with her skinny frame.

'Right, shall we go and get the paperwork out of the way then?' she suggested and then added as an afterthought, 'I'm Miss Budd, by the way. I am the house-mother here. You can leave your luggage there for now, Madeleine, and take it to your dormitory when Miss Maddox leaves. Not that you'll be needing much of it.'

Miss Budd began to stride away as if she was on a mission and they followed her along a labyrinth of corridors all painted in a dull grey colour. Maddy watched the woman as they moved along, trying to gauge how old she might be. The term 'plain Jane' might have been invented for her, but she could have been any age from thirty to fifty. The severely cut navy suit certainly did nothing to flatter her. She was quite tall for a woman, at least a head taller than Sue, and she was painfully thin. Her hair had obviously been very dark at one time but now it was a curious salt and pepper colour and her eyes were a watery grey, almost the same colour as the walls. But it was her nose that was her most striking feature. It was absolutely enormous and reminded Maddy of an eagle's beak. All this, added to her very angular features, did not make a pretty picture at all.

Eventually she paused at one of the many doors leading off the corridor and, flinging it open, she ushered them inside. They found themselves in an office that was immaculately tidy. Even the pens on the desk were neatly lined up in straight regimental lines.

'I assume you brought the necessary paperwork with you, Miss Maddox?' she snapped, as if time was of the essence.

'Er ... yes, of course.' Clearly flustered, Sue began to rummage about in her bag before producing a pile of forms. This wasn't turning out to be the sort of welcome she had hoped for, and if she was feeling so daunted by the woman she could only begin to imagine how Maddy must be feeling.

The woman instantly began to fill the forms in as Maddy and Sue settled into two hard-backed chairs in front of her desk. Moments later she pushed them back across the desk and, stabbing a pen at various papers, she told Sue, 'You sign there.'

Feeling thoroughly intimidated, Sue did as she was told, annoyed with herself because she couldn't seem to control the trembling of her hands.

'That all seems to be in order then.' Miss Budd turned her attention to Maddy. 'If you'd like to say goodbye to Miss Maddox we'll go and get your uniform sorted out.'

Uniform? Maddy gulped. She hadn't realised that she'd have to wear one of those, but that must have been what Miss Budd meant when she had said earlier that she wouldn't need much of her luggage. She glanced across at Sue, who was looking more uncomfortable by the minute. Rising from her chair slowly, the social worker raised a weak smile as she told Maddy, 'I suppose I ought to be going then so that you can get settled in.'

Only Maddy's desolate dark eyes showed any sign of emotion as she sat rigidly straight with her hands clasped in her lap. Sue wondered if she would cry but then dismissed the idea. Maddy never cried; at least not in public.

'Have a safe journey back, Miss Maddox.'

Sue had the notion that the woman couldn't get rid of her quickly enough. But then she had to begrudgingly admit that she was probably right. Nothing she said could make things any better for Maddy now. This awful place would be her home for at least the next five years. Sue wondered how she would bear it and wished wholeheartedly that she had had time to check it out before delivering Maddy there.

Pausing at the door she looked back at the girl. 'Goodbye then, Maddy. I'll be in touch soon, OK?'

Maddy stared straight ahead, giving no sign that she had even heard her as Sue left the room with a sigh. There was little more she could do for her now, and the realisation brought her no joy whatsoever. Apart from a statutory visit from herself about every twelve months, from now on, Maddy would be totally in the hands of Miss Budd.

God help her.

Chapter Nine

'Come along then, girl. We don't have all day, you know!' Miss Budd's voice was brusque.

Sliding from her seat, Maddy followed her back along the corridor to the front entrance. Through the window she glimpsed Sue's car heading off down the long driveway and she had to stifle the urge to run after her and beg her to take her back to Kirsty and Andy. If this place was a school, she dreaded to think what a prison would be like. The woman turned at the bottom of a wide staircase and hurried on down yet another corridor with Maddy having to almost run to keep up with her. Miss Budd led her into a room where the walls were lined with shelves before eyeing her up and down.

'Hmm,' she mused, and then her arms seemed to move like lightning as she began to lift various items of clothing off the shelves. 'You'll need two dresses, one to wash and one to wear. And here are six pairs of knickers and two vests. Oh, and you'll need two cardigans too.'

Maddy hadn't worn a vest for years but was too afraid to say so.

The woman added two drab grey cardigans to the pile in Maddy's arms and then snapped, 'What size shoe are you?'

'Size four,' Maddy mumbled.

The woman snatched a pair of flat black down-at-heel lace-ups from a shelf lower down and added them to the pile too, along with two faded cotton nightdresses.

'Right.' She rubbed her hands together. 'That should do you for now. Now come with me and I'll show you to your dormitory.'

Maddy's heart sank even lower, if that were possible. A dormitory. That meant she would be sharing with other girls, but then she supposed she shouldn't have expected to have a room to herself in a place like this.

'Are ... are there any boys here?' she dared to ask as she followed Miss Budd up the sweeping staircase.

The woman glanced at her disparagingly. 'Of course there aren't,' she said, as if she was talking to a complete imbecile. 'River House is a *girls'* school.'

They were at the top of the stairs now where two long corridors led off at angles. The woman took the right-hand one and marched along as if she was in a race as Maddy tried valiantly not to drop the pile of clothes and shoes that were teetering precariously in her arms.

'Here we are then. This will be your room.' Miss Budd had stopped in front of a door with the number 18 written on it in tall black letters. The woman ushered Maddy ahead of her and she found herself in a large room with six beds, three along two walls. Between each of them was a battered chest-of-drawers, but other than that the room was bare apart from washed-out curtains that framed a large sash-cord window. A couple of the beds had teddy bears propped up

101

against the pillows, and the sight of such personal things in this impersonal room made the lump in her throat swell even bigger.

'This will be your bed.' Miss Budd motioned to the bed on the right nearest to the door. 'You can put your things in there,' she told her, pointing at the chest-of-drawers. 'And we expect the room to be kept tidy at all times. There is a room inspection each morning before breakfast, and if your bed and your drawers aren't tidy, you will lose points. I'll explain how the points system works later on.'

Maddy nodded numbly.

'I'll leave you to get settled in. Your room-mates will be finished their lessons soon and they will show you down to the dining room for your evening meal. Is there anything you would like to ask me before I go?'

Maddy shook her head as the woman moved back to the door and then she was gone. Maddy sank onto the edge of the bed as despair coursed through her, wondering how she was going to be able to bear living in such a bleak mausoleum of a place.

After a while she heaved herself off the lumpy mattress and crossed to the window. The view from it was absolutely breathtaking – if you looked beyond the high brick walls that surrounded the place, that was. Within the walls was a small copse to the left of the house, which Maddy would soon discover was where a lot of the older girls liked to congregate during their free time, free from the prying eyes of the social workers who ran the place. To the side of it a small stream meandered through the grounds, and as Maddy looked beyond the wall she saw that it flowed into a fast-moving river running down into a deep valley. That's probably how the house got its name, she thought. Surprisingly, there was not another house or cottage to be seen for miles. The nearest were dotted here and there deep down in the bottom of the valley, and from here they appeared no bigger than her fingernail. The sight only served to make her feel even more isolated. There was not a single person here that she knew, and beyond the walls there was no one at all who cared about her or what became of her. It was a sobering thought.

Almost an hour later, the unnatural quietness was broken by the sounds of footsteps clattering up the stairs and girls' voices. She heard doors opening and shutting and then footsteps approaching the room she was in. She steeled herself to meet her room-mates. The door opened and three pairs of eyes surveyed her warily. Maddy stuck her chin in the air and stared back at them.

'I'm Holly,' a painfully thin fair-haired girl finally introduced herself. 'And this is Kim and that's Stephanie, but we all call her Steph. What's your name?'

'Maddy,' she mumbled.

She looked from one to another of them, trying to gauge their ages. She finally decided that they were probably about the same age as herself, or possibly slightly older. The girl who had introduced herself as Holly had an almost ethereal quality about her, with soft blonde hair framing a heart-shaped face. She was very dainty and petite, unlike the girl she had introduced as Steph, who was black and quite well-built. Her hair was very frizzy and cut short to her head, and she had the most enormous brown eyes that Maddy had ever seen, the whites of them startling against her dark skin. Kim was quite plain and the uniform she was wearing made her appear even more so. Her hair was mousy and poker straight, cut into an unbecoming style that looked as if someone had stuck a basin on her head and cut around it. She was on the plump side and her face was covered in the worst case of acne that Maddy had ever seen. All three were dressed in the same unbecoming uniform that Maddy had been issued with, and she was horrified to see that it looked even worse on than off, if that was possible. She could see them all eyeing her jeans and the bright sweatshirt she was wearing, and she scowled.

Eventually, Holly suggested tentatively, 'I should get your uniform on if I was you. Miss Budd won't like it if she spots you in them clothes.'

Maddy gazed resentfully at the pile of clothes on the bed. Steph and Kim drifted away to their own beds but Holly stood there smiling at her.

'It ain't so bad once you get used to wearin' it,' she told her, as if she could read her mind. 'An' we're all dressed the same so nobody takes any notice.'

'Where can I get changed?' Maddy asked, and now all the girls looked at her and laughed.

'Right where you are,' Kim piped up. 'Yer don't have no modesty in this place. Same as when we shower. We all go in together.'

Maddy blushed to the colour of a beetroot. She couldn't think of anything worse than having to walk about naked in front of other people, but these girls seemed to accept it. Turning her back on them, she removed her sweatshirt then hastily pulled the drab grey dress over her head; then she wriggled out of her jeans and smoothed the dress over her hips. It buttoned to the neck with a small collar and hung shapelessly from her shoulders to mid-calf.

'I should put your cardigan on an' all,' Holly told her. 'This place is really draughty in winter. The only time you're really warm in here is when you're in the shower or in bed.'

Maddy looked at the cardigan disdainfully but put it on as Holly had suggested. The flat ugly shoes completed the picture and she was glad that there wasn't a mirror in the room. She could only guess how awful she must look and thanked God that she had never been a particularly vain person.

'It's about an hour to dinner,' Holly now told her. 'Have you been given any jobs to do yet?'

When Maddy shook her head she grinned, revealing a set of straight white teeth. 'Lucky you then. Make the most of it while you can. We've all got to get off to do our chores now, but we'll see you downstairs. Oh, and while you've got time I should put your things away too. Old Budd is a stickler for tidiness.' Smiling, she then added as an afterthought, 'Do you know the way to the dining room?'

When Maddy shook her head, she offered good-naturedly, 'Not to worry, I'll pop up and fetch you down, shall I?'

'Please.'

The three girls began to troop towards the door and once again Maddy found herself alone. She began to ram her clothes into the chest and slid her case under the bed. There didn't seem to be anywhere else she could put it. And then she lay on the bed with her hands behind her head and stared up at the cracked ceiling wondering if there were any more room-mates she hadn't met as yet. There were six beds in the room, after all. Holly seemed quite nice, and so did Kim, but she felt she had detected a slight coolness in Steph. Perhaps she felt that she shouldn't have muscled in on their space? Finally the trauma of the day she had just spent caught up with her and she slipped into a doze. She began to dream and in the dream Oliver was calling for her.

'Maddy, wake up... It's time to go to dinner.'

Maddy started awake to find Holly standing over her with a look of concern on her face.

'I think you were having a bad dream.' Holly looked sympathetic but Maddy was determined to keep her distance. She had never had a real friend and she certainly didn't need one now. Running her fingers through her thick dark hair to tidy it, she followed Holly to the door. Once they reached the hallway Holly led her towards the back of the house, and Maddy soon found herself in a large room in which bare tables were laid with mismatched cutlery. A large number of girls of all shapes and sizes, all dressed in the same unbecoming grey uniform, were standing about in little groups and they all looked towards her curiously.

'This is our table over here.' Holly led her to where Steph and Kim were already seated. Kim smiled at her but Steph continued talking to a girl on the next table.

The room suddenly became silent when Miss Budd bustled in with two other adults closely following her. One of them was a fairly young, attractive-looking woman. The other was a man who was so obese he seemed to roll across the room rather than walk.

'That's Mr Dumbarr,' Holly whispered to Maddy. 'He's resident here with Miss Budd. The other one is Miss Gay. She's a social worker. She and three others work here in shifts.'

The adults took a seat at the top of the room and Maddy noticed that their table had a crisp white cloth on it.

Miss Budd rose and banged the table with her fork. 'Now, girls, we shall say grace,' she said, and bowing her head she muttered, 'For what we are about to receive, may the Lord make us truly thankful.'

'Amen,' the girls said in chorus and then they all stood and formed an orderly queue at a long table where women in white starched caps and white uniforms were ladling food onto plates.

Maddy stared down in dismay at the lumpy spoonful of mashed potato one of the ladies had just dolloped onto her plate. The next lady along slid a slice of meat next to it. And so she went along the row until finally someone ladled a spoonful of gravy onto the whole unappetising meal. The gravy was so watery that Maddy had to be careful it didn't slosh over the side of the plate as she carried it carefully back to the table.

'What is this?' she whispered to Holly as she tried to cut her meat. It was so tough that Maddy was sure she could have soled shoes with it.

Holly shrugged. 'Probably pork or beef,' she whispered back. The carrots were so overcooked that they were almost colourless and they were tasteless too, but Maddy was hungry now so she tackled the meal as best she could. She glanced enviously at the sizzling pork chops the dinner ladies were carrying to the adults' table but wisely held her tongue.

The pudding wasn't much better. It was some sort of sponge with very thin custard trickled over it. None of the other girls commented on how awful the meal was, so Maddy could only assume that they were used to it. No wonder half of them were so scrawny, she found herself thinking. She drank at least three glasses of water to wash the whole sorry mess down, but had to admit she felt slightly better now that she had eaten something, even if it had been horrible. Holly barely touched her own food and Maddy noticed her wipe sweat from her forehead halfway through the meal. She found this rather strange as it was chilly in the dining room, to say the least. The girl was very pale, and Maddy wondered if she was unwell, not that it was any of her business.

Now that the meal was over Maddy saw the other girls carrying their dirty plates to a large table at the end of the room, so she did the same and then stood there feeling rather like a fish out of water as she wondered what to do next.

Despite being determined to keep herself to herself, she was relieved when Holly approached her and asked, 'Do you fancy a bit of fresh air? We all usually have a stroll outside before they lock the doors at seven.'

Not knowing what else she could do, Maddy nodded and followed the stream of girls who were heading towards the French doors in the dining room. It was bitterly cold outside and very dark, so she was surprised to see them making for the little copse she had spotted from her bedroom window. When they reached it, Maddy found that the trees were denser than she had expected, and she picked her way along the uneven ground beneath the barren branches to a place in the centre of the copse where the others were all congregated. Here they were out of sight of the house. Some of them were smoking and she wondered where they had got their cigarettes from.

Steph was amongst them and she peered at Maddy through the gloom before asking, 'Do you want a smoke?'

'No, thanks,' Maddy said, before daring to ask, 'How do you manage to get your cigarettes? Are you allowed out of here?'

'Huh! I wish.' Steph took a long drag and blew a perfect smoke ring into the air before going on, 'It's the dinner ladies who come in from the local villages that bring us stuff in. You'd be surprised what we are able to get hold of. And then of course those who are lucky enough to have visitors get them to bring in stuff too. What they don't want, they trade.'

'Oh, so are we never allowed out of here then?'

'Only if you need to go to a hospital or the dentist,' Steph told her glumly.

'So how do you get toiletries and personal things?' Maddy asked.

'There's a van that comes round each week and we buy them with our allowance,' Steph informed her. 'And, if we have relatives who are prepared to take us, we're allowed to spend holidays with them now and again.'

Plucking up her courage, Maddy then asked the question that had been burning her. 'Is this like an approved school for girls?'

'Not really.' Steph's dark skin glowed like warm chocolate in the dim light. 'But it might as well be, the way they treat us. It's more like a school for misfits. You know ... kids that have had problems. Some are in because their parents reckoned they were beyond control. Some are in because they have nowhere else to go and because they are too old to be adopted, and others are in because they have done things wrong but are too young to be sent to prison.'

Maddy gulped as her worst fears were confirmed. 'Have you been here long?' she asked.

'About eighteen months or so now. I'll be here till I'm eighteen which is still a long way away. Me mum died, see, an' I went to live with me uncle but he wasn't able to take proper care of me, so I ended up here. There ain't many who'd want to take in a thirteen-year-old Jamaican girl, is there?'

Steph went on, 'Kim is here 'cos her mum put her on the game when she was twelve. Her mum was a pro too an' the authorities thought she'd be

110

safer here.'

'And what about Holly?'

Steph snorted with disgust as she glanced towards the other side of the copse where Holly was standing. 'Her mum an' dad split up an' she went to live with her dad for a while but she didn't get on with her step-mum. Holly ain't in the best of health so I reckon they dumped her here 'cos it was easier than havin' to keep takin' her to the doctor's all the while. She's always in the sick bay though no one seems to know what's wrong with her yet. She's had loads of tests. They had a new baby of their own an' all, an' I think things got more difficult for her after that. Personally I just think they didn't want her, but I wouldn't tell her that, of course.'

As Maddy followed Steph's eyes she felt sorry for the girl. 'An' why are *you* here?'

Steph's question took Maddy by surprise but after a moment she muttered, 'My mum and dad died and I had nowhere else to go.' That was all she was prepared to divulge for now, even though she was more than grateful that someone was actually speaking to her.

'What ... they both died at the same time?'

'Yes. There was a fire and they didn't get out.' Maddy was glad of the darkness that hid her discomfort.

'An' I suppose, judgin' by the way you talk, they were quite well-to-do, were they?' Steph was intrigued now.

'I suppose they were,' Maddy mumbled. Thankfully, Holly joined them at that moment and spared her from having to answer any more difficult questions.

When she flashed Maddy a friendly smile the girl felt herself warming to her, as she recognised someone who seemed to be just as abandoned and unwanted as she herself was.

'So what are the staff like?' Maddy asked next.

'Well, Miss Budd is a tartar,' Steph warned her. 'Upset her an' you'll find yourself in the Quiet Room before you can say Jack Robinson.'

'The Quiet Room?'

'Yes, it's downstairs in the cellars. I once spent a whole week in there for fightin' with one of the other girls, an' I don't mind admittin' it was the worst time of me life. It's just a little room with no window. They lock you in with nothing to do, so you have no way of knowing whether it's day or night, and the only time you see anyone is when they bring you your meals.' Steph shuddered at the memory. 'You don't have to get shut in there many times before you start toeing the line, I don't mind tellin' you. Anyway, then there's Miss Gay. She's about the best of the lot of 'em, to be honest. We also have teachers who come in to give us lessons, an' some of them are all right an' all. An' then there's Mr Dumbarr ... ugh! Whatever you do, try not to *ever* get left on your own with him. He likes young girls – if you know what I mean.'

Maddy frowned. She didn't like the sound of this at all. 'Has he ever touched you?' she whispered.

'He's touched nearly every girl in the school,' Steph said scathingly. 'But some quite like it. They get special favours, see, if they're nice to him. He'll have an eye on you because you're new, so be warned.'

'But why doesn't anyone tell somebody what he's doing?' Maddy was indignant.

'And just who are we supposed to tell?'

'Well, I don't know. We all have social workers, so why hasn't anyone spoken to them?'

Steph grinned at Maddy's naivety. 'Oh, plenty have. But no one ever believes them. Who's going to take our word against his? Miss Budd idolises the fat old git, and one word against him an' you find yourself in the Quiet Room. An' believe me, that makes it even worse. When you're in there he can come to you whenever he wants and do whatever he wants. No one can hear you screaming down there. We hardly ever get to see our social workers anyway. Once they've dumped us here we're on our own, apart from a visit from them every blue moon.'

Maddy felt fear trickle through her. Whatever Steph said, this place *was* like a prison – and she had five whole years of it ahead of her.

Chapter Ten

Maddy had been at River House for a week and that week had felt like a year. She hated every single thing about the place and constantly asked when her social worker would be coming to see her. Sue Maddox would get her out of there as soon as she told Sue how awful it was, she was

113

sure of it. But up to now, each time she had approached a member of staff to ask when Sue would be coming they had just told her to be patient. Thankfully, she had avoided being alone with Mr Dumbarr up to now but sometimes she had caught his eyes following her and she had scuttled away like a startled rabbit. Just the sight of the man made her shudder with revulsion. She was sure he was the ugliest man she had ever set eyes on, and she avoided him like the plague.

River House was run on a strict routine, beginning every morning at six-thirty when a member of staff would come and pound on their doors to wake them all. The girls would then file into the shower block where they were allowed four minutes each to get washed. Maddy had almost died of embarrassment for the first few mornings as she was herded under the water like a sheep with the other girls. They would then be allowed a few minutes to get dressed and tidy their room before Miss Budd came to check, and then it was time for breakfast. This usually consisted of lumpy porridge and cold toast. After breakfast they were all expected to tidy the pots away and prepare the tables for the midday meal before going off to lessons. These lasted until twelve-thirty, with a ten-minute break mid-morning when they were given a glass of milk. Then at lunchtime they would once again file off to the dining room for yet another unpalatable meal. Lessons resumed at one until four and then the girls all had chores to do. Up until now Maddy had been allocated washing-up duties, which was no easy task considering the mountain of dirty pots and pans she had to tackle each day. Still, she didn't complain – she was no stranger to household chores. And some of the girls had to clean the toilet and shower blocks, which Maddy considered was even worse than washing up. Even so she knew that soon she too would have to do it as the chores were done on a rota.

After evening dinner the girls were allowed within reason to do as they pleased for one hour. Some of them chose to go to the Day Room, a gloomy place that boasted a few well-worn books and a table-tennis table that was so wobbly no one ever bothered with it. There was a television in there that many of the girls opted to watch, but the older girls tended to head to the spinney for their nightly crafty fag.

The worst time for Maddy was when Miss Budd came to switch off the lights in the dormitory each evening. She would lie there in the darkness listening to the sounds of the old house settling around her and to Holly tossing and turning in her sleep. The girl would whimper as if she was in pain, and sometimes Maddy had to resist the urge to go to her and comfort her. She discovered that the girls in the home were aged from ten to eighteen and Maddy had been told that they were allowed visitors on the first Saturday of every month.

Maddy was dreading visiting day already. She knew there would be no one to come and see her, and this only served to increase her deep sense of loneliness. Often she thought back to her comfy little bedroom at Kirsty and Andy's and she wished now that she had tried harder with them.

Perhaps then they might have allowed her to stay?

There was one particular girl in the home who seemed to have taken a dislike to Maddy, and she tried to keep out of her way. The girl's name was Stacey, and Maddy learned through Holly that she was fifteen and a great favourite of Mr Dumbarr, or Dumbo as the girls had nicknamed him. Maddy wondered if he had come by the nickname because of his elephant-like ears or his name. She decided it was probably because of his ears. They stuck out on either side of his head like wings. Stacey was often to be seen disappearing into his office, and when she came out, she would always have a broad smirk on her face. Stacey was a well-built girl with a figure that would have looked fitting on a woman twice her age. Unlike the other girls, her dress had been shortened to above the knee, and the buttons on it revealed a deep cleavage of which she was inordinately proud. She had also been blessed with naturally blonde hair and eyes the colour of bluebells.

On this particular evening the girls made their way to the copse as they usually did following dinner and Maddy was dismayed to see that Stacey was there with a little band of girls who seemed to hang on her every word. Maddy stayed behind Kim, trying to make herself as inconspicuous as possible, but Stacey had already spotted her.

'Well, well.' The older girl's teeth curled back from her teeth in a sneer. 'If it ain't Little Miss High an' fuckin' Mighty.'

'Calm down, Stacey. There ain't no call for

that.' Steph's deep Jamaican voice echoed eerily through the leafless trees as she took a stand at Maddy's side. Maddy was touched that Steph was standing up for her. No one had ever done that before.

'I've seen the way you look at Mr Dumbarr,' Stacey continued as if Steph hadn't spoken. 'An' I'll warn yer now, you snotty little bitch, you keep away from him else you'll have me to answer to.'

Maddy's fists clenched in indignation. 'You can *have* Mr Dumbarr,' she answered haughtily. 'I wouldn't touch the likes of him with a bargepole.'

A silence settled amongst the girls as Stacey slowly ground out the stub of her cigarette with her heel and sauntered over to Maddy.

'Now don't start bein' cocky with me,' she snarled. 'I'm the kingpin around here an' you better fuckin' remember it, if you know what's good for you.'

Maddy decided that she would walk away rather than have a full-on confrontation and she turned ready to do just that, but Stacey had other ideas. All the girls were watching avidly and she had her position in the home to maintain. Catching Maddy by the elbow, she swung her about.

Caught offguard, Maddy stumbled and Stacey's hand snaked out and caught a handful of hair that she tugged at viciously.

'Ouch!' Instinct made Maddy lash out and purely by luck the blow caught Stacey full on the mouth. She staggered backwards as her hand flew to the blood trickling down her chin.

Maddy looked on in horror.

117

'I ... I'm sorry,' she stuttered. 'I didn't mean to do that.'

Stacey advanced on her menacingly but then suddenly stopped dead, realising that she could play this to her advantage. Staggering dramatically through the trees, she emerged onto the lawn wailing loudly enough to waken the dead. The rest of the girls followed her, eager to see what happened next. They led such boring lives that anything out of the daily routine was a welcome distraction.

'Whatever is going on here?' Miss Budd demanded as Stacey almost fell through the French windows in the dining room, clutching her lip.

'It ... it was that new girl.' Stacey forced a very convincing sob. 'I caught her smoking in the copse, miss. And when I told her that you wouldn't be pleased with her, she attacked me.'

'*I did not!*' Maddy declared indignantly as she followed her into the room.

Mr Dumbarr, who had been sitting beside Miss Budd, heaved himself out of his chair and rolled over to Stacey, his face a mask of concern.

'I think we'd better get the nurse to look at that, my dear. It looks quite nasty,' he said, as he tipped Stacey's chin and stared at her split lip. 'Come along. I'll take you to the Medical Room right now and hope that the nurse is still there. I trust I can leave you to handle this, Miss Budd.'

'Of *course*, Mr Dumbarr,' Miss Budd simpered and then turning towards Maddy she hissed, 'How *dare you* come here using violence? Why, you've only been here for two minutes and you're wreaking havoc already.'

118

Maddy's hands clenched into fists at the injustice of it. 'It wasn't like that at all,' she retaliated. 'It was Stacey who attacked *me*.'

'That's true, Miss Budd,' Holly volunteered, and now the woman directed her wrath at her.

'*One* more word out of you and you'll be in trouble too, my girl.' Her eyes were flashing fire and Holly hastily clamped her mouth shut as Miss Budd advanced on Maddy. 'I think a night in the Quiet Room might do you good and give you time to think on what you've done,' she said. As her scrawny hand clamped about Maddy's arm she tried to shake her off, but despite the woman's thin frame she was remarkably strong and the girl felt herself being dragged towards the door.

'Stop it!' she cried as panic gripped her. 'This isn't fair, I haven't done anything wrong.' She'd had a fear of enclosed spaces ever since Michelle had taken to shutting her away under the stairs, and from what the other girls had told her, the Quiet Room was not a nice place at all. By the time they were halfway along the hall, Maddy was sobbing and struggling with all her might but it was like battling against the wind, and soon she found herself being shoved down some dark stone steps. She fell halfway down and grazed her knee, but Miss Budd hauled her on relentlessly.

'There,' she panted with satisfaction as she flung a door open. 'Perhaps you'll be more ready to apologise to Stacey in the morning when you've had a cool-down in here.' She flung Maddy into the room and the girl landed in an undignified heap on the floor. Before she could stagger to her feet she heard the sound of a door slamming and a key turning in a lock.

'NO!' Flinging herself at the door, she began to hammer on it with all her might. 'Let me out! I haven't done anything wrong, I tell you!' She could hear the sound of Miss Budd's footsteps retreating, and as despair washed through her she stopped her hammering and stared around miserably, wrapping her arms tightly about herself. The room she was in was just long enough to house a single bed and a bucket that she assumed was for toilet purposes. The ceiling was high and a single dim bare light bulb dangled from it. There was no window and the walls were bare plaster, the floor cold concrete. Tears squeezed out of the corners of her eyes as she sank onto the side of the narrow metal bed. It was cold down here and the place smelled damp and musty. After a time she again began to pound on the door but only silence answered her. Panic made the breath catch in her throat as she strained her ears for sounds, any sounds at all, but it was as if she had been buried alive and the silence was profound.

Perhaps if I lie down and try to sleep it will be better, she told herself as she slid beneath the thin blanket on the bed. The bare mattress smelled of stale urine and she felt her stomach revolt. She was shivering uncontrollably and feeling more alone than she had ever felt in the whole of her young life. Now she knew without a shadow of a doubt that there was truly not a single person in the whole world who cared about her. She could die down here and no one would grieve. Burying her head in the pillow, she eventually cried herself to sleep.

In Plymouth at that very moment, Kirsty was staring off into space. Andy was sitting beside her on the settee and he asked, 'Are you all right, love?'

'What? Oh yes, I'm fine. I was just wondering how Maddy was doing.'

He sighed as he looked at his wife. She had been fretting ever since Maddy had left them.

'Look, it isn't your fault that she wasn't allowed to stay here,' he pointed out. 'The decision on Maddy's future was taken out of your hands, so why are you whipping yourself?'

'Because I didn't tell her that we wanted her to stay,' Kirsty replied. 'At the time I thought it would be easier for her if Sue just moved her on. But now I realise I should have told her we wanted her. At least then she would have known there was *someone* who gave a damn about her.'

'Well, it's no good getting upset about it now.' Andy stroked her arm tenderly. 'Maddy will be all right. She's a survivor.'

'I'm not so sure about that,' Kirsty muttered. 'I think underneath all that bravado was just a very young girl who wanted to feel she belonged. I'm going to ring Sue Maddox tomorrow and ask her if we can visit her.'

Andy looked concerned. 'Are you sure that's such a good idea? What I mean is, won't it just make her feel worse?'

Kirsty glared at him. 'How could we make things any worse? And who else will bother going

121

to see her if we don't? The poor kid doesn't have anyone, Andy. Can you even *begin* to imagine how that must feel?'

Andy sighed resignedly. 'All right then. If it will make you feel any better, go ahead and ring Sue. But don't be disappointed if she tells you she'd rather we didn't go.'

'I doubt she'll tell me that.' Kirsty's chin was set with determination. 'And if she does, she'd better have a bloody good reason why we can't.'

Andy picked up the paper and made a great pretence of reading it. He knew better than to try and reason with his wife when she had her stubborn head on.

Maddy had no idea how long she had lain there in the dank and musty room but finally she heard footsteps outside in the corridor and then the sound of the key turning in the lock. Pulling herself up onto her elbow, she peered towards the door at Mr Dumbarr, who was standing there with a smirk on his face. His enormous frame seemed to fill the doorway.

'Ready to come and apologise to Stacey now, are you, Madeleine?' His tongue snaked out and slid wetly around his thick lips.

'No, I'm not,' Maddy retorted. 'I didn't do anything wrong. I was only defending myself.'

'Hm!' A twinkle of amusement shone in his eyes. She was a feisty little thing, he had to give her that, and she was developing nicely. Just the way he liked them. 'You know, you can make your time here as easy or as difficult as you please,' he purred as he advanced on her. As he bent towards her, his hand dropped to stroke her exposed thigh. Maddy shuddered with revulsion as she wrapped the thin blanket protectively around her.

'If you were to be nice to me, I could ensure that you wanted for nothing and I think you would find that I can be *very* generous.'

'I don't need anything,' Maddy snapped before she could stop herself.

He stared at her for a moment before sighing heavily. 'Do you know, I don't think you've quite learned your lesson yet.' He was standing erect again now, his huge shadow dwarfing the small space of her prison. 'Perhaps a few more hours in here will make you a little more amenable, eh?'

'No!' Panic gripped her as she sprang off the bed. 'I want to come out! I haven't done anything wrong, really I haven't!'

He moved towards the door without even answering her, and seconds later it banged shut again and she heard the key turn in the lock once more.

'Let me out!' She was hammering at the door and it shook in its frame at the force of her blows, but all she heard was the sound of Mr Dumbarr's footsteps retreating again before the terrible silence once more pressed down on her. A sense of claustrophobia engulfed her, but then she scuttled to the bed once more and buried her head beneath the scratchy blanket as she prayed for this latest nightmare to end.

Hours later, the door opened and Miss Budd appeared, balancing a tray in one hand.

Crossing to the bed she plonked it down and

some of the lukewarm tea in the mug on it slopped over its rim to splash onto the dried-up sandwiches on the plate beside it.

'Your lunch, Madeleine,' she told her as she turned to leave. Then, pausing, she said icily, 'You only have to apologise to myself and Stacey, you know, and then you can come out of here.'

Maddy opened her mouth to tell her where to go but then clamped it shut again. If apologising was the only way of getting out of here, she would have to do it. She didn't know how much longer she could bear being locked away.

'I ... I'm sorry, Miss Budd.' Colour burned into her cheeks as the woman nodded.

'That's better.' There was a measure of satisfaction in her voice. 'Come along then and bring your tray with you. You've missed lunch, I'm afraid. We'll go and find Stacey right away and once you've apologised to her we'll put this whole unfortunate incident behind us and hope that you've learned a lesson from it. Bullying and fighting will not be tolerated in this school, is that *quite* clear?'

'Yes, Miss Budd.' Anger was simmering away like boiling liquid in Maddy but she managed to conceal it behind a meek façade.

Lifting her tray, she passed the woman and quietly followed her back through the labyrinth of corridors beneath River House until they came to the roughly hewn stone steps that led up to the ground floor.

Once they entered the hallway, Maddy blinked as her eyes adjusted to the daylight.

'Take your tray through to the kitchen staff,'

Miss Budd ordered. 'And then wait in the dining room while I go and fetch Stacey from her lesson. Once you've apologised, you can get back to your own lessons.'

Minutes later, the woman appeared in the doorway of the dining room with a smug-faced Stacey standing at the side of her.

Maddy had the satisfaction of seeing that Stacey's lip was split and swollen, but she managed to keep the smile from showing on her face as she stared at her.

'Well, I believe you have something to say to Stacey, don't you?' Miss Budd demanded impatiently. 'Come along, girl. We don't have all day, you know!'

'I apologise for hurting you yesterday.' Maddy looked her straight in the eye and although the girl was head and shoulders above her, Stacey realised in that moment that she might have met her match. Maddy was saying all the right things, but the expression in her eyes told another story.

'May we have a response, Stacey?' Miss Budd snapped.

Stacey shuffled from foot to foot before mumbling, 'It's all right.'

'That's better now, isn't it, girls?' Miss Budd rubbed her hands together before flapping them at the two of them. 'Now be off with you both. We don't want you missing valuable lesson time, do we?'

The two girls followed her into the hallway and then both shot off in different directions. Maddy was fuming at the injustice of it all and struggled to concentrate on what the teacher was saying for the rest of the afternoon. But she had learned a valuable lesson from the episode. It appeared that only the strongest survived in this place and she was determined to survive. At any price.

Chapter Eleven

When dinner and the chores were finally done that evening, Maddy found her room-mates waiting for her in the dormitory.

'Are you all right?' Holly asked, the instant she set foot through the door. Maddy noticed that there were dark circles under Holly's eyes but she didn't comment on it, she merely shrugged.

'I told you it was horrible in that Quiet Room, didn't I?' Steph shivered as she thought back to the times she had been shut in there.

Maddy took care to make light of it. 'I suppose there are worse places,' she answered nonchalantly. The attention was taken off her then when Holly suddenly sat down heavily on the side of her bed.

'Are you OK, mate?' Kim crossed to the girl, flicking her lank hair out of her face as she told Maddy, 'She hasn't been too well again today. Miss Budd sent her along to the sick bay an' the nurse took some blood tests to send off to the hospital.'

Of all the girls, Holly was the one that Maddy felt the most affinity with and now she asked, 'Is there anything I can get for you?'

126

Wiping the sweat that had broken out on her upper lip away with the cuff of her cardigan, Holly smiled weakly. 'No, I'll be fine, honestly. You lot get off and get some fresh air. I reckon I'll stay here and put my feet up for a while.'

'I'll stay with her,' Maddy said, and with a nod the other two girls left the room.

'I'm sorry about what happened to you,' Holly whispered. 'We did try to tell Budd and Dumbo what had gone on, that Stacey had started the fight, but they wouldn't listen to us.'

'Don't worry about it,' Maddy replied. 'At least I'll know to keep out of her way in future. Why is she here anyway?'

Holly giggled now as she settled back against her pillows. 'Well, you wouldn't believe it but Stacey's father is actually a vicar. She comes from Stoke-on-Trent and her mum and dad are *ever* so posh. Apparently she got in with a bad crowd right from when she was just twelve, and got herself into all sorts of trouble. Then last year, just before they sent her here, she had a baby. It went for adoption apparently, and her mum and dad said then that she was beyond parental control and they put her in here.' Suddenly becoming serious again, Holly said quietly, 'I ought to warn you, Maddy, there's a rumour going round about you. They're saying that you set fire to your parents' home and that they both died in the fire. They reckon you did it to be rid of them because you didn't get on with them. Is that true?'

'What if it is?' Maddy said wearily. 'I'd be a liar to say I cared about them. They weren't my real mum and dad anyway. I'm glad that they're dead,

127

if you want the truth. I do miss my brother though.' Crossing her arms tightly across her chest she held back the tears.

'How old is he?' Holly asked softly.

'He's nine now and his name is Oliver. And *one day* when I get out of this hell-hole I'm going to find him – *and* my other brother and sister – and nothing and no one will ever part us again,' Maddy stated with conviction.

She saw Holly blink with shock and quickly looked away again, fearful that, due to her confession, she might just have lost the nearest thing to a friend that she had ever had.

After a while she risked a glance to find that Holly was fast asleep. Her face was as white as the pillowcase she was lying on and Maddy felt sorry for her. Holly was trapped in here through no fault of her own from what she could see of it, and she thought how unfair it was. But then life, as she was fast discovering, *was* unfair. The only things that were getting her through this difficult time were Holly and Miss Parr, the fair-haired English teacher who came to the home three times a week. A plump middle-aged woman, she had taken a shine to Maddy, and although she was too professional to make a teacher's pet of the girl, she always made sure that Maddy had enough books to read and a kindly word from her. Crossing to Holly now, Maddy gently pulled the blanket up around her and then dropping onto her own bed she began to read the latest book that Miss Parr had loaned her. It was *Four Past Midnight* by Stephen King, and within minutes she was engrossed in the story and all her worries melted away for now.

It was the first Saturday of December and the house was alive with excitement as the girls who were lucky enough to have them prepared for their visitors to arrive.

Miss Budd had made sure that all the girls were clean and tidy, and no one would ever have believed that this was anything other than a happy place to be. Maddy could have told a different story, had she had anyone to tell it to, but she knew there was fat chance of anyone visiting her.

The visitors began to arrive shortly after lunch and the girls escorted them to the Day Room. Holly and Maddy watched enviously from the staircase. Holly had spent most of the previous week in the sick bay and seemed to be sleeping more and more – a fact that was not lost on Maddy. She and Holly had become quite close; at night when Kim and Steph were fast asleep, they would lie and whisper about what they wanted to do with their futures, and once or twice when Holly had been feeling really ill, Maddy had even lain next to her, whispering words of encouragement.

'You'll be all right,' she would tell her. 'Just as soon as the results of your latest blood tests come back, they'll be able to treat you for whatever is wrong with you.' Holly would nod unconvincingly in the darkness. She wasn't so sure.

As they were sitting there, Maddy suddenly received a sharp dig in the ribs from Holly's elbow and following her pointing finger she saw a smartly dressed middle-aged couple enter the hallway. The man was wearing a dog collar.

'That's Stacey's parents,' Holly hissed in her ear, and even as she said it, Stacey appeared as if by magic and sauntered over to them.

'Have you brought me the things I asked for?' she said ungraciously by way of a greeting.

'Of course we have, darling,' the woman flustered. 'How are you?' She was tall and slim and very attractive, and Maddy instantly saw where Stacey had got her good looks from.

'How d'you expect me to be, locked away in here?' Stacey grumbled as she snatched two of the carrier bags that her mother was holding out to her.

'Now, let's not start that again, my dear,' the vicar trilled as he yanked nervously at his starched white collar. 'You know you are only here for your own safety. Had you listened to what your mother and I tried to tell you, there would have been no need for us to resort to such measures. But at least while you are here we know that you are safe and out of the way of temptation.'

'Oh, spare me all that bleeding malarkey again,' Stacey groaned as she stamped off towards the Day Room. The woman almost swooned as she snatched a flimsy lace handkerchief from her smart leather handbag and held it to her nose. Her husband then took her by the elbow and they started after Stacey at a trot as Holly tittered.

'Oh, dear. Fancy a vicar havin' a daughter like that, eh?'

Seeing the funny side of it, Maddy grinned too. 'She must have been a disappointment to say the least,' she agreed. 'Perhaps they got given the wrong baby at the hospital when she was born.'

'I very much doubt that. Stacey is like a younger version of her mother,' Holly pointed out, still smiling, and then suddenly she leaned heavily against the banister as the colour drained from her face.

'I feel a bit funny,' she whispered, and then to Maddy's horror she crumpled in a heap at her feet. Maddy flew down the stairs and along to the sick bay where she found the nurse sitting writing a report.

'Come quickly,' she gasped. 'Holly has just fainted and she looks ever so poorly.'

The nurse followed her back along the corridor at a trot. Holly was halfway up the stairs where Maddy had left her, and once the nurse had taken her pulse, she told her, 'Run and fetch the first two members of staff you can find. We need to get her into bed.'

Maddy pounded back down the stairs only to be brought to an abrupt halt when she almost collided with Miss Budd.

'The nurse needs some help. She's up there,' Maddy pointed back up the stairs. 'Holly has fainted.'

'I see.' Miss Budd looked as if she was sucking on a lemon. 'Then I suggest you leave me to go and deal with it while you get along to the Day Room to your visitors.'

'*Visitors?*' Maddy's face betrayed her shock. 'What visitors? I didn't know I was having any.'

'Neither did I,' Miss Budd retorted indignantly. 'It's really most irregular. Visitors should apply to me for a pass, but seeing as these people had come some distance I have made an allowance on this occasion. You should think yourself lucky, girl. Now get along with you.'

In an agony of indecision, Maddy glanced back towards the stairs. Holly had looked really ill and she was loath to leave her. But then she realised that there was nothing that she could do to help her so she started off in the direction of the Day Room, wondering who might have taken the trouble to come and see her.

She stood in the doorway and looked about. There were people everywhere, and for once most of the girls were smiling. And then she saw Kirsty and Andy, and her heart began to pound. What were they doing here? They had seemed keen enough to get rid of her, so why the sudden concern? Picking her way through the tables with burning cheeks she finally stood in front of them.

'Maddy.' Kirsty leaped out of her seat looking genuinely pleased to see her as she took her hand. 'How have you been, love? And how are you settling in?'

Maddy was aware of Stacey watching her from the next table with a wide smirk on her face.

'I've been fine,' she mumbled, as she lowered herself into a chair and stared down at the floor. An uncomfortable silence settled, broken by Andy when he asked quietly, 'Are you eating enough, Maddy? You look as if you might have lost a bit of weight.' The girl had always been slim but now in her shapeless uniform she looked positively skeletal.

Maddy could have told him that the food they

were served was not much better than pigswill, but she was conscious of Stacey's eyes on her so she merely shrugged. Half of her wanted to throw herself into their arms and beg them to take her away from this godforsaken place, but pride would not allow her to. She had managed on her own up to now, after a fashion, and she was determined to carry on doing so. She didn't need anyone and almost wished that they hadn't come. It only served to remind her of what she had lost and what might have been, if they had allowed her to stay with them.

Sensing her discomfort, Andy leaned towards her and whispered, 'Why don't you run and get your coat? We could take a stroll outside. It's a little noisy in here, isn't it?'

Maddy nodded, and as she made for the door, Kirsty and Andy followed her. They waited in the hallway while she ran to her room to fetch her outdoor coat and soon after they were strolling towards the copse in the grounds.

Kirsty drew Maddy's cold hand through her arm as she said cheerfully, 'It's very pretty here, isn't it?'

'I suppose it is – on the outside,' Maddy said.

Andy began to tell her about a block of flats he was building, hoping to fill in the awkward silences as they meandered along. He could see how unhappy the girl was and it almost broke his heart.

'Have you made any friends yet?' he enquired pleasantly.

'Just one.' They were at the banks of the stream now and Maddy stooped to lift a handful of pebbles which she began to skim across the water.

Andy and Kirsty exchanged a concerned glance.

'And what's this friend's name then?' Kirsty asked, desperately trying to put Maddy at ease.

'Holly. But she's not very well. In fact, she's in the sick bay right now.'

'Well, I'm sure they'll soon get her well again. There are lots of coughs and colds and bugs about at the minute with the weather being so cold,' Kirsty told her.

Maddy glared at her. 'It's nothing like that. She'd been poorly for some time before I even came here and she had to have some blood tests not long ago.'

'Oh ... then I hope they soon find out what's wrong.' Kirsty was beginning to feel like she was swimming against the tide. She certainly hadn't got the welcome she had hoped for. She had thought that Maddy would be pleased to see them. That it would be a nice surprise for her – but instead the girl seemed to resent them being there. She supposed deep down she could understand why. Maddy must have thought that they didn't want her, and once again she grappled with her conscience as she tried to decide whether she should tell her otherwise or not.

'I was thinking I might ask Sue Maddox if you could come and stay with us from time to time,' she said instead, but Maddy shook her head.

'There wouldn't be any point. We're not allowed out of here. It's like a prison camp,' she informed her gruffly.

Kirsty had a lump in her throat. From the outside, River House was beautiful, but the inside was cold and uninviting and she could well see why Maddy was so unhappy.

'Why have you come?'

Maddy's question was so abrupt and unexpected that for a moment both Kirsty and Andy were speechless.

'We came because we were worried about you,' Andy replied eventually. 'We *do* care about you, Maddy. I know you may not believe it, but it's true. We were hoping that you might write to us and keep in touch and that we might be able to come and see you from time to time.'

'Why bother?' Maddy pulled her coat more closely about her as she turned to face them. 'I appreciate you taking the trouble to come but I'd rather you didn't in the future, if you don't mind.'

'But why not?' Kirsty looked so genuinely distressed that Maddy felt guilty, but only for an instant.

'I don't need anyone.' The words that tripped out of her mouth might have been spoken by an adult instead of a thirteen-year-old girl. 'I've got to stay here for almost five years, but they can't keep me here for ever, and when I come out I'm going to find my family again. My *real* family. All of them.' The last words were uttered almost as a threat and Kirsty could think of nothing to say.

'Now if you don't mind, I'm going to go along to the sick bay and see how Holly is. Thanks for coming.' She turned and began to walk away with her shoulders hunched as if she had the weight of the whole world on them and now the tears that Kirsty had held back finally began to course down her cold cheeks.

'It seems coming here wasn't such a good idea after all,' she choked as Andy put his arm around her. She half-expected him to say 'I told you so', but he wisely held his tongue.

'Come on, love,' he encouraged instead. 'Let's head for home, eh? It's more than obvious that Maddy doesn't want us here.'

Kirsty nodded miserably as she followed him back to the car park.

Holly was back in the dormitory when Maddy returned to the house and she flashed her a weak smile.

'How are you feeling?' Maddy folded her coat and stuffed it into the bottom drawer next to her bed.

'A bit better. I don't know what happened, but Nurse Law is going to chase up the results of my blood tests on Monday and then she says we'll take it from there.' To Maddy's horror, the girl then burst into tears.

Approaching her bed, Maddy patted her arm. 'Try not to worry too much,' she comforted. 'It will probably turn out to be something and nothing.'

'I don't think so,' Holly whispered. 'I think I might be dying, Maddy.'

'Don't say such awful things.' Maddy was appalled. 'Of course you're not dying! You're only the same age as me. And anyway, I won't let you die ... you're the only real friend I've got.' Hardly able to believe that she had said such a thing, she went to turn away, deeply embarrassed, but Holly caught her hand and squeezed it.

'Thanks for that,' she said softly. 'I could really do with a friend right now. But come on – tell me about your visitors. The nurse said you had some. Was it family?'

Maddy's head wagged from side to side as she sank onto the edge of the mattress. 'No, it wasn't family. It was the foster-carers I lived with for a time in Plymouth after the fire.'

'Oh, they must think a lot of you then, if they came all this way to see you.'

'Huh! They think so much of me they allowed me to be put in here,' Maddy spat as all the hurt she was feeling exploded out of her.

'Perhaps they couldn't stop it,' Holly pointed out.

Maddy tossed her head. 'Perhaps they didn't try,' she grunted, but then she tried to turn the conversation in another direction. It was too painful to talk of Andy and Kirsty.

'What are you going to do when you get out of here?' she asked.

Holly's face lit up in a smile. '*If* I get out of here I'm going to meet a wonderful boy and get married and have lots of children,' she sighed dreamily. 'I shall have the most beautiful wedding dress that you've ever seen and I shall make sure that my children are loved and that they *never* feel unwanted or sad. What are you going to do, Maddy?'

'I'm going to find my family and make sure that all of them are all right. And then we'll all live together and never be separated again.'

Swallowing the lump in her throat, she took Holly's hand and they sat staring towards the window as they planned their glorious futures.

Chapter Twelve

The following morning as the girls showered, Maddy noticed some angry red marks on a younger girl's spine, and nudging Holly, who was showering beside her, she hissed, 'Have you seen those marks?'

Glancing at the girl, Holly shook the water from her wispy blond hair. 'Oh, that's Caroline. She wets the bed, so Miss Budd took her mattress away and made her sleep on the bedsprings.'

Maddy was horrified, but bit back a protest. She was fast learning that it was the safest thing to do in this place.

It was as she and Holly were heading back to their bedroom that they bumped into Stacey and her little band of followers on the landing. Up until now, Maddy had managed to avoid her, but now there was nothing she could do but try to walk past with her chin in the air.

'Enjoy your little rest in the Quiet Room?' the girl sneered, and then turning to her gang she told them, 'And she apologised *so* fucking beautifully the next day for Budd.'

Anger began to bubble through Maddy's veins but she clamped her lips together, not wanting another confrontation.

Stacey's eyes dropped to the thin towel that Maddy had wrapped around herself and she giggled as she pointed at Maddy's chest.

'Lookie here then, girls. The little 'un is just beginning to sprout tits.'

Maddy squirmed with embarrassment as she began to elbow her way roughly through the little throng of girls.

'Now don't be in such a rush,' Stacey tormented, and before Maddy was even aware of what she was intending to do, the older girl grabbed the corner of the towel and whipped it away, leaving Maddy mortified and naked as she tried to cover herself with her hands. She lunged at Stacey in an attempt to snatch her towel back, just as Mr Dumbarr appeared at the head of the stairs.

'What the devil is going on here?' he roared, as his eyes fastened greedily on Maddy's developing breasts. She managed to grab the towel from Stacey and hugged it to her, wishing that she could just die of shame there and then.

Stacey instantly took on the role of the injured party again. 'Please, sir. Maddy dropped her towel and I was just picking it up for her when she attacked me again,' she simpered, fluttering her eyelashes becomingly at him.

'*Did* she now?' His steely eyes fastened on Maddy once more. 'Perhaps it's time she had another little cooling-down time in the Quiet Room again, eh?'

'It wasn't Maddy, sir, it was—'

'Shut up, girl, and speak when you are spoken to,' he stormed at Holly, and then turning back to

Maddy he snapped, 'Come with me, girl.'

'B ... but I'm not even dressed yet and I haven't done anything wrong again,' Maddy objected hotly as the fat man bore down on her.

'You won't need clothes where you're going,' he told her as he gripped her arm spitefully. 'There will be no one to see them. And I think this time we should leave you in the Quiet Room for two nights, as one night obviously didn't teach you a lesson.'

As he began to haul her along the landing, Stacey watched with a satisfied smirk on her face.

Maddy was bubbling with rage but she also realised how futile it would be to fight this great bear of a man, so she wrapped her towel around her as best she could and went with what dignity she could muster. The journey to the room in the cellars seemed to take for ever, and Maddy's cheeks burned with humiliation as other girls stared at her on the way.

This time she entered the room on her own and sat on the end of the bed with her chin proudly in the air. She would not give Mr Dumbarr the satisfaction of seeing how upset she was, although her heart was racing at the thought of being shut away again.

Trailing a fat finger down her cheek he smiled at her almost lovingly. 'Don't forget what I told you, Maddy,' he said softly. 'All of this could be avoided if you would be nice to me.'

'Go away!' Maddy spat as she recoiled from his touch.

His mouth instantly set in a grim line. 'I find you very unruly, girl. But there's plenty of time to knock some manners into you, and by the time I've finished you'll be grateful for my attention. Have a good day now.'

He left the room, slamming the door behind him, and she began to shiver uncontrollably. Now she wished that she had told Kirsty and Andy just how awful this place really was: the unwholesome food the inmates were expected to eat. The poor young girl she had seen in the shower who was forced to sleep on bare bed-springs. Mr Dumbarr's unnatural sexual leaning towards certain of the pupils, herself included. The cruelty that she had already witnessed here was unbelievable, and she had an awful feeling that there was more to come that she hadn't seen as yet. But then despair washed over her. No one would take her word against those of the adult staff here, would they, Andy and Kirsty included. The way she saw it, the only thing she could do now was keep her head down and try to get through the years ahead. Taking the thin blanket off the bed, she wrapped it around herself and huddled into a ball on the stained mattress.

Maddy was let out of the Quiet Room on Monday morning. She went straight to her room to get dressed and then on to her lessons. One of the classes was with Miss Parr and she glanced at Maddy curiously as she took her seat. When the lesson was over she asked the girl to stay behind. 'Is everything all right, Maddy?' she wanted to know. 'It isn't like you to be late for a lesson.'

Maddy opened her mouth to tell the kindly teacher about the awful room she had been con-

141

fined to, but then she clamped it shut again. Her room-mates had already told her what happened to teachers who tried to deal with the way the girls were disciplined. Budd and Dumbarr would quickly tell them that their services were no longer required, and she didn't want to put Miss Parr in that position.

'I ... er ... had a bit of a headache,' she mumbled, and then she scuttled away to the next lesson, leaving Miss Parr with a bemused expression on her face.

At lunchtime when she entered the dining room she looked about for Holly but there was no sign of her as she joined Steph and Kim at their table. She studiously avoided eye-contact with Stacey, who was watching her every move with a smug grin on her face.

'Where's Holly?' she asked as Steph and Kim looked at her with concern. Maddy was as white as a sheet but she wasn't worried for herself right now.

'The nurse took her off to the hospital first thing this morning,' Steph informed her. 'They got the results of the blood tests back and then whipped her off straight away, so we'll have to wait and see what she says when she gets back.'

A feeling of foreboding settled around Maddy like a damp blanket as she thought back to what Holly had said. *I think I might be dying.* But of course, she reassured herself, that couldn't possibly be true. Holly was only thirteen years old.

'Come on,' Steph encouraged, seeing how worried Maddy was. 'Let's go and get in the dinner queue, eh? I've no doubt Holly will be back

142

before we know it.'

But two days later, Holly still wasn't back and Maddy finally plucked up the courage to ask Miss Gay, 'Have you heard how Holly is, miss?'

The young social worker shook her head sadly. 'Actually, Holly is quite poorly, Maddy,' she confided. 'I don't suppose I should be telling you this, but I've no doubt word will get out eventually, so you may as well know. Holly has been diagnosed with leukaemia. They're keeping her in for her first dose of chemotherapy, but then hopefully she will be coming back here and then just be going to the hospital for regular treatment.'

Maddy felt as if the floor was coming up to meet her. Surely leukaemia was a form of cancer. Her adoptive mother's friend had suffered from it and she had died, so Maddy knew that it must be very serious.

'She won't die, will she?' she asked fearfully.

Miss Gay put her arm about Maddy's slight shoulders. She had seen how close the two girls had become and her heart went out to her. 'I hope not,' she said. 'They're talking about doing a bone-marrow transplant if they can find the right donor. But she's going to need a friend more than ever now, so you must stay strong and be there for her.'

In that moment, Maddy realised that somehow, Holly had taken the place of Oliver in her affections. And now it looked like she might lose her too, just as she seemed to lose everyone she cared about.

'Look, why don't you skip your English lesson and go and have some quiet time in your room?'

Miss Gay suggested kindly. 'I'll tell your teacher that you weren't feeling too well and have gone for a lie-down. You look like you could do with a bit of space to come to terms with what I've told you.'

Maddy stumbled blindly towards the staircase but unfortunately, halfway up she came face to face with Stacey, who stopped abruptly and sneered, 'Enjoy your latest little break in the cellar, did you?'

When Maddy made to push past her, she snatched at her arm and Maddy roughly shook her off, much to Stacey's amusement. The girl only reached up to her shoulder, after all. 'Word has it that you're in here because you burned your parents to death,' she taunted, and then she shrank back against the wall as Maddy suddenly turned on her furiously. She wasn't trying to get away from her now, she was actually standing up to her, and Stacey wasn't used to anyone doing that. She was a bully through and through, and only picked on people who couldn't defend themselves.

'If you really want to know, yes. I *did* kill my parents,' Maddy snarled. 'And do you know what? I'd kill again if I had to, so be warned. Keep out of my way or *you* might be next.'

Stacey paled to the colour of putty. Maddy was standing on tiptoe and was so close that Stacey could feel her breath fanning her cheek. For one awful moment she thought that the girl was going to strike her, but then Maddy's lips curled back from her teeth with contempt and she took the rest of the stairs two at a time as Stacey watched

144

her go with her eyes on stalks.

Once in the sanctuary of her room, Maddy let out a deep breath. It was then that her eyes settled on the teddy bear propped up against Holly's pillow, and at last the tears she had tried so hard to control began to fall. Life was so unfair, but somehow she would have to be strong for her friend now. Holly would need her when she came out of hospital and Maddy intended to be there for her.

Holly came back to River House the following morning looking incredibly fragile and with her eyes sunk into her head. She looked absolutely dreadful, but Maddy greeted her cheerfully.

'I missed you,' she told her shyly.

Holly smiled. 'I missed you too,' she replied, and from that moment on their friendship was sealed and Maddy became her protector.

The girls at River House were each allotted a small allowance every week, and just before Christmas, Maddy gave the money she had saved to one of the dinner ladies and asked her if she would get a present for Holly for her. The dinner lady came back two days later with a pretty little jewellery box and Maddy could hardly wait for Christmas morning to give it to her friend. Many of the girls who had family who were willing to take them were going home to spend the holiday with them, and luckily Stacey was amongst them, so Maddy was looking forward to the break from routine. She had been told that the meals that they were served over Christmas were actually quite nice, so all in all things were looking up, although

Holly appeared very ill. She'd had three doses of chemotherapy now and only this morning had woken up to find great clumps of her hair on her pillow.

'Oh, Maddy, I'm going to be bald! The doctors warned me that this might happen,' she wailed.

Maddy forced herself to sound upbeat. 'Well, that will be a small price to pay if the treatment makes you better,' she pointed out optimistically. 'And you never know. You might start a new trend. The rest of the girls might start shaving their heads.'

Holly giggled at the picture Maddy had conjured up. 'I don't think that's much of a possibility, but I suppose you're right if this chemo makes me better. I *am* going to get better, aren't I?'

'Of course you are!' Maddy exclaimed as she put her arms around Holly's shoulders. She seemed to have lost even more weight and looked as if a puff of wind would blow her away.

After dinner that evening, Holly went to the dormitory to rest. Steph was in the Day Room valiantly trying to knit a scarf for her grandma as a Christmas present and Kim had joined the older girls in the copse. Maddy had avoided the place for some time, deciding that it was best to keep out of Stacey's way, so instead she put her coat on and took a wander about the grounds on her own.

It was bitterly cold and although it was only six o'clock in the evening, the grass was already stiff and standing to attention with hoar frost.

Maddy shuddered as she thrust her hands into

146

her coat pocket and walked around the perimeter of the high wall that enclosed the home. From here she had a good view of the house and she glanced towards the west wing where Miss Budd and Mr Dumbarr had their private quarters. No one was allowed in there except them and the cleaners, and Maddy often wondered what their living accommodation was like. She had no doubt it would be a million times more comfortable than the cold draughty dormitories.

A light was on in one of the upper windows, and sheltered by the darkness, Maddy paused and stared towards it. It was then that she saw the most curious thing. There was a woman in Mr Dumbarr's room, she was sure of it. It was difficult to tell exactly what the woman looked like from this far away, but Maddy could see that she was quite enormous, with a shock of long blonde hair. She wondered how the man had managed to smuggle her in without anyone seeing her, and grinned as she thought of what Miss Budd's reaction might be if she were to find out. The woman obviously adored him, although Maddy could see no reason whatsoever why she should.

It had been Mr Dumbarr's day off today and she had watched from the classroom window as he roared off down the drive in his low-slung Porsche. That was another source of amusement to Maddy as she wondered how he ever managed to lever himself into such a small car. Perhaps he had brought the blonde woman back with him while they were all still in their lessons. She wondered if the woman would stay the night with him and shuddered at the thought. It would certainly put Stacey's nose out of joint if she were to find out. She seemed to think the slobbering obese man was her sole possession, and she was welcome to him. Just the thought of him touching her made Maddy shudder with revulsion.

Briefly she considered walking a little nearer to the house so that she could get a better view of Mr Dumbarr's fancy piece, but dismissed the idea almost immediately. Here she was sheltered by the wall, but closer to the building he might spot her watching him and then all hell would break loose. And so she stood watching the woman avidly, her breath hanging on the air like a plume of fine lace in front of her. The woman was wearing what appeared to be a shocking pink satin blouse or jacket that did nothing to enhance her enormous bulk. She had a glass of what Maddy supposed was wine in her hand and she could see her gesticulating with the other hand as if she was talking to someone on the other side of the room. No doubt that someone was Mr Dumbarr.

Eventually, Maddy got so cold that she gave up her vigil and started back to the house. Stacey and her cronies appeared at the edge of the copse at almost the same time but thankfully they ignored her, just as they had since the day Maddy had stood up to the bully on the stairs. Maddy made her way to the Boot Room where she hung up her coat and then slipped up the stairs to check on Holly. Steph and Kim were already there and they smiled at her as she entered the room.

'Ssh!' Kim put her finger to her lips. 'Holly's out for the count,' she whispered. 'So we're trying not to disturb her.'

148

Maddy nodded as she began to hastily slide out of her clothes and into her nightdress. It was the same plain white cotton affair that they were all issued with, and had no adornment at all, but this no longer bothered Maddy. In fact, she was so used to wearing the uniform now that she rarely thought back to what it was like to be able to choose what she wore.

Once they were all changed, the girls slid into their beds and not long afterwards, they heard Miss Budd in the corridor outside.

'Lights out now, girls, if you please.'

Maddy snuggled down into the cold cotton sheets. Soon there would be another night to tick off the time she would have to stay there. As her eyelids drooped, she once again pictured Mr Dumbarr's colourful girlfriend and fell asleep with a wry smile on her lips.

Chapter Thirteen

It was Christmas Eve and Holly and Maddy were in their room. Most of the girls in the school had gone back to their families for the holidays but Maddy didn't care. So long as she had Holly, she was happy. Or as happy as she could be under the circumstances. The day before, a card had arrived in the post for her and when she opened it she found that it was from Kirsty and Andy. She had been forced to swallow her disappointment as she had hoped that it would be from

Oliver. She wondered where he was and if he was happy. She also wondered if he ever thought of her as she did of him. They had never been apart before, and this Christmas would be especially hard for both of them. But at least she had Holly.

Looking across at the girl, Maddy felt sad. Holly was spending more and more time at the hospital. The doctors there were still desperately searching for a compatible bone-marrow donor for her, but as yet they had had no success.

Holly had explained that she had a very aggressive type of leukaemia but she was being incredibly brave about it and Maddy wondered if she could have been the same, had she been in Holly's shoes.

'You're quiet,' Holly said, as she looked up from the magazine she was reading.

'Oh, am I? Sorry, I was just thinking.'

'What about? Your brother?'

Maddy shrugged. 'I suppose I was,' she admitted, and forcing a smile to her face she asked, 'What are you reading?'

'Oh, just some sloppy short story.' Holly shut the magazine and becoming solemn asked tentatively, 'Maddy ... would you do something for me?'

'Of course I will, if I can,' Maddy told her obligingly.

Holly began to feel in her top drawer before producing a pair of scissors. 'I was wondering if you'd cut the rest of my hair off for me? The thing is, I look a freak with all these bald spots and I think I'd look better if I didn't have any hair at all.'

Maddy blinked hard to stop her tears from

falling. 'Are you quite sure about this?' Taking the scissors from Holly's hand she stood over her uncertainly.

'Yes, I am. I'd do it myself but the only mirror is in the shower block and I can't really do it in front of all the rest of the girls, can I? *Please* help me, Maddy. It's awful to wake up each morning and see clumps of hair on my pillow.'

Taking a deep breath, Maddy reluctantly lifted a lock of the silver-blonde hair and snipped at it with the scissors. Holly had had such beautiful hair and it broke her heart to see it now. All thin and straggly, or what was left of it.

In no time at all Holly's head was covered in a short fine down and the rest of her hair lay on the floor in between them.

The girl ran her fingers tentatively over her scalp. Grinning at Maddy, who looked absolutely devastated, she said encouragingly, 'Come on, cheer up. As you once told me, it will grow back – and at least I'm not half and half now.'

Maddy stooped and began to gather the hair together before depositing it in the bin. Unseen by Holly, she slipped a lock into her pocket.

'Right now, what about we go down to the Day Room and watch telly for a bit, eh? There's an old Morecambe and Wise show on tonight and Budd has told us that we can stay up to see it.' Holly slid off the bed. Because it was Christmas, many of the house rules had been lifted and the sick girl intended to make the most of every minute.

Side by side, they went downstairs. Some of the girls in the Day Room stared at Holly's new haircut, but thankfully none of them commented

151

on it. It was just as well because Maddy had been ready to do battle if they had.

Tonight a supper had been laid out for them in the dining room and every one of the girls took full advantage of the fact. There were turkey sandwiches and slices of pork pie, as well as mince pies that the dinner ladies had baked especially for them. The mood was light-hearted, made even more so when one of the girls suddenly shouted, 'Look, it's snowing!'

They all glanced towards the window and Maddy smiled as she saw the snowflakes fluttering down. Perhaps it wasn't going to be such a bad Christmas, after all. It certainly couldn't be any worse than the ones she had been forced to spend with her adoptive parents.

Her mind drifted back to another Christmas Eve and the sounds of the girls disappeared. She was with Olly again as they stared in wonder at the snow drifting down from his bedroom window. The street lights made the lawn look as if it had been sprinkled with diamonds and the little boy's voice was full of awe as he asked, 'Will Santa still come if it's snowing, Maddy?'

'Oh yes.' Maddy cuddled him, enjoying the warmth of his sturdy little body through his pyjamas. 'Santa will always come no matter what the weather is like.'

He sighed contentedly as he nestled against her until eventually she led him back to his bed and snuck away to her own room.

By morning the snow had settled and Maddy was woken by Olly's excited shouts as he emptied the contents of the sack that he had hung over the end of his bed the night before onto the carpet. Forgetting to look at her own gifts, she sped across the landing but before she could reach him her new parents came out of their bedroom door tightening the belts of their dressing gowns as they headed towards Olly's room.

'Ah, Maddy, go and put the kettle on, would you?' Michelle's eyes were as cold as the snow that lay on the ground. 'You can bring your father and me a cup of tea up while we help Oliver to open his presents. And then perhaps you could make a start preparing the vegetables for dinner.'

Swallowing her disappointment, Maddy looked towards Peter but she soon saw that there was no help to be found there. He was totally under Michelle's thumb and although Maddy thought she sometimes detected a look of sympathy on his face when Michelle was stern with her, he had never once stuck up for her, which was why she had come to hate him almost as much as her adoptive mother. It was then that the joy of Christmas died, for Maddy knew without another word being said that this day would be just like any other. She would spend it cooking and cleaning and waiting on her new parents just as she did every other day...

'Maddy ... did you hear me?'

'*What?*' Maddy started as she looked towards Holly, who was staring at her.

'I said, how do you fancy a game of cards?' Holly repeated for the third time.

Dragging her thoughts back to the present, Maddy forced a smile and nodded. 'Yes, we might as well.' But as they made their way to the Day

Room she was missing her brother so much that it was almost like a physical pain.

On Christmas morning, Holly screamed with delight when she opened the jewellery box that Maddy had bought for her. 'Oh, it's really lovely,' she gasped, as she turned it over in her hands. 'And one day when I meet my lovely boyfriend he'll spoil me with beautiful jewellery and I'll fill it right to the very top and think of you.' She now shyly handed Maddy a gaily wrapped package, and when Maddy opened it she found a warm pair of gloves in a pretty blue colour with a matching scarf inside.

'I thought they'd keep you warm when you go out in the evening for your stroll around,' Holly explained.

'They're fab.' Maddy wrapped the scarf around her neck, and smiling, the two girls went down to breakfast arm-in-arm.

Today they were served with crispy bacon and fat juicy sausages.

'I feel like I've died and gone to heaven,' Holly sighed contentedly as she tackled the tasty meal in front of her, and Maddy was thrilled to see her friend clear her plate. Maybe she had finally turned the corner. Her spirits rose. It was Christmas Day and she was determined to make it as good as she could for Holly. Even Miss Budd and Mr Dumbarr seemed to be in a jovial mood today.

After breakfast they went outside and had a snowball fight. Steph had gone home to her grandma in London for Christmas and Kim was spending the holiday with an aunt in Leicester, but Maddy and Holly were content in each other's company. There were only eight girls left at the home and it suddenly seemed enormous.

The grounds of River House looked breathtakingly pretty in the snow and when Holly tired of throwing snowballs she looked about with a dreamy expression on her face.

'Everywhere looks brand new, doesn't it?'

'Yes, it does. Shame the inside isn't the same,' Maddy said grumpily.

'Oh, don't think like that. You won't be here for ever,' Holly pointed out. Maddy knew that she was right, but five years felt like for ever at present, and she was missing Oliver so much that it hurt.

Holly brushed the snow from a bench and sat down, patting the seat at the side of her. 'Didn't Miss Budd look different in that dress this morning?' she grinned. 'I've never seen her in anything but a suit before.'

'She's probably making an effort because it's Christmas. But I wonder why she's here? I mean, if she had any family you'd think she'd have gone to spend the holiday with them, wouldn't you?'

'She probably doesn't have any family,' Holly said musingly. 'And neither can Mr Dumbarr or I dare say he'd have gone to them too. So you see, it's not just us that are abandoned.'

'Mm, I suppose you're right.' Maddy stared off into the distance, wondering what Kirsty and Andy were doing. Funnily enough, when she thought back to the time she had spent with them she found that she missed them. But of course she

155

would never let them know that. It didn't do to let your guard down, as she had discovered.

In the kitchen behind them they could hear the cooks busily preparing the Christmas dinner and Holly said excitedly, 'I wonder if we'll get turkey and Christmas pudding and all the trimmings?'

Not much caring one way or another, Maddy shrugged. She had grown used to the meagre fare they were usually served. Peeping at Holly out of the corner of her eye, she was disturbed to see the dark shadows beneath her eyes. This morning in the shower Maddy had noticed bruises on her friend's body. They were so prominent it would have been hard not to.

'Where did they come from?' she had asked, shocked. Had someone been hitting her?

'Oh, apparently it's normal to bruise with leukaemia. It's something to do with the chemo I'm having, I think.'

Maddy could have cried for her. Holly was being remarkably brave but she knew how hard it must be. After each dose of chemotherapy, the poor girl would be in bed for at least two days being violently sick, and yet she never complained. They sat there for a while watching a small red-breasted robin digging in the snow until Holly shivered.

'Let's go in now, eh? It's starting to snow again and I'm frozen through.'

Maddy followed her back inside and then they went off to watch the television in the Day Room until dinner was ready. There would be no lessons for at least another week and it was nice to be able to do as they pleased for once.

Dinner proved to be yet another pleasant surprise when they were served with turkey and all the trimmings just as Holly had hoped for. Sadly, she couldn't eat much this time, but she enjoyed herself all the same. For dessert they had a rich Christmas pudding with thick creamy custard, and by the time they had finished, Maddy was so full she was sure she wouldn't be able to eat another thing for at least two days.

When the meal was over, Miss Budd and Mr Dumbarr went off to their private quarters.

'I reckon Miss Budd is a bit tipsy,' Maddy whispered to Holly as she watched Mr Dumbarr take her elbow and steer her up the stairs.

The woman was giggling like a schoolgirl as she stared up at him adoringly and Holly, who had a kind heart, remarked, 'It's a shame Dumbo can't see how much she loves him, isn't it? I mean, if they were to get married they could still live here as man and wife.'

Maddy snorted with derision as she thought back to the evening she had seen the large blonde woman in Mr Dumbarr's room through the window.

'I doubt there's much chance of that happening,' she retorted, and taking Holly's arm she led her back to their room so that she could rest for a while.

It was the day after New Year's Day when Holly took a turn for the worse. The girls who had been allowed home for the holidays were returning in dribs and drabs, and Maddy and Holly were keeping out of their way, sad that the brief respite from routine was over.

Steph had just come back from her stay in London and was busily telling them all about what she had been up to when Holly suddenly turned a horrible grey colour and swayed as she reached out to her bed.

Maddy rushed towards her, but Holly had slumped into a heap on the floor.

'I'll go and get help,' she told Steph, who was kneeling next to the girl, and she shot from the room like a bullet from a gun. She was nearly at the bottom of the stairs when she heard someone having a heated exchange – and to her surprise she saw that it was Mr Dumbarr and Stacey, who had obviously just returned from her visit to her parents. She was dressed in high heels and jeans that were so tight she looked as if she had been poured into them. Dangly earrings hung from her ears and her long blonde hair had been permed. Maddy was briefly reminded of Madonna and thought that Stacey looked at least eighteen years old.

Completely ignoring her, Maddy shouted, 'I need some help! Holly has fainted again.'

Mr Dumbarr turned startled eyes towards her and then barked at Stacey, 'Go and get the nurse from the sick bay and then get changed into your uniform *immediately.*'

Stacey glared back at him through eyelashes heavy with mascara before turning about and stomping away. Mr Dumbarr then panted up the stairs after Maddy, who had raced ahead. By the time he reached the girls' dormitory, Maddy was already kneeling on the floor with Holly's head in her lap, Kim and Steph either side of her, each holding one of Holly's hands.

'Nurse Law should be here at any minute,' the fat man puffed, as he tried to get his breath back. Maddy didn't bother to answer him. She kept her attention firmly fixed on Holly.

When the nurse arrived, she quickly checked Holly's pulse before turning to Mr Dumbarr and telling him, 'I think you'd better phone for an ambulance, and tell them to hurry.'

After a cursory nod he heaved his enormous frame out of the room as Maddy looked at the nurse from troubled eyes.

'She *is* going to be all right, isn't she?' Her voice was loaded with concern.

'Well, I don't think I need to tell any of you that Holly is very ill indeed, do I, Maddy?' the woman answered kindly. 'And the problem we're up against is finding the right donor. The longer it goes on...' She sighed as she looked at the girls' stricken faces. It was obvious that they were very fond of Holly.

'I'm her best friend. Can I at least go with her in the ambulance?' But Maddy knew the answer to her question before the woman even replied.

The nurse shook her head. 'I don't think Mr Dumbarr would allow that, but try not to worry. I shall go with her and as soon as I get back I'll let you know how she is, eh?'

Maddy nodded miserably. Once again she was reminded how much like a prison this place really was. Unless you were lucky enough to have family outside who were willing to allow you home now and again for special occasions, you were completely cut off from the world. Or at least that's how it felt.

Shortly after, two ambulancemen rushed into the room carrying a stretcher, and after gently lifting Holly onto it they whisked her away.

'She'll be all right, you'll see.' Steph placed her hand gently on Maddy's shoulder but the girl shrugged it off. This was what you got for caring – and suddenly she wished that she had never allowed herself to get close to Holly. She wouldn't be hurting then.

'I'm fine,' she told Steph shortly as she stamped out of the room, snatching up her new scarf and gloves. A good brisk walk around the grounds might make her feel better, although she very much doubted it. All she could do now was wait for the nurse to return with news of her friend.

Chapter Fourteen

July 1991

'What do you mean you've stopped responding to treatment?'

'Just what I say.' Holly was lying in bed in the sick bay. 'My white blood cells and my red blood cells are all over the place again apparently, but I'm not very medically minded so that's all I can tell you.'

Maddy was so disappointed she could have cried aloud. Since her stay in hospital in January, Holly seemed to have become slightly better, but now the illness was back with a vengeance.

Maddy spent every second of her leisure time with her and worried about her constantly. She had grown accustomed to living at River House now, and often went for days without wondering what it would be like to get out of there again. She had always done well at school, but now she put all her efforts into her lessons, especially her English, at which she excelled. One day, she hoped her learning would stand her in good stead. She intended to get a decent job and make something of herself when she did eventually get out of there, and was determined never to be answerable to anyone again. Letters had arrived regularly once a month for her since Christmas, and she knew that they were from Kirsty and Andy because she recognised the handwriting from the card they had sent her. But she never even bothered to open them. She simply pushed them into her drawer and forgot all about them. The way she saw it, the couple hadn't wanted to keep her and corresponding with them would only have reminded her of what she had lost.

Stacey had kept her distance for some time, although whenever they bumped into each other Maddy could feel the animosity coming off her in waves. Rumour had it that she wasn't quite so close to Dumbo nowadays and Maddy could only assume that this was true. She certainly hadn't seen Stacey disappearing off into the west wing to his private quarters as often as she had used to. And the other girl didn't seem to be getting as many privileges as she had before, either.

What was worrying was the fact that the man now seemed to be showing her a lot more attention. It was completely unwanted – but Maddy couldn't tell him that, of course. He allowed her to spend as much of her free time as she wished in the sick bay with Holly, and whenever he got the chance he would stroke her arm or smile at her, which made her stomach lurch.

It was a small price to pay for being allowed to be there for Holly. The poor soul had no one else and Maddy wanted to support her as much as she could.

As the two girls sat there chatting, the nurse came into the room and smiled at them.

'So how are you feeling now, Holly, love? Did that injection I gave you take the pain off a little?'

'Yes, thanks, it did.'

As Holly returned her smile the woman's heart went out to her. Mary Law was thirty-five years old and had worked as a nurse at River House for the last five years. During that time she had seen things that had horrified her. A slim attractive woman with brunette hair and soft brown eyes, she had a big heart. For most of the time her job entailed dealing with everyday illnesses – such as coughs and colds, heavy periods, upset stomachs and the odd case of German measles or chicken pox. But from time to time she had also had to deal with far more serious injuries, like the poor little girl from dormitory ten who had come to her with open wounds on her back because she was forced to sleep on bare bedsprings. The child had suffered sexual abuse at the hands of her father and numerous uncles before coming here, but Miss Budd was not prepared to make any allowances for that. Wet mattresses were not acceptable and that was that, she had informed her coldly.

When Mary had challenged her about it, the house-mother had told her quite clearly that if she wasn't happy with her decision, then she could leave.

Nothing would have given Mary more pleasure than to tell the woman she could stick her job where the sun didn't shine. But jobs in this remote area of the Cotswolds were like gold dust and Mary needed the money. Her husband had left her three years ago for his blonde secretary who had legs that went on for ever, and now Mary was the sole breadwinner and had to provide for three children. And so she closed her eyes to what went on there, praying that the day would come when she could shout from the rooftops just what an evil place this really was.

During the previous year, one of the resident girls had become pregnant. No one could understand how this could have happened. No one but Mary, that was, who had her suspicions. There were no boys at River House and the girls were rarely allowed out of the place. But she had seen the way Mr Dumbarr favoured the girl and drew her own conclusions. Shortly afterwards, some aunt who had never been heard of before had miraculously crawled out of the woodwork and taken the girl away to God knows where, or at least that was what Mr Dumbarr had told them. He was responsible for finding the girls places to go when they left here, so Mary had only had his word for it.

Within days of the other girl leaving, Stacey

163

had become the chosen one. But now Mary was concerned for Maddy. Over the last six months she had seen the child begin to develop into a very attractive teenager, and she had watched the way Mr Dumbarr's eyes followed her lasciviously. The sight had struck terror into her heart, but she was powerless to do anything about it. Maddy was a stand-offish sort of girl, but the nurse suspected that beneath the cold front she showed to everyone there was a young girl who was hurting. And she was certainly kind to Holly. In fact, nothing seemed to be too much trouble for Maddy when it came to her friend.

As Mary took Holly's temperature, she wondered if Maddy did comprehend just how seriously ill Holly really was.

Smiling, she shook the thermometer. 'That's not too bad at all, but I think you ought to stay here for another night. We'll see if you're well enough to be up and about again tomorrow, shall we?'

Holly sighed. She would have liked to return to the dormitory to be with Maddy and Kim and Steph, but she supposed the nurse knew best.

'If you should need anyone tonight while I'm off duty, I'm sure the night nurse will get Miss Budd to fetch the doctor in for you.' And a fat lot of good that will do, she thought to herself. The doctor just happened to be a very close friend of Mr Dumbarr's and Mary didn't trust him as far as she could throw him. Miss Budd was no better. She was so besotted with Mr Dumbarr that it was painful to see, though Mary for the life of her couldn't understand the attraction. Mr Dumbarr was a bully, and together, he and Miss Budd

164

ruled the young girls who were unfortunate enough to come into their care with a rod of iron.

Some of the social workers who worked there or visited the girls from time to time were good sorts, but sadly they came and went during office hours and never got to see half of what went on behind the scenes. Like the poor kid who was suffering from terrible nightmares because of the times she had been shut away in what they termed 'the Quiet Room'. There was another room down in the cellars that the social workers were shown into, should one of the girls complain, which was entirely different to the one they were locked up in. The one Miss Budd showed them was well-lit and comfortable, and they never got to see the punishment room. And of course, Miss Budd always went to great pains to point out the girls who were trouble, so the social workers never questioned the fact that they should be punished. Once, Mary had sneaked down into the cellar to see what the room was like for herself, and she had been appalled. She knew that it would have driven her mad, had she been shut away down there, so she could only presume that it would have long-term effects on the youngsters.

Glancing at her watch, she saw that it was past five o'clock. The night nurse would be here soon to take over from her. Sadly, she would be another agency nurse. They came and went, just like the social workers, and barely lasted for more than a month.

'Are you going to stay for a while?' she asked Maddy now, and the girl nodded.

'That's fine then, but don't be late for dinner,

165

will you? Otherwise Miss Budd will blame me.'

Maddy smiled at her. 'I won't.'

She and Holly watched the kindly nurse leave, then turning towards Holly, Maddy asked, 'So what do you fancy for your supper then? I could bring you a tray in.'

'I'm not really hungry, to be honest.'

'But you've got to eat something,' Maddy protested. 'You have to eat to keep your strength up.'

Holly knew that Maddy meant well but her appetite had disappeared completely over the last couple of weeks. Perhaps after she'd had her next lot of chemo later in the week it would come back.

'You get off and have yours,' she encouraged. 'I'll read some of this book you got me out of the library.'

'Are you sure you'll be all right on your own?'

'I won't be on my own,' Holly pointed out. 'The night nurse will be here in a minute, so get off with you.'

Maddy nodded and made her way back to the hallway, where she almost collided with Mr Dumbarr, who was coming in the opposite direction.

'Slow down,' he said jovially as his hands reached out and grasped her arms. His tongue flicked out to wet his fat lips as he stared at her appreciatively. She's filling out nicely now, he thought to himself, and she's a pretty little thing an' all, though she doesn't seem to know it.

'Been in the sick bay with Holly, have you?' he asked, still with a firm grip on her arms.

Maddy nodded mutely. She felt like a rabbit caught in car headlights. She wanted to run but didn't dare to. Memories of the Quiet Room were still too fresh in her memory.

'It's later this week when she goes for another dose of chemo, isn't it?' he asked now, and bewildered, Maddy nodded.

'Mm, well, if you were to play your cards right I just might wangle it that you could go with her.'

Maddy's eyes almost popped out of her head. 'What do you mean, if I play my cards right?'

Glancing over his shoulder to ensure that they weren't being watched, the big man leaned down to her and whispered, 'Come to my room in the west wing tonight after lights out and I'll show you.'

Maddy recoiled as the implications of his words sank in. Sexually, she had led a very sheltered life, but she had heard enough whispers from the other girls to know what Mr Dumbarr and Stacey got up to. That's why she had always been favoured and now it seemed that he wanted to target *her*.

Seeing her indecision, he grinned. 'Have a think about it, and if you decide to come, I'll be waiting. I don't think you would regret it.'

Maddy disentangled her arms from his grasp and stumbled away as shock coursed through her. Just the thought of him touching her made her want to vomit, and as much as she would have loved to be allowed to accompany Holly to her hospital appointments, she didn't think she could bear to do it. She was no stranger to physical abuse, her adoptive mother had seen to that, but what Mr Dumbarr was suggesting was another thing altogether. Suddenly she wasn't hungry any more and she headed for her room to give herself

167

time to think. Thankfully, Steph and Kim had already gone in to dinner and she was grateful for the space.

It was almost an hour later when the door creaked open and she saw Mr Dumbarr standing there. 'Why didn't you come in to dinner?' he asked.

'I wasn't hungry,' Maddy muttered, crossing her arms protectively over her chest.

'I see – and have you had time to consider my invitation?' His voice was cold now.

'Yes, I have, and the answer is no – I won't be coming,' she answered boldly.

His face was so red now that Maddy feared he was going to burst a blood vessel. 'I've been trying to be nice to you, girl,' he spat, as his fists clenched and unclenched, 'but it appears that you are doing your best to be uncooperative. So ... I think it's time for a little gentle persuasion.'

Crossing to her chest-of-drawers he flung each one open in turn and scattered her clothes across the floor. 'Now just *look* at that mess! Miss Budd will have a fit when she sees what you've done. I think this deserves a night in the Quiet Room.'

'B ... but it was *you* that did it,' she protested as he bore down on her.

'You know that and I know that, but no one else will. And the cheek! Why, you swore at me so I had no choice but to take you to the Quiet Room to calm you down.'

'That's unfair!' Maddy cried as he caught her arm and started to yank her towards the door.

'Life, my dear, *is* unfair – as you'll discover when you go out into the big, wide world. I am doing you a favour, if you did but know it. But now ... are you going to come quietly, or do I have to drag you there kicking and screaming?'

Knowing that she was beaten, Maddy's shoulders sagged as resentment coursed through her. She followed him mutely, and minutes later she walked into the Quiet Room, waiting for the sound of the door closing behind her. But it didn't close and when she turned round to find out why, she found Mr Dumbarr standing so close that his breath fanned her cheek.

'Now *that's* better,' he said hoarsely, as his fat arms encircled her waist.

Maddy forced herself to remain rigid although every nerve in her body was screaming at her to push him away.

She could feel his hands stroking up and down her back, and then one of them found its way to her breast and she could not stop the shudder that ran through her. Fingering her small nipple through the worn material of her dress, he sighed with pleasure.

'You have a rest and I shall be back later.' His words were like a threat. 'And when I *do* come back we'll get a little better acquainted, and I assure you, you won't regret it. If you're nice to me, you can have everything you wish for – within reason, of course. And that will include being allowed to accompany your little friend on her trips to the hospital. Now just think how much better that will make her feel.'

Maddy knew then that he was blackmailing her and she watched as he turned away and ambled towards the door. 'Until later,' he whispered, and

169

then she was alone and the full horror of the position she was in came home to her. But what could she do about it? If she complained to Miss Budd she would never believe her word over Mr Dumbarr's, and the rest of the staff would just think she was trying to cause trouble. And then of course there was Holly. Maddy knew how terrified she was of going to the hospital on her own, and it would mean everything to her if Maddy was allowed to go with her.

And there *would* be perks ... look at Stacey. She had seemed to get away with murder until recently, although things seemed strained between her and Mr Dumbarr these days. She had heard some of the girls say that Stacey was too old for him now. He had lost interest because he liked them a little younger, when they were just developing ... as she was.

Shuddering, Maddy sat on the edge of the bed to wait. There wasn't much else she could do. She could scream till her lungs felt fit to burst down here and no one would hear her. But worse still, no one would care.

Chapter Fifteen

By the time Maddy heard the key turn in the lock she was completely calm.

After all, she didn't have a choice, did she? What was about to happen was inevitable, just as everything else in her life had been up to now.

She had no way of knowing what time it was but she rightly guessed that it must be very late. The man had changed into beige cord trousers and an open-necked shirt, and he looked even larger than he did in the suits that Maddy was accustomed to seeing him in. He was holding a bottle and two glasses in his hand and greeted her like a long-lost friend.

'Had a good rest have you, my dear?' His voice was oily.

Maddy didn't bother to answer as he closed the door behind him and advanced on her. Pushing a glass into her hand he then opened the bottle and filled her glass to the top before filling his own.

'This is a rather nice Chardonnay,' he informed her, as if she was a wine connoisseur. 'I thought it might help to relax us a little.'

Maddy had never tried wine before, but she decided now was as good a time as any and took a great gulp of it. She was surprised to find that it was quite pleasant, and to the man's great amusement she quickly drained the glass and cheekily held it out for a refill.

'I can see that you and I are going to get along just fine, little lady.' His eyes were shining with lust as he again filled her glass to the brim and Maddy again drained it before he could blink. And then the strangest thing happened; suddenly the man didn't look quite so repulsive and she felt more relaxed than she had for a long, long time.

In no time at all the bottle was empty and now he pulled her down onto the bed next to him and began to stroke her cheek. She knew that she should be pushing him away but she was too

171

tired to fight any more.

She had no idea how she came to be naked but was suddenly aware that she was, and so was Mr Dumbarr.

He was murmuring sweet nothings in her ear and Maddy discovered that it was actually quite nice to have someone be kind to her, although she wasn't too sure about the way he was touching her intimately. She could feel his slavering lips roving around her neck, and then suddenly he rolled his great weight on top of her and nothing was nice any more. She felt as if she was being rent in two and opened her mouth to scream, but his great hand closed across her mouth and all she could do was lie there wishing that she could die. At last it was over and she coiled into a tight ball trying to cover her nakedness as the man clambered from the bed and pulled his clothes on with a broad smile on his face.

'Now wasn't that nice?' His breathing was still erratic but he looked inordinately pleased with himself.

Maddy was crying now and could only see him as a blur; a huge *revolting* blur. And then he collected the empty bottle and the glasses together and he was walking towards the door and at last she was alone again. She listened until his footsteps had died away before rolling off the bed and then crawling to the bucket that served as a toilet, where she vomited until her stomach was empty. She was sure that she would never feel clean again even if she scrubbed herself to within an inch of her life. Her humiliation was complete. And she also knew then without a doubt that her life would never be the same again.

When Miss Budd came to fetch her the following morning she grimaced as the overpowering stench of vomit hit her. Maddy was fully dressed, lying on the bed, staring at the ceiling.

'When will you ever learn, girl?' she asked contemptuously. 'Mr Dumbarr informed me of how rude you had been to him and what a dreadful state your room was in. Perhaps now you will learn a few manners.'

Maddy climbed from the bed and followed the woman without a word. It was as they were approaching the staircase that Miss Budd informed her, 'By the way, I should tell you not to bother going along to the sick bay to see how your friend is. She took a turn for the worse during the night and we had no alternative but to send her back into hospital. I really can't think why they don't just keep her in. It's so inconvenient to have to keep calling the doctor in to her all the time. But there you are.'

Maddy stopped dead in her tracks and stared at the woman as if she had grown another head.

'Will I be able to go and see her?'

'Of course you can't go and see her. It would mean a member of staff having to run you all the way into—'

'Perhaps you would allow me to handle this?' Mr Dumbarr's smooth voice made them both look towards the dining-room door. He flashed the older woman a charming smile as he advanced on them and she blushed like a schoolgirl.

'Well ... I ... if you're quite sure?' she simpered.

173

'Of course I am. Now you go about your business, dear lady. I know how busy you are. I'll deal with this.'

'Very well, Mr Dumbarr.' Miss Budd cast one last glare in Maddy's direction and tripped away as the man turned his attention to the girl in front of him.

'Why don't you slip upstairs and get washed and changed and then we'll see about getting you off to the hospital to visit Holly,' he suggested.

Maddy felt sick as she thought back to the despicable things he had done to her the night before. But for now her overriding need was to see her friend, so she obediently hurried up the stairs, although her legs felt like lead and she had a splitting headache from the wine. But at least Mr Dumbarr was allowing her to go and see Holly, so the things she had endured had not been all in vain.

Ten minutes later, she was back in the hallway looking slightly tidier with her hair brushed and a fresh uniform on. 'What about my lessons?' she asked as he led her towards the door.

'Don't you go worrying your pretty little head about things like that.' He smiled at her as they stepped out into the bright sunshine. 'I shall speak to your teacher and explain what's happened when we get back.' And so Maddy meekly followed him, wondering if this was really the same man who had raped her the night before.

It was strange to be out of the confines of River House after so many months, and stranger still to be sitting beside the man in his shiny Porsche. Everywhere seemed enormous and Maddy felt

174

vaguely uneasy. All the way to the hospital, Mr Dumbarr kept up a running commentary of the places they passed, and anyone seeing them together might have thought he was a kindly uncle. Only Maddy knew what he was capable of, and the knowledge ate away at her like a cancer.

On the drive to the hospital in Cheltenham, Maddy tried to concentrate on the beautiful villages they were passing through rather than on the man sitting beside her until at last they pulled into the hospital car park.

When they left to return to the home almost an hour later, Maddy was close to tears and feeling utterly wretched. Holly had looked awful and had been so pleased to see her that Maddy was deeply touched.

While Maddy had been sitting with Holly, Mr Dumbarr had taken the opportunity to speak to the specialists who were treating the sick girl, and the news they had given him was far from good.

'I'm afraid you should prepare yourself for the worst, my dear,' he told Maddy as he steered the car away from the hospital. 'Holly has become very weak, and unless they can find a suitable donor for her within the next couple of weeks it will be too late for her to have a transplant.'

'Is she going to die?' Maddy asked fearfully.

The man paused before answering, 'I fear there is a grave possibility of that. Her doctor told me that she is asking to come back to River House, and as there is nothing more they can do for her at the hospital, I have agreed to ask Nurse Law if she is prepared to take on the responsibility of her. Of course,' his hand dropped from the steering wheel to caress Maddy's bare knee, 'I'm only doing this to please you. I know how much you think of Holly, and as you are being so nice to me ... well, it's the least I can do for you. I did tell you that I could be generous, didn't I?'

Maddy nodded, understanding exactly what he was saying. And she knew then that her worst nightmare had only just begun, but for Holly's sake she must endure it.

Kim and Steph were deeply upset when Maddy told them just how poorly Holly was. They were also rather confused about how Maddy had managed to get Mr Dumbarr to take her to the hospital to visit Holly.

'I can't understand it,' Steph muttered. 'I ain't never known him to take anyone out before except Stacey...' Her voice trailed away as she stared at Maddy suspiciously. But then she pushed the idea away. She knew how much Maddy detested the man, and she would *never* allow him to touch her ... would she?

Maddy was as pale as a ghost and very tearful, but then Steph supposed that was to be expected. She knew how close Holly and Maddy had grown.

'Things will pan out, you'll see,' she said with a conviction she was far from feeling, and the three girls then lapsed into silence as they thought of their absent room-mate.

Two nights later, as Maddy was leaving the dining room following the evening meal, Mr Dumbarr beckoned her over to him. She could feel her skin crawling as if it was covered in insects as she stared up into his moon face, but she went to him without question.

He waited until the last of the girls had left before smiling at her with anticipation.

'How would you like to come along to my room this evening when your room-mates are asleep?' he asked suggestively. 'I have another bottle of that Chardonnay that you enjoyed so much, and I thought it might be rather nice if we shared it.'

Maddy's heart sank into her drab black shoes but she knew there would be no way of refusing. He smiled with satisfaction before telling her, 'I rang the hospital today and apparently your little friend will be coming home tomorrow. She's feeling a bit better.'

'Oh!' That was good news at least, and Maddy was grateful he had shared the information with her.

'Right, you'd better get off then,' he said, and flicked a nervous glance across his shoulder, afraid that Miss Budd might magically appear from nowhere as she had a habit of doing. Maddy's stomach revolted at the thought of the night ahead. She had no doubt what would happen, but what could she do but go along with it? As far as Dumbo was concerned, she was his now; he had made that more than plain.

The evening progressed much as any other, but as the three girls lay in bed chatting, Steph and Kim's words went over Maddy's head. She found it hard to concentrate on what they were saying as she thought of what lay ahead of her. Slowly, the house began to quieten and Maddy peered from beneath her bedclothes. Steph and Kim were fast asleep, their gentle snores echoing off the plain drab walls. Slipping out of bed, she pulled her dressing gown over her nightie before padding silently to the door. After inching it open she peered up and down the corridor and when she was sure that no one was about, she crept along it towards the west wing where Mr Dumbarr had his living-quarters. She was terrified of bumping into Miss Budd along the way, but thankfully she met no one. The house was as silent as a grave.

Dumbarr was hovering by the door waiting for her with a wide smile of anticipation on his face. He was wearing a silk smoking robe that did nothing to flatter his enormous frame, and Maddy had to stop herself from shuddering as she looked up at his great bulbous nose.

He lifted his finger to his lips, warning her to be quiet, then took her arm and led her towards a door at the far end of a long corridor.

When Maddy entered his room she felt as if she had stepped into another world. The room was so luxurious it looked like something out of a magazine. A thick gold patterned carpet stretched from wall to wall, and heavy damask curtains hung at the window. The furniture in there was mahogany, so highly polished that she could see her face in it, and the bed that stood against one wall was huge, piled high with silk-clad pillows and an elaborate silk bedspread.

'Sit down, my dear,' he told her as he crossed to a table on which stood a number of cut-glass decanters and glasses. Maddy perched nervously on the edge of a velvet chaise longue as she peered around at the heavy gilt-framed pictures on the walls. This was a world away from the bare dormitories the residents were forced to live in, but then she supposed he was entitled to furnish his own rooms as he wished.

Briefly she thought of the woman she had once seen through his bedroom window and wondered why the man was interested in her when he obviously had a lady friend. But then there was no more time to think because he was bearing down on her with a full glass in his hand. 'To calm your nerves,' he informed her as he passed it to her.

Maddy gulped at it, glad of anything that would soften what was about to happen... And then the nightmare continued.

Holly arrived back at River House the following morning. Miss Gay, the young social worker, had fetched her from the hospital and although she was deathly pale, Holly was in good spirits and glad to be back with her friends. She was taken to the sick bay where she was told she would be staying from now on. Although she was sorry not to be going back to the dormitory that she shared with her room-mates she was so pleased to be back that she agreed to it without argument.

'You may spend all your leisure time in there with her,' Mr Dumbarr informed Maddy, and she acknowledged that that was something to be grateful for at least. As she was fast discovering, there were perks attached to being the man's favourite. But at what price?

Chapter Sixteen

'Hello, Maddy.' Nurse Law looked up as Maddy entered the sick bay. Holly was fast asleep, but then that came as no surprise. She seemed to sleep for most of the time now. The nurse cocked her finger towards the other end of the room and once Maddy had joined her there she whispered, 'I've asked Holly's social worker to get in touch with her father. I know he hasn't been to see her for an awfully long time, but ... Well, I thought we should let him know how very sick she really is. We did inform him some time ago that Holly had leukaemia, and he signed all the consent forms for her treatment. I just hope for her sake that he will come now.'

'I see. Have you told Holly?'

Mary shook her head. 'No, I haven't. I didn't want to raise her hopes until we know whether he's going to respond or not.'

As Maddy looked towards her friend, her heart ached for her. Holly seemed to be fading away before their very eyes.

'Do you think she'd want to see him? I mean, he did abandon her, didn't he?'

'Oh, I think she still would,' the nurse assured her. 'She often talks about him, and I think she still loves him. It's just a shame she couldn't have got on with her step-mum.'

At that moment, Holly stirred and Maddy

rushed to her side with a fake smile on her face.

'So how are you feeling this evening then?' She kept her voice light.

'Fine.' Holly pulled herself up the bed a little and pointed to a magazine on her locker. 'Nurse Law brought that for me. You should see how the fashions have changed since we've been stuck in here. Our clothes are going to be really outdated by the time we get out of this place. That's if they'll still fit us.'

'It doesn't really matter, seeing as we're going to have all new clothes when we leave.' Maddy took a seat at the side of the bed. 'We'll have everything all brand new, right from our bras and knickers, and we'll rent a little flat together. We'll both get a really good job and no one will *ever* tell us what to do again.'

Holly sighed dreamily at the picture Maddy had conjured up.

'And my hair will grow back and we'll live happily ever after,' she murmured.

Mary Law quickly walked from the room and once outside the door she pressed her hand to her mouth. Poor little sods, she thought. But at least they could dream.

It was a beautiful evening, and once Holly had slipped off into a drug-induced sleep again, Maddy wandered off outside to get a bit of fresh air. Thankfully, it was Mr Dumbarr's day off, and as usual he had gone out early in the morning, only returning in time for his evening meal which he had with Miss Budd in the dining room. He hadn't approached her today, and Maddy was praying that she wouldn't have to go to his room tonight. She had seen him when he returned from his shopping trip, loaded down with bags, and wondered what it was that he spent his money on each week.

Unfortunately, she had gone no more than a few yards from the door when Stacey appeared out of the copse with her little band of followers. It was only a few months until she was due to leave River House now and Maddy had been hoping to avoid her, but tonight it was impossible. Stacey had spotted her, and judging by the look on her face she was spoiling for a fight.

'Well, bugger me if it ain't Dumbo's latest little blue eyes,' she cooed sarcastically. Stacey was always brave when she was surrounded by her cronies.

Maddy started to walk in the opposite direction, but Stacey was hot on her heels.

'Don't get too fond of the perks.' Her voice was heavy with malice. 'Dumbo likes them young, and he'll soon have his eye on some other poor little sod.'

Deciding to play her at her own game, Maddy rounded on her, her dark eyes almost black as they flashed with hatred.

'And is that supposed to worry me?' she spat.

Stacey went down like a balloon. As Maddy had found once before, she didn't like anyone to stand up to her, but for now she had to save face in front of her friends.

'He was all over me like a rash. Couldn't get enough of me – until *you* batted your eyelashes at him, that is. But you'll see. Any time now, someone else will catch his eye and then you'll be on

182

the scrapheap too.'

'And that will suit me just fine. You might have enjoyed having him paw at you, but I think he's repulsive.'

The words were said with such venom that Stacey was momentarily lost for words. It was then that all their eyes were diverted to where screams were echoing from the open door behind them. As they looked towards it, they saw Miss Budd dragging one of the younger girls along the hallway. It was the child who had been forced to sleep on bare bedsprings and she was crying loudly.

'She must have been sick again after dinner,' one of Stacey's mates muttered. 'She's having terrible nightmares, and all. Keeps me awake half the night, she does, and I heard Budd tell her that if she kept it up she'd be due for some more time in the Quiet Room.'

Maddy's face wrinkled in disgust. Why couldn't Miss Budd see that the girl was deeply disturbed? The way she saw it, the girl needed help, not punishment. But then what else could she expect in this place? It was like hell on earth.

Stacey flounced away now as if she sensed that Maddy wasn't going to rise to her bait, and alone again, Maddy began to wander about the grounds. These were maintained by a couple of gardeners who came in once a week. It was then that an idea began to form in her mind. What if she were to somehow hide in their van and get out of River House that way? She knew exactly what time they left each week, and if she timed it right she would be long gone before anyone had had time to miss her. But then reality kicked in. Where could she go, once she was out of here? And what would happen to Holly?

Maddy's shoulders sagged. She didn't know how much longer she could endure the despicable things that Mr Dumbarr did to her, but if what Stacey said was true, perhaps he *would* soon lose interest in her. Her thoughts turned to the un-opened letters piling up in her drawer. They still came each week with monotonous regularity and she still refused to open them. But sometimes, just *sometimes* she was tempted to. Andy and Kirsty were her only link with the outside world at present. Her thoughts raced on and once again she wondered where Oliver was. Sue Maddox had visited once, since she had been here, but Maddy, always her own worst enemy, had stubbornly refused to see her. Now she wondered if she might have made a mistake, as the social worker might have had word of Oliver at least. It could be months now before Sue Maddox came again, if what the other girls told her was anything to go by. It seemed that once they reached this place they were forgotten, like lost souls.

But it wouldn't be for ever, and one day, Maddy promised herself, I'll make them pay, every last one of them.

As she kicked idly at a stone, her eyes strayed to Dumbarr's bedroom window and she stopped dead in her tracks. He had the woman in his room again – the same large blonde that she had seen in there once before. But how had she got in? Maddy had seen him return alone. She could only suppose that the gateman, George, must have let her in whilst they were all at dinner. Afraid of being seen, she shrank back against the wall. It had been dark the last time she had watched the woman, but tonight it was still bright with the sun slowly sinking in a cloudless blue sky. Skipping over to a nearby tree she hid behind it, peeping towards the man's window. Yes, the woman was definitely there, dressed in a garish lilac outfit this time, with her fair curls tumbling about her ample shoulders. Maddy wondered what would happen if she were to storm off to his bedroom and tell this other woman all about the things he did to her in the dead of night. The terrible, diabolical things that made her sometimes wish she could just die. Half of her was ready to go ahead and do just that. The other, more cautious half instantly began to wonder what she would gain from it. Dumbarr would obviously strenuously deny everything she said, and would the woman really believe her word against his? Maddy thought it was highly unlikely.

With her head down, she walked dejectedly back to the house. Holly might be awake again now and she still had a little time she could spend with her before Miss Budd put the lights out.

After lessons the following day, Maddy headed for the sick bay. She knew that she was on kitchen duty today and should have been there helping prepare the vegetables for the evening meal, but she was determined to see Holly first, even if it meant facing Miss Budd's wrath.

Once outside the door, she forced a bright smile to her face before flinging the door open –

185

only to stop abruptly. A man was sitting at the side of Holly's bed and he was holding her hand.

'Maddy, this is me dad.' Holly's face was alight with pure joy. 'He's come to see me – but better than that, he's takin' me home with him.' She now turned her face to her father, saying, 'This is Maddy, Dad. The friend I was telling you about.'

The man rose and extended his hand. He was tall and very good-looking in a Nordic sort of way, and Maddy saw that his eyes were kindly.

'Hello, Maddy. Holly's told me a lot about you,' he said. 'And I think I ought to thank you for taking such good care of her. She's told me how good you've been to her.'

Maddy eyed him suspiciously. He was saying all the right things, but if he thought so much of his daughter, why then had he abandoned her here in the first place? As if he could read her mind he dropped his hand and looked towards Holly regretfully. 'As I've just been telling Holly, I've made a lot of mistakes in the past but I intend to make it up to her now. In fact, her step-mum and I can hardly wait to have her home. This is going to be a brand new start for all of us.'

Maddy bit back the sarcastic retort that was hovering on her lips as she saw Holly's face. The girl was positively glowing with happiness and looking better than she had for months.

'I ... er ... ought to be off now,' Maddy told the man self-consciously. 'I have work to do in the kitchen. But I'll be back to see you later, Holly.' She turned to leave but then as a thought occurred to her, she paused to ask, 'You *will* still be here, won't you?'

'Oh yes, she will,' Holly's father answered for her. 'Mr Dumbarr is going to arrange for an ambulance to come and bring her home within the next couple of days or so. We thought she might be more comfortable travelling that way, rather than in a car. And of course, you will be very welcome to come and see her.'

Maddy knew that there was about as much likelihood of that happening as a snowball's chance in hell, but wisely refrained from saying so. She nodded at them both and hastily left the room before her feelings got the better of her. Now that the initial shock of seeing Holly's father there had worn off, her emotions were in turmoil. She was thrilled for Holly that she would be returning home, and yet selfishly she was wondering how she would cope without her. She and Holly told each other everything; or almost everything. Up to now, Holly had no idea what Maddy was being forced into with Mr Dumbarr. Neither had Maddy's other two room-mates – and that was how Maddy wanted it to stay. Even so, she guessed that it would only be a matter of time before word got around. Nothing stayed private in this place for long.

She had taken no more than a couple of steps along the corridor when Nurse Law appeared from the room next door, where one of the other girls was isolated with a severe chest infection. Maddy could hear her hacking cough through the door that the nurse had just closed behind her.

'Ah, Maddy, I take it you've met Holly's father and heard the news, then?' She took in Maddy's

187

glum expression and felt sorry for her.

Maddy nodded, too full up to speak. She wasn't in the mood for talking to anyone right now. Nurse Law watched her go before hurrying on her way with a loud sigh. Sometimes she wished she could just wave a magic wand and make everything right, but in this particular case she feared there would be no happy ending. There rarely was for the girls who ended up in River House.

Maddy kept her promise and visited Holly again after dinner. Her friend was ecstatic at the prospect of going home and Maddy smiled as she listened to her rambling on. Thankfully, Holly soon tired herself out and after she had slipped into a doze Maddy quietly crept from the room and made her way up to the dormitory. She had a lot to think about tonight and would be relieved when it came time for lights out. Halfway up the stairs she met Mr Dumbarr, and when she saw him smiling at her, her heart sank. She had come to know all too well what that look meant.

'Come to my room when all is quiet,' he whispered as she passed him, and eyes straight ahead she continued on her way.

Steph and Kim were already there, and as she entered the room they immediately stopped talking. Maddy had the distinct feeling that they had been talking about her, but simply began to get ready for bed. Shortly afterwards, Miss Budd's heavy footsteps sounded on the landing and within minutes the room was plunged into darkness.

'G'night,' Steph muttered.

'G'night,' Kim replied, and soon there was only silence as the huge old house began to settle around them.

Eventually, Maddy wriggled out of bed. She had just slipped her arms into her dressing gown when Steph's voice carried to her.

'Where are you going?'

Maddy gulped before whispering, 'I'm just going to the toilet.'

'No, you're not. You're going along to Dumbo's room, aren't you? It's true what the girls are saying, isn't it – that you're the latest one he's targeted.'

Maddy opened her mouth to deny it but then clamped it shut again.

'Yes, it is true and before you say anything, what am I supposed to do about it? I either do as he says or he makes my life a misery.'

'Couldn't you try speaking to Miss Budd?'

'Huh! What use would that be?' Maddy hissed. 'You know as well as I do that she thinks the sun shines out of his arse. She'd never take my word against that slimy git's... Now go back to sleep and don't worry about it. Just think yourself lucky it isn't you he's after.' And with that she slipped away, leaving Steph to stare after her with a look of horror on her face.

She had barely taken more than a couple of steps along the landing when Miss Budd suddenly appeared and Maddy felt the colour drain from her face.

'What are you doing out of bed?' the woman demanded.

'I ... er ... need the toilet,' Maddy stammered.

189

Miss Budd folded her arms across her chest. 'Just make sure that you go before lights out in future,' she told her sternly. 'Now look sharp about it. I shall wait here until you're back in your room.'

Maddy's heart felt as if it was trying to escape from her chest as she skittered away to the toilet block. There was no way she dare risk going to Dumbarr's room now with Miss Budd on the prowl. She knew that he would not be happy about it, but what could she do? Worse still, what would *he* do when she didn't turn up? She had a horrible feeling that she would find out soon enough and she was proved right the very next morning.

As Maddy was making her way to her first lesson, Mr Dumbarr called her into his office.

'And where did *you* get to last night?' he demanded.

Maddy explained what had happened so quickly that the words tripped off her tongue.

'Hm, I see. Then in that case I suppose it was no fault of yours,' he remarked. 'But tonight you *will* come to my room. And you will be more careful about it, do you understand? Otherwise I shall be forced to think of some other way we can be together, like putting you in the Quiet Room where I can visit you.'

'Yes, sir.' Maddy's eyes burned with hate as she kept them fixed firmly on a spot on the ceiling.

'Very well, you may go.'

Turning on her heel, she stalked out of the room feeling utterly wretched until suddenly she thought of something. Once Holly was gone, she would no longer need to ask for favours, like being allowed to visit her friend. Perhaps something good would come out of Holly leaving, after all? Only time would tell.

Later that day, the home was full of muttered whisperings. The young girl whom Miss Budd had made sleep on bare bedsprings had managed to escape – and if what Maddy heard was true, she wasn't the first. Maddy wondered if that was why Miss Budd had been on the prowl the night before. Perhaps she had been looking for her – but how had the girl managed to escape from the Quiet Room? Good luck to her, Maddy thought to herself. I just hope they don't find her and force her to come back. She felt almost envious of the girl as she went on her way.

It was much later that evening when Maddy stole to Dumbarr's room to find him waiting for her. He was all smiles as he pressed a large glass of wine into her hand and she gulped at it greedily. She would gladly have drunk arsenic if it took her mind off what he was about to do to her. And then the nightmare began all over again.

Chapter Seventeen

'I'll write to you every single week, I promise,' Holly told her as they clung together for one last time.

'Make sure that you do,' Maddy said through her tears. 'And you just get well again now, do you hear me?'

'I hear you.' Holly raised a frail hand to wipe the tears from her friend's cheeks as the ambulancemen helped her into a wheelchair, and then they were pushing her towards the waiting ambulance and Maddy waved with a brave smile on her face.

'Don't forget, we'll go flat-hunting when you get out, and we'll live together happily ever after,' Holly called across her shoulder.

'I won't forget.' The doors slammed and suddenly Maddy felt very alone as she watched the only friend she had ever had disappearing off down the winding drive.

'Come on, love. How about I make you a nice cup of tea before you go back to your lessons, eh?' Nurse Law asked as she placed a comforting hand on Maddy's thin arm.

As ever, the girl could not bear to be touched. She shook it off. 'No thanks. I'll be fine,' she mumbled before rushing away. The woman watched resignedly before slowly making her way back to the sick bay.

True to her word, Holly wrote every week for the next two months, and then the letters suddenly stopped coming.

Two weeks later, on a cold clear day early in October, Nurse Law called her into the sick bay.

'Maddy,' she began uncomfortably, 'I'm afraid I have some very bad news for you. Holly passed away yesterday morning. Her family assure me that her end was very peaceful. My dear, she left this for you. She actually gave it to me before she went away, and asked me to give it to you when she died, as she knew she would.' She passed a sealed envelope to Maddy, who took it numbly as she tried to digest what the nurse had just told her.

'Now I want you to go to your room and have some quiet time to yourself,' the woman said. 'And don't get worrying about your lessons. I shall speak to Miss Budd and explain what has happened.'

'Thank you,' Maddy said dully as she turned towards the door in a daze.

Once in the privacy of her room she sank onto the end of her bed and stared at the envelope in her hand before slowly tearing it open. Inside was a single sheet of paper and on it was written:

My dear Maddy,
By the time you read this letter I will be dead. But I just wanted you to know how much your friendship has meant to me. All our plans for the future have kept me going throughout the last months, although deep down I think we both knew that our hopes were

nothing more than pipe dreams. I know in my heart that I am never going to get better, but you helped me to believe that I just might. So go on and do all the things we planned for me. Have a lovely home and find someone who will love you unconditionally. Fill your home with children who will never feel abandoned as we have, and never let them feel lonely. I will never be far away from you and I want you to know that you are the best friend I could ever have wished for. Be happy.

All my love for ever,
Holly xxx

The letter slid from Maddy's hand – and at that moment Mr Dumbarr stuck his head around the door.

'Ah, here you are, my dear.' He was gasping from the effort of climbing the stairs. 'Nurse Law said that I would find you here and I just came to say–'

'GO AWAY!'

'*What* did you say?' he asked indignantly.

'I said *go away* – or as God is my witness, I'll scream this place down.'

Mr Dumbarr seemed to swell with rage but then as he saw that Maddy meant every word she said, he tried to control his anger.

'I can see that you are distraught so I will ignore your outburst just this once,' he told her through gritted teeth. 'But just remember who the boss is here, and I shall expect to see you in my room tonight after lights out.'

And then he was gone, closing the door none

too quietly behind him.

The rest of the day passed in a blur. As word spread of Holly's death the girls became hushed and crept past Maddy's room. They knew how close she and Holly had become and didn't want to disturb her grieving, which she undoubtedly was, if the sobs echoing from the other side of the door were anything to go by.

In the middle of the afternoon there was a tap on her door and Nurse Law walked in. 'Do you want anything, love? Perhaps a drink or something to eat?'

Maddy swiped her nose along the length of her cardigan sleeve as she shook her head miserably. The years stretching ahead of her had been bearable with Holly to share the time with, but now she felt as if she was doing a life sentence. She was not even fourteen years of age yet, but suddenly she felt like a very old woman with nothing to look forward to.

Sighing heavily, the kindly nurse turned to leave but then remembering something, she took a letter from the pocket of her starched white apron.

'This other letter came for you today so I thought I'd bring it up to you.' After placing the envelope on Maddy's bed she slipped quietly from the room, respecting the fact that for now at least, Maddy preferred to be alone.

Maddy looked at the writing. It was obviously another letter from Andy and Kirsty. Normally she would have flung it into the drawer to join the others, but today she felt the need to hear from someone outside these drab four walls so she slit it open and started to read it. It was from Andy.

195

He spoke of ordinary everyday things. He told her how the dogs were doing and that Kirsty hadn't been herself lately. Maddy briefly wondered what he meant but was too upset about Holly to dwell on it. Eventually she tossed it aside, not even bothering to finish reading it. The way she saw it, if the couple had offered her a permanent home, there would have been no need for them to write to her. She would still have been at home in Plymouth with them, and all the terrible things she was being subjected to here could have been avoided. Like everyone else in her life, they hadn't loved her enough to keep her.

Now a terrible feeling began to bubble up inside her. Perhaps it was something about her that caused everyone she cared about to leave? Maddy had no way of knowing, but what she did know was that from this day on she would never let anyone get close enough to hurt her again. Forming any kind of attachment only caused pain – and she had already had enough of that to last her a lifetime.

Steph and Kim found her curled up on the bed in a foetal position when they returned to the dormitory later that afternoon, and they looked at Maddy sympathetically.

'How you doin'? Steph asked softly. When Maddy looked at her, Steph was surprised to see that her eyes were hard.

'I'm fine.' Maddy dragged herself up onto the pillows. 'You have to be in this place, otherwise you'd go mad. But I'll tell you now – one way or another, I'm going to get out of here.'

Steph and Kim exchanged a worried glance.

'You're bound to feel like that. You've just had an awful shock,' Kim said awkwardly. 'But you'll soon settle down again once you've gotten over it a bit.'

'I won't!' Maddy glared at her. 'I've been to hell and back since I set foot in this place, but Dumbo's power over me has gone now. I only went along with what he wanted so he would allow me to spend time with Holly. But now she's gone he's got no hold over me any more and he can kiss my arse.'

Kim eyed Maddy warily. She had never seen her so angry and wasn't sure what to say to her. All she did know was that Dumbo wasn't someone to be messed with lightly and Maddy might make things worse for herself if she went against him. However, she was wise enough to realise that now wasn't the right time to voice her concerns so she simply nodded towards the door and Steph hastily rose and followed her.

'We'll give you a bit of space,' Kim muttered feelingly. 'But if you decide you don't want to be on your own, just come down an' join us, eh?'

Silence was her only answer as she and her friend quietly left the room.

That evening, when Miss Budd did her usual tour of inspection and turned out all the lights, Maddy lay in her bed as still as a statue. She had no intention of visiting Mr Dumbarr, and as far as she was concerned, he could do what he liked about it. She was sick of being used, and in the future he would find that she was no longer the submissive girl she had been while she'd had Holly to worry about. From now on, Maddy in-

197

tended to do things *her* way – and woe betide anyone who tried to stop her.

Mr Dumbarr caught up with her mid-morning the following day and bore down on her like an avenging angel.

'My office – right *now!*' he barked as they came face-to-face in the corridor.

Maddy followed him, wearing an insolent expression. Once inside his room he closed the door and turned on her, demanding, 'And just where did you get to last night? I spent a long time waiting for you.'

'You can wait as long as you like in future but I won't be coming again,' Maddy told him clearly as she folded her arms and leaned against the door.

He looked momentarily stunned. Mr Dumbarr was not used to being disobeyed but then he composed himself with a great effort and ground out, 'Oh, but I think you *will*, Madeleine. Much harder girls than you have disobeyed me in the past, and believe me – they soon wished that they hadn't. You *will* come to my room whenever I choose you to. Is that quite clear?' He was leaning so heavily on his desk that his pudgy knuckles were white but Maddy faced him fearlessly although she said not a word.

Deciding to take a gentler approach, the man now rose to his full height and forced a sickly smile to his face. 'I know you've had a great shock, my dear, so I am prepared to overlook this outburst. But don't cut off your nose to spite your face. Haven't I been good to you? I've never known you

198

to refuse all the little treats and surprises I buy for you, and you wouldn't want them to stop, now would you?' His voice had a cajoling edge to it but Maddy stood her ground.

'You're nothing but a dirty bullying old pervert, and you can just fuck off,' she told him with contempt.

His face coloured to such an extent that for a moment, Maddy was sure he was going to burst a blood vessel.

'How *dare* you speak to me like that?' he spluttered. He had never even heard Maddy swear before. But then this girl standing in front of him was nothing like the girl he had enjoyed abusing.

'Oh, I dare all right,' Maddy retorted with a toss of her head. 'And I'll tell you something else as well. If you so much as try to lay one more finger on me, I'll shout from the rooftops just what you are. You just see if I don't.'

Turning about, she marched from the room as her threat echoed in his ears – and he was so dumbfounded that he allowed her to leave without a word.

It was at lunchtime, as Maddy was making her way to the dining room with her room-mates, that they spotted Miss Budd showing a handsome young man about. He flashed them a friendly smile as they passed and Steph almost swooned.

'Cor, he's a bit of all right, ain't he?' she said dreamily. 'I wonder if he's the new social worker who's due to start here? I heard Dumbo speaking to Budd about a chap that was due to start yesterday as I passed Miss Budd's room.'

'Ooh, I hope it's him,' Kim giggled. 'He's just gorgeous on legs!'

Maddy grinned at her friends. It was nice to hear them laughing for a change. In fact, it was nice to have something to laugh about.

The excitement of the new social worker starting evaporated two days later when Maddy began to discover just what the consequences of upsetting Mr Dumbarr were.

She had just entered the dining room for her evening meal when the overweight man bore down on her.

'Come with me,' he told her in a voice that made the whole room fall silent.

'What for?' Maddy squared her slim shoulders as she glared back at him.

'You've been caught out, girl,' he retaliated. 'Stealing!'

'Stealing!' Maddy repeated, painfully aware that every pair of eyes in the room was trained on her. 'I'm no thief,' she protested hotly. 'What is it I'm supposed to have stolen?'

'Miss Budd had her solid gold pen go missing from her room this morning,' he told her coldly. 'At round about that time you were seen in the hallway out of your lessons.'

'But I was just going to the toilet,' Maddy protested.

'Even so, you were not where you were supposed to be and that singled you out as a prime suspect. So, we decided to search your room and Miss Budd's pen was found hidden in one of your drawers.'

'*No!* It couldn't have been!' Maddy's head wagged from side to side in distress. She had never stolen a single thing in her whole life and could never even recollect seeing a gold pen in Miss Budd's room. She avoided the place like the plague and had set foot in there no more than three times in the whole of her stay at River House.

As realisation suddenly dawned on her, her distress turned to anger and she pointed a trembling finger at Mr Dumbarr.

'You've set me up,' she screeched accusingly. 'Because I've refused to let you have your way with me any more!'

The silence in the room was almost deafening now as Miss Budd bore down on her.

'I might have known you would come up with such disgusting claptrap. But it won't get you anywhere, I assure you. Such wicked allegations will only earn you yet more time in the Quiet Room, which is where you are going right now, my girl.'

'Oh no, I am not!' Maddy turned to run but they were on her before she had taken more than two steps. Both adults had a firm hold on her arms, and although she struggled and kicked out she knew that she was no match for them.

'You'll be sorry for this!' she screamed as they dragged her from the room, but they totally ignored her and continued to haul her along. When they came to the dark staircase that led down to the Quiet Room, Maddy dug her heels in after kicking out with all her might, catching Miss Budd a glancing blow on her shin.

201

The woman howled with pain but her grip on the girl did not lessen in the least. If anything it increased, and now Maddy could feel her sharp nails digging into the soft skin of her upper arm.

She refused to walk another step and so they dragged her down the roughly hewn concrete steps as she felt the skin being peeled painfully from her knees.

Once at the door of the Quiet Room, Miss Budd flung it open. She was sweating profusely now with the exertion of getting Maddy there, and the smell of stale deodorant was coming off her in waves. Mr Dumbarr was sweating too and was so red in the face that he looked likely to have a heart-attack at any moment. Maddy prayed with all her being that he would.

'There, that's the best place for you, my girl,' Miss Budd spat breathlessly as she shoved Maddy into the room. 'Perhaps you'll learn to keep your thieving fingers to yourself now and learn some manners into the bargain. I just knew you were going to be trouble the second I set eyes on you.'

Maddy landed in a painful heap on the cold concrete floor and for a second she was winded with the force of the fall. But then she scrabbled to her knees and threw herself towards the door just as it clanged resoundingly shut. The sound echoed in the cold room as she began to pummel the wooden surface with her fists.

'Let me out, you bastards!'

It was then that the bare light bulb dangling from the ceiling suddenly went out and she found herself in pitch darkness. Panic gripped her, robbing her of speech. Maddy had always been terrified of the dark from when she was just a tiny girl. But this was darkness as she had never known it. So black that she couldn't even see her hand in front of her.

Her anger and frustration were quickly replaced by hysteria, and suddenly she was a little girl again being locked in the pitch black cupboard beneath the stairs. 'Please,' she implored as she slid to the ground. 'Turn the light on. I don't like the dark.'

A throaty chuckle full of spite floated from the other side of the door. 'I'm afraid I have no choice but to turn the light off. It seems that it's the only way we can get you to calm down.'

Maddy's hatred of the woman who had imprisoned her grew tenfold but she wouldn't give Miss Budd the satisfaction of hearing her cry, so she wrapped her arms about her knees and screwed her eyes up tight. Seconds later she heard her jailers walk away, their footsteps echoing hollowly on the bare concrete floors. And then there was nothing but silence, and to her mortification she felt warm urine trickle down her leg. She sat there for what seemed like an eternity as every story of bogeymen she had ever heard flashed through her mind. This was fear as she had never known it. Eventually she crawled across the floor, her hand held out in front of her as she blindly felt for the location of the bed. It was bitterly cold and she could feel her breath fanning out in front of her. Her knickers and the back of her dress were wet through and humiliation swept over her as the sickly-sweet smell of urine filled her nostrils. When she found the bed she hoisted herself painfully up onto it. And now her knees began to throb where the skin had been grazed from them. Tentatively she put her hand down and when she felt something warm and sticky she knew that they were bleeding. Quickly wrapping the blanket around herself she hid her head beneath it and there she cried as if her heart would break. She cried for Holly and her lost siblings, for the mother whom she could no longer even picture in her mind, and for the life that she might have had if just one single person had ever loved her.

Chapter Eighteen

When the light finally came on again, Maddy blinked as her eyes tried to adjust to it. She had stopped crying long ago. There was no one to hear her and anyway, even if there had been, she was sure that there was not a single tear left in her.

She heard the key grate in the lock and there was Mr Dumbarr standing in the doorway with a tray in his hand and a self-satisfied look on his face.

'Ready to be nice to me again yet, are you?'

Maddy made no move to rise from the bed but simply stared at him from listless eyes. He smirked as he advanced on her – and when she suddenly lunged from the bed and sent the tray flying from his hands, he gasped with surprise. She was fiery, he would have to give her that, but then that was just how he liked his girls to be.

'Now now.' He stepped over the puddle of luke-warm tea that was spreading across the floor. 'That's no way to greet me, is it? Especially after I went to all the trouble of bringing you some food. You'll just have to go hungry until morning now, won't you?'

As he pushed her hard up against the wall and began to fumble with the buttons on her dress, Maddy felt herself stiffen. She already ached all over from the way she had been treated earlier, but she knew now that the pain she had felt then was nothing compared to the pain Dumbarr was about to inflict on her. And all too soon she was proved to be right. He used her body viciously, making her cry out, which only seemed to increase his pleasure. There was no fear of anyone hearing her down here so he took her roughly, grunting with pleasure the whole time. At last it was over and he rolled off her to lie panting on the narrow bed, waiting for his heart to slow to a steadier rhythm.

Minutes later, he stood up and began to drag his clothes back on.

'You won't be quite so ready to go stealing again, will you?' he jeered.

'I didn't steal anything. You know I didn't.'

'That's exactly right – I do know. But perhaps now you'll see what I'm capable of doing, if you try to cross me.' He leaned in so close that she could smell his whisky breath fanning her face. 'And in future you'll perhaps know your place. Just remember, until I tire of you, you are *mine*. Now think on what I've said.'

With that he turned and left, and seconds later the room was plunged into darkness yet again. Maddy was so sore that she felt as if she had been torn apart, and now she staggered from the bed and blindly felt about the cold floor for the bucket that would serve as her toilet. She felt dirty and humiliated, and just wished that she could die there and then. But the night wasn't over yet, and in her distress she overturned the bucket. Seconds later, she found herself kneeling in stale urine. The smell was overpowering, and lowering her head she wept in despair.

Two mornings later, Nurse Law stopped Miss Budd in the corridor outside the sick bay. 'You haven't seen anything of Maddy this morning, have you?' she asked innocently. 'Only I've been trying to keep my eye on her since Holly died. She was deeply upset about her death but I haven't seen her about for a while.'

Miss Budd pursed her lips. 'Maddy was caught with my gold pen hidden in her room,' she rasped. 'And so I had no choice but to teach her a lesson. She has been in the Quiet Room for the last couple of nights.'

'For *two* whole nights?' Nurse Law was appalled. 'Is there really any need for her to be left there for so long? Particularly in the state of mind she's in?'

'There is every need,' Miss Budd snapped pompously. 'We cannot tolerate thieves here under any circumstances. When she shows some remorse I will let her out. And in the meantime, Nurse Law, I suggest you should mind your own business.'

She then stuck her chin in the air and stamped away.

Mary chewed on her lip. Maddy stealing? Somehow she just couldn't picture it. Maddy was a difficult girl in some ways, admittedly, but she had always come across as a generous person to Mary. Any treats she had, had always found their way to Holly while she had been in the sick bay. There was a sinking feeling in the pit of the nurse's stomach as she thought of the poor girl locked away down in the cellar. But what could she do about it? She was only the school nurse, after all. Shrugging, she hurried back to the sick bay where she had a girl suffering from a severe case of tonsillitis.

The rest of the morning passed quickly, but by lunchtime Nurse Law still could not stop thinking of Maddy. As she stepped into the hallway she saw Nick Preston, the young social worker who had recently started working at River House. Nick was a lovely young man in his early twenties. He was still at university but had been commissioned to work at River House for six months as part of his PhD. Mary smiled. She was aware that half the girls had already developed a crush on him, which was understandable. He was a good-looking young chap.

'Nick?' As Nurse Law beckoned to him, he came across to her with a wide smile on his face. 'Would you happen to know if Miss Budd has let young Maddy out of the Quiet Room yet?' she asked, keeping her voice deliberately low.

Nick scratched his head. 'I wasn't even aware that they'd put her there,' he said. 'What's she done?' Up to now he had only seen the Punishment Room that the authorities were shown into on their once-yearly inspection of the home, so he could have no idea of how awful the place Maddy was in really was.

'Miss Budd reckons she was caught with a valuable gold pen that she had stolen from her study, but between you and me, it just doesn't ring true. Maddy is not the type to steal.'

He nodded in agreement. 'I think I know the girl you're talking about and I have to agree with you. Maddy's a quiet kid but I can't see her stealing from anyone. How long has she been down there?'

'Two nights.'

He could see the concern on the nurse's face and frowned. 'That's a bit harsh, isn't it? Has she had food taken down to her?'

'I don't know,' Mary Law wrung her hands together. 'As far as I'm concerned no one should ever be put down there. It's enough to drive the poor kids mad, being shut away like that. I mean, I accept that in a place like this there have to be rules, but surely there are more apt forms of punishment if they've done wrong?'

'What's Maddy here for?' he asked now, his curiosity aroused.

'I'm not really sure. I don't have access to the girls' files, seeing as I'm only the school nurse. But rumour has it that Maddy started a fire that killed both her parents, hence she ended up here. She never has any visitors as far as I know, so it could be that she has no one on the outside.'

'Well, I can soon check that out,' he told her.

208

'But of course, I'll have to choose the right time. I don't think Miss Budd would be too happy to find me rummaging about in the records willy nilly.'

'Thanks, I'd appreciate that. I don't mind telling you I'm really concerned about the girl. She seems as taut as a wire lately and I put it down to the fact that her best friend has recently died of cancer after a long illness. But I wonder now if there isn't something else bothering her too. She looks sort of haunted, and she seems to have lost a tremendous amount of weight. She almost jumps at her own shadow.'

'Leave it with me,' he answered as he patted her arm. 'As soon as the right moment comes I'll open her file and find out all about her and then I'll come back to you, OK?'

'Thanks, I'd really appreciate that. But don't go getting yourself into trouble. This place isn't quite what it appears to be from the outside and I'd be the first to admit I don't approve of some of the things that go on here, like locking the girls away in the cellar for the least little things for a start-off. And that Mr Dumbarr ... ugh! There's something about the man that makes me shudder.'

At that moment the person they were talking about appeared out of his office and the nurse and the young social worker hastily parted to go their separate ways.

Once Mr Dumbarr had disappeared off into the dining room, Mary stood there chewing on her lip indecisively. But then she straightened her shoulders and strode towards the corridor that led to the cellars. If she was discovered she would simply say that as the school nurse she had felt obligated to check that Maddy was all right.

Picking her way cautiously down the stone steps, she wrinkled her nose as the smell of damp pervaded her nostrils. There was no form of heating down here and it was bitterly cold and dismal.

When she reached the door of the Quiet Room she slipped open the hatch that fastened from the outside and peeped through it. For a moment she thought she must have the wrong room as the inside was in total darkness, but then a whimper came from within and her blood turned to ice. Surely Miss Budd hadn't left the girl with not even a light on?

Her hand scanned the wall at the side of the door, and when she located a light switch she clicked it on and the room was suddenly illuminated. Maddy was curled up in a tight ball on a damp mattress and Mary Law had to stop herself from crying aloud at the pathetic sight of her.

'Maddy,' she whispered urgently. 'Are you all right, love?'

The shape on the mattress slowly raised its head and Mary's hand flew to her mouth as Maddy's tear-stained swollen face appeared from beneath a grimy blanket.

Mary looked around for a sign of the key that would unlock the door but it was nowhere in sight and now frustration flooded through her. The smell that was emitting from the hatch was making her gag and it took all her willpower to try and keep her voice light.

'Have you eaten, Maddy?'

The girl woefully shook her head. 'When can I come out?'

'Just as soon as I can speak to Miss Budd,' Mary informed her. 'Now try and keep warm. I'm going to leave the light on for you while I go and have a word with her.' And with that she was gone, racing along the damp corridors as cold anger lent speed to her legs.

Once upstairs she headed towards the dining room and almost collided with Miss Budd who was just leaving the room.

'Ah, here you are,' Mary said without preamble. 'I was just coming to try and find you. I went down to the Quiet Room to check on Maddy and I think it's high time you let her out now. As a nurse it's my duty to keep an eye on the health of the girls in my care and I think any longer down there could have a very bad effect on her. Did you know that she was in total darkness?'

Miss Budd swallowed the hasty retort that sprang to her lips. She was of a mind to tell this meddling woman to mind her own damn business but she was also aware that she must be careful not to do anything to bring disrepute to River House.

'In the dark you say? Oh, how *dreadful*.' Miss Budd looked suitably flustered as she fingered the strand of pearls at her throat. 'I must have turned the light off by mistake the last time I took a meal to her. And funnily enough, I was just on my way there now to let her out. I suggest you go about your business now, Nurse. *I* shall see to Maddy.'

211

As Mary walked away with clenched fists Miss Budd's mouth narrowed into a thin straight line. Just who did that damn nurse think she was anyway, and how *dare* she tell her what to do? Miss Budd had had no intention of letting Maddy out just yet, but now she felt as if she had been backed into a corner. Still, she consoled herself as she felt in her pocket for the key to the Quiet Room, there would be other times. She hadn't finished with Maddy yet, not by a long chalk. And she would have strong words with Dumbarr too. What was he thinking of, interfering with the girls here? She'd had her suspicions for some time about the way he favoured Maddy. But what was he thinking of, jeopardising their positions? If he wanted to satisfy his desire for young girls there would be plenty of time for that later on, that was their agreement, but certainly not now when busybodies like Mary Law might poke their noses in and learn more than was good for them.

Glancing at her watch she tutted with annoyance. She had been about to go to her rooms to enjoy a quiet after-dinner drink as she did most days, but now she supposed she had better go and release the girl first.

When she unlocked the door to the Quiet Room, Maddy blinked with surprise.

'Come on, girl, up with you,' the woman barked as she held the door wide. As Maddy stumbled past her, the woman pulled a face. 'Get yourself off for a shower and change your clothes,' she ordered. 'And then get back down here and clean this place up. It stinks, and when I come back I want to find it spotless. Do you understand?'

Maddy nodded as she slipped past her with her head down so that Miss Budd wouldn't see the raw hatred on her face. And as she followed her back through the labyrinth of corridors she knew without a doubt that had she had a knife in her hand that minute, she would have stabbed the woman to death there and then.

Chapter Nineteen

It was two days later when Nick Preston turned up at the door of the sick bay looking very furtive. Mary was cleaning her instruments and quickly beckoned him in before closing the door behind him.

'I managed to get a look at Maddy's files,' he told her, 'and I have to say they don't make very good reading. The poor kid has been pushed from one place to another all her life, from what I can make of it. It seems her father left the family when she was quite young, leaving the mother to cope with two little children. She then went on to have two more to different fathers, and it appears that Maddy had to be a mum to them.'

'Oh, so Maddy has siblings then?'

'Yes, she does – one sister and two brothers, all younger than her. It seems that her mum hit the bottle after her husband left her, and if the notes are anything to go by, things got so bad that they were all taken into care. Maddy and her brother,

213

Oliver, were then adopted by the couple in Plymouth, and apparently Maddy never really gelled with them although her notes don't say why. Anyway, her birth mum ended up in a rehabilitation centre for alcoholics, although it doesn't say what happened to her after that. I suppose it would have been too late for her to try and get the kids back by the time she got out because they'd all gone for adoption. The two younger siblings, Molly and Ryan, are somewhere in Nuneaton and Birmingham and following the fire, Oliver has gone to a couple on the outskirts of Plymouth. And that's about all I know, though I could make a few discreet enquiries if you wanted me to. I have a few social-worker friends who are very good at ferreting out addresses, although it's strictly against the rules.'

'Rules are sometimes made to be broken,' Mary told him stoically. 'And from where I'm standing that poor kid has no one. Perhaps if we could track down her siblings it might make her feel that she had someone who cared?'

'Well, I'll see what I can do but don't hold me to it,' he replied. 'These things can take time. Meanwhile, all we can do is keep an eye out for her. How does she seem?'

'Very withdrawn and quiet,' Mary admitted. She studied him for a moment and then, deciding that she could trust him, she lowered her voice as she told him, 'I have a horrible feeling that Dumbarr is more interested in certain of the girls here than is healthy – if you get my drift.'

'No!' Nick's face betrayed his horror. 'What, you mean he–?'

'I have no proof whatsoever,' Mary added quickly. 'But I've seen the way he watches Maddy. Up until a few months ago it was Stacey, but I think Maddy has caught his eye now. I've tried to question her discreetly but as soon as I mention his name she just closes up like a clam.'

'But why doesn't she tell her social worker?'

'Huh!' Mary shrugged. 'As far as I know, the one time her social worker visited her, Maddy refused to see her. You know how stroppy she can be. And anyway, even if she had agreed to see her, I doubt she would have said anything. None of the girls here do. I think they're too afraid to.'

'Stacey will be leaving here soon, won't she?' Nick now asked.

Mary nodded. 'Yes, she will, and if she has nowhere to go it will be up to Dumbarr to find her somewhere to live and to help her get a job.'

'I see.' Nick stroked his chin thoughtfully. 'Don't the girls' social workers do any follow-up care?'

'Not as far as I know. That's Mr Dumbarr's job, bearing in mind that most of the girls are too old to stay in care when they leave here.'

'Well, look, I'll see what I can find out and in the meantime you keep an eye out for her as best you can, eh?'

Mary nodded and once Nick had gone she crossed to the window and stood gazing out across the grounds. There but for the grace of God go my kids, she thought, and shuddered as if someone had stepped on her grave.

'Oh, Stacey, I'm gonna miss yer,' her friend told her as she hugged her tightly.

Stacey, who looked like the cat that had got the cream, hugged her back. 'Well, I'll miss you too but I can't say I'm gonna miss this place,' she replied.

'Ain't it a shame that yer mam an' dad wouldn't let yer go back home?' her friend went on.

'Is it *hell*.' Stacey flicked her long blonde hair over her shoulders. 'I wouldn't have wanted to go back to live with those two Bible-bashing, self-righteous old gits! They'd have driven me barmy. I didn't mind them coming to see me and supplying me with treats, but living with them again is a different kettle of fish altogether. No, thank you very much, I shall be just fine and dandy in this little flat Dumbo's found for me. Soon as I get settled, I'll write and give you the address, shall I?'

As Mr Dumbarr stepped from his office with his car keys dangling from his plump hand, Stacey lifted her small suitcase and waved airily at her friend.

'See yer, wouldn't wanna be yer!' she shouted, and then she and Mr Dumbarr left together, leaving Stacey's friend staring forlornly after them.

'Lucky sod,' she muttered, before turning and heading off for her next lesson.

Maddy had been watching the whole thing from behind the banisters on the stairs and breathed a sigh of relief as she stood up. At least now Stacey had gone that would be one problem out of the way, although Dumbarr would still be there, and he was the biggest problem of all.

She'd had strict instructions to go to his room after lights out that very night, and already her

216

stomach was doing somersaults at the thought of it. Her body was still sore and inflamed from the last time he'd used her.

'Ah, Maddy!'

The sound of her name being called made the girl quickly look up to where Nurse Law was standing at the top of the stairs.

'I've been looking for you,' she told her with a cheery smile. 'I was wondering how you were feeling. You've been looking awfully pale just lately. Why don't you pop into the sick bay and let me check you over. You look as if a tonic might do you some good.'

Maddy shook her head, mumbling, 'Thanks, but I'm fine, honest.'

'That's as maybe but I'd like to check you out all the same.' Nurse Law's voice was firm. 'Come to the sick bay after classes, please.'

Maddy sighed with resentment. She knew that Nurse Law meant well. In fact, she was about the only person in the whole place who seemed to give a jot for the girls, apart from the new trainee social worker, Nick. He seemed a good sort and all but she wished they would just leave her alone. All she really wanted to do was keep her head down and hope that the time she had left to spend here would pass quickly.

After classes, Maddy reluctantly made her way to the sick bay where Mary Law was waiting for her. The nurse smiled a welcome before motioning towards a chair.

'Sit yourself down over there and let's have a look at you, shall we?'

Maddy sat down, squirming in her seat and wishing that she was a million miles away.

Mary quickly checked her eyes and then looked into her throat and ears.

'Everything's fine there,' she assured her. 'Now take your cardigan off and hop onto the bed, would you, please.'

'What for?' Maddy hugged her scratchy cardigan more tightly about her and stubbornly stayed where she was.

'Well, I can't examine you properly sitting there, can I? Now come along, it won't take more than a minute. Have you started your periods, Maddy?' She continued to ask questions as Maddy reluctantly slipped her cardigan off and lay down on the bed. Mary Law frowned as she saw the bruises on Maddy's arms and began to inspect them.

'However did you get these?' she asked.

'I slipped on the stairs,' Maddy muttered as colour flamed into her cheeks.

Convinced that she was lying, Mary stared at her. These bruises were in completely the wrong place for a fall on the stairs, but what could she do if Maddy refused to tell her how she had really got them?

The woman gently pressed around Maddy's stomach before unfastening her dress so that she could listen to her heartbeat. 'That's it then – all done. You can hop down now.' She kept her voice light as she placed her stethoscope down on the trolley.

'Can I go now? The hairdresser is coming in today and I want to get my hair trimmed.'

'Of course you can, love. But Maddy, if ever

218

you need to talk to anyone or anything is troubling you, you can always come to me.'

Inclining her head, Maddy bolted as Mary stared thoughtfully after her. Those bruises hadn't been caused by any fall, she would have bet a week's pay on it. So could it be that someone was bullying the girl? She had certainly not seen any evidence of this. In fact, since Holly had died, Maddy tended to keep herself very much to herself and the rest of the girls had very little to do with her. With a shake of the head, Mary went about her business. As her mother had been fond of saying, 'You can only help those who help themselves.'

Later that night when the house was finally quiet, Maddy crept along the corridors to Mr Dumbarr's room. She tapped at his door and when there was no reply, she glanced fearfully up and down the landing. Normally, he was waiting for her and it wouldn't do if Miss Budd were to find her there. Maddy tried the door, sighing with relief when it opened soundlessly. The room was in darkness and after hastily slipping inside and closing the door behind her, she fumbled for the light switch. When bright light flooded the room she blinked and looked about. There was no sign of the man but now that she came to think about it, she hadn't seen him since he had left with Stacey earlier in the day.

For a moment she stood there indecisively but then curiosity got the better of her and she began to stroll around the room. She poured herself a large glass of wine from the bottle that stood on the table to one side of the window and swallowed it in two gulps. Instantly the nerves that were fluttering in her stomach began to subside so she poured herself another, enjoying the warm sensation as it burned its way down her throat.

Crossing to the large polished wardrobe, she threw the door open and stared at the shirts and suits all hung neatly away. To one side of it were some long clothes bags and she undid the zip on the first one before gasping with astonishment. It was full of brightly coloured women's clothes. Hastily dragging it out of the wardrobe, she carried it to the bed and tipped out its contents. There were gaudy silk blouses and skirts and a long chiffon dress that looked so big it was more like a tent. Hurrying back, she took out the next bag and after tipping that out too she found that it was full of enormous padded bras and knickers. Now she thrust the suits aside and began to rummage in the bottom of the wardrobe where she found three pairs of stiletto shoes that were as big as boats.

'Crikey, his girlfriend must be as large as a house,' she muttered with a smile on her face. Next she turned her attention to the large chest-of-drawers. The top two were full of neatly folded men's underwear but the next one revealed a collection of make-up. Inside the bottom one was a long blonde wig, and after lifting it out she frowned. The woman whom she had seen on two occasions in Mr Dumbarr's room had had long blonde hair...

Glancing back at the shocking pink blouse on the bed she frowned thoughtfully – and then as realisation suddenly dawned on her she gasped and dropped the wig as if it had burned her.

These clothes didn't belong to any girlfriend. They were Mr Dumbarr's. He dressed up in them himself. He had to be one of those strange men she had read about and seen on the telly who liked to strut about in women's clothing.

Suddenly the effects of the wine had worn off and as she backed towards the door shock coursed through her. She had to get away before he returned.

Once out in the corridor she ran as if the devil himself was after her, heedless to whether Miss Budd saw her or not, and she didn't slow her steps until she was safely back in her own dormitory.

After scrambling into bed she lay there with her mind spinning. She had known for some time that Dumbarr was a pervert, but this on top was unbelievable. Not that anything could be worse than child abuse. There was a name for men like him and she lay there until it came to her. Transvestites, that's what they were called, she was sure of it. Grown men who liked to dress as women.

She wondered what he would do when he returned to find his things strewn about the room. Would he guess that it was her? And if he did, what would he do about it? Her heart was thumping so loudly that she was sure it would wake Steph and Kim up, but thankfully they slept on, totally oblivious to Maddy's turmoil.

Her thoughts raced on. What would Miss Budd do if she were to discover the truth about him? It was common knowledge that the woman worshipped the very ground he walked on, but would he still be her idol if she knew about his fetish?

It came to Maddy in a blinding flash. She could use this to her advantage! Dumbarr would die of shame, should his secret ever come to light, she was sure of it. And on top of that he would lose his job as well as his home. Perhaps if she were to tell him that she knew all about his fetish he might leave her well alone? The way she saw it, she had nothing to lose and everything to gain. It was certainly worth trying a little bit of blackmail if she was forced to. With a wide smile on her face she lay there until exhaustion finally claimed her and she slept. It never occurred to her for a second that Miss Budd might already be aware of her colleague's 'private' interests.

Chapter Twenty

The following two weeks were the most peaceful Maddy had known since coming to River House. Mr Dumbarr would eye her warily every time he saw her and skirt around her as if she had the plague. This suited Maddy down to the ground. As long as he left her alone she was happy to leave him alone, but it would be God help him if he tried it on with her again.

Maddy had told no one that it was her birthday, so it was a shock when after classes on a day in October, Nurse Law called her into the sick bay where she was confronted with a birthday cake complete with fourteen candles that were flickering brightly.

'Happy birthday, love,' the kindly woman said.

Maddy's mouth dropped slackly open. Nick was there too and he grinned at her, saying, 'Happy birthday, Maddy.'

'H ... how did you know?' Maddy muttered as embarrassment washed over her.

'Well, we do have your date of birth on file, you know!' Pressing a small, gaily wrapped package into her hand, Nick told her, 'This is from Nurse Law and myself. It's not much but we hope you'll like it. Now blow your candles out before they melt all over the icing, will you?'

Maddy obediently did as she was told as unfamiliar emotions ripped through her. She wasn't used to people being kind to her and wasn't sure how to react.

'Well done, Maddy. Now open your present while I cut us each a slice of this cake. I'm afraid my latest diet is going straight out of the window again.' Mary Law smiled at her as she cut wedges of cake, and Maddy fumbled with the paper on her present. When she finally managed to get past the many layers of sellotape she looked down at a small jewellery box and her throat clogged with tears. It was white with tiny roses painted on it, and Maddy thought it was the prettiest thing she had ever seen. It also reminded her of the one she had bought Holly for Christmas.

'We were going to get you something to wear, but seeing as you girls are never allowed out of uniform there didn't seem much point,' Mary explained as she bit into her cake. 'Open the lid,' she urged, spraying crumbs everywhere.

Maddy did as she was told and was confronted by a tiny ballerina who slowly turned as the box played the haunting music from *Swan Lake*.

'I ... it's really lovely,' Maddy assured them as she took the plate Mary was holding out to her. 'Thank you both very much.'

Suddenly River House didn't seem quite such a prison, after all. Dumbarr was leaving her well alone and now this kindness. Perhaps things were finally looking up.

Maddy's happier state of mind lasted for another three whole weeks, but then the nightmare looked set to begin again when Mr Dumbarr cornered her on the landing one morning.

With her back to the wall she glared at him as she hissed, 'What do *you* want?'

Painfully aware that a few of the girls were still trickling down to breakfast, he kept his smile fixed firmly in place.

'I was just wondering how you are,' he told her, his voice dripping with charm. 'I've missed our little meetings.'

'Well, I haven't.' Maddy stared him out, happy to see that he looked vaguely uncomfortable.

'I needed to have a word with you because ... the thing is ... someone went into my room on the day I moved Stacey and I found certain things flung all about the place when I returned home.'

He was watching her closely for a sign that she knew what he was talking about, but Maddy never so much as blinked. She wanted to keep what she had discovered to herself for now.

'And why are you asking me about it?' she

224

asked innocently. 'I didn't go to your room that night because I knew you weren't back.'

She watched the relief on his face and had to stifle the urge to grin. It was pay-back time now for all the terrible things he had forced her to do and she wanted to make him squirm until the time was right.

'Oh, I see.' The look she had come to dread was back in his eyes now as they dropped to her breasts. Maddy had developed over the last year and was now a very attractive teenager.

'I thought perhaps you could come to my room this evening?'

'Did you?' Maddy pulled herself from the wall and walked past him insolently with her chin in the air. She could see that he wanted to threaten her again but didn't quite dare. Not until he was quite sure that she had no idea about his secret.

'So ... can I expect you then?'

'You'll have to wait and see, won't you?' Maddy said carelessly, and then skipped down the stairs as he stared after her in confusion.

Once he was out of sight, her steps slowed and she frowned. He had had time to get rid of the evidence now, and should she shout out what he was, there might be nothing left in his room to substantiate what she was saying.

Her eyes moved to the window just as the gardeners' van pulled up and, once again, Maddy thought of trying to escape.

She had a free study period after Computer Studies this afternoon, and if she could manage to sneak into the van before the gardeners left, there was every chance she could be long gone from here before anyone missed her. After all, what was there to keep her here now? Holly was gone and was never coming back. Chewing thoughtfully on her lip, Maddy continued on to breakfast.

By mid-afternoon she had made her mind up. Nothing ventured, nothing gained. She was going to try and escape.

A short while later, she, Steph and Kim were making their way to the small library at the back of the house when she told them, 'I think I'll go and do my homework in our room this afternoon. I've got a bit of a headache after staring at that monitor screen, and it will be quieter there.'

'Suit yourself,' Kim told her obligingly, and she and Steph continued on their way, happily gossiping about Stacey's friend who was now complaining loudly because the girl still hadn't bothered to write to her as yet.

Once upstairs, Maddy hastily dragged the bag she had arrived with from under the bed and began to stuff her clothes into it, along with the little jewellery box that Nurse Law and Nick had bought for her. They were the only two people she would really miss in this place and she wished that she could have said goodbye to them. But of course that was totally out of the question. Tossing aside the hated uniform, she struggled into the clothes she had arrived in. The jeans were above her ankles now and the top strained across her newly developed breasts, but thankfully she could just about still squeeze into them. The ill-fitting clothes didn't trouble her, since Maddy didn't much care what she looked like just so long as she could get out of there.

She glanced around the room for what she hoped would be the very last time before cautiously inching the door open. With her heart in her mouth she peered up and down the landing. Everywhere was as quiet as the grave, so she tiptoed towards the top of the stairs. It was then that she heard footsteps coming from the opposite corridor and she shrank back against the wall as her heart pounded in her chest. Thankfully the footsteps finally receded as whoever it was went down the stairs and she stood there until the sound of them had died away altogether. Then, hitching her bag onto her shoulder, she moved on, expecting to be stopped and challenged at any second.

By the time she reached the front door she was sweating with fear. On top of that, she had recently started her periods and had terrible stomach cramps but she was determined to go on now that she had come this far. She slipped outside, gasping as the icy wind took her breath away. She would have to hurry now. The gardeners never stayed long in the winter as there was not so much to do and they could be leaving at any minute. With her head bent she made a sudden dash for the back of their van and sighed with relief when the rear door opened at her touch. Flinging her bag ahead of her she quickly followed it and pulled the door shut behind her. For a moment she squinted as her eyes adjusted to the dim light but then as she looked around she saw a selection of gardening tools sprawled about the floor, along with a number of tarpaulins. She quickly slid beneath one, pulling her bag in behind her, and then squatted down to wait. Soon after, she heard the sound of voices and held her breath as the gardeners approached the van. There were two of them and she could hear them laughing together. The back door of the van opened and something was flung inside, then it slammed shut again and she listened as the men walked round to the front and clambered in. The engine roared into life and suddenly she was rolling from side to side on the slippery floor as the van trundled off down the drive.

When it stopped shortly afterwards, tears sprang to her eyes. She was afraid that she had been caught out – but she needn't have worried because the next moment she heard one of the men say, 'See you next week then, George. Ta-ra for now.'

'See yer, lads. Have a good weekend now.'

George was the gateman who was obviously opening the enormous gates for them. They were moving again, and somehow she just knew that she was free. Escaping had proved to be far easier than she had dared to hope it would be. Almost too easy – but Maddy was no fool and she knew that staying out might prove to be far harder. She had no doubt at all that as soon as they discovered she was gone, they would have every policeman for miles around looking for her. And here she was with just the few measly pounds she had managed to save from the small amount of pocket money the girls in the home were given each week, and with nowhere to go. Still, she consoled herself, she was free ... for now at least.

The van seemed to drive for a long while, but then she heard the noise of traffic and cautiously squeezed from beneath the stained tarpaulin. It sounded as if they were in a town now, if the noise of the cars whizzing past was anything to go by, so she inched along the floor on her hands and knees and peered out of the dirty back window.

Within seconds, Maddy guessed that this must be Cheltenham. They were driving by sweeping classical terraces of Regency townhouses, many boasting intricate ironwork balconies and painted stucco façades. She supposed that the people who lived in such houses must be very rich, but had no time to ponder on it because just then the van began to slow down and she panicked. Scrambling back across the floor, she disappeared beneath the tarpaulin again and seconds later the van stopped and the sound of the engine died.

She heard the van doors slam as the two men in front got out and then the back doors opened and she heard them speaking.

'Just a tidy-up here, isn't it?' one of them asked.

'Yes, it is. Shouldn't take us no more than an hour,' his workmate replied.

They were dragging something across the floor dangerously close to her, and Maddy was terrified that they would lift the tarpaulin and discover her, but thankfully they didn't and seconds later the back doors were slammed shut again. After waiting for what seemed an eternity she cautiously ventured out, peering through the back window to make sure that the coast was clear. She tentatively tried the door and sighed with relief to find that it was unlocked. Quickly snatching her bag, she inched the door open, and after checking first one way and then the other, she jumped down onto the road and started to march smartly away. She had absolutely no idea what direction she was going in, but for now that didn't matter. All that mattered was getting as far away from the van as was possible. All the streets were tree-lined, and Maddy stared about in awe. Everywhere felt absolutely enormous after being confined to the grounds of River House for so long, and she felt very small and vulnerable. She also felt euphoric and terrified all at the same time, and her heart was racing painfully fast.

At the end of the road she followed the signs towards the town centre, feeling slightly less conspicuous amongst the many people who thronged the streets. She was suddenly painfully aware of her ill-fitting clothes and the grass stains on the knees of her jeans that she had acquired in the back of the gardeners' van, but there was nothing she could do about that for now, so she simply hurried along. A bitterly cold wind was blowing and as the afternoon lengthened, the light began to fade and Maddy's stomach grumbled with hunger. She was in a slightly less salubrious area now on the outskirts of the town, and was convinced that she must have walked for miles. Up ahead she could see a small baker's shop, so she slipped inside and bought herself three crusty batches and a custard cream for afterwards. She then moved on until she came to a small park and after going into it she sat on a bench and began to eat her meagre meal, saving two of the batches for later.

Within an hour it was dark and Maddy began

to shiver as she wondered where she might find shelter for the night. She certainly didn't relish the thought of being out in the open, but where could she go? Deciding that anything would be better than just sitting there, she ventured out of the park again and continued walking until she came to a main road. Cars and lorries were thundering along it and without thinking she stuck her thumb out. She had never hitch-hiked in her life before, but decided there was always a first time for anything and she could think of no better alternative.

A cold drizzle began to fall now and soon Maddy was soaked to the skin and shivering uncontrollably. After the solitude of River House and the surrounding countryside the noise of the traffic was deafening and she was feeling miserable and dejected. Added to that, her trainers, which were now at least two sizes too small for her, were rubbing her heels painfully and she began to limp.

When a large lorry suddenly indicated and pulled into the side of the road ahead of her, Maddy gulped. It had *Astbury's Abattoir* written on its large canvas sides. Limping towards the cab, Maddy reached up and opened the door and stared up at the driver. He was a middle-aged man with greying hair and a kindly face.

'Where yer headin' luv?' he asked with a friendly smile.

Maddy shrugged before gabbling, 'Where are *you* heading?'

'I'm off up north to Leeds. Is that any good to you?'

'Fine, thanks very much.' Maddy threw her bag

into the cab and clambered up the steep steps behind it, wincing with pain as the tight trainers rubbed at the soft skin on her heels. The warmth of the cab wrapped itself around her like a cosy blanket, and she was grateful for that at least, although the smell was appalling.

'It's the meat in the back. It pongs, don't it?' he said as he saw her wrinkle her nose.

When he had steered the lorry back out into the traffic again he peered at his passenger out of the corner of his eye. She only looked a slip of a kid and he wondered what she was doing out all alone accepting lifts from strangers. It was something he had warned his own kids that they were never to do. There were too many freaks and perverts about nowadays to take the chance.

'Got family in Leeds then, have yer?' he asked conversationally.

Maddy nodded as she wrapped her arms about herself. She felt bad about lying to him after he had been kind enough to give her a lift, but what choice did she have? She could hardly tell him that she was a runaway or he'd probably turn her in at the nearest police station.

'My gran lives there,' she lied glibly. 'And I lost the money she'd given me for the train back. I've been visiting my aunt.'

'Hm.' He didn't believe a word of it but refrained from telling her so. This kid looked like she was in trouble and she looked frozen and wet through too.

'There's a towel behind yer seat if yer want to dry yer hair off a bit,' he told her kindly, and Maddy smiled gratefully before turning to find it.

232

As she rubbed at her wet face and her hair she slowly began to warm up and felt slightly better. It was surprisingly comfortable in the cab, and decidedly better than sitting on a park bench or traipsing the streets. And Leeds was a long way away, which was an added bonus. Surely there would be less chance of her being found there?

'I'm Ronnie,' the man informed her.

'I'm Holly,' Maddy replied. She didn't want to tell him her real name, and Holly was the first name that had sprung to mind. Maddy still missed her friend every single day and thought about the time they had spent together constantly.

'Nice name,' he commented. 'And how old are you, luv?'

'Sixteen.'

'Hm,' he said again, and Maddy had the distinct impression that he didn't believe her, although he didn't challenge her about it.

'I've got three kids,' he now told her, opening a Mars bar as he went along. He passed another one to Maddy and she accepted it gratefully and polished it off in seconds.

'Two lads and a little girl,' he went on, and she could hear the pride in his voice. 'An' a nice old woman into the bargain. Salt o' the earth she is, so I'm a lucky man, ain't I?'

Maddy nodded, not really wishing to get into a conversation. The warmth of the cab and the gentle throb of the engine was so very soothing ... and when Ronnie looked at her again he saw that she was fast asleep, with her chin drooped onto her chest and her arms folded protectively across her chest.

He blew out his lips and sighed deeply. Poor little sod looked as if she didn't have a single soul in the world who gave a cuss about her. But then he'd seen enough kids in exactly the same predicament in his time and it never failed to make him feel heartsore. If she was heading to Leeds hoping to become lost in the crowds she was certainly going to the right place. There were enough kids living rough there to fill Wembley Stadium, God help them.

Chapter Twenty-One

'Wake up, luv. This is as far as I go, I'm afraid.'

Maddy's eyes popped open and for a moment she was disorientated and panic engulfed her. But then she realised where she was and hastily pulled herself up in the comfortable old worn leather seat.

'Thanks.' She knuckled the sleep from her eyes before fumbling about at her feet for her bag. 'Where are we?'

'That's Cross Flatts Park over there.' He pointed through the cab window into the darkness beyond. 'We're close to Beeston Hill. Is that near enough to your gran's for yer?'

'Oh ... er ... yes, thank you,' Maddy stuttered as she tried to find the door handle.

The man called Ronnie felt bad about abandoning her in this area. It was notorious but the abattoir he worked for was just down the road and his wife would be waiting up for him just as she always did, God bless her heart. She'd probably have a nice hot supper on the table an' all.

As Maddy tumbled down the steps she remembered her manners and smiled up at him. 'Thanks for the lift,' she said.

'Yer very welcome, luv. You just take care now, do yer hear me?'

Maddy nodded solemnly as she slammed the cab door. It was strange, she thought, that she always felt far closer to tears when someone was kind to her than when they were abusing her.

As she watched the lorry drive away she stood forlornly clutching her bag to her on the pavement. Then she glanced up and down the street. On one side of it was a row of terraced houses. Many of them were boarded up and the ones that weren't looked neglected and uncared-for. On the other side was a long metal railing with a gate in the centre of it, which she assumed led into the park that Ronnie had mentioned. A gang of youths were walking towards her, kicking a can ahead of them and shouting and laughing noisily, and so she hastily slipped through the gate and walked across the grass, which was now thick with hoar frost. At least it had stopped raining, but it was so cold now that her teeth began to chatter as she strained her eyes into the darkness, hoping to find shelter for the night. She wandered aimlessly on for some time, getting colder by the second, but all she came across was a scrawny tabby cat who looked at her disdainfully as he darted off in search of his supper. There were usually plenty of rats to be found round this area.

Eventually Maddy sank down onto a bench and finally the tears came. Hot scalding tears that threatened to choke her. Everything seemed so different now from when she had gone into River House. Most of the young people she saw walking about were wearing acid-washed jeans and jackets, or oversized slouch-shouldered leather jackets with puffy sleeves. It was as she was sitting there that she became aware of someone watching her, and she started as she peered towards the shape.

'Lost yer way, 'ave yer?' A boy who looked to be not much older than herself stepped towards her and she stared at him suspiciously.

'Not exactly,' she told him guardedly.

He came and sat down next to her, balancing the carrier bag he was carrying on his lap. He then fumbled in his coat pocket and after a time he lit a cigarette and inhaled deeply as he offered the packet to her.

'No thanks, I don't smoke.' She nervously edged further away along the seat.

'Run away then, 'ave yer?'

Maddy gulped deeply before shaking her head in denial. 'No, of course I haven't. I was just sitting here having a rest for a while.'

'Oh yeah, o' course yer were,' he replied cynically. 'It's great fun sittin' 'ere freezin' yer fuckin' balls off, ain't it? Still, if that's what turns you on, get on wi' it. I was gonna say that I know somewhere where yer could doss down fer the night if you ain't got nowhere, that's all – but suit yerself.'

He rose and began to walk away, and suddenly Maddy jumped up and hurried after him.

'Actually, I could do with somewhere to sleep – just for tonight,' she said hastily.

'Fair do's. Foller me then.' The youth carried on walking and Maddy had to almost run to keep up with him. When they reached the road again she took a better look at him in the glow of the street-lights. He was so thin that he looked almost emaci-ated. He was wearing some sort of sweatshirt with a hood on that he had pulled across his face, and denim jeans that looked none too clean. He didn't smell too nice either, but at that moment in time, Maddy was feeling so cold and miserable that she would have taken shelter with the devil himself.

She continued to follow him along the road at a trot until eventually he stopped in front of one of the boarded-up houses and lifted the wood that was propped against the door.

'In yer go,' he invited, holding it aside for her to squeeze past. Maddy did as she was told and walked straight into a room where candles were burning, leaving an acrid smell floating on the air.

There were at least three other young people in there and they stared at her curiously as the boy who had rescued her squeezed in behind her and pulled the board back into place.

'She needed somewhere to kip,' her rescuer ex-plained as he placed the carrier bag he had been holding onto a table that was leaning at a danger-ous angle. No one seemed to take much notice of her, but seemed far more interested in the con-tents of the bag.

'So what we got fer supper tonight then?' A girl with short blonde hair peered into the bag as Maddy watched in silence. Her eyes were the

237

bluest that Maddy had ever seen, and these, combined with her blonde hair, made her very striking-looking.

She extracted a pack of bacon and a small bundle of sausages, saying coarsely, 'Come on, Kat. Get off yer fat arse an' get that Primus stove lit, mate. We'll eat like kings and queens tonight.'

A heavily pregnant young girl heaved herself up off a large cushion on the floor and after striking a match she lit a small stove that was standing in a corner of the room. She was very pale, with a shock of long brunette hair that looked as if it hadn't been washed for months, but when she caught Maddy's eye, her smile was friendly. A second youth was lounging on another cushion smoking what looked like a roll-up cigarette. There was a faraway look in his eyes and he showed no interest in Maddy, nor any of the others, whatsoever.

Following Maddy's eyes, the boy she had met in the park grinned at her. 'That's Joey an' he's well out of it,' he told her. 'He likes his spliffs, does our Joey. In fact, he likes *any* drugs he can get his fuckin' mitts on, but he's 'armless enough. An' I'm Jimbo, by the way. That there is Kat.' He pointed at the pregnant girl. 'An' this is Abbi. She's me girl.' The blonde girl had gone to stand at Jimbo's side and she stared at Maddy suspiciously.

'An' what are we to call you?' he now asked.

'I ... er ... I'm Maddy.' Somehow she sensed that she didn't need to lie here. At least not about her name.

'Run away from home, have yer?' Abbi asked.

'Not from home exactly, but I have run away,'

Maddy replied.

'Fair enough.' The girl's hair was naturally curly and waved about her head like a halo, although her clothes were shabby. Kat had produced a loaf of bread from somewhere and as each rasher of bacon and sausage was fried she made sandwiches and passed them around.

Maddy accepted hers gratefully and after sitting cross-legged on the floor, she looked more closely at the room. In places, faded flowered wallpaper still clung to the walls and a carpet covered the floor, although it was so threadbare now that it was impossible to see what colour it might once have been. Odd chairs and pieces of furniture were dotted haphazardly about, along with old mattresses covered in grubby blankets and coats.

No one seemed to take much notice of her, they were all far too busy eating, but when the supply of food finally ran out, Jimbo wiped the back of his hand across his mouth and told Maddy, 'You can sleep on that mattress over there, if yer like. It ain't very posh but it's better than bein' out there.' He cocked his thumb towards the wood that covered the front door. 'It'd freeze yer bollocks off, out in that tonight. Oh, an' if yer need the toilet, it's upstairs, but you'll have to take a candle up wi' yer.'

'Thanks,' Maddy told him. She had never seen such a set-up in her life, but then tonight she was grateful for small mercies.

There was a wireless standing on the table, and when Jimbo crossed to it and turned it on, the sounds of the Sex Pistols blasted about the room.

The girl he had addressed as Kat was now piling the dirty pots into a bowl and as she saw Maddy watching her she told her, 'I'll boil the kettle an' wash them in the mornin'.'

Maddy remained silent, unsure of what to say as she eyed her new housemates curiously. There was an electric fire standing in the grate and it blasted out heat, so it was surprisingly warm in there. The following day she discovered that Jimbo had broken into the electric meter and somehow tapped into the electricity supply. There seemed to be very little that Jimbo couldn't accomplish, as Maddy was to find out as the days passed.

After a while she went and crouched on the mattress next to the girl called Kat and asked tentatively, 'Have you been here long?'

Kat shrugged wearily as her hand stroked her swollen belly. 'A couple o' months or so, I should say. Eventually the council will find out we're here an' come an' turf us out, but then we'll just find another empty house an' start all over again.'

'Oh.' It sounded a very bleak sort of existence to Maddy but she was wise enough to refrain from saying so. No doubt these young people had reasons for being in this predicament, just as she did.

'When is the baby due?' she asked.

'About another six weeks or so, I should think.' Kat's voice was heavy with regret.

'Are you going to keep it?'

Kat raised her eyebrows. 'How am I supposed to do that, livin' like this?' Spreading her hands, she looked about the room. 'Ner, I'll dump it some-

240

where safe once it decides to put in an appearance, an' that way it will at least have a chance of a good start in life wi' somebody who really wants it.'

Maddy smiled at her sympathetically as memories of how awful it had been to be taken away from her own mother flooded back. 'So how do you all manage to live?' she asked tentatively.

Kat snorted. 'Any bleedin' way we can,' she retorted. 'Jimbo there has got his fingers into all sorts o' pies, yer know? A bit o' wheelin' an' dealin'. There are always folks willin' to take stolen goods off his hands at the right price. Joey works for a drug dealer an' is usually out on the streets sellin' most nights. He does really well in the clubs in the city centre. An' Abbi there is a brilliant shoplifter. She nicks things to order, and me ... well, lookin' at this I should think it's pretty obvious how I earn my livin'. But what am I supposed to do? I have to eat, don't I? I shall just be glad to see the back o' this bump now so I can get properly back to work.'

Maddy blinked as she tried to take it all in. It appeared that for tonight at least she would be sharing a room with a drug dealer, thieves and a prostitute. But then beggars couldn't be choosers and they all seemed to be friendly enough, at least. Easing her trainers off she sighed with relief then snuggled down onto the mattress, surprised to find that she was desperately tired. And within minutes she was fast asleep.

The following morning Jimbo watched as Maddy tried to put her trainers back on. Her heels were

241

raw and blistered and she was obviously in a lot of pain.

'Looks like you're due fer a new pair,' he commented as he bit into a slice of bread liberally spread with margarine.

'I am, but I'm afraid my funds won't stretch to that at the minute,' Maddy admitted.

'Hm.' Jimbo looked at her thoughtfully then turning to Abbi he asked her, 'You could sort her out wiv a new pair, couldn't yer, luv?'

Abbi appeared to be none too pleased, but all the same she looked at Maddy resentfully before asking, 'What size are yer?'

'I think I'd probably be a size six now,' Maddy grimaced as the back of the shoe finally slid across her sore heel.

'A couple o' pairs o' new socks wouldn't go amiss either by the look of it.' Jimbo gave Abbi a squeeze and she forced a smile to her face, but Maddy had the distinct impression that she wasn't too happy about her being there.

'We've all got things to do,' Jimbo now told her. 'But you stay here today an' give them heels a rest. Abbi will sort you out, won't yer, luv?'

Maddy felt colour rise in her cheeks. She hated to stay where she wasn't wanted, but at present didn't feel that she had any other option. The police would no doubt be looking for her by now, and so she welcomed the chance of lying low for a while.

Shortly afterwards, Jimbo, Abbi and Joey went off to go about their business, whatever that might be, and Maddy found herself alone with Kat, who began to rather haphazardly tidy the room up.

'So where yer headin' for?' she asked after a time as she poured the hot water from the kettle into a small plastic washing-up bowl.

Maddy shrugged. 'I don't really have anywhere to head to,' she admitted.

'So stay here with us then.' Kat began to wash the dirty pots from the night before.

'But how would I earn my keep? I can't expect you lot to feed and clothe me for nothing,' Maddy pointed out. 'And I got the impression that Abbi isn't too happy about me being here.'

'Oh, don't get worrying about her,' Kat told her airily. 'She's jealous of anything female with a pulse that comes within ten yards of Jimbo. She was just the same wi' me till I landed meself wi' this lot. There's lots o' ways to earn yer livin'. Yer could go shopliftin' or yer could go on the game. There are two options to start with.'

Maddy was horrified but tried not to let it show. 'Couldn't I just try and get a *proper* job?' she asked in a small voice.

'Huh! Fer a start-off you ain't even sixteen yet, are yer, by the look o' yer? An' for another thing, everyone round here lives on the dole. Jobs are like gold dust though there ain't many hereabouts as would want 'em anyway.'

'Oh.' Maddy felt strangely deflated. She needed to work so that she could save enough money to go searching for Oliver, but the options that Kat had proposed were daunting, to say the least. A prostitute or a shoplifter. She suddenly had a vision of Dumbarr's fat fingers roaming over her and decided that she would rather be a thief than submit to that again.

'Abbi will show yer the ropes if yer decide to go on the nick, an' I'll show yer the ropes if yer want to go on the streets,' Kat offered, as if she was doing Maddy a great service.

'I think I'll do the shops,' Maddy muttered, and so her choice was made, although it wasn't a choice that gave her any pleasure.

Chapter Twenty-Two

It was Christmas Eve and the mood in the small squat that had become Maddy's temporary home was almost festive.

Her feet had healed since Abbi had stolen a comfortable pair of new trainers for her, and she was becoming quite adept at shoplifting. In fact, it had turned out to be much easier than she had thought. Each day she would head for the city centre and hit the shops, returning home with her takings which could be anything from baby's clothes to small electrical goods. Jimbo seemed to have an outlet for them all and always gave her half of what he sold them on for.

As well as the things she stole to sell on, Maddy had also taken a few new outfits for herself, and the modern clothes made her look much older than she really was.

They had all agreed to look out for Kat until after the baby was born, and in return she cooked and cleaned for them all as best she could. She was waddling around like a duck now and suffered from terrible heartburn and cramps that would have her dancing around the room in the dead of night.

'I just can't wait fer this to be over now,' she confided to Maddy one day when they were in alone as Maddy was getting ready to go out.

'Why don't you consider keeping the baby?' Maddy ventured.

'What? Are you *completely* off yer rocker?' Kat looked horrified. 'I ain't bleedin' Mary Poppins, yer know. An' what would *I* have to offer a kid? The poor little sod would 'ave to be pushed from pillar to post while I was out on the game. It'd end up bein' *dragged* up, so I ain't even thinkin' o' goin' down that road.'

Maddy could clearly understand what Kat meant, but the thought of her having to part with her baby hurt her all the same. None of their futures was safe, she realised that now. The council could turn up and evict them any day, and then they would have to go looking for another house to break into and squat in as none of them were old enough to be offered council housing. Even if they had been, no one wished to be traced, for various reasons, and so, for now, living in squats was their only option. As Kat had quite rightly pointed out, it wouldn't be much of a life for a baby. It wasn't much of a life for them either if truth be told, but at least they were all old enough to muddle by.

'Anyway, on a brighter note, Jimbo's got us some lovely snap in fer Christmas,' Kat told her cheerily. 'We ain't got an oven to cook us a turkey, o' course. But he's got us some gammon that I can fry up an' loads of other goodies. Mince pies, Christmas cake – you name it an' we've got it!'

Maddy headed for the door. It was time to hit the shops again and she was having to be very careful. Most of the big department stores had hired extra store detectives for the holiday period and so she had to be very picky where she targeted.

'I'll see you later then,' she called, and so another day of her new life began.

It was four-thirty in the afternoon before she headed back to the squat and already it was dark and bitterly cold. She left the city centre with the goodies she had managed to steal secured inside her coat and tucked away in two large shopping bags. She was passing a row of houses in the better part of the town when she paused. Through the window of one particular house she could see a family trimming their Christmas tree and the sight brought a lump to her throat. There was a mother and father and two little girls, and the room they were in looked warm and inviting through the open curtains. A great fire was blazing in the hearth, and as she stood there the man lifted the smaller of the girls so that she could place the fairy on the top of the tree. As he put her back down on the floor he kissed her tenderly and the act made tears squeeze out of the corners of Maddy's eyes. A long time ago she could remember her own father doing the same to her, and it was one of the memories that she cherished. She too had been part of a real loving family then, but all too soon it had been snatched away from her and now she felt utterly alone.

Oh, she had her housemates admittedly, but it wasn't the same as having her own family about her. It had never been the same since the family had been torn apart, and she missed being a little mother to her siblings.

Jimbo and Kat had made her feel welcome. Joey was oblivious to her presence half the time, lost in the drug-induced world he inhabited, but Abbi was sometimes openly hostile, terrified that Jimbo would transfer his affections from her to Maddy. Could she have known it, there was no fear of that happening. After being subjected to the abuse she had suffered with Mr Dumbarr, Maddy knew that it would be a long, long time before she wanted male company again – if ever. But still, she counted herself lucky that she at least had somewhere to stay while she got a little money together. Once she had enough she intended to start her search for Oliver in earnest, and that thought kept her going from day to day. When she eventually found him, she planned to whisk him away to a safe place where no one could ever separate them again, but she was wise enough to know that she would need money to be able to do that.

She had no conscience at all about the things she stole. After all, the way she saw it, she wasn't stealing from individuals. She was stealing from shops, and with the inflated prices they charged and the profit they made, she reasoned they could afford to lose the odd item or two. Now she lifted her bags again and continued on her way, but the thought of the happy family she had just witnessed stayed with her and her heart was heavy.

Once back at the squat, she banged on the wood panel that covered the door and Kat pulled it aside for her while Maddy ducked and slipped beneath it, dragging the heavy bags in behind her.

Jimbo smiled a greeting. 'Did you manage to get the toys I asked you for?'

Nodding, Maddy began to unload the bags, revealing two Cabbage Patch dolls, two Care Bears, two Ghost-busters and two wheeled warriors, along with a number of other toys.

Jimbo whistled through his teeth in appreciation as he began to ram them back into the bags again.

'These will fuckin' *fly* tonight, with it being Christmas Eve,' he assured her. 'The blokes down the pub will snatch me hand off for 'em. I'm hopin' Abbi will be able to get some too, but she ain't back yet so I'll hang on till she arrives afore I set off.'

Kat had placed the kettle on the Primus stove and now as she looked across at Maddy she smiled sympathetically, saying, 'You look all in.'

'I am,' Maddy admitted as she took her coat off, revealing yet more small toys. 'The shops were heaving today with everyone doing their last-minute shopping.'

Glancing across at Joey, who was comatose on a large floor cushion, she sighed. His arms were a mess of pinpricks. Even the skin between his toes was bruised from the needles he had inserted there. But then as she had soon discovered, Joey would take drugs any way he could get them, be it snorting, smoking or injecting them.

Following Maddy's eyes, Jimbo shook his head. 'Looks like he's out of it fer the night again. That'll mean yet another visit from his boss, no doubt. The silly fucker. I reckon he's usin' more than he's sellin' just lately an' I can't see his boss puttin' up wi' that fer long. Still, it ain't no business o' mine at the end o' the day. Joey is old enough an' ugly enough to know what he's doin'.'

Maddy nodded in agreement but she felt sorry for Joey all the same and wondered what had brought him to this. She wondered what had brought any of them here, if it came to that, but no one ever volunteered any information and so Maddy tactfully didn't ask for any. It was a little like at River House where the girls had only ever been called by their Christian names – as if, from the second they set foot through the door, they all lost their identity. But at least that was all behind her now. Here, she could come and go as she pleased, which was something at least. The worst part of living in the squat for Maddy was the fact that she never felt truly clean. Jimbo had managed to fiddle the electric meter so that they could plug the electric fire in, but the old immersion heater in the airing cupboard upstairs was broken and so the best she could do was fill the kettle with hot water and wash in a bowl.

Kat regularly took all their clothes to the launderette for them, but Maddy had soon discovered that it didn't feel right putting clean clothes on a dirty body. Not that she could do much about it.

They were all in the same predicament and it was something she was going to have to get used to. Looking about the squalid little room, she thought of Oliver and hoped that he was happy. She still missed him so much that it hurt, but now that she was beginning to save a few pounds she was feeling more optimistic. He could be anywhere by now, but she was determined that somehow, someday soon, they would be together again.

A banging on the door roused them, and thinking that it was Abbi coming back from her shoplifting spree, Jimbo quickly drew the wood aside. Almost immediately, two burly men pushed their way into the room. After glancing around, their eyes came to rest on Joey and their lips curled with contempt.

'Our boyo out of it again, is he?' The older of the two men, who was immaculately dressed in a long black overcoat, stepped towards him and nudged him with his foot. Joey didn't even move as the other young people in the room looked on fearfully. Maddy had no idea who the two men were, but Jimbo obviously did if the look on his face was anything to go by.

'H ... he'll probably be OK in a bit,' he stammered.

The younger man turned his attention to Jimbo now and sneered. 'Will he now? Well, yer coulda fooled me. The stupid little bastard is as 'igh as the proverbial kite an' the boss ain't gonna be none too pleased about it.'

He too was smartly dressed and quite good-looking – a fact of which he was obviously aware.

250

His hair was naturally blond with a tendency to curl about the crisp white collar of his shirt, and he had strikingly blue eyes. But those eyes as they glanced about the room were as cold as ice.

'Where's the gear the boss give 'im to sell?' he asked Jimbo shortly

Jimbo shrugged. 'I ain't got a clue, mate, I swear it.'

'Then we'd better fuckin' find it, 'adn't we? Else yer mate there is gonna be dead meat. He's pulled this stunt just once too often.'

The two men then began to ransack the room as Maddy crept fearfully towards Kat, whose mouth was hanging slackly open.

Mattresses were upturned and cushions flung about, but within minutes it was clear that the search was proving to be fruitless.

The men were both red in the face now and looked very angry.

'Get the little bastard out into the car,' the older of the men ordered his mate, his eyes narrowed slits. 'We'll let the gaffer deal wi' him when he comes round.'

Jimbo took a tentative step towards them. 'Couldn't you just let 'im sleep it off an' come back later? I'm sure he'll find it fer yer then.'

'Piss off out me way,' the man growled as he and his mate bent to grab Joey under his arms. 'Unless you wanna come an' 'ave a chat to the boss an' all.'

Jimbo hastily shook his head and stepped back as the men began to haul Joey none too gently towards the door. Seconds later they dragged him out onto the cold pavement and the young people heard the sound of car doors slamming before the car roared away.

'Christ almighty!' Kat lit a cigarette with shaking fingers and took a deep drag on it. 'I hope Joey can come up wi' the money or the goods. I didn't like the look o' them two.'

'Well, there ain't nowt we can do about it now,' Jimbo retorted as he began to right what little furniture they had. The place looked as if a hurricane had swept through it. They all began to help him, and it was then that Abbi appeared.

'What the bloody hell's been goin' on here?' Dumping two hefty bags on the floor she put her hands on her hips and looked around in amazement.

'Joey's boss sent two of his heavies round for him,' Jimbo informed her, as he lifted the rickety table back into position. 'An' between you an' me, I reckon it's gonna take some smart talkin' on his part to get 'im out o' the shit this time.'

Abbi shrugged. 'Well, that's his silly bleedin' fault then, ain't it?' she rapped casually. 'I certainly ain't gonna lose no sleep over him. Now come an' look at this lot. Me arms feel like they're droppin' off but I reckon you'll be pleased wi' what I've got. Take this lot down the pub tonight an' they'll be queuing up fer 'em.'

Instantly forgetting all about the predicament Joey was in, Jimbo started to rifle through the goodies as Kat and Maddy exchanged a worried glance. Both girls were clearly shaken by what had happened, but Abbi and Jimbo had obviously dismissed him already.

'Are you all right?' Maddy asked, noting how

pale Kat was.

Kat nodded as she sat down heavily on a mattress, clutching her stomach.

'Yeah, I'm fine. It's just a twinge. I reckon it's 'cos o' the shock o' them pair burstin' in as they did. Don't look so worried, it'll go off in a minute if I sit still.'

'Right – there's no time like the present so me an' Abbi are off to shift this lot,' Jimbo told them as he headed to the door with Abbi following behind like an adoring puppy. 'See yer both later.'

The couple disappeared out into the bitterly cold night and Maddy quickly pulled the wood that served as a door back into place before turning to Kat once more.

'Shall I make you a hot drink?' she offered.

Kat tittered despite the look of pain that was flitting across her face. 'Cor, yer don't 'alf talk posh,' she commented.

Maddy lifted a box of matches and lit the Primus stove and placed the kettle on it before replying, 'That's because the people who adopted me were posh. Or they thought they were. They would have died if they'd seen the state of this place.' She spread her hands to encompass the filthy room. 'Everything had to be *just so* for them.'

There was so much bitterness in her voice that Kat eyed her curiously. Maddy had never really opened up about her past before and she was interested.

'The adoption break down then, did it? Or did yer just run away?'

'Something like that,' Maddy muttered, feeling that she had said too much already.

253

Kat fell silent until Maddy joined her on the mattress with two steaming mugs of tea five minutes later. Kat had taken no more than a few sips before she doubled over in pain, sending tea slopping everywhere.

'Ouch, that bastard really hurt.' She was clutching her stomach and Maddy felt the first stirrings of panic. What if Kat had the baby right now? What would she do? She had never had anything to do with babies being born before.

'Sh ... shall I run and fetch a doctor?' she suggested tremulously.

'Don't talk so bloody daft,' Kat ground out. 'It can't be the baby comin' just yet. It ain't even due for another few weeks.'

'From what I've heard of it, babies tend to come when they're good and ready whether it's time or not,' Maddy told her sensibly.

'Yeah, well this one won't 'cos *I* ain't ready for it yet – got that? Phew, it's gone off now. I told yer it would, didn't I?'

Maddy breathed a huge sigh of relief as her heart steadied to a more normal rhythm. For a moment there she'd had the awful feeling that she was going to have to play midwife.

Now Kat lifted her cup again and glanced at Maddy as if nothing had happened to disturb their conversation.

'Do you think you might change your mind when the time comes ... I mean about keeping the baby?' Maddy asked eventually.

'No chance.'

Maddy thought she detected a hint of regret in Kat's voice but decided to change the subject, having no wish to upset her.

'Will Joey be all right, do you reckon?'

Kat sighed as she swirled the dregs of her tea in her mug. 'I couldn't say, to be honest. Joey is about as straight as a corkscrew. He'd steal off his own granny if it meant him gettin' his drugs, but yer still can't help but feel sorry fer him. Although…'

'Although what?'

'Well, the thing is, Joey's card was marked any road. He's HIV, poor sod.'

'No!' Maddy was shocked. 'But I thought only gay men got that?'

'Not on yer nelly. Anyone can get it. Though Joey is known to swing both ways, if yer get me drift. An' the worst of it is, if he don't come back we'll have to move an' pronto. We've seen too much, see? An' the blokes might come back to finish us all off an' all.'

Maddy fell silent again. She had thought that nothing could shock her any more, but what Kat had just divulged had shown her how wrong she was. And it was then that the truth came home to her. She had sunk just about as low as she could get.

Chapter Twenty-Three

A low moaning woke Maddy in the early hours of the morning. As she peered into the darkness she saw the shapes of Abbi and Jimbo curled up together on the mattress at the other side of the room. She then turned over and looked at Kat who was whimpering softly. In the light of the candle they had left flickering she could see the sweat standing out in beads on the girl's forehead and as she lifted it and carried it closer she saw that the mattress Kat was lying on was drenched in blood.

'Kat, what's happening?' she asked with a note of urgency in her voice.

'Yer were right,' the other girl gasped. 'I reckon this babby has decided to put in an early appearance.'

'Oh!' Maddy could hear Abbi and Jimbo's soft snores echoing around the room. 'What should I do?'

'*I* don't know! I ain't never had a babby before, have I?'

'I'll wake Jimbo,' Maddy told her and hurried across to him, urgently shaking his shoulder. Abbi was instantly awake and glaring at her as she put her arm possessively across her boyfriend.

'What do yer want my Jimbo for?' she hissed.

'Kat's having the baby and I need some help,' Maddy told her.

Jimbo blinked up at her blearily as he asked, 'Whassup?'

'It's Kat's baby,' Abbi told him, keeping a suspicious eye on Maddy.

'It's coming.'

Pulling himself together, Jimbo hurried over to Kat who was writhing in agony now. 'Is this it then, gel?' His voice was surprisingly gentle and when she nodded he turned to Abbi and told her, 'Put the kettle on an' get some hot water in a bowl.'

'What for?' she gasped, horrified. 'You're not goin' to try an' deliver it yerself, are yer?'

'Do you 'ave a better idea?' His voice was cold now. 'I can 'ardly fetch a doctor or phone fer an ambulance, can I, else we'll all find usselves out on the streets. Is that what yer want?'

'O' course it ain't,' she sputtered indignantly and then reluctantly scuttled away to do as she was told.

'Maddy ... you find some towels,' he told her with authority and nodding, she too hurried away to fetch what he was asking for.

There then began the longest two hours that Maddy could ever remember. Occasionally when the pain became more than she could bear, Kat would cry out like an animal caught in a trap and Maddy would put her hands over her ears to try and shut out the sound. And then just when she thought that it was never going to end, a tiny mewling cry echoed around the room and she heard Jimbo sigh with satisfaction.

'You've done it, gel,' he told her triumphantly. 'You've got yerself a right fine little lad. He's a

257

bruiser an' all, from what I can see of 'im.'

Turning, he handed the child to Maddy, who had a clean towel ready, and she stared down at the tiny being with wonder shining in her eyes.

'Is ... is he all right?' Kat asked weakly as she sagged back onto the scruffy pillows on the mattress.

Maddy nodded, too full to speak as she studied the perfect little face. Just as Jimbo had said, he really was a bonny little thing with a shock of dark hair and squinty blue eyes that seemed to be staring enquiringly up at her.

She kept her eyes averted from Jimbo, who was leaning over Kat once more until he wrapped something in a towel and put it to one side.

'There, that's about it, I reckon. Have we got any clothes fer 'im?' He wiped the sweat from his forehead as he sat back on his heels and Maddy shook her head.

'I'm afraid not,' she admitted. 'I was going to steal some but he arrived before I got the chance.'

As she spoke she held the child out to his mother, but Kat averted her eyes. 'I don't want to see him,' she said dully. 'There ain't no point if I ain't keepin' him.'

'B ... but what are we going to do with him then?' Maddy asked nervously.

'I want yer to take him to the Social Services office in the centre an' leave him on the steps there,' the girl told her matter-of-factly.

'But it's Christmas Day. No one will be there and he'll freeze to death,' Maddy protested.

'No, he won't, 'cos when you've taken him there, Jimbo can call the Old Bill from a phone

258

box an' they'll be straight round to collect him.'

It was obvious that Kat had everything worked out in her mind.

'I'll go wi' Maddy an' call the cops. Jimbo's done enough fer one night an' he looks all in,' Abbi offered.

Maddy looked at her in surprise. It wasn't like Abbi to be so obliging, but then she supposed she shouldn't knock it.

As her eyes dropped to the baby again she had to stifle the urge to cry. She knew that Kat was probably doing the right thing. She had nothing at all to offer the child, whereas there were probably dozens of childless couples who would die for this beautiful little boy, Kirsty and Andy amongst them. But even so, it seemed heartbreaking that his real mother couldn't keep him.

'Are you quite sure that this is what you really want?'

Kat nodded before turning over and burying her face beneath the blankets as Maddy began to wash the baby. She had no baby clothes to put on him, so she fashioned a nappy out of an old towel and wrapped him in one of the warm jumpers she had stolen on one of her shoplifting sprees.

And then they all sat down to wait for the dawn to arrive.

At last there was a break in the darkness and Maddy and Abbi wrapped up for the outdoors.

'Why, bugger me, it's started to snow,' Abbi told them as she poked her head out into the street.

'Are you really, really sure this is what you want, Kat?' Maddy asked again as she snuggled the baby inside her coat. He was getting restless

259

now and hungry for his first feed, but Kat still adamantly refused to even look at him, let alone feed him.

The only answer was a bob of the girl's head so Maddy sadly followed Abbi out into the cold early morning, cuddling the baby protectively. The snow had started to settle and everywhere looked surprisingly clean and bright. They walked briskly in silence until they came to the outskirts of the city centre where Abbi stopped to point ahead. 'The Social Services office is just down that road there. I'll give you ten minutes then I'll call the cops. That will give you time to get away an' I'll meet you back at the squat. All right?'

Maddy nodded as she watched the girl march away. Something didn't feel right but there was no time to worry about it now. First she had to make sure that the baby was sheltered and safe before she left him.

She moved on and sure enough within minutes the building she was looking for came into sight. She was thankful to see that there was a deep porch leading to the doors and after hastily looking up and down the street, to make sure that no one was about, she quickly stepped inside it and began to lift the child from the warmth of her coat.

'You'll be all right,' she crooned as she gently laid him in the farthest corner. Tears were dripping onto his face and he began to cry lustily as if he could sense that he was about to be abandoned. She straightened, but as she turned to leave she heard a siren and panic lent speed to her feet. Racing down the path, heedless of her coat flapping about her, she saw the police car speeding towards her. Turning in the opposite direction she ran until she felt as if her lungs were about to burst, but then she heard a car screech to a halt behind her, followed by the sound of footsteps pounding closer and closer. When a hard hand gripped her arm she began to kick and lash out.

'It's all right, pet,' a soothing voice told her. 'You're safe now an' so is your baby. Now come on, let's get you both to a hospital to get you checked over, eh?'

'B ... but he's not *my* baby,' Maddy told the police officer frantically as his grip on her arm tightened. His colleague had come to join him now and between them they were hauling her towards the police car.

'Now come on, love. Maddy, isn't it?'

Maddy blinked at him in confusion. How could he have known her name? And then it came to her. Of course – *Abbi!* That explained why the girl had wanted to go with her, so that she could turn her in to the police and get rid of her once and for all. And it looked like she just might have succeeded.

Back at the squat, Kat asked anxiously, 'Is there still no sign of Maddy?'

Jimbo shook his head as he sponged her forehead with an old piece of rag. She was burning up with fever and he was getting seriously worried now.

'Abbi's been back for ages,' Kat fretted. 'So where can she be?'

Abbi examined her nails with a bored expres-

261

sion on her face as she told her, 'She's probably done a runner back to wherever she came from. The ungrateful little cow. An' after we were good enough to take her in out o' the cold an' all.'

Jimbo raised an eyebrow but refrained from saying anything as Kat looked up at him. They both knew that Abbi had never taken to Maddy but neither of them wanted to start an argument over it now.

'An' what about Joey? Ain't he back neither?'

'No, he ain't, an' I 'ave the most awful feelin' he won't be now.' Jimbo dropped the rag back into the dish and swiped his forehead with the back of his hand. He looked at Kat with concern. 'I reckon we're goin' to 'ave to think about gettin' you to a doctor if we can't get this temperature o' yours down soon,' he commented.

'We'll do no such thing!' Abbi snapped. As usual she was jealous of anyone who commanded Jimbo's attention. 'Kat will have to find her own way to a quack if she needs one. It's bad enough that we may have to do a runner from here if Joey don't come back, without havin' to worry about *her*. She's big enough to take care of herself. Unless there's some special reason why yer so concerned about her, that is?'

'Oh, don't talk such fuckin' *rubbish*,' Jimbo retorted angrily as he realised what she was insinuating. 'Ain't you got a single ounce o' compassion in yer whole body, Abbi? I'm beginnin' to think you ain't the gel I thought yer were.'

Realising that she had gone too far, Abbi edged up to him and rubbed his arm tenderly as she batted her eyelashes at him. 'Sorry,' she

262

muttered. 'I suppose I'm just a bit het up about all that's gone on.'

The words had barely left her lips when the sound of the wood that covered the door being moved back made them all look towards it. Jimbo stood up, but he had no time to see who was there before a milk bottle full of an amber-coloured liquid with a flaming cloth stuck into the neck of it was swung into the room. It landed against the wall with a resounding crack as Jimbo shouted, *'Fuckin' hell!* It's a petrol bomb! Get down onto the floor – *quick!'*

Neither he nor Abbi had time to do anything before there was a loud explosion that knocked them off their feet – and suddenly there were flames racing towards the three inert figures sprawled across the grimy floor. And then there was only silence, save for the sound of the fire greedily eating everything in its path.

'So, what can you tell me about our little runaway then, Sister?' The police officer stared at the straight-backed nurse sitting across the desk from him and she smiled grimly.

'Not a lot,' she said. 'But what I *can* tell you is the girl is definitely not the mother of the baby. The doctor who examined her is quite clear on that point.'

'Not the mother? But then who is?' The inspector scratched his head in bewilderment.

'I have no idea. But it certainly isn't her, although the doctor can confirm that she has been sexually active.'

'Sexually active?'

'Precisely, she is not a virgin.'

'Well, that doesn't really surprise me,' he muttered. 'Kids grow up too quickly nowadays and half the runaways who end up on the streets earn their living on the game. Has she told you anything at all?'

The sister shook her head. 'Not a dickie bird. She refuses to speak at all, even to confirm that her name is Maddy.'

'Hm.' The inspector strummed his fingers on the desk thoughtfully. 'Well, they're going through the files of missing kids at the station even as we speak, so we should discover who she is soon – if she's been reported as missing, that is. In the meantime I'm more concerned about who the mother of the baby is. She might be in urgent need of medical treatment. How is the baby, by the way?'

'He's absolutely fine,' the sister assured him. 'They have him down in the neo-natal unit as a precautionary measure at present, but from what I've heard he's perfectly healthy. But what will happen to him now?'

'I dare say Social Services will foster him out if we don't manage to locate the mother? The inspector sighed sadly. It was heartbreaking when a mother abandoned her child, but the fact that it was Christmas Day seemed to make it even more so. He thought of his own children who would be happily playing at home with their Christmas presents right now and shuddered. It just didn't bear thinking about. What state of mind must the mother have been in? And how had the young girl who was in the next room come by him?

As he rose to leave the sister asked him, 'What do you want us to do with Maddy?'

'Keep her here for the time being, if you wouldn't mind. I've posted an officer on the door of the ward just in case she decides to try and do a runner. Hopefully we'll know a little more about her later today when they've gone through the Missing Persons files and then we'll take it from there. Goodbye for now, Sister, and thanks for all your help.'

She inclined her head and once he had left the room she walked to the window and gazed out at the hospital grounds, which were now beneath a thick blanket of snow. Sometimes she wondered what the world was coming to.

It was mid-afternoon before the solemn-faced inspector returned to the hospital, along with a WPC. After a hasty word with the ward sister he strode into the small private room where Maddy had been placed, and as he came to the end of the bed he asked, 'How are you feeling, love?'

Maddy kept her eyes fixed on the ceiling, ignoring him as if he wasn't even there.

The policeman glanced at his female colleague before beginning cautiously, 'Maddy, we have reason to believe that you are, in fact, Madeleine Donovan. You ran away from River House in the Cotswolds some weeks ago, didn't you?'

Maddy blinked but other than that she showed no sign of having heard him.

'We have already contacted the staff there and a Miss Budd will be coming to see you tomorrow,' he went on. 'If she can identify you as the person we believe you to be, you will be returning to River House with her. In the meantime, I suggest you don't even think about trying to run away. I have an officer posted at the doors of the ward. And it would make things considerably easier for me if you would cooperate with us, Maddy. We need to know whose baby you had with you when we found you. Whoever the baby belonged to may be in urgent need of medical care, so you're not doing the mother any favours by remaining silent. What do you say?'

Once more, Maddy remained obstinately silent and the inspector sighed. 'Well, if you're going to continue to be uncooperative there's no point in me staying any longer, is there?'

He nodded disconsolately towards the door to the female police officer who had accompanied him, and they both rose to leave. Once outside the door, which was left slightly ajar, the sister bore down on them like an avenging angel.

'Did she tell you anything?'

Inspector Crane took a handkerchief from his pocket and noisily blew his nose.

'Not a word,' he told her regretfully. 'But we're ninety-nine per cent sure that she *is* Madeleine Donovan. She certainly looks remarkably like the pictures we were issued with when she was reported missing, and she's the right age too. I don't mind telling you I'll be glad when today is over, Sister. Some Christmas Day this has turned out to be. First her ladyship and a newborn baby to deal with, and then a terrible fire in Wheat Street this morning. It appears that some kids were squatting there in one of the houses that are due to be demolished. Two of them were already dead when the firemen got them out. Burned to a crisp, by all accounts. The third one, a young girl, is downstairs in the ITU right now. I'm just on my way down there to see her. Poor little sod. Anyway, good day, Sister. If she decides to open up, give me a ring, eh?'

'Of course, Inspector,' she assured him, and then as he strode away she straightened her starched white frilly hat and went about her business.

After passing through a maze of corridors that all smelled of stale disinfectant and something indistinguishable, the inspector paused at the doors of the Intensive Care Unit and rang the bell.

An attractive young nurse with soft green eyes opened the doors and looked at him enquiringly.

After hastily fumbling in his overcoat pocket, he flashed his identity card at her as he told her, 'Inspector Crane to see the young woman who was brought in with severe burns this morning.'

'Oh.' She held the door wide, and as the two police officers stepped into the corridors she told them, 'I'm afraid I can only allow one of you in to see her and you'll have to gown up.'

'Of course.' Inspector Crane followed her to a small room where a number of gowns were hanging. He slipped his arms into one before asking, 'How is she?'

'Not good, I'm afraid. She suffered very severe burns but the doctor is in with her now and I'm sure he'll be able to tell you a lot more than me. I doubt you'll be able to talk to her. She's very heavily sedated because of the pain,' she explained.

'I see.' The inspector followed her down the passage until she came to double doors with glass windows in the top of them.

'She's in there. Do go in. I'm sure the doctor will be happy to talk to you.'

'Thank you, Nurse.' The inspector took a deep breath before pushing the doors open. He hated hospitals at the best of times, but today he was sick of the sight of the place and the end of his shift couldn't come quickly enough as far as he was concerned.

He was immediately confronted with a young woman lying on a bed with tubes and drips seemingly hooked up to every inch of her. Part of her hair had been burned away and she was swathed in bandages. One side of her face was red raw and the inspector had to swallow the bile that rose in his throat.

'Inspector Crane,' he introduced himself to the doctor who was leaning over her.

The doctor took his hand out of the rubber glove that it was encased in and shook his hand firmly before turning his attention back to his patient.

'So how's she doing?' Crane asked, keeping his eyes averted from the poor soul on the bed.

The doctor stretched wearily. Like the inspector he had had a long day. He gestured for the policeman to follow him away from the bed and then said in a low voice, 'Between you and me, I doubt if she'll last the night. Her burns are horrific. And on top of that, I found when I examined her that she had just given birth. God alone knows where the baby is. The firemen said there was no sign of a newborn in the squat.'

The inspector's eyes stretched wide as a thought occurred to him and he said quietly, 'I think I just might know, as well as Him Upstairs.' And with that he turned and walked away, with the doctor's uncomprehending eyes boring into his back.

Chapter Twenty-Four

Maddy was surprised when the Inspector strode back into her room some minutes later. She hadn't expected to see him again so soon.

'Madeleine Donovan, I'd like to ask you a few questions,' he told her without preamble, and Maddy was quick to note that the softly, softly approach he had tried on her earlier in the day had flown out of the window.

'Have you been living at a squat in Wheat Street?'

Maddy kept her eyes fixed on the glass light-fitting above, although her heart was starting to pump so loudly she was afraid that the inspector would hear it.

'Come along now,' he told her harshly. 'The time for playing silly, games is over. If you *were* living in Wheat Street, then one of your housemates is dying downstairs in the Intensive Care Unit even as we speak, and I need you to identify her for us. The poor soul deserves that much, at least. If we can find out who she is, there may be relatives that we can inform. She should have her family with her.'

Maddy was listening intently now and raised herself on her elbow to stare at him. What was he talking about?

'Y ... yes, I was living in a squat there,' she confessed.

The inspector let out a sigh of relief. Things were beginning to come together if he wasn't very much mistaken.

'Then are you prepared to come downstairs with me and identify the girl?'

Maddy nodded reluctantly, not relishing the thought at all. But then she would have to do it, to put her mind at rest now. It must have been another squat. Surely the girl downstairs couldn't be Kat! It just didn't bear thinking about. Maybe her condition had worsened after she and Abbi had left the house...

Slipping off the bed, she followed the inspector from the room. He had a hurried word with the ward sister and then taking Maddy by the arm he began to march her through the hospital. In no time at all, Maddy was hopelessly lost, but the inspector seemed to know where he was going, so she accompanied him meekly until they came to the doors of the ITU where he rang the bell once more.

The same nurse who had admitted him earlier opened it yet again and the inspector ushered Maddy into the gowning-up room. When they were both suitably attired he told her, 'I want you to look at the girl and tell me if you know her. Are you prepared to do that for me?'

Maddy nodded as she followed him from the room and along the corridor. At the door to the ward he paused to tell her, 'I'm afraid you might find what you are about to see quite distressing. The girl has suffered very severe burns. In fact, the skin on one side of her face has been completely burned away. But I think she may still be recognisable to anyone that knows her. Are you ready?'

Severe burns? Maddy didn't understand. She gulped deeply, drawing air into her lungs as she prepared herself for the ordeal ahead. And somehow she knew that it *was* going to be an ordeal. Particularly if the girl did turn out to be Kat.

'Yes, I am ready,' she told the inspector who was holding the door open for her. Once at the foot of the bed, she raised her eyes, and the sight she saw brought her hand flying to her mouth as she cried out in distress.

'Oh, Kat, what's happened to you?' She was round the bed in a minute but was afraid to touch the girl's heavily bandaged hands for fear of hurting her even more.

'I gather you do know this person then?' The inspector's voice was cold.

Maddy nodded miserably. 'Yes, we lived in the squat together for a time.'

'In that case I think it might be a good idea if you came to the police station with me. I have a few questions I'd like to ask you.'

Maddy's shoulders drooped. After one last glance at Kat, she went with the inspector to complete the formalities that would allow her to leave the hospital for a couple of hours.

At the police station she was placed in a small room with nothing but a table and two chairs in it. After a while the inspector joined her and sat down opposite.

'Now this is a purely informal interview, Maddy,' he informed her, glancing at the young policewoman who was standing behind him with an open notebook. 'To interview you properly you are entitled to have your social worker present. But as you can appreciate, time is of the essence at the moment. That young girl lying in the hospital is seriously ill, so the more we can find out about her, the better. Let's start by you telling me her name, eh?'

'I only knew her as Kat,' Maddy said as she wrapped her arms about herself.

'And where did Kat come from?'

'She never told me that either.'

The inspector sighed with frustration before changing tack. 'How about telling me about the baby then? Was it Kat's baby?'

Maddy stared stubbornly at the table.

'You may as well tell the truth. The doctor has already told me that the girl in the hospital had just given birth, and seeing as how you definitely hadn't, it stands to reason that the child was hers. Am I right?'

Still she remained silent so now he asked, 'What about the other two young people that were brought out of the squat? Who were they?'

'One was called Jimbo and the other was his girlfriend, Abbi. But that's all I know about them.'

'Did none of them ever talk about where they had come from?'

'No, none of us did,' she answered truthfully. 'Where are they? What's happened to them?'

The inspector sighed before beckoning the young policewoman to him. He'd had more than enough for one day and was ready for home. 'Constable, please explain to this young lady what has happened at Wheat Street. It seems she's had a narrow escape. Then arrange for a car to take her back to the hospital. And tell the sister there that I will be in touch tomorrow before Miss Budd arrives from River House.'

'Yes, sir.'

The inspector ran his hand wearily across his face. Deep down he supposed that he should ring the Social Services out-of-hours number to arrange for a bed for the night for Maddy with emergency foster-carers. But he also knew that trying to get through to that particular department on Christmas night of all nights would be virtually impossible and he was just too tired to go all through the rigmarole. Perhaps this Miss Budd would be able to enlighten him about Maddy's background and the reason for her being in River House. One thing was for sure, he certainly wasn't going to get any more out of Maddy. He left the room and Maddy looked towards the policewoman expectantly.

'I'm Sarah,' the woman told her and, as she went on to explain what had happened at the squat, Maddy's face crumpled. It seemed that there was no end to the misery.

Once the police car had taken her back to the hospital Maddy sat up all night chewing on her nails as she thought of Kat lying downstairs. She watched the first fingers of dawn streak the sky as the snow softly fell, and over and over again, she asked herself how the fire might have started. Suddenly she thought of something Jimbo had said, and her heart skipped a beat. He'd commented that if Joey didn't come back, it wouldn't be safe for them to stay there any more. Could Joey's boss have ordered the fire to be started? The heavies he had sent in certainly seemed capable of doing it without a qualm. But then she had no way of proving that, so she decided that it might be a case of least said, soonest mended. If she told the police too much they might start questioning how she and the others in the squat had earned their living – and that would open up yet another can of worms. How could she admit that she and Abbi had been shoplifters, Joey had dabbled in drugs and Jimbo had handled stolen goods? It would be yet another thing to go on her record.

The prospect of being returned to River House was weighing on her heavily. She had briefly thought of escaping but had no idea how to go about it. There was a police officer at the doors leading into the ward and one glance from the window assured her that she was far too high up to try and escape that way. And then there was Kat. How could she go anywhere until she knew that her friend was going to pull through? Thumping her pillows to make them more comfortable, she waited to see what the next day would bring.

Later that morning, Miss Budd perched neatly

on the edge of the chair in the hospital day room and balanced her handbag primly on her lap as she stared at the inspector sitting opposite her.

'Madeleine Donovan came to River House because there was a suspicion that she started the fire that killed her parents,' she told him calmly. 'The police could never prove it, but by her own admission, Maddy never cared for them. In fact, she didn't even grieve when they died.'

'I see.' The inspector tapped his chin thoughtfully before asking, 'Do you personally believe that she would be capable of doing such a thing?'

'Maddy is a difficult girl, very uncommunicative and surly, as you may already have found out,' the woman told him, smoothing her skirt over her knee. 'And yes, I *do* think she did it – although I have no evidence, of course. And even if I did, she is still a minor, so what would the courts do about it? If you were to ask me, I'd say that young people nowadays can literally get away with murder. And now this on top...' She allowed her voice to trail away for effect.

'The fire at the squat was started by a petrol bomb,' the inspector informed her. 'Surely a girl her age wouldn't know how to make one of those. And why did she go off with the baby? None of it makes any sense and there is absolutely no evidence to suggest that she is in any way guilty of anything except running away from your establishment.'

'Well, I'm sorry, Inspector, but I really do need to get on,' Miss Budd told him impatiently. 'Perhaps we could go and see Madeleine now.'

He nodded and they both rose from their seats.

As they entered Maddy's room, she was standing at the window and she glanced towards them, her eyes full of scorn.

'So, miss, we meet again. You didn't really think that we wouldn't find you, did you?' Miss Budd said smugly.

Maddy didn't even bother to answer; she just continued to look from the window with a fixed expression of boredom on her face.

'Your social worker is on the way.' Miss Budd was clearly struggling to control her temper. 'And once she has arrived and we have filled in all the necessary paperwork, you will be coming back to River House with me. *And,* may I add, we shall make quite sure that it isn't so easy for you to escape again. It's Boxing Day for heaven's sake! You have caused a lot of trouble for a lot of people, and at Christmas, too. I just hope you are proud of yourself.'

As Inspector Crane listened to the woman ranting on he almost felt sorry for Maddy. Miss Budd was a right vinegar-faced old witch and he was glad that he would never have to be trapped in River House with her, else he might be tempted to do a runner as well.

Suddenly looking at the inspector, Maddy asked, 'Please may I go and see Kat before I leave, sir?'

His heart melted at the sight of her pale face and sad eyes. She was just a kid, after all.

'I'll go and have a word with the sister for you,' he answered before scuttling away.

He came back solemn-faced moments later. 'Maddy,' he began, wondering how to tell her, 'Sister has informed me that Kat is very seriously

276

ill. Under normal circumstances she would not be allowed any visitors other than close family, but seeing as they haven't been located, Sister has spoken to the ITU and they have agreed to you seeing her. Are you quite sure that you want to, though?'

Maddy's head bobbed eagerly. She hated to think of Kat lying there all alone with no one she knew about her.

'Well *really!*' Miss Budd puffed her chest out indignantly. 'This is most irregular. I don't have time to sit about here all day, you know – I should be getting back.'

'There is a young girl downstairs dying all on her own,' Crane told her caustically. 'Would you begrudge her seeing a friendly face?'

Miss Budd gulped so hard she looked in danger of swallowing her Adam's apple. 'Well, if you put it like that I dare say we can spare a few minutes,' she conceded.

'The social worker isn't even here yet, and by your own admission there is paperwork to do when she arrives, so I suggest you wait for her here while I take Maddy down to the ICU.'

With that he beckoned to the girl and they left the room without giving Miss Budd so much as a sideways glance.

On the way downstairs the inspector ventured, 'That Miss Budd is a bit of a tartar, isn't she?'

'Huh! You haven't seen the half of it. She's like a prison warden,' Maddy told him resentfully and he glanced at her, feeling sorrier for her by the minute. One way or another it looked like this kid had had a raw deal.

Once they were gowned up they were shown to Kat's bed, and Maddy's heart sank into her shoes as she stared down at the girl. Kat's skin had a grey pallor to it and she was gasping, as if each breath she took was an effort. There was a young doctor standing at the side of the bed and he sadly shook his head at the inspector, who stood well back.

'You can talk to her. I think she'll hear you,' the doctor told Maddy quietly.

Maddy swallowed back tears as she stroked the only part of Kat's arm that wasn't swathed in bandages. And it was then she realised that, over the previous weeks, Kat had taken Holly's place in her affections and become her friend.

'Kat, I'm here,' she whispered. For a moment it appeared that the girl couldn't hear her, but then her eyes flickered open and she managed a weak smile as recognition showed in her eyes.

'Maddy.' She raised her hand slightly and Maddy took it heedless of the bandages.

'My baby ... is he all right?'

'He's fine.' Tears were sliding down Maddy's cheeks now despite all her attempts to stop them. 'He's being well looked after and he's going to have everything you wished for him.'

Kat sighed with satisfaction. There was a machine at the side of the bed that was monitoring her heartbeats and Maddy found herself glancing nervously towards the erratic lines on the screens.

'You have to get better now,' she told Kat. 'We've got a lot of living to do yet.'

Kat's eyes had fluttered shut again but now they opened and she held Maddy's stare. 'Thanks,' she

278

murmured, 'for what you did...'

Suddenly a flat line appeared on the screen and Kat's head fell to one side as the young doctor rushed forward. All hell seemed to break loose as nurses arrived, and the inspector and Maddy were hustled from the room.

'She's going to be all right, isn't she?' Maddy asked fearfully as they stood helplessly in the corridor.

'I don't know, love. But ... well, you have to remember she suffered horrendous burns and she'd just given birth on top of that. Her body's had an awful lot to cope with.'

They stood there in silence as the minutes ticked away, each one seeming like an hour, until the door opened again and the doctor appeared. He looked tired as he told them, 'I'm so sorry.'

Deeply concerned, the inspector turned to Maddy. He had expected her to burst into floods of tears, but the girl simply stood there as if she had been carved from stone. The pain she was feeling went far beyond tears.

Back upstairs, Miss Budd was waiting for them with Sue Maddox, who eyed Maddy anxiously.

'I would like a few moments alone with Maddy, if you wouldn't mind,' she said.

'But we should be leaving now,' Miss Budd blustered. One stern glance from the inspector, however, silenced her as he took her elbow and led her from the room.

'I'm so sorry to hear about your friend,' Sue told Maddy. 'Sister filled me in on what happened. But why did you run away from River

279

House, Maddy? Is there something you're not telling me?'

Maddy stared past her and Sue sighed. If only Maddy would open up to her she might be able to help her, but she was getting nowhere.

'Please talk to me,' she implored. 'I so want to help you, love.'

The look that the girl turned on her made her blood run cold.

'*Nobody* can help me,' Maddy told her in a voice barely above a whisper, and with that she turned and went to join Miss Budd in the corridor.

Chapter Twenty-Five

Maddy stared straight ahead as River House loomed in front of her at the end of the drive. Everything looked just as it had when she'd left, and yet somehow everything was different. She'd had a brief taste of freedom and nothing could ever be the same again now. Miss Budd had said barely two words to her on the journey, not even to offer commiserations over Kat's death, but that suited Maddy down to the ground. From now on she was determined to keep herself to herself and not get close to anyone. She would study every spare minute she could, so that when she finally walked away from here she could get a good job and become the person she wanted to be.

Mr Dumbarr was waiting in the hall for them and he eyed Maddy up and down. She had left as a young girl but now the look in her eyes was that of a woman; a woman who had seen too much too soon.

'You realise that you will be going straight to the Quiet Room,' he said nastily. 'Running away cannot pass without punishment.'

Maddy didn't even bother to argue. The Quiet Room held no fears for her any more. In fact, she would welcome time to herself to put her thoughts into some sort of order. She felt numb inside and was sure that nothing would ever be able to hurt her again.

Stepping forward, the big man made to take her arm but Maddy moved out of his reach.

'There will be no need for that,' she told him icily. 'Let's just go, shall we?'

Mr Dumbarr looked towards Miss Budd with his eyebrows raised but then turned and began to shamble away, and Maddy followed him without argument. At the door to the Quiet Room she stepped past him without protest and he scowled as she walked calmly to the bed and sat down.

'So ... what have you got to say for yourself?' he demanded.

When Maddy ignored him he slammed the door and turned off the light. He stood there for a time, expecting her to bang on the door and beg him to let her out, or to turn on the light at the very least. Maddy had always hated the darkness. But there was nothing but silence and so eventually he walked away. He sensed that the Maddy who had returned to River House was no longer the subservient child she had been when she ran away. Then he had been able to control her, but now he realised that she might be a threat to him and the possibility made him break out in a cold sweat.

Maddy stayed in the Quiet Room for four nights, and never once did she protest or say so much as a single word. Strangely, she found the darkness and her own company comforting now. Miss Budd periodically brought trays of food to her and Maddy ate it without comment, much to the woman's amazement.

The house-mother had been in regular contact with the police in Leeds, who eventually informed her that there would be no charges brought against Maddy because of insufficient evidence, although Miss Budd had her own thoughts on the matter. As far as she was concerned, it was just too much of a coincidence that Maddy should be connected to yet another fire, and in her mind the girl was as guilty as sin.

Once released from the Quiet Room, Maddy was shown to the dormitory that she had shared with Steph and Kim before escaping, only to discover that Steph had been gone for almost a month.

'She seemed to just suddenly go off the rails,' Kim explained to her as she chewed nervously on her nails. 'An' between you an' me, I reckon it was something to do with Dumbo. He showed a lot of interest in her after you'd gone an' she began creepin' out at night, just like you did. Then she started havin' nightmares. I don't mind tellin' you, she scared the pants off me when she started. She'd scream the place down in the dead o' night an' wake everyone up. Then suddenly she just disappeared. Dumbo an' Budd reckoned that she did a runner the same as you did, but I ain't so sure. You know how hard it is to get out o' this place. It's like Fort Knox. They knew how you'd escaped 'cos the gardeners found one o' your tops in the back o' their van the next day. It must have rolled out of your bag. Anyway, after that they checked the gardeners' van every time they left, so how else could she have got out?'

'I don't know,' Maddy answered musingly. It did seem strange, but then she wouldn't lose any sleep over it. She didn't intend to ever lose sleep over anyone again, barring her brothers and sister, that was. The thought of finding them again was all that kept her going now and she just lived for the day when she could do that. She spent every spare minute revising and doing homework, and began to get excellent reports from the teachers. However, this did nothing to endear her to Miss Budd. In fact, if anything, the woman's dislike of her seemed to grow daily as did her frustration, because Maddy never put a foot wrong and there was no excuse to send her off to the Quiet Room.

It was on a day in early February that Miss Budd came to her dormitory and informed her tartly, 'You have a visitor. I suggest you make yourself look fit to be seen and then you'd better get yourself off to the Day Room.'

'A visitor?' Maddy was baffled. Who would bother coming to see her? She laid aside the copy of *David Copperfield* she had been studying and

283

went downstairs.

Her eyes snapped open with surprise when she saw Andy Tranter sitting looking very awkward at a table by the window.

'Maddy.' He stood up to greet her as she looked around for Kirsty.

'Er ... Kirsty isn't with me,' he told her.

'Oh, why is that then?'

'To tell you the truth, we split up some months ago.'

Maddy was shocked but sat down and looked at him as she waited for him to go on. When he didn't volunteer any further information, she asked bluntly, 'Why are you here, Andy?'

He shrugged before deciding to tell her the truth. 'I don't know, really. I suppose I just wanted to make sure that you were all right. It was in all the newspapers about the fire in the squat, and your name was mentioned as you were the only survivor. Anyway, I rang Miss Budd and she admitted that you had run away but that you were back here again, and as I knew you didn't have anyone else to look out for you I thought I'd just come and check that you were OK. You *are* OK, aren't you, Maddy?'

It was her turn to shrug now and he was shocked at the change in her. She seemed to have grown up overnight but there was a haunted look about her that made her seem as vulnerable as ever.

'Why didn't you ever reply to any of the letters we sent you?' he asked suddenly.

Maddy lowered her eyes. 'I was angry with you both, thinking that if you and Kirsty had been that concerned about me, you would have kept me back home with you. I lay in the bath one night and heard you both saying that that was what you were going to do, and the next minute you were shipping me off to this horrible dump!'

'That's not quite true.' He stared at her steadily. 'In actual fact, we *did* want to keep you, but the decision was taken out of our hands because of what happened to your parents.'

'So why didn't you tell me this before?' Maddy's eyes were blazing.

'Because we thought it would just make things worse for you – that it would be easier for you to adjust to somewhere new if you didn't know that we had wanted you to stay with us. Looking back, I realise we were wrong, but it's too late to change that now. What I can say, if it's any consolation to you, is that once you get out of here you can always come and stay with me – just until you get on your feet, of course,' he added hastily. 'I hate to think of you having nowhere to go.'

'Won't Kirsty mind, if you're back together?'

He snorted with disgust. 'There's no chance of that happening, I can assure you. Kirsty is gone for good, as far as I'm concerned. She changed after you left. She'd always longed for a baby but it became an obsession with her, to the point that she couldn't think of anything else.' Obviously distressed, he ran his hand distractedly through his hair but then pulling himself together he went on, 'Anyway, that's water under the bridge now. How are you *really* doing? You look well. A bit on the skinny side but then you were never further through than a line-prop.'

'I spend a lot of time studying. I want to get a good job when I leave here so that I can save enough money to find my real family again.'

Andy's heart went out to the girl and suddenly he was glad that he had taken the trouble to come and see her. In her short life she had suffered more than most people did in an entire lifetime, and from where he was standing it was a bloody shame.

'Would you like a cup of tea?' Maddy suddenly asked, and visibly relaxing, he nodded gratefully. Smiling, she went off in search of the tea trolley. The rest of the visit was spent discussing more impersonal things, and when the bell heralding the end of visiting sounded, Maddy was almost sorry. Andy was the first person she had really spoken to since Kat, and that seemed like a lifetime ago now. Strangely, she barely thought about her – or Holly, for that matter. The memories were too painful and so she buried them away.

'Right, I'd better be off then. I've a long drive ahead of me.' Andy looked at her awkwardly. 'Would you mind very much if I came to see you again some time?'

'I'd like that,' Maddy told him, and it was true. 'But I'll come to the door with you.'

As they left the room side-by-side she suddenly asked, 'How are your parents?' She saw his fists clench and the colour rush into his cheeks as he said, 'Mum and Dad have split up too. It must be something in the water round our way, eh?' Pausing at the entrance, he held his hand out to her and asked, 'Are you going to answer my letters if

286

I write to you now?'

Maddy nodded and with a final smile he was gone and she turned to head back towards the dormitory. Nurse Law stopped her en route.

'So who was the handsome visitor then, young lady?' she teased, delighted to note that someone had taken the trouble to come and see the girl.

'It was my former foster-carer,' Maddy told her. 'I lived with him and his wife for a time before I came here, but he just told me that they'd split up. It's a shame because I thought they were really happy together.'

'I thought *I* was happy with my husband till he took it into his empty head to clear off with a blonde bimbo,' Mary Law told her with a rueful grin. 'But it taught me a valuable lesson – that things aren't always what they appear to be. But there, that's another story entirely.' She suddenly glanced about to make sure that they couldn't be overheard before lowering her voice to a whisper. 'Could you come to the sick bay, Maddy, in about an hour?'

'What for?' Maddy asked.

'Just come and you'll find out. Now off you go and I'll see you soon.' And with that the nurse turned and hurried away, leaving Maddy to stare after her.

Once back in her room, Maddy found it hard to concentrate on the homework in front of her. Her head was full of the surprise visit from Andy and wondering what it might be that Nurse Law wanted to see her about. The woman had made whatever it was sound very cloak and dagger, and she had seemed on edge too, almost jumping at her own shadow.

At last, after an hour had passed, Maddy went along to the sick bay to find Nurse Law changing the beds in there. She prided herself on keeping everything clean as a new pin within her little domain and hated things to be out of place.

'Ah, Maddy, here you are. Come into the office, would you?'

Intrigued, Maddy followed her into the small room that served as her office and looked at her expectantly.

The nurse opened a drawer and after taking out a folded piece of paper she told her, 'I have something here that just might make the rest of the time here pass a little more quickly for you. Now before I give it to you, you must promise me faithfully that you will put it away somewhere very safe. Should anyone ever find out that I've given you this, my job will be well and truly up the Swannee!'

'What is it?' Maddy asked curiously.

'It's the addresses of where your brothers and sister are living.' The nurse watched the colour drain from the girl's face and hastily pulled a chair out for her. 'Sit yourself down,' she urged. 'I know this must have come as a bit of a shock, but Nick got them for me. With working for Social Services he has contacts, you see. But I can't express enough how important it is that no one ever finds out about this. Nick would get his marching orders too if Miss Budd or Mr Dumbarr ever found out what he'd done. Do you understand, Maddy?'

'Yes.' Maddy felt euphoric. There would be no

more worrying about where her siblings were any more. At least she would know – and that gave her inexpressible comfort. It would also make it a lot easier to find them once she got out of here.

The nurse passed her the slip of paper and Maddy jammed it straight into the pocket of her cardigan.

'Why have you done this for me?' she asked suddenly.

Mary Law shrugged. 'I don't really know, to be honest,' she admitted. 'I suppose I just feel you've had a raw deal of it, one way and another. And Nick does too, which is why he agreed to help when I asked him. But you know, as I've said before, I'm always here if you need to talk about anything. Anything at all.'

The closed look came over Maddy's face again now and she rose hastily. When she reached the door she paused to look over her shoulder. 'Thanks again,' she muttered, 'for everything.' And then she was gone, leaving Nurse Law to stare after her with a concerned frown creasing her brow.

Chapter Twenty-Six

January 1995
'Not long to go now then, eh, Maddy?' Mr Dumbarr blocked her path as she was leaving the schoolroom.

Since returning to River House after her short

289

time of freedom, Maddy had been left alone by him. It didn't surprise her in the least. She was well aware by now that Dumbarr favoured the younger girls.

She was now seventeen years old, and had developed into a very attractive young woman. Her long dark hair, which she tended to keep tied back in a severe ponytail, reached almost to her waist now and she was fortunate enough to have a clear complexion. But it was Maddy's deep brown eyes that were still her best feature.

For over a year she had been doing a secretarial course with the tutor who came in each week from a college in Cheltenham to teach the older girls, and he was full of praise for her. 'You'll walk out of here into a top-class job with your grades,' he assured her, and Maddy could only hope that he was right.

Very often, she would remove the slip of paper with her siblings' addresses on from the small slit in her mattress where she had hidden it and hug herself when she thought of seeing them again. It wouldn't be long now. In October when she reached eighteen she would be able to walk out of here and hopefully never have to set eyes on the place again.

Now she rose to her full height and stared at Mr Dumbarr, although she said not a word. She was careful now never to give him cause to have her taken to the Quiet Room. Clutching her books to her chest she made to move past him, but he put his arm out to stay her.

'I was thinking, why don't you come along to my room this evening for a glass of wine? If I remember rightly, you always enjoyed a drink.'

'Actually, I only liked it because it took the edge off the despicable things you did to me she retorted daringly, and had the satisfaction of seeing him colour to a dull brick-red.

He glanced about nervously, worried that someone might have overheard them.

'I think what you need to remember is that *my* word is law here,' he ground out. 'And I'm not asking you, girl, I'm *telling you* that I want you in my room tonight!'

'Aren't I a little too old for you now?' Maddy shot back, as the colour in her cheeks rose to match his. He was so angry that he looked as if he might explode but Maddy had no fear of him any more. She knew too much about him, and should he so much as offer to lay a hand on her again she would scream what he was from the rooftops and shame the consequences.

'I ... I don't know what you're talking about,' he stuttered.

'*Really?*' Maddy's voice dripped with sarcasm although she was shaking like a leaf. It seemed that he still had the power to strike terror into her heart despite her brave words. 'Still dressing up and abusing little girls, are you?' she asked scathingly, and now the colour faded from his face and seemed to drain out of him as if someone had turned a tap on. He might have forgotten that she knew about his fetish but Maddy certainly hadn't.

'I think you're old enough to be able to control that tongue of yours,' he snapped, the picture of indignation. 'Who do you think would believe you if you made such a ridiculous allegation?'

'Andy would,' Maddy brazened. 'He's the foster-carer I lived with before I came here and he still comes to see me from time to time. I'm more than aware that the girls here are too afraid to tell their social workers what goes on, but I assure you that if I told him what I knew, *he* would follow it up.'

The man took a step back and allowed her to pass him now but she could feel his eyes boring into her back. She held her head high until he was out of sight and then her legs nearly gave way. During her time in River House she had seen sights that had turned her blood to water. Young girls suffering nightmares because of the unwanted attentions of Mr Dumbarr. Girls hauled off to the Quiet Room for the least little thing and left there for days on end. And worst of all, girls just disappearing without trace. Maddy had always found it hard to believe the reasons Miss Budd gave for this, and the fact that the girls were never found or mentioned again. They had certainly soon hauled *her* back when she had tried to escape the place.

Steph had been the last to disappear and Maddy couldn't understand it. She knew that she had been one of Dumbarr's victims after listening to what Kim had told her about Steph's erratic behaviour. The signs were all there. Creeping out of the room in the dead of night only to return and cry herself to sleep. Nightmares that woke Kim on a regular basis. Maddy shuddered as she recalled her own experiences, and knew that she would never forget a second of them for as long as she lived. The things she had been forced to endure at Dumbo's hands were branded into her very soul.

Steph had been gone for ages now and Maddy had had no word from her. Neither had Kim, which was strange because the two of them had been close. Kim had told Maddy that she had just returned to their room one day to find all of Steph's things gone. She had asked Miss Budd where Steph was, only to be told, 'Oh, she's just another runaway. No doubt she'll be found eventually and hauled back here. In the meantime you'd do well to forget all about her.'

But Kim *hadn't* forgotten about her – and Maddy knew that she still missed her every single day.

As she now hurried towards the stairs the sound of Sinead O'Connor warbling 'Nothing Compares 2U' floated from the Day Room. No doubt some of the younger girls were trying to play a few music tracks before they began their pre-dinner chores. Poor little sods. It was about the only pleasure they had and Maddy sometimes wondered how the old record player managed to keep going.

'Maddy, is everything all right?'

Her head snapped up to see Nick, the young social worker, watching her with a worried look on his face. She gulped as she realised that he must have seen her talking to Dumbarr.

'Er ... yes, everything is fine, thanks.'

He sighed with frustration. Nick had long since finished his PhD and as soon as he had got his doctorate, had returned to River House as a fully-fledged social worker. He worked Monday to

Friday and was extremely popular with the girls, many of whom had a huge crush on him. It wasn't surprising really, Maddy thought, seeing as he was one of the very few young men they ever set eyes on.

'Are you quite sure? To me, it looked as if you and Mr Dumbarr were having words.'

'I told you, everything is fine.'

'All right, all right, keep your hair on. I was only asking.' He grinned as he held up his hands as if to ward off a blow, but once Maddy had slipped past him he stared after her thoughtfully.

Sometimes his feelings for Maddy concerned him. She was just seventeen years old and yet she came over as a much older person. She had a quick wit and a keen sense of humour when she cared to use it, and over the last year, Nick had felt drawn to her. He knew it was wrong and totally unprofessional, but attraction was a funny thing and it often struck in the most unlikely of places. Not that anything could ever come of it. He knew that Maddy would be gone in a few months' time and he doubted that he would ever see her again. She seemed to be living for the day when she could begin the search for her siblings, and he couldn't blame her. Having come from a very loving home environment himself, with parents who had put their children before themselves, he could only imagine how awful it must have been for Maddy to be ripped away from the people she cared about at such an early age.

The same applied to most of the kids who had ended up here, if it came to that, but for some reason Maddy was special to him. He had read her file time and time again, but could never envisage Maddy setting fire to her adoptive parents' home deliberately. And then there was that other fire that had started at the squat in Leeds, where she had briefly lived. Three more people had died as a consequence of it, but once again, there was no evidence to implicate her – although Miss Budd and Mr Dumbarr clearly thought she was guilty. They had made that more than obvious, so why then was Dumbarr singling her out again?

The harsh ringing of a phone coming from the direction of his office brought him sharply back to the present. Hurrying away, he tried to push thoughts of Maddy from his mind, painfully aware that if he didn't, his career could well be over before it had begun. His tutors certainly hadn't taught him how to deal with the feelings he was currently experiencing.

Once in her room, Maddy flung her books onto the bed and crossed to the window with her hand pressed to her mouth. She knew that she couldn't bear it if Mr Dumbarr laid so much as a finger on her again and began to seriously think of whether she should confide in Andy. There would be no point whatsoever in trying to tell any of the social workers here what went on in this place. It would all just be swept under the carpet and put down to spite. Miss Budd was exceptionally good at persuading the social workers who visited how disruptive the girls were, so no one would ever take their word against hers.

Suddenly reaching a decision, Maddy took a pad and pen out of her drawer and whilst she had the courage, she began to write a letter to Andy. He was the only one whom she felt she could trust now, and she knew that he would believe her. She told him everything. About Miss Budd's brutal treatment of her; how Dumbarr had raped her and numerous other girls at the home ... and as her pen raced across the page her confidence began to grow. Finally she told Andy of the Quiet Room and the way the girls were locked away there if they so much as put a foot wrong. And finally it was done. All the things she had longed to talk about were down on paper, and once Andy received the letter she knew he would act on it. No one here would believe her if she disclosed to them what was happening, but they *would* listen to Andy. It was like a calming salve to her soul and suddenly she knew that she had done the right thing.

Quickly addressing the envelope, she carried the letter downstairs and placed it on the tray in the hallway. The letters from the girls were posted twice a week, and this time tomorrow it would be winging its way to someone who just might be able to help her and all the other girls at the home who lived in fear of Miss Budd and Mr Dumbarr.

That night, she slept easily for the first time in months. She had no intention of going to Dumbarr's room as he had ordered her to, and after tomorrow he would never be able to force her to again.

It was late the following evening when the house was sleeping that someone urgently shook

Maddy's arm, awakening her from a deep sleep. Her eyes blinked open and she found herself staring up at Miss Budd who was hovering over her with a smile on her face.

'Come along, my dear,' she urged. 'There is someone downstairs to see you. It seems there's been a family crisis and they need to talk to you.'

'A family crisis?' Maddy looked confused.

'I think it's about your brother.'

Maddy's heart sank. 'I'll be down in two minutes. I just have to get dressed,' she muttered as she began to yank her clothes on over her night-dress.

She glanced across to where Kim was softly snoring, and after slipping her feet into her flat black shoes she joined the older woman on the landing.

'I don't understand. I didn't even know that Oliver was aware of where I was.'

'Ah well, Sue Maddox must have informed his new family of your whereabouts,' Miss Budd told her as they headed for the top of the staircase.

'Oliver *is* all right, isn't he?' Maddy was beginning to panic now.

'I have no idea, but we'll soon find out, won't we? They're waiting for you in the Day Room.' The woman's voice was soothing and Maddy was more than ever confused. This was a caring side of the woman that she had never seen before, and she began to wonder if Miss Budd did have a heart instead of a swinging brick, after all.

The rest of the short journey was made in silence as they crept through the sleeping house. Once they reached the door of the Day Room,

Miss Budd pushed it open for her and Maddy stepped inside. It was in darkness and for a moment she wondered if Miss Budd had directed her to the wrong room. But then suddenly a thick arm closed around her neck from behind and a familiar smell of stale sweat assailed her nostrils. It was Dumbarr's smell – she would never forget it.

'What the–' Maddy began to fight but then a reeking cloth was placed across her mouth and suddenly everything began to fade away until there was nothing but blackness.

Chapter Twenty-Seven

'Where am I?' Maddy tried to pull herself up onto her elbow but she felt as if there was a lead weight in her head and dropped heavily back onto the pillows.

'Just lie still, you'll start to feel better in a while,' a soothing voice told her.

Squinting, Maddy tried to focus on the shape that was leaning over her but it was useless. Everything was blurred. Taking great gulps of air, she forced herself to think of what had brought her to this state, and as it all came rushing back, a sense of panic engulfed her. She kept her eyes screwed tight shut until she felt a little calmer and then slowly opened them again as everything began to swim into focus.

A sallow-faced girl was standing beside her and

Maddy realised that she was lying on a bed although she had no idea where she was. She certainly wasn't in the dormitory in River House. Turning her head to the side with an enormous effort, she saw that she was in a small room with nothing but a bed and a huge mirror on the wall opposite it. A window set into one wall was draped with lovely red silk curtains and the wallpaper looked expensive, like silk, and had an oriental feel about it.

'That's better.' The girl's voice was gentle. 'Here, drink this.'

Someone lifted her head and she felt cooling water trickling down her throat. The feeling was coming back into her limbs now, giving the sensation of pins and needles as she flexed her fingers.

At that moment the door opened and a very tall thin man entered with a small tray in his hand.

'Ah, so she's awake then, is she?'

Maddy scowled. There was something about his voice that was strangely familiar, but for the life of her she couldn't think where she had heard it before.

'I'm going to give you your first taste of paradise,' he told her with a smile as he lifted a syringe and squirted a tiny amount of liquid into the air. He then took her arm and she felt the prick of a needle as it slid into her vein. She wanted to fight and lash out, but her arms were not back to normal as yet and so all she could do was lie there and watch helplessly.

Seconds later he sighed with satisfaction as he placed the syringe back on the small silver tray. 'You can go now,' he told the girl. 'She'll be out of it again, once that takes hold.'

The girl obediently left the room as the man leaned over Maddy and sneered. 'A few of these and you'll be begging for more of the same,' he chuckled, and then he too left the room as Maddy's head lashed from side to side. What had he injected her with? She wondered if it was poison and whether she was going to die, but then common sense took over. He had told her that this would be the first, so he must intend to keep her alive. But who was he, and where was she?

Suddenly, she felt herself relaxing again as vivid colours began to flash in front of her eyes. There were deep purples fading into mauves and lilacs before changing to electric blues, followed by oranges and reds and all the colours of the rainbow – although they were more intense than anything she had ever seen before. And then suddenly Oliver was there and she felt a rush of happiness. He was standing at the end of the bed, looking at her with love. Her mother was there too, smiling and holding her arms out to her. Maddy reached out to the wonderful vision, but even as she did so, the woman faded away. And then she was floating and it was the most heavenly sensation she had ever experienced. Suddenly it didn't matter where she was – and she lay back to enjoy it...

'You didn't really think I would let you blow the whistle on me, did you?'

As Maddy's eyes struggled open she found herself staring into Dumbarr's bloated face. There was a smirk playing about his thick lips and a

300

cruel glint in his eyes. She groaned as her hand reached up to stroke her forehead. There was a raging headache thumping away in time to her heart behind her eyes, and her mouth felt dry.

'After your threats I decided to intercept your mail,' he went on smugly. 'And wasn't it lucky for me that I did, eh?'

'Wh ... what have you done to me?' Maddy whimpered.

He laughed – a hard, cold sound that echoed about the room. 'You tell her,' he said to someone who was standing behind him, and turning, he headed to the door. He had done what he had come to do and now it was time to return to River House and his other life.

Maddy's eyes popped wide with shock when a young woman stepped forward. It was Stacey.

'What are *you* doing here?' she gasped. Was she still dreaming?

Stacey laughed bitterly. 'The same as you'll be doing from now on,' she informed her callously. 'You just had your first dose of the old brown, mate. A few more of them and you'll be begging Dumbo for more. That's how it gets you.'

'Brown?' Maddy frowned in confusion.

'Heroin to you,' Stacey said flatly. 'That's how he keeps us all here. That – and a few locked doors.'

'But why? Why would he want to keep us locked up?'

'Let's just say he's got a nice little money-spinner going.'

'What sort of a money-spinner – and how did *you* come to be here? Dumbarr told us all at

River House that he had found you a job and a flat to live in.'

'Well, he would, wouldn't he? That's his job as far as the Social Services Department are concerned – to find us somewhere to go when we reach eighteen. The Department don't wanna know after that. As far as they're concerned, they've done their job then and we're on our own. But this is where the girls with no families to care about them end up. With my track record, my old dears were quite willing to believe that I'd simply run away. Old Dumbo isn't quite what he appears to be, believe you me.'

'I know he dresses up in women's clothes,' Maddy volunteered, and Stacey chuckled dismissively.

'Huh! That ain't the half of it,' she assured her. 'You'll find out soon enough. But for now, I'd rest if I were you. You'll probably feel like shit for the next few hours, bein' as it was yer first fix. The funny thing is, once it's properly worn off, you'll wanna do it again. The high you get from it is worth the comin' down, see?'

Maddy shook her head. She had no intentions of getting hooked on drugs.

'I won't want to do it again,' she spat savagely. 'And I'm not staying here either! And nor would you, if you had any sense.'

Stacey stared at her. 'And where would I go if I were to leave here?' There was a hint of sorrow in her voice. 'This is about as good as it's gonna get for me and half the other kids that end up here. I'm fed and clothed and I can have a fix whenever I want it. It's what I have to do in return

302

that's the bit that ain't so pleasant ... but then nothing's ever perfect, is it?'

'And just what *do* you have to do?'

Stacey turned to the door. 'You'll see, all in good time. Goodbye, Maddy.'

As the door closed quietly behind her, Maddy sighed in frustration before dragging her legs to the edge of the bed. They felt as if they had turned to jelly and she felt sick and wobbly.

Eventually she managed to get to the window where she leaned heavily on the sill as she gazed through the glass. There was no other house, or building for that matter, in sight; all that was visible were rolling fields stretching away into the distance. Much like River House, the building she was in was surrounded by a high brick wall with an enormous lake circled by trees within the grounds, but there was no sign of a drive leading up to it, so Maddy assumed that she must be at the back of the building.

Crossing to the door, she tried the handle and was not surprised to discover it was locked. But where was she, and why had Mr Dumbarr brought her here? She began to pound on the door but no one answered, and eventually she returned to the bed where she fell into a restless doze. Some time later, the sound of the key in the lock woke her and she looked towards it. The room was in semi-darkness, so she knew that she must have slept for some time. The same girl she had seen when she first regained consciousness walked into the room balancing a tray in her hand and smiled at her.

'I've brought yer somethin' to eat an' a drink.'

303

Placing the tray on the end of the bed she asked, 'How yer feelin'?'

'As if I've been run over by a steamroller. I ache everywhere.'

The girl nodded. 'Yer will, seein' as it were yer first fix, but you'll get used to it.'

'Oh no, I won't,' Maddy told her indignantly, as the girl now put a light on. 'I won't be staying here long enough to get used to anything.'

'Just mind who you say that to,' the girl warned her as she glanced nervously towards the door. 'Believe me, if yer don't toe the line here yer get sent somewhere far worse. If yer want my advice, you'll buckle down an' take the lesser o' two evils.'

Maddy had just opened her mouth to ask her what she meant when a huge, heavily made-up woman entered the room. She was so large that she seemed to fill the doorframe. She looked Maddy up and down as if she was a piece of meat before commenting in a deep voice, 'Mm, a bit old but I dare say we'll find a slot for you.' Then, turning her attention to the girl, she told her, 'Ginny, go and get yourself ready. We have a party tonight.'

The girl nodded before scuttling away like a frightened rabbit as the woman returned her gaze to Maddy.

'Hurry up and eat your meal and then we'll go and find a proper room for you.'

'What do you mean, a proper room? What is this then?'

'This is one of the party rooms – look.' As the woman pointed to a far corner with a fat finger,

304

Maddy saw a small camera on the wall that was trained on the bed, and frowned with confusion. Just what sort of place was this anyway?

Seeing her bewilderment, the enormous woman chuckled, setting her double chin wobbling. 'You're in a nonce house, my love. Do you know what a nonce house is?'

Maddy shook her head.

'Well then, let me try and explain it to you. We cater to people with ... shall we say ... different tastes?'

'Different tastes in what?'

'Do you know what a brothel is?'

Maddy nodded as she swallowed her growing fear.

'Then for now let's just say that a nonce house is a brothel with a difference.' The woman laughed as if she had just told a huge joke. 'And that's about all you need to know. The rest will be explained to you as we go along.'

Maddy was so horrified that she was momentarily speechless.

'Now come along. If you're not going to eat that, we may as well go and get you settled.' The woman's voice was stern. 'And don't even think of trying to run away. I promise you wouldn't even get to the gates. We have dogs prowling the grounds that would tear you apart in two seconds flat. Are you ready?'

Maddy rose and followed the woman without a murmur. Although the girl prided herself on the fact that she had feared no one for some long time, there was something about this giant with the gravelly voice that told her she would do well not to cross her. As she followed her along a corridor with a deep pile carpet that stretched from wall to wall, she peeped at the woman out of the corner of her eye. She was wearing a bright flowered dress in garish colours that did nothing to flatter her ample figure, and her enormous feet were squeezed into high-heeled shoes. She had shoulder-length dark hair that was cut into a bob and her face was plastered with make-up. Maddy briefly wondered if the woman was wearing a wig. She was certainly no spring chicken yet there was not a single grey hair in sight, although she supposed that could have been due to a bottle of hair-dye. Her fingers were heavily ringed and she wore a number of necklaces that cascaded across her enormous breasts. Maddy was so intent on studying her jailer that she took little notice of where they were going until the woman came to a door that she unlocked with a key. They then entered another corridor but there were no carpets here, only bare floorboards and drab walls painted in a dull cream colour.

A door further along suddenly opened and a young boy who looked to be about ten years old appeared. He had shocking ginger hair and the bluest eyes that Maddy had ever seen.

'*Charles!*' At sight of the person standing at Maddy's side he ran to him and flung his arms about his ample hips as Maddy's mouth gaped open. *Charles!* No wonder she had thought there was something strange about her. This woman was actually a man!

'How you doing, son?' The person at Maddy's side rumpled the boy's hair affectionately before

306

turning his attention back to Maddy.

'Young Jimmy here and me are best mates,' he informed her as she blinked in bewilderment. Now more doors began to open and yet more children of various ages appeared one by one.

'I've brought you a new friend,' the person called Charles informed them, as he ushered Maddy ahead of him into a bedroom. There was yet another shock waiting for her there when she saw Steph lying on a single bed next to the window.

'Steph!' Crossing to her, Maddy gently shook her arm before realising that her old room-mate was totally out of it. She was no doubt high on drugs if what Maddy had seen in this place up to now was anything to go by.

'Of course, you must know Steph from River House,' Charles commented. 'She's proved to be very popular with our customers, although even after three years she isn't quite house-trained yet.' He chuckled as Maddy glared at him. 'The blokes like a bit of black from time to time.'

'Charles, Charles ... come an' see me jigsaw. It's nearly done now,' Jimmy implored as he tugged at the skirt of the garish dress.

Charles grinned down at him. 'All right then. Just let me show Maddy where everything is and I'll come along to you.'

The small boy nodded before scooting out of the room and now Charles told her, 'This wardrobe here is yours, and that chest-of-drawers. Once we know your size you'll be supplied with a whole wardrobe of new clothes. We like to look after our kids here. This will be your bed and the toilet is just along the corridor. So is the bathroom. At the end of the corridor you'll find the Day Room. There's a telly, a tape machine and everything you could want in there. None of the doors on this wing are ever locked so you can come and go as you please. I'm sure you'll soon settle, especially as you already have friends here. Now I must get off and look at this jigsaw of Jimmy's. I'll get no peace until I do.' He tutted as if he was a mother speaking of an errant child as he turned and left the room, leaving Maddy to stare after him. She felt as if she was trapped in a nightmare. What had he meant when he mentioned 'customers' and why did he have children locked up here?

Turning her attention back to Steph she again shook her arm, whispering urgently, 'Steph, please talk to me.'

'She can't. She's too out of it.'

Wheeling about, Maddy saw Stacey standing in the doorway. It was no secret that she and Stacey had never got on at River House, but Maddy didn't feel that now was the time for holding grudges. There was too much she needed to find out.

'Stacey, where the hell are we?'

The other girl shrugged. 'I couldn't rightly tell you. I only know we're still somewhere in the Cotswolds and miles from anywhere. This used to be a Victorian gentleman's residence years ago apparently, and we're stuck up in the servants' quarters. We do get let out for fresh air though. At certain times of the day Charles locks the dogs up and we're all allowed out into the gardens.

There's about nine of us here at present. Four of us older kids and five nippers. The clientele Charles and Dumbo cater for like 'em young. The younger the better, in fact.'

'B ... but what about the children's families? Aren't they looking for them?'

'I dare say some of them are, but you'd be surprised who visits here. There are more bent coppers than enough, believe me. Some of them favour girls and some of them like the lads.'

Maddy visibly shuddered. 'And what about Charles?'

'He's a big mate of Dumbo's. They're both trannies,' Stacey told her matter-of-factly as she studied her bright purple nail varnish. 'Lots of the blokes that come here are the same, though you'd never believe it if you saw them when they first arrived. Suits, briefcases – the lot – till they get into their gear, that is. They're all fucking perves, every last one of them, but so long as we do as we're told, we're treated well.'

'And what if we don't behave?'

A shadow flitted across Stacey's pretty face. 'Then let's just say we get sent on a long journey. There's a lot of foreign blokes come here from Bucharest and places like that. Apparently, from what I've heard off Charles, they love child prostitutes in certain areas over there, and so the kids end up in brothels. That poor little sod that Budd used to make sleep on bedsprings was the last to be shipped off 'cos she wouldn't play ball.'

'So *this* is where all the girls that disappeared from the home ended up,' Maddy breathed, appalled. 'They just used to tell the rest of us that

309

they'd run away.'

'And that's what they'll say about you and all, but you know different now, don't you? Anyway, I'm off for a bath now. Come and join us when you're ready, eh?' With that, Stacey turned and sauntered away as if she hadn't a care in the world.

Maddy scuttled away in the direction of the toilet. She had suffered a lot in her life, but she had the most awful feeling that her worst night-mare was just about to begin.

Chapter Twenty-Eight

Maddy returned to her room and stayed there for an hour or so but then curiosity finally got the better of her and she ventured out onto the land-ing and went towards the room where Charles had told her the kids who lived there congre-gated.

As she tentatively opened the door she was confronted by what appeared at first glance to be a sea of faces all looking towards her.

The television was on and Tom and Jerry were chasing each other across the screen. The younger children were sitting cross-legged in front of it whilst Stacey was lounging in an easy chair by a high sash-cord window reading a magazine.

'Come on in,' she invited, as if they were the best of friends. The small ginger-haired boy she had met earlier smiled at her as she passed him. He was sitting at a large table that took up the centre of the room, struggling with a jigsaw puzzle.

Maddy looked around in surprise. It was actually a very nice room with toys and books scattered about the place. There was also an enormous bookcase standing against one of the walls with books that would appeal to all ages placed neatly upon it. A tape-player stood on another smaller table and Maddy saw a pile of tapes beneath it. All the children were well dressed and most of them appeared to be content, apart from one scrawny little girl who stared at her from haunted eyes. She appeared to be no older than six or seven and resembled a little angel. She had long blonde hair that had been tightly woven into plaits, and sea-green eyes. She looked tired and Maddy was saddened to see that her eyes held a wisdom beyond their years.

'That's Chloe,' Stacey told her as she saw Maddy smiling at the little girl. 'She ain't been here long and ain't none too settled yet. She's only nine but she looks younger, doesn't she? That's why she's so popular with the punters. The younger the better here.'

Maddy joined Stacey at the window and gazed down to the courtyard below. This room was obviously on the front of the house, approached by a long winding drive that was bordered by trees. As she stood there, two huge Dobermann dogs appeared and she shuddered. She could well believe that these animals could tear someone to shreds if they so chose, judging by the look of them.

'They're called Rip and Satan. The names suit them, don't they?'

Maddy nodded solemnly. They were certainly a far cry from the little shih-tzus she had become so fond of at Kirsty and Andy's. As she thought of them now, a flicker of hope rose in her. *Andy!* Surely he would realise that something was wrong when he discovered that she had disappeared. Perhaps he would search for her? They had become close. In fact, he was just about the only person she trusted now, and he would know that she had had no intentions of running away again. She was too near to finishing her time at River House to risk it. Now she wished she had confided in him earlier and told him of the awful things she had been subjected to during her stay there, but it was too late to do anything about it now. She could only pray that his instincts would warn him that something was wrong.

As if Stacey could read her mind she warned her, 'Don't get thinking that someone is going to come along and save you. Budd and Dumbo are too good at covering up their tracks. To all intents and purposes, Budd is the ideal house-mother and Dumbo is the perfect home-finder. They choose the ones that will come here well. Only the ones that don't have no one on the outside who gives a shit, see?'

'But who actually *owns* this place? Someone must be in charge?' Maddy snapped.

'It's Budd and Dumbo's place.' Stacey sighed. 'They've been lovers for years, by all accounts.'

Maddy's eyes stretched wide. 'But how can that be? Dumbo loved messing with the kids at River House. Surely Miss Budd wouldn't have allowed that if they were lovers?'

312

Stacey chuckled. 'Of course she would. Or should I say, *he* would! You *still* ain't worked it out, have you?'

Suddenly Maddy gasped in shock. The thin, grey-haired man who had injected her when she first arrived here ... *he* was Miss Budd! It was all clear. The deep gravelly voice. The angular features. But why hadn't she twigged it before?

'Budd likes the little lads,' Stacey went on. 'Dumbo prefers the little girls, although they both swing both ways, if you get my meaning? *She's* his favourite at the minute.' She stabbed a finger towards Chloe. 'She's popular with the men that come here and all. Poor little sod. Sometimes when they've gone she cries enough to fill a bucket. But then she is only a babby, ain't she? It's different for us older ones. We can cope with it.'

Maddy felt bile rise in her throat. She had never dreamed that such things went on.

'I'm not staying here,' she said flatly as her hands balled into fists. 'I think I'd rather die.'

'And you well could do, if you don't do as yer told,' Stacey rejoined without an ounce of sympathy. 'The sooner you resign yourself to the fact, the easier it gets. Think about it. What would've happened to you when they tipped you out into the big wide world? For kids like us who have no one who cares it's a tough life. At least here you're taken care of. And if you play ball there's a chance that you could become a big star. In porn films, I mean.'

Maddy pursed her lips, too disgusted to even reply. Stacey might be prepared to stay here and accept her lot, but she certainly wasn't.

313

As they stood there they saw Budd, now dressed as a woman again in a staid tweed suit, leave the building and approach his car. The two dogs bounded towards him barking furiously but the instant the man held his hand up they quietened and allowed him to go on his way. Seconds later the car roared off down the drive and Stacey sighed as she rubbed her stomach.

'It'll be dinnertime soon. The snap here is great, which is just as well. I'm starving and me stomach thinks me throat's cut. I shall need me energy tonight. I'm entertaining.'

'Entertaining?'

Stacey flicked her long fair hair across her shoulder. 'Yes, I've got a punter to entertain. But don't look so worried, they won't bother you just yet. They'll let you settle in before they set you to work.'

Maddy shuddered violently at the thought of it before turning her attention back to Chloe. There was something about her that reminded her of Molly, the younger sister she had been torn away from so many years ago. The little girl was still watching her closely and she smiled tentatively as she rose and crossed the room to take Maddy's hand.

'How about we do some colouring?' the older girl suggested softly, spotting the colouring books and crayons laid out on the table. The child nodded and so for the next half an hour Maddy kept her entertained. The rest of the children paid her no heed. They were well used to people coming and going and had little interest in her.

Soon after, the door opened and a stout woman

appeared. 'Come on then, kids,' she told them. 'It's dinnertime.' She looked Maddy up and down with an appreciative look in her eyes before turning back to the corridor.

The children all followed her from the room and Maddy tacked on behind them, with Chloe keeping a tight grip on her hand.

As they descended a beautiful staircase with carved balustrades, Maddy looked about her with interest. The luxurious foyer looked like the entrance to one of the lovely hotels she had seen in magazines. Her feet sank into a deep plum-coloured carpet as she marched along, looking conspicuous in her worn grey school uniform, since all the others were dressed in fashionable clothes.

Stacey held her back and whispered as she pointed towards a woman who was standing in the hallway, 'That's Belle. She's the madam of the place and lives in.'

'Is she a man too?' Maddy whispered back.

'No, not as far as I know. But she does have a tendency to like the lads. Especially the little ones.'

Maddy's head was whirling as she tried to take everything in. So much had happened in such a short space of time that she was still reeling from the shock of finding herself there.

Eventually the woman led them into a very pleasant dining room. A row of tables were laid with cutlery and on a long sideboard that stood against the far wall a number of steaming dishes were waiting for them.

'Help yourselves, kids,' the woman told them

315

amiably. 'And make sure you eat your fill. It's a long time till breakfast.'

The children all lifted plates and formed an orderly queue as they moved along helping themselves to vegetables and meat from the tureens. Once they had their meals they then sat at the tables as Maddy eyed them all cautiously. They all seemed so accepting and she couldn't for the life of her understand why.

At a table set slightly apart from the others were two more adults who supervised the children as they tucked into their meals. Maddy found herself sharing a table with Stacey and Chloe and asked, 'Who are they?'

Stacey paused in the act of loading a forkful of roast lamb into her mouth. 'That's the rest of the staff. They help organise the parties for the punters. The food is brought in from outside by a catering firm.'

'Don't the catering firm question what sort of place this is?' Maddy enquired.

'I don't suppose they much care, so long as they get their money,' Stacey pointed out. 'I expect they think it's some sort of a children's home or hotel.'

Maddy shook her head in disbelief. The situation seemed to become more bizarre by the minute. It was as if she and the other young people here had been forgotten about by the rest of the world. But Andy would find her, she just knew he would. As long as she could cling on to that hope, she could cope.

Just as Stacey had said, the meal was delicious compared to the culinary disasters she had become used to at River House. But still, Maddy couldn't eat a thing. Her stomach was in knots as she racked her brain to think of ways she might escape this place and she pushed her food aimlessly about the plate.

When the meal was finally over, the children were allowed to go outside for some fresh air and Maddy was relieved to see that there was no sign of the dogs. The house must have been stunningly beautiful once, but now it was sadly neglected and looked almost derelict, with its crumbling tall chimneys and turrets. The grounds surrounding it could have been breathtaking, but were now overgrown. Snowdrops grew in wild profusion amongst the long grass and the weeds, and the large trees swayed in the early-evening breeze as if they were dancing in time to the wind that blew through their branches. There was nothing but the sound of birds to be heard.

Already Maddy was wondering if she could somehow escape in the caterers' van that Stacey had told her delivered food to the house, just as she had once escaped in the gardeners' van from River House. But that was something she would have to look into properly if it was to become viable.

Chloe skipped ahead of her and as Maddy watched the child her heart ached for her. She was so young and small, but already her innocence had been snatched away from her. Somehow I'm going to get her out of here, Maddy promised herself, and her chin jutted with determination.

The light faded quickly and soon the children were stamping their feet to keep warm. The moment Belle appeared at the French doors at the rear of the house, the children filed back inside before being led upstairs to their living quarters.

On entering her bedroom, Maddy saw that Steph was now awake. She was lying on her bed with tears streaming down her face. She looked mildly surprised to see Maddy, but remained silent until the girl crossed to stand at her side.

'So they got you too then?' Steph said dully.

'Yes, they did, but I'll tell you now, there's no *way* I'm staying here.' The note of determination in her voice made Steph look at her again.

'You won't have any choice. They have ways of making us behave.'

'Huh! They can try.' Maddy's eyes glittered dangerously as she stared down at Steph. It was as if someone had sucked all the spirit out of her friend and she looked broken.

'The things they make us do...' Steph's voice trailed off miserably as she burst into a fresh torrent of tears. 'The men come and then they film them with us.'

Maddy bit down on her lip at the image Steph had conjured up. It didn't make a pretty picture in her head.

'Have you tried standing up to them?' she asked in a small voice as Steph's hand curled in her own.

'Of course I have. Or at least I did when I first came here, but if you put up a fight they just inject you and then you're putty in their hands.'

'But why would they film you?'

'Because there's a world market for that sort of film. I've no doubt Dumbo and Budd are raking

318

it in at our expense. But that's not the worst of it. Sometimes men come from abroad and take the kids away with them.'

Maddy shuddered. What Steph was telling her linked in with what Stacey had said.

'It's even worse for the little ones,' Steph went on as she heaved herself up against the headboard. 'Little Chloe cries every time they drag her off to what they call the party rooms, and when she comes back she's inconsolable for hours. Poor little girl.'

Maddy screwed her eyes up tight as she tried to shut out the picture that was flashing before her eyes.

'So that's all the more reason for us to try and get out of here and blow the whistle on what's going on,' she said after a time.

'Show me a way and I'll be right behind you. But I wouldn't hold your breath. From what I've seen of this place, there's no way out unless they want you out.'

'We'll see. I was surprised how rundown the outside of the place is, compared to the inside,' Maddy remarked.

'Well, I dare say the punters who come here prefer it this way; they don't want to draw attention to it,' Steph replied wearily.

At that moment, a high-pitched scream sounded from along the corridor. 'That'll be Chloe,' Steph stated flatly. 'Charles will be getting her ready for a punter. She'll look like a little Barbie doll by the time he's done with her.'

Unable to help herself, Maddy stepped out into the corridor and, as Steph had predicted, was just in time to see Charles dragging the child off into the bathroom. The man had a pretty frilly dress folded across one arm and Chloe was fighting him every step of the way. Not that it was any use; he was hauling her along as if she weighed no more than a feather.

Ten minutes later he emerged with the little girl sobbing inconsolably at his side. Her hair had been released from its plaits and now hung down her back in shimmering gold tresses. Her beautiful sea-green eyes looked at Maddy imploringly as they passed her but all Maddy could do was stand and watch helplessly as Charles headed for the door at the end of the corridor.

'He'll be takin' her to one o' the party rooms,' Steph informed her. 'That's where they would have put you when you first arrived. Did you notice the big mirror on the wall at the end o' the bed? Well, that's got a camera behind it, see?'

Maddy's stomach felt as if it had been twisted into knots as she thought of what was ahead of the poor child. But for now there was not a single thing she could do about it.

Chapter Twenty-Nine

'What do you mean, she's run away again?' Nurse Law said the following morning as she stared at Miss Budd disbelievingly.

'Just what I say!' There was a harsh glint in the house-mother's eyes as she stared back at Mary.

'B ... but why would she do that?' the nurse persisted. 'She only had a few more months to go before she'd be out of here for good, and Maddy is no fool – she'd realise that running away again would only get her into yet more trouble.'

'Well, as you should have learned by now, some of the girls who come here *don't* stop to think.' Miss Budd obviously had no intention of discussing the matter further and was already backing away as she snapped over her shoulder, 'I suggest you get back to work now, Nurse. Your job is to see to the physical welfare of the children and nothing more. Mr Dumbarr and I will deal with this and in the meantime I advise you to stop worrying about it. No doubt Maddy will be found in time.'

Mary chewed on her lip as she watched the older woman stride away. There was something fishy here; she would have staked her life on it. Maddy had been so positive about leaving River House in the near future, so why would she suddenly have decided to run away again? It just didn't make sense.

Turning about, Mary Law headed for Nick's small office. She wanted to know what he felt about it.

She found him poring over a pile of paperwork.

'Were you aware that Maddy had gone missing again?' she asked him.

The friendly smile slid from his face as he gasped, 'She's *what?*'

'I couldn't find her this morning, and when I asked Miss Budd where she was, she told me that Maddy had run away again.'

Nick's forehead creased into a frown. 'I can't believe she'd do that. She only had a few months left to go – it just doesn't make sense.'

'I agree,' Mary said. 'Why would she suddenly just up and go? And how did she manage to get out of the grounds? There were no deliveries or gardeners here. It's visiting today and her friend, Andy, is coming to see her. She was looking forward to it. I know she was, because she told me so.'

Nick steepled his fingers as he gazed off thoughtfully into space. 'It might be worth having a chat with him and seeing if he has any idea where she may have gone.'

Mary nodded. For now it seemed that was all they could do – but every instinct she possessed screamed that something was not right here, and she would not rest until she had got to the bottom of it.

'Here you are then.' Charles had a bright smile on his face as he entered Maddy's bedroom with an armful of clothes. 'I think you'll find there's everything you need there. I had to guess at your size but I guarantee that everything will fit.'

Maddy gazed at the pile of clothes with no interest whatsoever. There were jeans and tops, all seemingly brand new with the labels still attached. There was pretty underwear and shoes and trainers but the sight of them brought her no joy. She had worn her old grey uniform for so long now that it was like a safety blanket, and the thought of wearing normal clothes again was frightening. In her uniform she was anonymous,

322

but dressed in these clothes she would take on a new identity. It was a scary thought.

Before she could stop him, Charles reached out and fingered her hair which was scraped back unbecomingly into a tight ponytail on the back of her head.

'You'll look brand new once this is loose and you've got all your new togs on,' he said approvingly. 'From what I can see of it, you've got a fine little figure underneath that monstrosity you're wearing. Now come along. Let's have you into the bathroom, eh? This little lot cost an arm and a leg, and it would be a shame if it were all to go to waste.'

'I don't want your new clothes. In fact, I don't want *anything* off you,' Maddy stated defiantly as she crossed her arms protectively across her breasts.

'Oh, it's going to be like that, is it?' Charles sighed dramatically before pulling a syringe from the pocket of the gaudy dress he was wearing. 'Perhaps another taste of this will make you a bit more compliant, eh?'

Maddy backed hastily away as terror coursed through her. She had no intention of becoming hooked on drugs as Stacey obviously was.

'All right,' she quickly agreed. 'Put that away and I'll go and change now.'

'Not without me you won't,' Charles warned her. 'I need to have a good look at you so as I know which punters might be best pleased with you. I know what they all like, see?'

Swallowing the bile that had risen in her throat, Maddy walked past him with what dignity she could muster. The way she saw it, anything was better than being drugged again.

Once at the bathroom, Charles followed her in, locking the door behind him before telling her, 'Strip off then.'

Maddy blinked to hold back the tears of humiliation that were threatening to fall before slowly doing as she was told. Once she was naked she bowed her head as he looked at her appraisingly.

'Mm. I know a couple of punters who you'll be just right for,' he commented as he handed her a pair of lace knickers with a matching bra. Just as he had said, they fitted her perfectly. She then snatched the jeans and top he handed to her, hastily putting them on. Once she was dressed, he turned her about and after releasing her hair from the tight band that held it, he began to brush it. The feel of his hands made her skin crawl, but she stood perfectly still, not wishing to incur his wrath. The sight of the syringe he had in his pocket was still uppermost in her mind.

At last he was done and he smiled at her approvingly as he snatched up the uniform she had discarded on the floor.

'There now, that's better. Look in the mirror.'

Maddy did so, and gasped at the transformation. A young woman with serious eyes stared back at her and she barely recognised herself.

'It just so happens that I have a punter coming tonight who'll really go for you,' Charles said approvingly.

'B ... but Stacey said I would have some time to settle in,' Maddy objected.

'Normally I would give you a little time, but the

thing is, this is an important client and you're right up his street.' He smiled disarmingly as Maddy tensed at the thought, but she remained silent as Charles unlocked the door.

In seconds they were out in the corridor again and the sound of *The Addams Family* wafted from the television in the Day Room. It was one of the younger children's favourites and they rarely missed it.

Maddy sighed with relief when Charles sashayed away before hurrying back to her room to join Steph, who was now up and about and looking absolutely dreadful. Her huge dark eyes were sunk deep into her face.

'You look nice,' she commented, but Maddy snorted in disgust. The unfamiliar pink lace underwear felt strange and scratchy against her skin, and after being used to the baggy uniform she normally wore, the jeans she was now wearing felt incredibly tight and uncomfortable.

'It's who Charles is making me look nice *for* that's the worry,' she said gloomily as her imagination took hold.

Steph looked at her with sympathy. She wanted to offer words of comfort, but what could she say? 'Well, I suppose the way yer have to look at it is, after havin' Dumbarr's maulers all over yer, nothin' can be as bad.'

Maddy nodded miserably, supposing she was right, and she then settled down to wait for the nightmare to continue.

As soon as the girls and the staff at River House had gone into the dining room for dinner, Mary

Law sneaked upstairs to Maddy's room and hastily opened her drawers. All her clothes were gone and yet Maddy's battered old suitcase was still there under the bed. It just didn't make sense. She chewed on her lip but then, not wishing to be caught, she hurried back downstairs and hovered by the door of the sick room as she waited for the first visitors to arrive.

Some time later they began to stream in and Mary bided her time. Sure enough, Andy Tranter eventually came in bearing a pile of magazines and a bright smile. The smile was instantly wiped from his face when Miss Budd cornered him and dragged him to one side. Mary watched the woman's mouth working and slipped outside to stand in the shelter of the enormous porch.

Soon after, Andy walked out despondently, and as he headed towards his car Mary hissed, 'Excuse me, could I have a word with you, please? Round here.' She beckoned him to follow her and once they were out of sight of the entrance she said, 'I suppose Miss Budd has told you that Maddy has run away again?'

He nodded, his eyes never leaving her face as he realised that something was amiss.

'Do you believe that?' the nurse demanded.

Andy shook his head. 'Not really,' he said. 'The last time I was here, Maddy seemed resigned to waiting until she was eighteen to get away, and it seems strange that she should have had such a sudden change of heart. We'd even discussed her coming to stay with me until she found somewhere of her own. She didn't fancy the thought of Mr Dumbarr finding her somewhere to live so

I agreed that she could come to me and I'd help her find a job.'

'That's exactly what she told me,' Mary agreed. 'Between you and me, I think there's something more going on here than meets the eye.'

'Such as what?' Andy was bemused.

Mary Law took a deep breath, knowing full well that what she was about to divulge might cost her her job. But then she felt that Maddy was worth it and so she continued, 'There are things that go on here that I'm not entirely happy about. Miss Budd and Mr Dumbarr rule this place with a rod of iron. Maddy isn't the first girl to go missing from here, and what's more... She gulped nervously. 'I have a feeling that Dumbarr shows a rather unhealthy interest in certain of the girls.'

'*What?* You mean he interferes with them?' Andy was horrified.

'I have no proof, of course,' Mary hurried on, 'but he's certainly shown a lot of interest in Maddy from time to time. And she's not the only one. The funny thing is, though, that all the girls he's picked on like this have conveniently run away. Don't you find that rather strange?'

'Yes, I must say I do,' Andy answered as he stared off across the grounds. 'But what can we do about it?'

'I've been thinking about that,' Mary told him, 'and I reckon that if either Budd or Dumbarr do know where the girls are, they could lead us to them. They both have a full day off each week and I wondered if we couldn't perhaps follow them and see where they go.'

'That would be difficult with me living so far

327

away,' Andy muttered. 'What days do they usually have off?'

'Budd usually has Wednesday off and Dumbarr Thursday – but this week for some reason they both had Thursday off. And that isn't all. Nick, the young social worker here, told me that Maddy was really upset about something on Wednesday night and then, when I came in on Friday, Budd informed me that she'd run away. I know that I must sound paranoid but Nick feels the same way.'

'I see.' Andy tapped his chin thoughtfully with his forefinger before saying, 'In that case I could get here early next Wednesday and follow Miss Budd when she leaves.'

'You could come the night before and stay at my place if you'd like,' Mary offered, and as a blush rose to her cheeks she hoped that he understood that she just wanted to help Maddy. There was something about Andy that made her feel she could trust him.

'That would make sense,' Andy admitted. 'Thank you. I could be here nice and early then, to make sure I didn't miss her going out.'

Mary hastily took a pen from her pocket and scribbled down her home phone number on it. 'Ring me and I'll give you my address. But I'd better be going in now. If Miss Budd saw us talking she might begin to suspect we were on to something.'

'Well, in all fairness we might be totally barking up the wrong tree,' Andy pointed out, but deep down he didn't think so. Maddy had seemed so focused on her future the last time he had come to see her and there had been no mention of running away.

'Until next week then.' He smiled before turning and heading for his car and, bracing herself, Mary slipped back inside.

It was nine o'clock that night when Belle appeared in the doorway of Maddy's room. 'Come with me,' she said curtly before turning on her heel.

Maddy glanced at Steph apprehensively before following the great Amazon of a woman down the corridor. The sound of *Miami Vice* drifted from the direction of the Day Room and she wished fervently that she could be allowed to go in there and watch it. But she knew there was no chance of that happening. Her evening was mapped out for her and she felt sick inside as she imagined what lay ahead.

At the end of the corridor, Belle led her through the door and on towards the rooms that Charles had referred to as 'the party rooms'. Pausing, she told her brusquely, 'Go in there and wait. Someone will be joining you shortly. And I *strongly* suggest you behave. If you don't, I shall have no choice but to come in and give you something to calm you down.'

Maddy nodded expressionlessly, knowing all too well what that something would be. Belle nudged her none too gently into the room and when the door slammed shut behind her, Maddy stared about. Just like the other room she had woken up in there was nothing in there but a huge bed and a massive mirror on one wall. Knowing now what was behind that mirror, Maddy began to tremble. The next room was obviously already occupied and Maddy could hear noises through the wall. The loud giggling she instantly recognised as Stacey's. The girl seemed to be under the misguided impression that she would one day become a porn star, but Maddy seriously doubted it and wondered what did become of the girls once they became too old for the customers who frequented the place. She supposed that they would be carted off to brothels abroad like the younger children, and the thought struck terror into her soul. At least while she was here she had a chance of escaping and finding Oliver again, and that thought kept her strong. The sound of the door opening made her swing about to see a middle-aged man with a bald head staring at her with a smirk on his face.

'Ah, Belle told me that I was in for a treat and she wasn't wrong,' he said approvingly.

Maddy gritted her teeth. She had always thought of child abusers as dirty old men in macs, but this smartly dressed man could have been anyone's favourite grandad, and she would have passed him on the street without giving him so much as a second glance. It just went to prove how wrong you could be, she thought as he raised his hand and stroked her hair.

Much later that night, Belle escorted her back to her room and Maddy followed like a wounded animal. Her companion had been unnecessarily rough with her and she had been shocked to hear the string of obscenities that had spewed from his mouth. It was as if he had shed all sense of decency with his clothes, and she was sure that she would never feel clean again. But worse was to come when Belle ushered her back into the wing that housed the other youngsters, slamming the door resoundingly behind her. Maddy was limping towards her own room when the sound of someone sobbing broken-heartedly made her pause. Gently inching a door open she peeped around it to see Chloe lying in a heap on her bed, clutching her teddy bear and crying as if her little heart would break.

'Aw, sweetheart, don't cry,' she soothed as she crossed to the little girl and wiped the damp hair from her brow.

'I ... I want my mummy,' Chloe hiccuped as she threw her scrawny arms about Maddy's neck. Maddy's heart melted as she rocked the youngster to and fro.

'We'll find your mummy,' she promised, and slipping into the bed beside the child she held her tight against her.

'The chap *I* were with last night said I could go on to become a big star,' Stacey swooned the next morning as they all sat together in the Day Room.

Maddy rolled her eyes to the ceiling. Stacey was obviously living in cloud cuckoo land but then she supposed if the thought comforted her there was no harm in it.

'They all tell you that,' Steph rejoined sulkily. 'An' if you believe that, you'll believe anything.'

'That's not true!' Stacey strutted up and down

331

the room, her long blonde hair flying out behind her. It had lost some of its sheen now and her eyes looked hollow, no doubt due to the drugs of which she had become so fond.

Jimmy had just gone off with Charles like a lamb to slaughter. The rest of the children seemed resigned to their fate too and it made Maddy's resolve to get away even stronger. She would never accept this way of life and if need be, she would commit murder to escape it.

Chapter Thirty

When Andy arrived at Mary Law's neat semi-detached house early the following Tuesday evening, she greeted him warmly. Andy was surprised to see how different she looked with her hair loose about her shoulders and dressed in jeans and a T-shirt. He had never seen her out of her nurse's uniform before and found himself thinking what an attractive woman she was. He supposed that she was a few years older than him, perhaps somewhere in her late thirties, but she carried her age well.

'Come on in. The dinner is just about ready,' she said, making him feel welcome.

He held out a bottle of wine. 'I ... er ... brought you this,' he told her self-consciously. 'Seeing as you were so kind as to offer to cook dinner, I thought it was the least I could do.'

She took it with a smile. 'The kids are all out

but no doubt you'll meet them when they decide to come back in.' She sighed in mock annoyance. 'It's not easy being a single mum to three teenagers, but they're good kids thankfully.'

'Have you been on your own for long?' Andy asked, feeling as ill at ease as she obviously did.

'Yes, for some time now,' Mary sighed. 'My husband got lured away by a blonde with legs up to her armpits. It didn't last for long, mind you. She soon found herself someone else and then he came crawling back to me with his tail between his legs. Needless to say I showed him the door. You know the saying – once bitten twice shy.'

'Yes, I do,' Andy mumbled, as thoughts of Kirsty crowded into his mind. But he didn't want to talk about that for now, so instead he asked, 'Has there been any news of Maddy?'

'Not a peep.' Mary led him through to a pleasant kitchen where the table was set for two and put the wine down before crossing to the oven. 'It's only chicken casserole, I'm afraid. You do like it, don't you?'

'Love it,' he assured her as he settled into a chair and watched her carry a piping-hot dish to the table. 'Shall I pour the wine?'

'Please.' She ladled a generous portion of casserole onto his plate, together with some roast potatoes and broccoli, and as they ate, slowly they began to relax.

'It's a nice place you have here,' Andy said conversationally as he loaded his fork.

Mary glanced around as if she was looking at her house for the very first time. 'I do my best, though with working full time and having three youngsters to pander to I don't do as much as I'd like to it. How do you cope on your own?'

'All right really,' Andy answered. 'It was tough for a while after Kirsty left. The washing and ironing was the worst. I'd never had to do that before, and I tended to put more creases into the clothes than I ironed out of them, but I'm quite an expert now.'

They both lapsed into a temporary silence as they thought back to the partners who had abandoned them, but then the conversation started up again when Mary told him, 'I made a discovery at work today.'

'Oh yes, and what was that then?'

'I discovered that Nick Preston, who works at River House, has a soft spot for Maddy.'

'Really?' Andy was slightly put out, although he had no idea why he should be. 'But isn't he a little old for her? I mean, Maddy is just a kid.'

'She's nearly eighteen, Andy,' Mary sensibly pointed out. 'And Nick is only about twenty-five, so the age difference between them is nothing really. He didn't exactly *say* that he had feelings for her in so many words, but looking back, I see now that he's always gone out of his way to help her. And Maddy is an attractive young woman, or she would be if she didn't have to wear that damn drab uniform all the time. I've tried to get her interested in make-up and her hair and such, as girls her age normally are, but Maddy just wanted to keep her head down and get out of there. All she seems to live for is finding her younger brother again. That's what makes me believe she wouldn't have run away again. Between you and me, Nick found out some time ago where all her siblings are living for her, and since then she's seemed quite content to let the time pass until she could set off to find them.'

Andy paused with a forkful of food halfway to his mouth to ask, 'Why don't the kids' allocated social workers take more interest in them? Sue Maddox always seemed a good sort.'

'She may well have been, but the problem is, once the girls enter River House, Budd and Dumbarr take over the responsibility for them. Budd, as you know, is the house-mother and Dumbarr is the one who finds the girls homes when they're due to leave, so apart from receiving the odd progress report and doing their statutory visits, their former social workers have very little contact with them, more's the pity. Most of the girls don't leave until they're eighteen and the Social Services are not responsible for them after that anyway.'

Andy took a sip of his wine. 'Seems to me that Maddy's had a hard time of it all along the line,' he said. 'She came to us shortly after her parents' home burned down, when there was still a police investigation going on. Maddy has never denied that she started the fire with the chip pan, but they could never prove that she had started it *deliberately.*'

'It was exactly the same when she ran away and went to live in the squat that burned down,' Mary agreed. 'It was obvious that the police thought she was involved in that too, but there was no evidence so they couldn't bring charges.'

Mary then speared a roast potato and asked

Andy, 'Are you still quite sure that you want to go ahead with following Miss Budd?'

Andy nodded adamantly 'Yes, I am. Of course, I realise that I might be going off on a wild-goose chase, but there's something... I don't know, something that leaves a nasty taste in my mouth about all this and I want to get to the bottom of it.'

'Good, then let's hope that you do.' Mary raised her glass and they drank a toast to Maddy.

The following morning, Andy got into his car and followed Mary, now wearing her uniform again, along the winding road that led to River House. He parked beneath the shelter of some trees and waited.

Shortly after eight o'clock, Miss Budd appeared in her battered old Mini – a far cry from the low-slung sports car that Dumbarr drove – and Andy hastily started the engine and began to follow her at a safe distance.

They drove for miles until eventually they came to Tewkesbury. Once through the town they hit open countryside again and now Andy pulled back for fear of Miss Budd spotting him. There was nothing but open fields and rolling hills on either side of him, and he knew that under other circumstances he would have enjoyed the scenery, but for now he was too intent on staying as close to Miss Budd's car as he dared. Suddenly she pulled off the road and went bumping off down a dirt track. Andy waited for a couple of minutes before following her, and was just in time to see her car disappearing through a massive pair of high iron gates. He thumped the steering wheel with frustration as he realised that he had come as far as he dared. After hastily parking the car, he got out and walked towards the enormous gates, keeping well out of sight of the CCTV camera he had spotted on the wall, but there was nothing to be seen but some turrets and chimneys in the distance above the treetops. The gates were securely locked so he began to walk around the perimeter of the high brick wall with his hands tucked deep in his coat pockets and his breath hanging on the air in front of him like flumes of lace.

Beyond the wall he could hear dogs barking furiously and they sounded big. He had gone no more than a few yards when the undergrowth became thick with thornbushes and brambles, and he was glad he was wearing sturdy denim jeans or he would have been cut to shreds. Retracing his steps, he stood at the gates once more and peered about thoughtfully. As he stood there, two enormous Dobermanns appeared and flung themselves at the gates in an attempt to get at him. Their teeth were bared and Andy stepped back hastily. To the left of him was a hill and now he began to walk towards it with the sounds of the dogs' growls ringing in his ears. The hillside was thickly wooded, so keeping to the shelter of the trees he started to climb. It was a grey overcast day with a hint of snow in the air and bitterly cold, but soon Andy was sweating with exertion as he continued to climb, the muscles in his legs aching with the effort. Beneath the trees it was even gloomier, but he continued without faltering until at last he saw daylight ahead.

Once out on the open hillside he stood for a few seconds to regain his breath and then turning, found himself looking down on an enormous old house. It had a stately look about it and he guessed that someone very rich must have lived there at some point. It was surrounded by grounds, but he could see Miss Budd's Mini parked outside the main entrance. His attention was then drawn to someone at the gates who appeared to be un-locking them, and minutes later he saw a large van go through them. On the side of it was written *Cotton's Caterers.*

Now Andy studied the house more closely. There were lights in the upstairs windows and what looked like a bunch of children congregated in one room, although from this distance he couldn't be sure. Two men had meanwhile got out of the van and were carrying large plastic containers inside. Andy guessed they must be full of food, but what sort of place was this? Could it be that this was yet another home similar to River House? That would certainly account for the children he could see through the upstairs window.

As he sat there, the first flakes of snow began to flutter down and he hastily retreated to the shelter of the trees as he continued to watch the house. His hands and feet were blue with cold now and he wished that he had worn extra clothing, but then he'd had no idea when he set off that he would end up hill-climbing. Suddenly making a decision, he hurriedly started the steep descent back through the woods until he was once again close to the gates of the house. There was no sign of the caterers' van as yet but he reasoned that it would have to come out sooner or later, so he began to saunter along the lane leading away from the place with his hands thrust deep down in his pockets and his coat collar turned up about his ears.

He had walked for about fifteen minutes when he heard the sound of a vehicle behind him and turning, he saw the van heading towards him. He hastily began to wave his hands and as it came abreast of him it drew to a halt.

'All right, mate?' he greeted the driver cheerily as the man wound down the van window. 'I was wondering if you might be able to help me. My car has broken down further along the road and I hoped you might be able to point me in the direction of the nearest garage?'

'Ooh, yer've got miles to go,' the man told him sagely. 'Nearest garage I know of is in Tewkesbury, an' that's a right good walk from here. Shame we can't give you a lift but we're late for our next job, see.'

'Oh, then do you know of any houses around here that might be able to help me?' Andy asked innocently. 'I notice there's a big place back there.' He cocked his thumb in the direction he had just walked from as the man shook his head.

'That's Lakeside Lodge but it's like getting into Fort Knox to try and get in there,' he warned him. 'They keep the gates locked 'cept for when we're due to deliver. I wouldn't recommend you tryin' there even if they were open though. There's a couple of hounds in them there grounds that

339

would rip you to shreds.'

'Really? Well, what sort of a place is it then? Does a pop star or a politician live there or something?'

'I ain't got the foggiest idea,' the man told him. 'But they be one of our best customers so we ask no questions an' we get told no lies. So long as they pay us, we mind our own business.'

'Of course.' Andy could almost taste his disappointment but kept the smile plastered on his face.

'Well, how about if we was to give yer a lift up to the main road?' the man now asked, anxious to be off.

'That's very kind of you, but I'll think of something,' Andy assured him.

'Have it your own way, pal.' The man then wound up the window and roared off, leaving Andy to stand there wondering what he should do next. There certainly seemed no point in loitering about for Miss Budd to reappear. She could be in there all day and he didn't want to run the risk of her seeing him. With his shoulders stooped, he returned to his car and drove away. All he could do now was wait until the next day and see if Mr Dumbarr visited the same place.

'So how did it go then?' Mary Law asked, the second she set foot through her front door that evening. She had given Andy a key and offered to let him stay for another night if necessary. He had accepted her offer gratefully. After all, the way he saw it he had nothing to rush home for as building work was in short supply during the cold snap

340

and his mother was looking after the dogs.

'Not brilliantly,' he confessed. 'Budd went to this great mausoleum of a place the other side of Tewkesbury but the gates were locked and there were two bloody great Dobermanns roaming about in the grounds. I reckon they'd have had my leg off soon as look at me, so I climbed a nearby hill and tried to see what was going on from there.'

'And what *did* you see?'

'Not a lot. I thought there were some children in one of the upstairs rooms but I couldn't be sure because I was so far away. Eventually, I went back down onto the road and waited for a caterers' van I saw going in there to come out. I made out that my car had broken down and asked the driver if I might be able to get help at the big house, but he didn't even know what sort of place it was, so that was a waste of time. It was snowing as well by then so I decided to come back and follow Dumbarr tomorrow to see if he goes to the same place. The van driver told me that it was called Lakeside Lodge.'

'I see.' Mary could not hide her disappointment. 'Well, Budd hadn't come back when I left. And I've never even heard of a place called Lakeside Lodge. Perhaps it's a private residence?'

Andy shrugged. 'Maybe. All we can do is wait until tomorrow and see what that turns up.'

Mary nodded in agreement. 'You're right, and now I'll go and get out of this uniform and do us all some dinner. Make yourself comfortable and I'll be back in a minute.'

Andy picked up the paper and tried to relax, but

341

no matter what he did he could not shift the terrible sense of foreboding that had settled about him like a shroud.

'Come on, Chloe, cheer up,' Maddy encouraged as she cuddled the little girl to her. The child was shaking like a leaf and was clearly traumatised, which was no wonder, considering what she had been subjected to the night before.

She had been taken to a room where two foreign men were waiting for her, and once again the child had been the object of their twisted lust. According to Stacey they were very taken with her because of her blonde hair and tiny stature, and Maddy was terrified that they might take her off with them. It wouldn't be the first time, if what Stacey had told her was true. Fair-skinned children were very popular in the brothels abroad, and once again Maddy's protective instinct was to the fore.

'Look, you wait here and I'll go and get you a drink from the Day Room, shall I?' she offered as she laid Chloe gently down.

Chloe instantly jammed her thumb in her mouth and clutched her teddy to her as she stared at Maddy from her soft green eyes. Maddy hurried from the room and set off along the corridor, only to pause outside Stacey's room. The door was open and she could see the girl leaning towards two straight lines of white powder lying on a piece of silver foil. Even as she watched curiously, Stacey bent to it and expertly snorted one of the lines up her nostril.

'What the hell are you doing?' Maddy stepped

into the room and stared at her appalled as Stacey wiped the palm of her hand across the bottom of her nose.

'Going to heaven. Would you care to join me? There's plenty more where this came from.'

There was a faraway look in her eyes and Maddy shook her head as she backed towards the door. There was no way she was going to get hooked on drugs. She had the most awful feeling that if she did, she would never get out of this place except in a wooden box.

'No, I'm fine as I am, thanks,' she mumbled as she beat a hasty retreat. Her hair was once more scraped back into a tight ponytail although she could do nothing about the new clothes she wore that showed off her trim figure.

Belle was in the Day Room talking to Jimmy when she entered, and clucked disapprovingly at the sight of her.

'Really, Maddy. Your hair does nothing at all for you, worn like that. Don't you want to look your best?'

'Not particularly.' Maddy shot her a withering look before picking up a soft drink for Chloe and turning on her heel. She was all too aware that she had no choice but to do as she was told while she was here, but she certainly didn't intend to let them think that she was happy about it.

As she left the room, Belle stroked her double chin thoughtfully. There was something about Maddy that made her feel uneasy. The girl had spirit, she was forced to admit, and that could be dangerous. Thank God, this place was as secure as a prison.

Feeling slightly better, Belle turned her attention back to Jimmy and tried to forget all about the girl for now.

Chapter Thirty-One

Tucked up warm and cosy on Mary's comfortable sofa bed in the lounge, Andy stared at the flickering patterns on the ceiling. Despite being worried sick about Maddy he had found that it was quite pleasant to have female company again.

Mary was remarkably easy to get on with and her children were friendly too. They had all made him feel at home and he thought that Mary had done a remarkable job with them. He knew that it must be hard, being a single parent to three boisterous youngsters, but she had somehow managed it as well as holding down a full-time job. Being with Mary's brood had also made Andy realise what he had missed, and the pain went deep. Kirsty had always longed for a child of their own and looking back now, he knew that she had felt inadequate because she was unable to give him a child. He sighed into the darkness, well aware that it was no use spending any more time yearning for what might have been. Kirsty was in his past now and it was time to move on. He had licked his wounds for long enough.

Earlier in the evening, when the children had retired to bed, he and Mary had sat together enjoying a glass of wine and chatting. Without saying a word Mary had conveyed to him that she found him attractive and at one point he had been tempted to kiss her. And yet he had been unable to bring himself to do it, which was strange because Mary was a very attractive woman. Perhaps I'm not as over Kirsty as I thought, he pondered, and then his thoughts slipped back to Maddy. He wondered where she was and if she was all right. He had grown very fond of her over the years and just wanted things to work out for her. God knew, she'd had a hard enough time of it in her short life.

Turning on his side, Andy burrowed down into the bed. All he could do now was try to get some sleep and wait to see what tomorrow would bring.

In her bedroom, Mary was also having trouble getting off to sleep. She'd had strong suspicions for some time that Dumbarr was taking advantage of the girls at the home, but there was more to it than that. She had concerns about Miss Budd too. Ever since the day Mary had gone for an interview at River House for a job, she had found something about Miss Budd puzzling, although for the life of her she couldn't put her finger on quite what it was. The woman would never win a beauty competition that was for sure. Her complexion was quite ruddy, so much so that on certain days she broke out in a rash and that teamed with her thick neck and large hands did not make for a pretty picture. But then Mary supposed that Miss Budd couldn't help the way she looked. She just wished that the woman could have shown a little more compassion to the girls in her care. Instead she seemed to find some perverse pleasure in locking them away in the Quiet Room. Sighing, she pulled the blanket over her head and told herself to switch off from it all but it proved to be a lot easier said than done. Maddy was out there somewhere and until Andy discovered what had become of the poor girl, Mary felt powerless to help her.

That evening, Belle collected Maddy from her room and she was once again led to one of the party rooms. She went without a fight, but inside she was rebelling and wondering how much longer she could bear it. She was still sore and bruised from the night before, but Belle paid no heed to that.

A dark-haired man who barely reached to her shoulder was waiting for her with a large glass of whisky in his hand and he eyed her appreciatively as Belle pushed her none too gently into the room. He was as far round as he was high, and Maddy shuddered with revulsion as she thought of what was ahead.

'Come in,' he invited as Belle discreetly slipped away, securely locking the door behind her. 'Here, drink this – it will help you to relax.'

Maddy took the glass he offered. The way she felt, anything that took the edge off would be welcome. She gulped at the amber liquid and then gagged as it hit the back of her throat and burned its way down into her stomach.

The man, who was very well-spoken, laughed as he loosened his tie and within minutes stood in front of her completely naked.

'Now it's *your* turn,' he said lecherously, and

346

suddenly she knew that she couldn't bear it, even if it meant being injected with drugs again.

'I don't want to get undressed,' she spat as she glared at him. Her defiance only seemed to excite him all the more, and gripping the neck of her T-shirt, he suddenly yanked it with such force that it tore to the waist and Maddy put her hands up to cover her breasts.

'*Leave me alone.*' She began to struggle but her strength was no match for his, and within minutes he had stripped her down to the lacy knickers and bra that she wore beneath her clothes.

'Stop – *please.*' She was really frightened now but he seemed oblivious to the fact. Seconds later, the bra had joined the rest of her clothes on the floor where he had tossed them, and now all she wore was her knickers. It was then that she lunged at him in desperation and, taken unawares, he toppled backwards, landing in an undignified heap.

'Why, you little bitch, you!' he roared as he jumped up and grabbed her. 'I'll make you sorry for that.'

Maddy looked about the room, searching frantically for something that she could use as a weapon, and spotting his smart black leather briefcase, she bent down and swung it at him as hard as she could. He howled with pain as it caught him full in the face and then burst open, scattering official-looking papers everywhere.

Maddy was genuinely terrified now, but she had come this far and there was no going back. She leaped towards him and he howled again as her nails raked down the skin of his cheeks. Blood began to pour from the wounds and he was shouting loudly enough to waken the dead. It was then that the door was unlocked and Belle appeared with an outraged look on her overly made-up face.

'What the hell is going on in here?' she demanded, and then seemed to puff up to twice her size as she rounded furiously on Maddy.

'I'm so sorry. I really can't apologise enough,' she gushed as she looked back at the man, who was clutching his face.

'Get her out of my sight,' he ground out, and Belle caught Maddy's arm in a painful grip as she dragged her from the room, telling him, 'I shall be right back to see to your face.'

All the way along the corridor she shook Maddy as a dog might shake a rat until the girl's teeth rattled in her head.

'Believe me, young lady, you're going to be *very* sorry for this,' she warned in a dangerously low voice. 'Mr Frost is one of our best customers, and you've just made a very grave mistake – as you'll soon find out.'

When they reached Maddy's room, she flung her inside as if she was so much rubbish and Maddy landed painfully against the bed. Pain ripped up her leg but Maddy glared back at the woman without an ounce of remorse.

'I'm not sorry for what I did,' she ranted breathlessly. 'And I'll do it again and again if you try to force me, do you hear me?'

'Oh, I hear you all right.' Belle's eyes were as cold as ice. 'And you'll hear *me* in a minute – and you might not like what I have to say. Now stay there!' The door was slammed so loudly behind her that it danced on its hinges as Maddy buried her face in her hands and began to cry, and all the while inside she was asking, *Andy, where are you?*

If Belle had expected to find Maddy in a quivering heap when she returned to the room with Charles ten minutes later, she was sadly disappointed. Maddy had thrown some clothes on and was facing the door with her head held high.

'Get out!' Her voice cracked across the room like a whip.

Charles chuckled evilly. The girl had guts, there was no doubt about it.

'I'd love to,' he told her with a smirk. 'But your customer is still waiting for you, and if you won't go willingly we shall have to help you on your way, won't we?'

Maddy paled as she saw the needle in his hand. She knew what was coming. She also knew that there was little she could do about it except put up a good fight – and that's exactly what she did, until Belle caught her to her ample chest in a bear hug. Charles slid the needle into the vein in her arm and almost instantly Maddy became calmer as lethargy crept through her.

'That's better.' Charles sighed with satisfaction as he watched her droop in Belle's arms. 'Now I think you're ready to go back to Mr Frost. And this time, you might be a little more amenable.'

One on either side of her they dragged her back to the despicable dark-haired man who now had a large plaster spread across his cheek.

He advanced on her with a cruel glint in his

eye, but Maddy didn't care any more. The drug was taking hold of her now and she knew that she would be putty in his hands.

Hours later, she woke in her own room to find little Chloe anxiously hovering over her.

'Maddy, wake up,' she whimpered fearfully. 'Are you all right?'

The first time Maddy tried to answer her, her tongue cleaved to the roof of her mouth, but the second time she managed to mutter, 'I'm fine, sweetie.'

Relief flitted across the little girl's face as she scrambled onto the bed at the side of her and snuggled against her.

'Th ... they hurt me again, Maddy.'

Maddy swallowed before answering, 'Never mind. It won't be for much longer now. I'm going to get you out of here – I promise.'

'Will I be able to go back to my mummy and daddy?'

'Of course you will. And no one will ever take you away from them again. Think how lovely that will be.' Maddy blinked back tears and prayed as she had never prayed before that somehow she would be able to make her promise become a reality. Her lip was split and one eye was almost closed from the beating that Mr Frost had given her, but all that meant nothing compared to what the little girl at her side was going through.

As they lay there with their arms entwined, the sound of Belle and Charles floated to her from the other side of the door, and Maddy strained to hear what they were saying.

'They've offered five figures for her. They reckon

she'll be in great demand in the nonce houses over there.' This was Belle's voice.

'I dare say she will. They like them little and blonde, and those lovely green eyes could charm the ducks off the water,' Charles hissed. 'But it isn't down to us, is it? We'll have to see what the gaffer thinks of the offer when he comes in tomorrow, won't we?'

Maddy's stomach flipped. They were talking about Chloe, she just knew it. Thankfully the little girl had dropped off to sleep and so she had no idea of the fate awaiting her. Maddy's brain began to work overtime and as she lay there, an idea began to form in her mind.

Dumbarr was due to come tomorrow. And she knew exactly what time the caterers arrived each day. Could she somehow persuade him to let her go downstairs for a time? The dogs were locked up while the caterers delivered the food, and if she could only sneak out of the house and into the back of their van she could perhaps get out that way.

It seemed a flimsy hope, but what alternative was there? Just the thought of going anywhere near that despicable man made her break out in goose bumps, but Chloe was at serious risk of being shipped abroad now and Maddy couldn't bear that. She also feared for the other inmates at River House, some of whom Dunbarr could be grooming for this even now. There were always about thirty girls for him to choose from so no doubt he would have his eye on at least one of them. She lay there with her arms tight about the child until the first cold fingers of dawn streaked the sky, when at last she slipped into an uneasy doze.

The following morning, Andy once more positioned himself outside River House and waited for Dumbarr's shiny sports car to appear. At last, George opened the gates and the car shot through. The snow had formed a thick carpet across the roads now and thankfully that slowed him down and enabled Andy to follow him at a safe distance. They had only gone a few miles before Andy realised that they were following exactly the same route as Budd had taken the day before and he guessed that Dumbarr was heading for the same place. By the time they had driven through Tewkesbury he was sure of it, and soon afterwards he pulled his car into the same copse of trees where he had hidden it the day before.

He watched Dumbarr's car disappear through the gates and then began the long ascent up the hill, clutching a pair of binoculars he had borrowed from Mary, carefully avoiding the camera as he went. There was nothing else he could do for now.

'I hear you were a naughty girl last night.' Dumbarr addressed Maddy as if she were a small child. He expected her to retaliate with some cutting remark as she normally did, but to his surprise she smiled at him sweetly. Her eye was swollen and almost closed today, and she looked bruised and battered, but she had loosened her hair and brushed it until it shone, which made her look strangely vulnerable.

'I'm sorry, Mr Dumbarr,' she said meekly as she lowered her eyes and looked contrite. 'I didn't mean to be unfriendly, it's just that ... well, after the lovely time we used to have together at River House I just didn't want another man near me. You were ... *special,* you see.'

'*Really?*' His eyebrows almost met in the middle with shock and his voice instantly took on a gentler tone as he told her, 'I'm surprised to hear that, Maddy. You certainly never *seemed* to be enjoying the times we spent together.'

'I suppose sometimes you don't know what you've got till it's gone,' she answered in a little girl's voice that made sweat break out on his lecherous brow. 'I just wish I could have another chance.'

'Perhaps you can.' Tugging at the tight collar of his shirt he looked at the firm little cleavage peeping out of her cotton top. 'How's about I take you into one of the party rooms? It's more private there and we could have a little ... *fun.*'

Maddy's heart began to thud painfully as hope rose in her. But it was too early yet. The caterers weren't due to arrive for another hour and the dogs would still be roaming the grounds. There was no chance of her escaping while they were out there.

'I'd rather come downstairs into your office,' she answered coyly. 'After last night I'm not too keen on going back into the party rooms just yet. I wouldn't be able to relax, but if we were downstairs ... well, I think it would be lovely – and would you mind very much if I had a soak in the bath first? I'm feeling quite sore and...' As she raised her hand to her bruised eye, he smiled at her sympathetically.

'Of course you may,' he purred. 'And if you would feel more comfortable in my office, that's fine too. What time would you like me to come and fetch you?' He might have been speaking to a lover and Maddy felt nauseated.

She fluttered her eyelashes becomingly. 'Shall we say in an hour? I want to make myself look nice for you.'

He nodded eagerly as his hand slipped to the unsightly bulge in his trousers.

'An hour it is then, my dear. I shall look forward to it.'

She flashed him another sweet smile as he turned on his heel and strutted from the room like a peacock, but once he was gone, panic gripped her. What if it all went wrong and she didn't manage to get away? She would have put herself all through this charade for nothing. Common sense quickly took over. This was about the only option she had, so there was no point in ducking out now. Chloe's future – and that of all the other children here – depended on it.

After waiting for a few moments she strode from the room, but instead of going to the bathroom, she headed for the Day Room. If this was going to work she would have to go prepared.

The older kids were lounging about watching the television, and the younger ones were amusing themselves with the toys that were scattered about, but Maddy hardly noticed them as she glanced around the room. Almost instantly her eyes settled on just the thing she needed, and crossing to the table she slipped it into the pocket of her jeans before hastily retreating back to her bedroom again. All she could do now was wait and pray that her plan would work. She was only too aware of what was in store for her if it didn't, and it would be God help her, because she knew that no one else would.

Chapter Thirty-Two

From his vantage point amongst the trees on the hillside, Andy gazed through his binoculars at Lakeside Lodge. His feet were frozen and he stamped them to try and get some feeling back into them as he rubbed his hands together. The landscape spread out before him had taken on a magical quality beneath its blanket of snow and the big mansion looked like a picture off a chocolate box. But he had an awful feeling that it was housing something sinister and was determined to find out what it was.

After a time he saw a man appear from the front door, and seconds later he saw him lead the dogs away around the side of the building. He then got into a car and drove up to the gates. Andy watched him get out of the car and unlock the gates before driving back to the house. And now in the distance he saw the caterers' van approaching along the snow-covered lane. He began to skirt around the hillside, looking for a gap in the wall or some way he could gain entry to the grounds other than going through the gates, and after a while he was rewarded when he saw that a small section of the wall had fallen away. Keeping to the shelter of the trees, Andy began to slither down the steep hillside towards Lakeside Lodge.

Maddy wiped her sweating palms down the side of her jeans as she heard footsteps approaching her room. Seconds later, the door swung open and Dumbarr grinned at her.

'Are you ready, my dear?' he gloated.

Forcing a smile to her face, she rose from the side of her bed and followed him meekly from her room, keeping close to his heels as they made for the door at the end of the corridor that led to the stairs.

As they descended the sweeping staircase he patted her buttock and Maddy had to force herself not to panic. She was determined to go through with her plan. Would allow nothing to get in her way.

Once downstairs, Dumbarr nodded at George who was helping the caterers to carry in the great containers full of food and then he led Maddy to a small room at the side of the front doors.

It was a very comfortable room that scarcely resembled an office. A large gilt-legged settee covered in a luxurious claret-coloured velvet took up the space in the deep bay window, and her feet sank into the deep-pile fitted carpet. There were also two wing chairs and a small desk on the opposite wall, and it was to the desk that Dumbarr headed now. He stood for a few moments studying some papers on it as if he had forgotten

Maddy's presence, before turning and crossing to the drinks table.

'How about a drop of Scotch, my dear?' He poured some whisky into two glasses and pressed one into her hand.

Maddy nodded mutely, praying that her courage would not desert her. She sipped at the drink, welcoming the warmth as it slid down her throat, but was careful not to swallow too much. It was imperative now that she keep a clear mind.

Dumbarr had made himself comfortable on the settee. He patted the seat at the side of him. 'Why don't you come and join me?'

Maddy forced herself to move forward, while her hand slid secretly to the pocket of her jeans. After placing the drink down, she perched at the side of him and within seconds his hands were all over her like a rash, just as she had envisaged.

The surge of pure rage that rampaged through her enabled her to carry out her plan. Quick as a flash, she removed the sharp-nibbed fountain pen that she had hidden in her pocket, and slamming her arm down with every ounce of strength she possessed, she buried the nib in his neck. So shocked was the man that he didn't even whimper. Taking full advantage of the situation, Maddy now snatched up one of the heavy decanters from the side table, and brought it crashing forward onto his forehead. Stunned, Dumbarr slithered from the settee to land like a beached whale at her feet. With no idea how long he might be incapacitated for, Maddy wasted not a single second but sprinted towards the door as if Old Nick himself was at her heels. Once there, she inched it open cautiously, just in time to see the caterers disappearing through the green baize door that led into the kitchen. Hardly daring to believe her luck, she fled for the front door, not stopping to look back as the cold air slapped her in the face. And then she was racing down the drive with her breath hissing out in front of her. As she ran, it occurred to her that if anyone should try to catch her, she would be clearly visible, so now she headed for the shelter of the trees on either side of the drive, although her steps did not slow.

It was bitterly cold, but she barely noticed. And then she heard a commotion somewhere behind her and knew that her attempt to escape had been discovered. Panicking now, she headed further into the trees, expecting to feel a hand clamp down on her shoulder at any second. She ran blindly, with no idea any more of which direction she was going in; she only knew that she mustn't stop. And then suddenly a sound brought her to a shuddering halt. Someone was calling her name and it sounded like Andy's voice. She shook her head, thinking that she must be imagining things, until the sound came again and this time it was closer.

'Andy – is that you?'

'Yes, I'm over here and hurry! We don't have a moment to lose. They're letting the dogs out.'

Stumbling, she headed in the direction the voice had come from and then suddenly, miraculously, there he was, beckoning to her urgently. 'This way – quick. *Now!*'

She broke into a run again as the faraway sound of the dogs barking reached them. Andy grasped her hand and began to haul her back through the trees in the direction he had come from, and with every step they took, the dogs drew closer. Maddy's ribs were hurting, but Andy's hold on her hand was relentless.

'You can't stop,' he panted raggedly. 'We're almost there now. Come on, Maddy, you can do it.'

The hairs on the back of her neck stood to attention as they pressed on, and the sound of the dogs' furious barking grew ever closer.

'I ... I can't go any further,' she sobbed with frustration. Her lungs felt as if they were about to burst, but Andy showed her no sympathy.

'Look, over there through the gap in the trees.'

She glanced ahead and sure enough, there was the wall that surrounded the house and part of it had fallen away. It was still about five foot high, but she knew that if they could only reach it, she would be able to scramble up and over it and then she would be free. *Free!* The word echoed round and round in her head, lending extra speed to her legs. And then they had reached it and Andy cupped his hands and told her, 'Put your foot in there and jump.'

'Andy!' As she bent to do as she was told, she saw the two enormous dogs emerge from the trees just yards away from them and terror coursed through her. They were barking and drooling as they bore down on them with their jaws snapping in anticipation.

'Don't look!' he shouted as he hoisted her up, and then she had the sensation of flying as he literally threw her across the wall. She landed in a heap on the other side, but thankfully the thick blanket

of snow broke her fall and for a moment she lay there winded. The sound of the dogs' howling was overwhelming now and she wondered fearfully if they had Andy fast in their jaws. And then suddenly there he was, and as she watched he hauled himself over the top of the wall and landed awkwardly at the side of her. She saw immediately that one of his trouser legs was torn and blood was pouring out of a long gash on his shin.

'*You're hurt!*' she gasped.

'It's nothing,' he snapped, waving her away as she tried to help him. 'Now come on, we don't have a moment to lose.'

The barking was deafening now and Andy slung an arm about Maddy's neck. He was limping badly but he merely gritted his teeth and hissed, 'My car's round at the front by the gates. If we can just get to it without them catching us we'll be home and dry.'

Maddy's fighting spirit was to the fore again now. They had come this far and she had no intention of being dragged back, so she gamely hurried on as best she could, with Andy hanging heavily on to her.

Once they came to the corner that led to the small copse by the gates, Andy held her back.

'I think we're clear. Come on, let's go for it. It might be our only chance.' The blood that was gushing from his leg was leaving a crimson trail in the snow and Maddy knew now that their only chance of escape lay in reaching the car.

They were almost there when an enraged voice shouted, '*Hoi there!*'

Not stopping to look back, they broke into a

360

run and soon Andy was fumbling with his car keys. Behind them they could hear the creak of someone opening the enormous gates again and then the hysterical baying of the dogs once more. Someone had set them loose outside and as she peeped over her shoulder, Maddy saw them racing towards them again.

'Andy, *hurry!*' she screamed, and suddenly she saw his door swing open and he fell into the car, leaning over to open her door for her. She leaped inside – and as she pulled the door shut, one of the Dobermanns slammed against it.

She shouted out with fright as Andy inserted the key into the ignition and then the engine roared into life – and Maddy was sure that it was the most wonderful sound she had ever heard.

He reversed erratically, narrowly missing the two dogs who were now throwing themselves at the car. People were running towards them, waving their arms and shouting, but Andy ignored them as he pressed his foot down hard on the accelerator. And then the car surged forward, its wheels slipping and skidding in the snow, and unbelievably the noise of their pursuers faded and they were on the lane that would lead them away from this terrible place.

Andy was ghastly pale and leaning heavily over the steering wheel as Maddy began to sob with relief.

'H … how did you manage to find me?' she choked out.

'I followed Budd and Dumbarr here two days on the trot. Mary Law told me when I came to visit you that Budd had given her some story that you'd run away again, but I wasn't swallowing that and neither was Mary, so we decided to follow them and try to find out what was going on. I was up on the hillside today when I saw you suddenly come haring out of the door – and the rest you know. Thank God I'd spotted the break in the wall from the hill, otherwise it might have been a very different story. But just what sort of a place is that, for Christ's sake?'

'They call it a nonce house,' Maddy said, shuddering. And then, pulling herself together, it all began to tumble out of her as Andy listened in horror.

'We have to get Chloe out of there,' she said finally, with a note of desperation in her voice. 'They're going to send her abroad and I can't bear it.'

'You won't have to bear it, sweetheart – we're going to get them *all* out,' Andy promised with a steely determination, and exhausted, Maddy sagged back against her seat. She felt as if a great weight had been lifted from her shoulders. All her life she had played the little mother. First to her siblings at home, and then to Oliver. In River House she had cared for Holly, and then Kat and Chloe, and now finally someone was caring about *her* and it felt wonderful.

Despite the pain he was in, Andy put his foot down. He had read about such places as Lakeside Lodge in the newspapers, but had never, in his wildest dreams, expected to become involved in one at such close quarters. The thought of what the youngsters who were incarcerated there had been subjected to made him want to vomit, and he knew that if he were to be confronted with Dumbarr or Budd at that moment, he could willingly have strangled them both with his bare hands. As far as he was concerned, such people should not be allowed to live.

Turning to look at him, Maddy was desperately worried. 'Are you all right?' The floor of the car beneath his seat was awash with blood now and his skin had taken on a deathly pallor. 'Shouldn't we stop and try to stem that bleeding?' she asked fearfully.

'No.' Andy shook his head. 'Not till we've sorted out those bastards back there. I'm going into Tewkesbury to the nearest police station, and once they know what's happening we'll worry about this.'

His eyes kept darting to the mirror and his heart was in his mouth. He knew that if they followed him, he would be too weak from loss of blood to fight them now – not that he wouldn't try. But thankfully as the miles sped by, the road behind him stayed clear. At last Tewkesbury loomed out of the snow that was now falling fast again, and Andy drove on, determined to help the children they had left behind.

Minutes later, he screeched to a halt outside the police station, telling Maddy, 'Get in there and tell them we need help. I'll wait here and lead them back to the house.'

Maddy lurched from the car and tumbled up the steps to the door that led into the police station. Her teeth were chattering with fear and cold, but she ran to the desk and began to babble at the desk sergeant whose head snapped up in surprise at her entrance. One side of her jeans was drenched with Andy's blood and her hair was dishevelled. This, added to the wild look in her eyes, made him fear that a madwoman had entered.

'Slow down, love,' he said kindly, lifting the counter and coming to join her. 'Now start again. *Slowly* this time, eh?'

Maddy took a deep breath as she tried to compose herself, waving her hand towards Andy waiting outside. 'You've got to help them. The children ... at Lakeside Lodge...'

As her story unfolded, the elderly sergeant's face stretched so wide it banished every wrinkle. Eventually he hurried back to the other side of the desk and lifted the phone, and the next minute, policemen seemed to materialise from everywhere.

A man in a plain suit appeared from the back of the counter and after a hasty conversation with the desk sergeant he told the men assembled there, 'Follow the chap outside. I'm going to radio for more back-up. Now get to it.'

Maddy almost sobbed with relief. She had been afraid that no one would believe her, but now at last there was hope on the horizon for the unfortunates back at the lodge.

Racing back outside, she jumped into the passenger seat as she told Andy, 'They're going to follow us. But are you up to driving all that way again?'

He nodded as he started the car and pulled it away from the kerb, and then they were on their way again with a trail of police cars following closely behind with their lights flashing. The journey seemed to take an eternity and every inch of the way, Maddy prayed as she had never prayed before that they wouldn't be too late. And then at last the gates of the house loomed up out of the fast-falling snow, and Maddy offered up a silent prayer of thanks that they were still open. Andy pulled into the side of the road and collapsed unconscious across the steering wheel as the police cars shot past and down the drive leading to the house. Would the nightmare now finally be over, Maddy asked herself as she clung to Andy's hand. All they could do was wait.

Chapter Thirty-Three

'So how are you feeling today?'

'I'm fine,' Maddy told the inspector as she leaned back against the hospital pillows. 'But how is Chloe?'

'Doing very well. Her parents are with her even as we speak and they said they don't know how they will ever be able to repay you. They had given up hope of finding their lass alive. What you did was very brave indeed.'

Maddy flushed at the unaccustomed praise. 'And what about Andy?'

'He's fine too. In fact, he'll be in to see you in a while. His leg has been stitched and of course, he lost a tremendous amount of blood, but after the past couple of days' rest he should be OK now. Thankfully the wound wasn't as bad as it appeared at first. All the children from Lakeside Lodge are here under observation whilst the social workers try to locate their families. Thanks to you, they all have a future ahead of them now.' The man shuddered as he thought of the den of vice that had been uncovered. It was hard to believe that such a place had been operating – and right under his nose too. It just went to show how clever the owners of the place had been. They had covered their tracks well – and had it not been for Maddy, the children's torment could have gone on indefinitely.

Her face solemn now, she asked, 'And Miss Budd and Mr Dumbarr?'

He blew his cheeks out. 'Don't you mean *Mr* Budd? You don't need to worry about them any more. They're locked away where they belong and I think I can safely say it will be a very long time before they walk free again. I don't mind telling you though, we were only in the nick of time when we got to the house. A few more minutes and the children would all have been whisked away. The creature called Belle and our friend Dumbarr had locked the caterers in a store room and loaded the youngsters into their van. God alone knows where they might have taken them if we hadn't got there when we did. It just doesn't bear thinking about.' The policeman blew his nose, feeling very emotional.

'Your social worker, Sue Maddox, will be here to see you later today he went on, 'and she should be able to tell you what's going to happen next. From my point of view, I can only think that anywhere you go now will be better than where

366

you've been. You're quite a hero if you did but know it, young Maddy.'

He rose now and smiling at her, he said, 'I have to say you've got some pluck for a little 'un. But I ought to get on now. My officers are interviewing the older kids and no doubt they'll be here to take your statement soon. Don't get worrying about it though. Just tell the truth and then you can start to put it all behind you. Goodbye, my dear.'

Maddy nodded at him as he left the room and then settled down to wait for the officers who were coming to interview her, and also for Sue Maddox. While she lay there, two unexpected visitors arrived and Maddy stared at them bewildered as they stood hesitantly in the door of her room.

'Are you Maddy?' the man asked.

'Yes, I am.' She liked him instantly. He was very tall with fair hair and kindly blue eyes.

Smiling now, the couple entered the room.

'We've come to thank you,' the man told her. 'We are Chloe's mum and dad, and if it wasn't for you we might never have seen our little girl again.'

The woman at his side nodded her agreement, the strain of the last few months showing clearly on her face. 'Chloe only went out to play with her little friend two doors away,' she confided with a tremor in her voice. 'And she never came back. You wouldn't believe the hell we've been through. It was as if she had vanished off the face of the earth and we'd almost given up hope of ever seeing her again. But thanks to you, we've got her back. Of course, after what she's been through, she's going to need a lot of counselling. I doubt she'll ever really get completely over it, but at least she's still alive and we have *you* to thank for that.'

'It's all right,' Maddy mumbled, deeply embarrassed. And then before she knew what was happening, the woman had crossed to her and wrapped her in a warm embrace. Maddy was so unused to shows of affection that she had no idea how to respond to it, so she just lay there like a statue.

'God bless you, and may you never know anything but happiness from this day on,' the woman whispered in her ear, and then with a final smile the couple turned and left the room, leaving Maddy with a warm glow in her stomach.

Soon afterwards, she fell into a doze and when she awoke she found Sue Maddox sitting at her side.

'Hello, Maddy. How are you feeling, love?' The guilt she felt for ever having placed Maddy in River House was writ large on her face.

'I'm fine,' Maddy assured her. The bruise around her eye was fading to yellow and purple now and her split lip was slowly healing, but other than that she had no visible physical injuries. Maddy's scars were all buried deep inside.

'What's going to happen to me now?' she asked.

'Well, we've called a big case conference for tomorrow so we should know more then. But hopefully if you have somewhere to go, you'll be released from hospital and become responsible for yourself from now on,' Sue told her. 'Let's face it, you are almost eighteen and you couldn't make any bigger a mess of your life than we have.'

'You weren't to know what sort of place River House was,' Maddy replied generously.

'No, I wasn't. But why didn't you ever tell me what was going on there, Maddy?'

'As Budd and Dumbarr drummed into us, who would have taken our word against theirs? And besides, I think we were all too afraid to speak up. We knew what would happen to us if we did.' An involuntary tremor ran through her as she thought back to the Quiet Room and felt Dumbarr's hands crawling all over her again.

'Well, at least it's over now,' Sue comforted. 'And soon you'll be free to go and be your own person. I've just spoken to Andy and he's offered to take you back to Plymouth with him until you get on your feet. How would you feel about that?'

'I'd love it,' Maddy replied without hesitation.

Sue nodded. 'In that case I shall tell them that at the meeting tomorrow and let's hope a decision will be made. But now I'm going to shoot off. I have piles of reports to get done before tomorrow. I just needed to come and see that you were all right.'

Maddy smiled. A real smile that made her bruised face light up the room. This time tomorrow she might be free. It was a heartening thought.

The rest of the day passed quickly. Police officers came and went and interviewed her until her head was spinning, but at last they were done. It was then that Nick Preston appeared with the most enormous bunch of flowers she had ever seen.

'Hello, Maddy. I ... er ... brought you these.

How are you feeling?'

'Fine,' she told him as a blush rose to her cheeks. No one had ever brought her flowers before – or looked at her as Nick was looking at her now, for that matter.

He placed them on the bedside table, saying, 'Sue Maddox tells me that you might be free to go tomorrow?'

'Yes.'

'I was wondering, would you mind very much if I kept in touch?'

Maddy shook her head, basking in the attention.

'Right, then, I'll get off now. But if you should need me, this is my home phone number. And don't get worrying about your sister's and brothers' addresses you left behind at River House. I can get them all again for you when you're ready.'

'You won't need to,' Maddy answered with a twinkle in her eye. 'I know them all off by heart.'

He grinned. 'In that case, get a good rest and I'll see you soon.'

Maddy sighed happily after he had gone. It seemed that for the first time in her whole life she was someone who mattered.

Andy was the final visitor of the day. He limped in bearing two enormous bags full of clothes that he had been out and bought for her.

'I had to guess at your size,' he said apologetically, 'but I hope they'll do you for now until I can take you shopping for some more.'

'Thanks.' Maddy beamed at him. 'Sue Maddox told me that I might be out of care tomorrow.'

He nodded. 'If all goes to plan, and I don't see why it shouldn't. You'll start to feel better once we get home and back to some sort of normality.'

Maddy wondered what normality was now, but didn't say so. 'Are you quite sure that you won't mind me living with you for a while?' she asked falteringly.

Andy laughed. 'Mind? I'll be glad of the company, to tell you the truth. It's been a bit lonely since Kirsty ... well, you know.'

'Actually, I don't know. You never told me why she went.'

For a moment it appeared that he was going to clam up but then with a shrug he told her, 'There's no reason why you shouldn't know, I suppose. You'll probably hear it from the neighbours once we get home anyway. The thing is, I was at work but the weather was diabolical so the lads and I decided to call it a day and go home early. It isn't easy laying bricks in a monsoon. When I got back there was no sign of Kirsty, so I decided I'd go up and have a bath and get changed. I was soaked through to the skin and thought she'd probably popped out to the shops. But when I walked into the bedroom she was there ... with my dad, in bed.'

Maddy's eyes almost started from her head. She had never felt easy around Andy's father but would not have thought him capable of doing this.

The young man spread his hands helplessly as the painful memories poured back. 'Of course, there was an almighty row and Kirsty admitted then that they'd been having an affair for some time. My mum was absolutely devastated when she found out and chucked Dad out on his ear, and the long and the short of it is, Kirsty chose to go with him. We haven't seen hide nor hair of them since, although I have heard from a solicitor. Kirsty has started divorce proceedings and it's all going through now. There seemed no reason to delay it. So there you have it.'

'Oh, Andy. How awful for you.' Maddy's eyes were brimming with tears. She could only begin to imagine how hard it must have been for him. It was bad enough that his wife chose to have an affair, but to have one with his own *father*... Kirsty had well and truly divided the whole family.

'The way I look at it, I have to put it behind me,' he commented optimistically. 'The same as you have to put all you've been through behind you. We've got a lot of living left to do and it's no good dwelling in the past.'

Even as he said it he wondered if Maddy would ever be able to move on after all she had suffered. The poor kid had become institutionalised and he knew that it wasn't going to be easy for her when she was back out in the big wide world. But that's where he could help. He wanted to offer her somewhere to live and a shoulder to cry on when she needed it – if Social Services would allow him to, that was. He was a single carer now that Kirsty had gone, and he was afraid that the Department might frown upon a young woman being placed with him. And with a little shock he realised that this was exactly what Maddy was now. She had grown up before his very eyes and he hadn't even noticed it. Time would tell though. By tomorrow afternoon they should have a decision, and if it went in their favour he could take Maddy home with him.

As he suddenly raised his hand to stifle a yawn, Maddy felt guilty. He looked absolutely dead on his feet, which was no surprise really, after what they had gone through.

'Why don't you get yourself off to bed?' she suggested. 'You look all in. Where are you staying tonight?'

'At Mary Law's. She sends her love and best wishes, by the way.'

'Oh.' Maddy suddenly realised that now River House had been temporarily closed down, Mary would be out of a job. 'How will she manage now?' she asked worriedly.

Andy shrugged. 'I doubt a good nurse like Mary will be unemployed for long. She's just relieved that you're all right, so don't start worrying about her. Now try and get some sleep and I'll be back tomorrow, hopefully with some good news, eh?'

Maddy nodded obediently, but once he had gone she began to fret again. What if the Department refused to allow her to go home with Andy? Would she be shipped off to yet another foster-home? There was no way she felt up to running away again. That had got her into enough trouble. Deciding that there was nothing she could do about it, she clambered into bed and within minutes was sound asleep.

Chapter Thirty-Four

'So I'm free to go then? Really free?'

'That's about the long and the short of it,' Sue Maddox told Maddy. 'Everyone agreed that it would be silly to try and keep you in care for the sake of another few months. That's not to say we won't be there if you need us though,' she added hastily.

Maddy beamed at Andy and Mary who had come with him to the hospital to see her.

'So how about we get you home then?' he teased, and Mary's heart fluttered. She had the strangest feeling that she wouldn't see Andy again after today. The night before, she had shown him again without saying a word that she was his for the taking, but he had scuttled away like a frightened fawn. It was a shame, because she knew that she could have become very fond of Andy. He was a truly genuine bloke, but he had made it more than clear that he wasn't ready to go into a new relationship just yet.

Maddy was whipping about the room like a whirling dervish, throwing the clothes that Andy had bought her into a bag with a wide smile on her face. But then suddenly she paused to ask, 'Do you think they might let me see Chloe before we go? I'd like to say goodbye.'

'I don't see why not. I'll just go and have a word with the sister for you.' Mary hurried away and within minutes was back with the good news. 'Sister's going to take you down to the children's ward right now,' she told her with a smile. 'Go on. Andy and I will finish packing your things for you.'

Maddy zipped out into the corridor where the sister was waiting for her, and together they took a lift to the ground floor.

At the entrance to the children's ward the sister told her kindly, 'Take as long as you like. The nurse will ring me when you're ready to come back and I'll come down to fetch you.' And with that she flashed Maddy a smile and strode away, her starched white apron crackling as she went.

The children's ward was very colourful, with an assortment of cots and beds placed down either side of it. There were brightly coloured posters on the walls and nurses rushing everywhere. Maddy started down the length of it, searching from side to side, and she soon spotted Chloe, looking lost in a big bed surrounded by dolls and teddies. Her parents were sitting either side of her and they welcomed her warmly.

'I'm going now,' Maddy explained, 'but I wanted to see Chloe before I left. Do you mind?'

'Mind?' her father chuckled. 'If it wasn't for you she might not be here. Of course we don't mind. In fact, I think it's time we had a tea break, so we'll leave you two in private. Back soon, pet.' With a loving wink at Chloe he took his wife's elbow and they disappeared off down the ward as Maddy approached the bed.

Chloe smiled at her shyly, delighted to see her. 'I'm going home soon with my mummy and daddy,' she informed her solemnly.

'I know you are and I think it's wonderful.' Maddy took her small hand in hers, relishing the feel of it. She had become very fond of Chloe but knew deep down that this would be their final goodbye. Chloe had a lot to get over, and Maddy could only be a constant reminder of what they had been through together.

'Will you come and see me?' Chloe now asked hopefully.

Choosing her words carefully, Maddy told her, 'Perhaps one day. But for now I think you need to go home and spend as much time as you can with your family. They've all missed you very much.'

Chloe nodded eagerly. 'They have, Mummy said so, and Nanny and Grandad are coming to see me later *and* all my cousins.'

Her little face was animated and Maddy thanked God that she had been able to save her from being shipped off to a whorehouse abroad. Chloe wouldn't have lasted six months in one of those hell-holes.

'I'm going home too now,' she said with a slight wobble in her voice. 'But I wanted to come and say goodbye first.'

'I'm glad you did.'

Maddy had just opened her mouth to say more when an elderly lady with grey hair and a man with a big moustache bore down on them.

'Chloe, my angel.' The woman caught the little girl to her in a bear hug as Maddy hastily stepped aside. Chloe whooped with delight as she clung to the woman.

'Nanny, I missed you so much!'

'Not half as much as we missed you.' The gentle-faced man added yet another soft toy to the pile on the bed and Maddy felt in the way. Chloe was safe now, surrounded by her family, just as it should be. She didn't need her any more. Turning about, she tiptoed away, pausing once at the doors to look back. Chloe's grandparents were ecstatic to see her and Maddy knew that it was time to go.

Upstairs, once Sue Maddox had left, Mary Law folded the last of Maddy's clothes into the bag before saying, 'I think that's about it then. As soon as Maddy gets back, you can be off.'

Shifting uncomfortably from foot to foot, Andy nodded. 'I dare say we can. Thanks for putting me up, Mary. If it wasn't for you suggesting that I should follow Budd and Dumbarr, those poor kids would still be in that terrible place.'

Mary flushed. 'It was a pleasure. Although I still can't believe that I didn't ever suss that Budd was a man. All the signs were there, yet I never put two and two together. Anyway just remember, if ever you need me I'm just at the end of the phone.'

'Thanks.' They both knew that this was really goodbye but didn't want to say it.

It was then that Maddy entered the room, looking pensive.

'How was she?' Andy asked.

Maddy blinked. 'Being spoiled rotten by her family just as a little girl ought to be.'

'And long may it last.' Mary had forced herself to sound cheerful and now she went over to Maddy and tenderly kissed her cheek. 'You be

377

happy and have a good life, eh?'

'I'll try.' Now the tears that Maddy had tried to hold back flowed freely as she clung to the kind woman. 'And thanks for all you've done for me.'

'It was a pleasure. And it's been a pleasure to know you too. Don't forget me.'

'Never.' Maddy sniffed as Mary slipped away without a backward glance.

Andy took her hand and lifted her bag with the other, saying softly, 'Let's go home, eh?'

Maddy swallowed her tears as he led her from the room, hardly daring to believe that she was really free at last. There would be no more looking over her shoulder. No more dreading the coming of night. For the first time in her life she was answerable to no one – and it was a fact that was going to take quite a bit of getting used to.

'Here we are then ... home at last!' Andy swung the car onto the drive as Maddy looked at him with concern. He was still very pale and she knew that the wounds the dogs had inflicted on his leg must be paining him, but he was in a good mood nonetheless.

As he took her bags from the boot and limped towards the front door he warned her, 'I ought to mention that the house might not be quite as tidy as it was when you lived with Kirsty and me. I do try to keep it clean, but what with work and one thing and another...' He shrugged sheepishly. 'I suppose I'm not cut out to be a housewife.'

Maddy saw what he meant the second she set foot through the door. Although the house was warm, as he'd left the heating on, piles of shoes were kicked about the hallway and the stair carpet looked as if it hadn't been hoovered for months. The lounge was untidy too, with empty mugs and newspapers strewn everywhere. But that was nothing compared to the kitchen, as she soon discovered. The sink was full of dirty pots, and barely an inch of work surface was visible. The floor was no better, with dirty dog bowls scattered here and there, and for a second she was back in Whizzer's house.

She was looking forward to seeing Lilibet and Talullah again, although she realised that they would be much older now – as she was too.

'I'll pop round and fetch the dogs from my mum's when we've had a cuppa,' Andy told her, as if he could read her mind.

Maddy rolled up her sleeves as Andy filled the kettle at the sink and began to collect the mugs from the lounge.

'There's no need for you to do that,' Andy objected, feeling ashamed. 'I didn't offer you a room so that you could become my skivvy.'

'I'm well aware of that,' Maddy retorted haughtily, 'but I shall have to find something to keep me occupied until I can find a job so I may as well start now.'

Filling the washing-up bowl with steaming hot water and a good squirt of Fairy Liquid, she put the dirtiest of the pots in to soak before taking her tea from Andy.

'It's funny, but it doesn't feel as if I've ever been away,' she remarked musingly. 'Everything is just as I remembered it.'

'Is that a good thing?'

Her head bobbed eagerly. 'Yes, it is. I was happy here, you know.'

'Then let's hope that you'll be happy here again.' Andy raised his mug, and as they chinked them together she grinned. This was going to be a brand new start. It felt good to be back in Plymouth and she intended to make the most of it.

Within a week of being back, Maddy had the whole house shining. The windows sparkled and the furniture was so highly polished that you could see your face in it. The dogs were happy to have someone at home with them in the day again whilst Andy was at work, but already Maddy was beginning to feel a little restless. She knew that Oliver was not too far away as the crow flew, and she was impatient to see him again. The addresses of all her siblings were burned into her brain, but Oliver was the one she longed to see first.

'Do you think he'll still remember me?' she asked constantly and Andy would reassure her.

The problem was, Maddy was still afraid of going out on her own. After the long years spent locked away, the outside seemed enormous – and the second she set foot out of the door she would have a panic attack and rush back inside.

'What if I'm *never* able to go out on my own again?' she wailed one evening as frustration ate away at her insides.

'You will,' Andy told her patiently. 'It just takes time. You're doing remarkably well, all things considered. Just take one step at a time, eh?'

She sighed miserably but knew that he was right. He was trying to get used to how neat and tidy the house was. Maddy was proving to be a remarkably good little housekeeper, although the same could not be said for her culinary skills. It had been a long time since she had cooked for the family who had adopted her, and now she was having to learn all over again, helped by Andy who had become quite a good chef since Kirsty's departure.

Her first attempts at a meal were disastrous, much to Andy's amusement.

'You could burn a boiled egg,' he would tease her, but Maddy took it all in good fun. Thankfully, Andy was very patient so between the two of them, they soon had the house running like clockwork.

'I ought to be out looking for a job,' Maddy fretted each evening. She felt guilty about letting Andy keep her, but he would repeatedly tell her to take things easy for the time being.

There were still lots of things that Maddy found frightening in this strange new world – simple things like answering the telephone being one of them – and he desperately wanted to give her time to adjust.

He was also trying to persuade her to take advantage of Sue Maddox's offer of counselling, but up to now Maddy had stubbornly refused it. The way she saw it, she had always muddled along with no help before, so she wanted to do the same now.

It was on a cold clear day in late February that Maddy ventured out on her own for the first time. She had read in the local newspaper of a library assistant's job that was going in a branch library near the town centre, and she was determined to apply for it.

The walk seemed endless, although in fact it was less than a mile, and Maddy was sure that everyone was looking at her, but she battled on regardless.

Despite her protests, Andy had bought her a smart black trouser suit and a crisp white blouse to wear beneath it, and in this ensemble Maddy looked sophisticated and older than her years. She had only accepted it when he agreed to let her pay him back out of her wages when she got a job, but now she was glad of the outfit. It gave her a little confidence, something she found she was sadly lacking at this moment in time. Andy had even offered to have the day off work to come with her, but Maddy had politely refused. She knew that at some time she would have to venture out into the big wide world again – and what better time than now, she asked herself.

As she neared the city centre, she smiled as places she recognised came into sight. In no time at all she was standing outside the branch library, taking deep breaths as she tried to control the panic that was threatening to overwhelm her. Just for a second she thought of turning around and running back to the safety of Andy's comfortable little house, but then common sense took over. She couldn't rely on him for ever; her pride would not allow that, so holding her head high, she marched into the library as if she owned the place.

An hour later, she came out again with her newfound confidence severely shaken. Miss

Miller, the head librarian who had interviewed her, had given no indication at all as to whether Maddy had got the job or not, although Maddy had gone to great pains to emphasise her love of books and her good grades at GCSE. The woman had merely replied primly that she still had at least three other applicants to see, as she peered at her over the reading spectacles perched on the end of her nose. Still, there was no sense in worrying about it, Maddy decided as she hurried home. It was all in the lap of the gods now, and all she could do was wait.

'So how did it go then?' Andy asked when he arrived home that evening and kicked his work boots off in the hallway.

Maddy tutted like an irate parent as she snatched them up and whisked them away to the kitchen, and he grinned with amusement.

'I can truthfully say I have no idea,' she said, as she deposited his boots in a box that she kept by the back door especially for the purpose. 'Miss Miller was very straight-faced and she asked me loads of questions. When she enquired why I hadn't had a job before, I just told her that I was orphaned and had lived in a children's home until recently.'

'Well, you weren't lying,' Andy said, as he switched the kettle on. 'And it's always hard to tell how an interview has gone.'

'I know,' Maddy chewed on her lip. 'But this job would mean such a lot to me and I'd love to work in a library. Now I have to sit back and wait for the letter telling me if I've got it or not, and that could be days away.'

'Did you tell her how good you were at English?' Andy asked.

'Oh yes, in a roundabout way. I told her about my favourite books and she seemed to listen.'

'Then you can do no more. But if at first you don't succeed then you try again. There are plenty of other jobs you could do,' Andy sensibly told her. 'Though I don't know why you're panicking. There's absolutely no rush.'

'I want to feel that I'm contributing towards the bills,' Maddy explained.

'Why? You more than earn your board and keep with all the housework you do, not to mention being a dogsitter while I'm at work.'

Ignoring the amused twinkle in his eye, she placed some spaghetti into a pan of boiling water. There were certain meals that she could manage very well now, like the spaghetti bolognese that they were having that evening.

'I'm doing enough for three if you don't mind,' she informed him. 'I had a phone call from Nick this morning and he asked if he could come over tonight.'

The young man had driven almost 160 miles from Cheltenham to see her twice since she had come to stay with Andy, and Maddy really liked him.

'I don't mind at all,' Andy said. 'After dinner I can go off to the pub if you like, and give you both a bit of space.'

'Why would you want to do that?' Maddy asked innocently. 'Nick is coming to see both of us.'

Dropping two tea bags into the mugs, Andy

chose not to answer. Despite all she had been through, Maddy was still terribly naive in some ways. It was more than obvious that Nick was keen on her, and yet Maddy didn't seem to realise it.

'Well, we'll see,' he said lightly and taking his mug off with him, he hurried away for a soak in the tub and a change of clothes.

When Nick arrived an hour later clutching a bunch of flowers and a large box of chocolates, Maddy flushed to the roots of her hair.

'Th ... thanks,' she mumbled, and snatching them off him, she fled to the kitchen, nearly tripping over the dogs in her haste.

'Come on in, Nick,' Andy told him, grinning to himself. 'Sit yourself down and I'll get you a lager. The dinner should be ready soon.'

Nick did as he was told as Andy followed Maddy to the kitchen where he found her arranging the flowers in a vase.

'Seeing as you reckoned he was coming to see us both, it's funny that he hasn't brought me a bunch, isn't it?' he teased, and Maddy flushed an even brighter red as she kept her eyes trained on the job at hand. Once he had returned to the lounge she leaned heavily against the draining board. Was Andy trying to tell her that Nick wanted to be more than friends? She shuddered at the thought. The mere notion of kissing a man, let alone anything else, brought her out in goose bumps now and she wondered if she would ever be able to have a relationship after what Dumbarr had done to her. But then she reasoned that now wasn't the time for worrying about it. The

385

meal was ready to serve, and seeing as she had gone to a lot of trouble over it, she didn't want it to spoil. After finally regaining her freedom she had promised herself that she would take each day at a time – and that was exactly what she intended to do.

Chapter Thirty-Five

Maddy answered a knock at the door the following week to find Sue Maddox standing on the doorstep. The colour fled from her face.

'It's all right,' Sue hastily assured her, 'I haven't come in a professional capacity, Maddy. I just wanted to call in and see how you are.'

'Oh!' The young woman held the door wide and let out a sigh of relief. 'In that case you'd better come in. I was just about to have a coffee break. Do you fancy one?'

'Not half,' Sue smiled. 'Specially if you've got a couple of custard creams to go with it.'

Beaming now, Maddy led her though to the kitchen where the kettle was boiling. 'Actually, I'm glad you came,' she confessed as she spooned instant coffee into two mugs. 'There was something I was hoping to ask you.'

'Then ask away.'

'Well, the thing is, I'm pretty desperate to see Oliver again now. I have his address but it doesn't seem right to just turn up on his doorstep. I was wondering if you could perhaps have a word with

386

the people who adopted him, to see how they'd feel about him seeing me again?'

She refrained from telling Sue that she had actually taken a bus past his home, which wasn't very far away, on a number of occasions, just in the hope of catching a glimpse of him. It had been another step towards getting used to being able to come and go as she pleased.

'I see.' Sue helped herself to some sugar. 'I suppose there couldn't be any harm in asking,' she said cautiously, 'but you have to understand that Oliver isn't eighteen yet. Until then, if his parents say that they don't want you to see him, there's nothing much I can do about it. Once he is eighteen, the choice will be up to him.'

'I know that,' Maddy told her solemnly. 'And if they say no, I'll just have to live with it. But ... could you at least try for me?'

Seeing the yearning in her eyes, Sue nodded but deep down she didn't feel too optimistic. The Drewers, Oliver's parents, were fiercely protective of him, and she had an idea they would have wrapped him in cottonwool if they could. Not that she was complaining. Oliver couldn't have wished for a better family and he had come on in leaps and bounds since going to live with them, and although his sight had deteriorated, his parents ensured that he had all the latest aids, including a computer and specially adapted screen, to enable him to keep up with his school work.

'Leave it with me.' Sue sipped at her drink then changed the subject, asking, 'And how are you doing?' Maddy certainly looked well, which was surprising considering all she had gone through.

'Really fine. Andy is very good to me,' Maddy confided. 'I don't know what I would have done without him, to be honest. I've applied for a job at the library too although I'm not holding my breath on getting it as loads of other people applied too. I'd like to feel independent now, Sue, and pay my way.'

'Well, you never know till you try, and if that one doesn't come about there will be plenty of other opportunities.'

'That's what Nick and Andy said,' Maddy agreed.

'Nick? Have you spoken to him then?'

'Oh yes,' Maddy told her. 'In fact, he comes to see me quite regularly. He's got a new job now, you know, at Social Services in Cheltenham.'

'So I heard.' There was an amused grin playing at the corners of Sue's mouth. It was as obvious as the nose on his face how Nick felt about Maddy, but the girl obviously hadn't clocked on to the fact as yet. Still, the way Sue saw it, there was plenty of time for things to develop and she could think of far worse people she would want to see Maddy end up with than him. Nick Preston appeared to be a thoroughly agreeable young man.

'And what about your other brother and sister? Have you got any plans to contact them?'

'Yes, but I need to get a job first and save some money to pay for the trips to where they're living.' Maddy bent to give the dogs a titbit. 'Trouble is, they were little more than babies when I last saw them. They'll be quite grown up now and I might not even recognise them.'

'You have to realise too that they might not even remember you any more, Maddy,' Sue said gently. 'They will have built their own lives with new families now. Are you quite sure that it's a good idea to get in touch? What I mean is – it could be very unsettling for them. Their new parents might not even have told them that they were adopted. You could be opening up a whole can of worms.'

Maddy frowned. This was something that she hadn't thought of.

'Of course, it's different for Oliver,' Sue hurried on, not wishing to pour cold water on Maddy's dreams. 'I'm sure he was old enough the last time you saw him to remember you clearly. But just think on what I've said, eh?'

'I will,' Maddy promised, and they then chatted about things in general until it was time for Sue to leave.

'Oh goodness me, look at the time!' she exclaimed, hastily putting her mug down on the worktop. 'I've got to be in court in less than an hour and if I'm late for it my boss will have my guts for garters.'

Maddy followed her to the front door where Sue paused to tell her tentatively, 'I don't know if you're aware of the fact, but Budd and Dumbarr are both in Crown Court next week.'

'Oh!' Just the sound of their names made Maddy feel as if the wind had been well and truly knocked out of her sails.

'Between you and me, I think they'll lock them both up and throw away the key,' Sue said reassuringly. 'The police investigations have uncovered so much. That house had been going for years, so God knows what happened to the unfortunates that they took there before you and the other kids that were brought out. I dare say we'll never know, but thanks to you, at least the youngsters you were there with are safe now. You have to hold on to that, Maddy. And don't get worrying about it. Because you aren't quite eighteen yet they won't be allowed to print your name in the newspapers, and you'll be spared from having to appear in court.'

'That's something at least.' Maddy shuddered at the thought of all and sundry knowing what she had been subjected to.

'They found out that Budd had originally got the job when he applied for it with fake papers,' Sue went on, barely suppressing a shiver. 'He had fake references, a fake passport, the lot. But then you can get hold of anything if you have the money. I can't believe now that, for all those years, no one realised that he was a man, but at least he's going to get his comeuppance, thanks to you, Maddy. Well, anyway, I'm really off now, but do let me know if you get news about the job.' Sue pecked her on the cheek and tripped off down the path as Maddy slowly closed the door behind her before bending to fuss the dogs. So Budd and Dumbarr were finally going to get what was coming to them. As far as she was concerned, it wasn't a moment too soon. The faster they were dealt with, the sooner she could really get on with her life again.

Andy noticed that Maddy was pensive that evening over dinner but wisely didn't comment on the fact. She often went into silent mode for a while – but then after what she had gone through, it was to be expected. Eventually she told him, 'Sue came to see me today.'

'Did she? Well, that was a nice surprise. What did she have to say?'

'She told me that Budd and Dumbarr are in court next week. Sue thinks they'll both get very long sentences.'

'Huh! No sentence could be long enough for those lowlifes,' he said in disgust.

'She also told me that it might not be a good idea to go looking for Molly and Ryan yet.'

Andy laid his knife and fork down and stared at the tablecloth before saying, 'To tell you the truth, I was thinking much along the same lines. They were so young when you last saw them, weren't they? And it could be that they won't remember you. But I didn't like to say anything. I know how intent you are on tracing your family again.'

Maddy sighed. She knew deep down that both Sue and Andy were quite right, but she wasn't willing to make a final decision on it yet.

Reaching across the table, Andy squeezed her hand gently. 'There's no rush,' he said softly. 'And at the end of the day it's up to you. You do what *you* feel is right in your own time. You still have a lot of adjusting to do, without worrying about that.'

Maddy flashed him a weak smile. Andy was always so sensible and she put a lot of store on his opinions. His hair was still damp from the bath and as a lock slipped across his forehead she suddenly had the urge to stroke it away. Instead she

391

slid a letter that had arrived for her that morning across the table to him.

'What's this then?' He swallowed the last mouthful of roast pork and lifted the envelope.

'It came just after Sue had left. It's from the library,' she told him self-consciously. 'I got the job and I can start next Monday. They say I can do a qualification later on, if I prove to be suitable.'

'*What!* Why, that's bloody marvellous!' Laughing aloud, he ran round the table to catch her in a bear hug. 'You clever thing. Just think of it – you a librarian. I bet you'll be brilliant.'

'I don't know about that,' Maddy said modestly, 'but I'm certainly going to do my best.'

He danced her around the room and soon they were both laughing uncontrollably as they fell in a heap onto the settee. And then the strangest thing happened. Their eyes locked and Maddy suddenly couldn't breathe.

'Right – well, er...' Andy released her abruptly and going to the table he took a large gulp of wine. 'I'm really pleased for you. I told you things would pan out for you in the end, didn't I?'

The embarrassing moment was gone and now Maddy grinned from ear to ear. 'I shall actually be able to give you some board money now.'

'Huh! You needn't worry about that. You just get some savings behind you.'

Misinterpreting what he'd said, Maddy flushed. 'So that I can find my own place, you mean?'

'No, of course I didn't mean that.' Andy was shocked. 'I just meant that once you've got some money behind you, you can–'

Maddy stood up quickly and headed for the

door. 'It's all right, Andy. I have absolutely no intention of being a burden on you. And now if you'll excuse me, I'm going up for a bath and an early night.'

'But it's only–' His words were stopped by the slamming of the door and his mouth gaped open in stunned disbelief. Why ever would Maddy have thought that he wanted to get rid of her? That was the last thing on his mind – not that there would be any point trying to tell her that. She was obviously in a funny mood. Shaking his head at the complexities of women, he turned the television on and sank despondently down into the cushions on the settee.

The atmosphere was strained between them the next morning before Andy left for work. Maddy then zipped through the housework as if there was no tomorrow. She hated being dependent on Andy, but deep down she knew that she had been a little hasty with him the night before. It was as she was taking her frustrations out on the oven with a large scouring pad that the phone rang and when she lifted it, Nick's voice wafted along the line. 'Hi, Maddy, how are things?'

'Fine,' she told him shortly and instantly feeling slightly guilty, she went on, 'I got my job in the library. I'm starting on Monday.'

'Why, that's absolutely wonderful.' Nick sounded genuinely pleased for her. 'And it's a damn good excuse for a celebration. How about I come and take you out for the day on Saturday? We could go and look at the John Piper stained-glass windows in St Andrew's Church that you said you'd like to see, and then I could take you out to lunch somewhere.'

Maddy opened her mouth to turn him down but then clamped it shut. 'All right, that would be nice,' she said instead. She usually helped Andy with the weekly shop on Saturday but he could manage perfectly well on his own for once.

'That's a date then.' Nick sounded happy. 'I'll pick you up at about eleven o'clock.'

The instant that Maddy put the phone down she wished that she had refused Nick's invitation. Still, it was too late to do anything about it now, she told herself, and if Andy didn't like it, he'd just have to lump it. And with that she snatched up the scourer and attacked the oven again.

The second phone call came just before lunch – and this time it was Mary Law.

'Hello, love,' she said pleasantly. 'Is Andy there?'

'No, he doesn't come home from work at lunchtime.'

'Oh well, never mind. I was just ringing to see if you were both all right.' Mary had promised herself that she would leave the two of them to their own devices, but the pull of Andy was too strong and she had phoned a few times since Maddy had been discharged from the hospital.

'We're both very well, thanks.' Maddy wondered why she wasn't more pleased to hear from her. Mary had been very kind to her whilst she had been in River House. The woman began to tell her all about her new job and they chatted of this and that until eventually Mary told her, 'Well, I must be off. Tell Andy I'll ring again soon. Bye for now.'

By early afternoon Maddy was bored. The house was sparkling, she had taken the dogs for a walk, the washing and ironing were done and now she needed something to fill her time. And then it came to her. She would go and see Whizzer. She had thought of him with affection over the years and remembered him as being the first person to show her any true kindness without asking anything in return.

Once the idea had occurred to her she hurried upstairs and tidied herself before she could change her mind, and in no time at all she was on her way to the bus stop. Half an hour later, she descended from the bus at the end of the street where Whizzer had lived and gazed around her. Everything looked so different. There was a large block of flats where the corner shop had once stood, and she could almost have believed that she was in the wrong street. She began to walk along the rows of terraced houses until she came to Whizzer's home, and blinked. The windows were gleaming with pretty curtains hanging at them. Windowboxes full of winter flowering pansies spilled colour onto the street and there was a smart new front door boasting a large brass knocker in the shape of a lion's head.

As she stood there, wondering what she should do, the next door opened and a young woman began to push a pram out of the house onto the street. Maddy wondered if this was some relation of Mrs Pike's, but before she could say anything the young woman smiled at her in a friendly fashion.

'Are you looking for somebody?' she asked. 'You look a bit lost.'

'Er ... I was actually looking for a man who was known as Whizzer. Would you happen to know if he still lives here?'

The woman bent into the pram to pop a dummy into her baby's mouth before saying regretfully, 'I'm afraid he doesn't. He died about two years ago, shortly after me and my husband bought this house off Mrs Pike. It was very sad. No one had seen him about for a while so in the end one of the neighbours got concerned and told the police. When they went in to check on him, they discovered that he'd been dead for some days. Sorry to be the bearer of bad news. Did you know him well?'

Maddy felt choked as she thought of such a gentle man coming to such a tragic end all alone, but she managed to smile as she said vaguely, 'Not that well, really. Thanks for the information.' And with that she turned and retraced her steps as the woman steered the pram in the opposite direction. All the way home she thought of the time she and Whizzer had spent together. It would have been nice to see him one more time and thank him for what he had once done for her. She just hoped that he was now at peace and reunited with his wife and daughter. He deserved that.

When Andy arrived home that evening he waved a white handkerchief through the door ahead of him, making her feel even worse.

'I'm sorry about the misunderstanding yester-day,' he said solemnly. 'The last thing I want is for you to leave just yet. I want to be sure that you can manage on your own first.'

He realised instantly that he had put his foot in it once again as Maddy bristled.

'I've been managing by myself since I was knee-high to a grasshopper,' she informed him scathingly.

'Yes, yes of course you have,' he said placatingly. 'I just meant—'

'It doesn't matter what you meant. Now why don't you go and get changed? Dinner will be ready to serve in fifteen minutes.'

Feeling as if he had been well and truly put in his place, Andy left the room. It seemed he couldn't say the right thing at the moment.

The atmosphere throughout dinner was frosty to say the least, and Andy was relieved when it was over.

'Why don't you go down to the pub for a drink?' Maddy suggested as she cleared the table.

'Since when have I been one for sidling off to the pub?' Andy was indignant. 'You know I don't go out except on high days and holidays, or at least you should do by now.'

'Then perhaps it's time you did,' she shot across her shoulder. 'I'm certainly going to start to get out more. In fact, Nick is coming to take me out for the day on Saturday.'

'Good for you,' he retaliated.

'Oh, and Mary rang for you. She said she'll try and catch you later on.'

Flinging himself into the chair, Andy disappeared behind the newspaper without bothering to answer as Maddy stamped away and clattered about in the kitchen. She had been bursting to tell him about her visit to Whizzer's house but now she wouldn't bother.

The next day, Maddy answered the door to find a very sheepish Sue Maddox standing on the doorstep.

'Called in for a cuppa, have you?' Maddy smiled as she held the door wide.

'No, this is just a flying visit as I have to be somewhere in ten minutes,' Sue told her apologetically. 'But I thought as I was passing I'd call in to tell you that I spoke to the Drewers yesterday afternoon.'

'Oh!' Maddy's heart started to race.

'I'm afraid it's not good news.' Sue started to fiddle with the buttons on her coat as she avoided Maddy's eyes. She knew that what she was about to tell her would upset the girl, but she had no other option.

'The thing is, Oliver's new parents have done a marvellous job with him since he was placed there. He was very traumatised then, but now he's a very well-adjusted young man. He's nearly totally blind now, which probably won't come as any surprise to you as it was always on the cards, but he has a guide dog called Zoop and he copes wonderfully. He goes to a special school and Amy Drewer tells me that his grades are very high. But ... well, the thing is, whilst she sympathises with the position you're in, she feels that having contact with you again now might set Oliver right back.'

'So she doesn't want me to let him know I'm here?'

'I'm afraid not. I'm so sorry, Maddy. I know how much this means to you. But when Oliver is eighteen the choice will rest with him. It could well be that *he* will come looking for *you.*'

Blinking back tears, Maddy nodded. It seemed that once again the odds were against her. 'Thanks for taking the trouble to find out.' She forced a smile to her face. 'And do keep in touch, Sue.'

'I will,' Sue promised as she turned to hurry back to her car.

Maddy waved her off and after closing the door she sank down to her knees and hugged the two little shih-tzus as she tried to come to terms with what she'd just heard. For years the thought of seeing Oliver again had kept her going, and somehow she just knew that they would be reunited, even if it meant waiting until Oliver was old enough to come looking for her. Deep inside, she knew he would do so. She had waited for such a long time, and now that she was free she could wait a little longer.

Chapter Thirty-Six

As Maddy made her way to work on a bitterly cold day in early October, kicking her way through the russet and gold leaves that were blowing across the pavement, she was humming merrily to herself. She had worked at the library for some months now, and loved every second of it.

Miss Miller, the head librarian who had interviewed her for the job, and who had once struck terror into Maddy's heart, had turned out to be a surprisingly gentle person and Maddy had grown quite fond of her. The girl had promised herself long ago that she would never grow too close to anyone again, since it brought too much heartache, but somehow as the barriers went down she had grown close to Nick and Andy too.

Nick still came to see her regularly and they had become good friends. As for Andy ... well, after the hiccup shortly after moving in with him, they had settled down to enjoy each other's company once more. Maddy supposed that this was due to the fact that she could now pay her way, although Andy had initially been against the idea. She hated being dependent on anyone, however, and got a little glow each time she drew her wages and saw her modest bank account growing.

Very soon now she would be eighteen and she had told Andy that after much thought she had finally decided that she would then head off to the Midlands to discover what had become of Molly and Ryan. Molly would be twelve and Ryan would be thirteen now, and she often wondered what they would look like. After much discussion with Andy on the matter she had agreed that if she was lucky enough to find them, she would not approach them or introduce herself. Knowing how much they meant to her, Andy went along with that because he understood that she needed to see that they were both all right.

In the meantime, Andy was planning a party for her, although Maddy wasn't overly keen on the idea. She had never been one for fuss, but didn't want to hurt his feelings.

'After all, it's not every day you reach eighteen,' he had pointed out when she had protested, and so she had given way. He seemed to be enjoying himself immensely with the preparations and she had no wish to spoil it for him.

She had matured over the last few months and had proved to be very popular with the people who visited the library. They had soon discovered that nothing was too much trouble for her. If they wanted a particular book, Maddy would go out of her way to find it for them, and if she couldn't find it then she would order it, and so all in all she was usually in great demand.

Never having had the chance to follow the fashions, Maddy now took a quiet pride in her appearance, although her taste in clothes was conservative compared to many girls her age. The trouser suit that Andy had bought her remained a firm favourite, and Maddy would alter the appearance of it with different tops and blouses.

Andy encouraged her to go out and treat herself to something new, but Maddy much preferred to watch her savings account grow rather than squander money on things that she considered unnecessary. However, she had decided that she would push the boat out for a dress to wear for her birthday party and intended to start looking for the right one that very day. She had no idea as yet what she wanted, but was sure that she would know it when she saw it.

Emma Bolton, one of the other young library assistants, had offered to go with her that lunch-time, and Maddy was looking forward to it.

Emma was the nearest thing to a friend her own age she had made since returning to Plymouth, and Maddy found her very amusing. Emma tended to be quite flamboyant with her clothes, although she had to tone them down for work, and she and Maddy got on famously.

Now as Maddy neared the library she saw her friend ahead of her and shouted, 'Hey, Emma, hold up!'

Emma turned and grinned, her frizzed shoulder-length blond hair flying out about her shoulders.

'Hi, Maddy.' She waited until Maddy caught up with her and slipped her arm through hers. 'So, is our shopping trip at dinnertime still on, then?'

Maddy nodded. 'It certainly is, but don't forget – I don't want anything too way out.'

'Oh, you're so *boring*.' Emma sighed dramatically. 'With your figure, you could wear anything and still look a million dollars. I just wish I could.' The girl was prone to be a little on the plump side, which Maddy supposed wasn't surprising, the amount of junk food she ate.

'Well, I'm sure we'll be able to find something we can both agree on,' she told her as they entered the library and headed for the staff room. Miss Miller was already there and smiled at Maddy while eyeing Emma cautiously. She was forever having to ask the girl to be quiet, whereas Maddy was the soul of discretion with never a word out of place, a fact that had greatly endeared her to the woman.

'Isn't that top a little *bright* for work, Emma?'

she asked primly as the girl slipped her coat off. The hint of criticism seemed to go over Emma's head like water off a duck's back.

'Red is all in at the moment,' the girl told her with a cheeky grin. 'You ought to try it, Miss Miller. It would suit you down to the ground with your colouring.'

'I rather think I'm a little old to be tripping around in red now,' Miss Miller answered, although she blushed at the compliment. 'But now, Emma, you finish the job you were doing last night. And you, Maddy, could you start to get the returns back onto the shelves, please?'

'Of course,' the girls chorused as they went their separate ways, and soon Maddy was immersed in the job at hand. It was almost mid-morning when a curious tap-tapping noise made her look up, and her heart leaped into her mouth. There was a tall, remarkably handsome teenage boy walking down the aisle towards her with the lead of his guide dog in one hand and a white stick in the other. Maddy instantly knew that this was her brother Oliver. Her heart was thumping so loudly that she was sure he must be able to hear it, and her mouth had gone dry. His thick fair hair was darker now, almost a honey-blond, and he was at least a head taller than her. But even so, she knew without a shadow of a doubt that it was him, and joy coursed through her.

He was almost level with her when he suddenly stopped and told his dog, 'Zoop, stay, boy.' The dog instantly sat down and now Oliver leaned his head to the side and asked, 'Is anyone there?'

'Y ... yes, may I help you?' Maddy forced herself to sound calm.

'Yes, please. I believe you have a Braille section in this library?'

'That's right, it's just over here.' Maddy clambered down from the library steps and wiped her palms down the legs of her trousers, her eyes never leaving his face for a moment. She longed to run to him and put her arms around him but knew that this wasn't the time or the place.

'Would you like to follow me?' she asked politely, and with a wide smile the young man told her, 'Yes, thanks.'

The dog instantly stood and began to follow Maddy with his master following close behind until they came to the section he was looking for.

'All the Braille books are here. Is there anything in particular you were looking for? I could get it for you if there was.'

'No, I'll manage, thanks,' he told her with another friendly smile as he ran his hand along the shelf of books. 'To be honest I'm only here to pass the time for a couple of hours. My mum has dragged my dad off on a shopping spree and I can't stand trailing around shops so they agreed to drop me off here.'

'Oh, I know exactly what you mean. I'm not much of a one for shopping either.'

'Really? I'm surprised. My sister would shop for England if you'd let her,' he joked. 'Dad is always moaning about how much she spends on clothes.'

His mum, his dad, his sister? It sounded like he was happy and whilst Maddy was grateful for that, it also hurt. *She* was his sister, if Oliver

404

could but know it.

'Do you go out on your own very often?' she asked now, hoping that he wouldn't think it was a chat-up line.

'Occasionally, but not as often as I'd like. I haven't had Zoop for long and Mum worries if I go too far afield just yet.'

'I dare say that's understandable,' Maddy replied solemnly. He had selected a book now and after tapping about with his cane for a second or two he located a table and sat down at it. She knew that she should be getting back to work but was finding it very difficult to drag herself away from him.

'Do you live close by?' she asked now, although his address was carved into her brain from the many times she had stared at it while locked away in River House.

'Not too far,' he answered pleasantly. 'I'll be going on to sixth-form college next September, so you'll probably be seeing a lot more of me. I need to get as much swotting done as I can until I go.'

'I see, and what will you be studying at college?'

'Well, I want to do A-levels in Economics, History and Law,' he told her, sending a thrill of pride coursing through her. It seemed that his blindness was no handicap at all to him, and she couldn't help but think what wonderful people the couple who had adopted him must be. He was certainly a happy boy, from what she could see of it. At that moment she saw Miss Miller eyeing her from the end of the aisle and she started guiltily.

'It's been lovely talking to you, but I'd better get

on with my work now,' she told him. 'I'll be back in a while to see if there's anything you need.'

He turned his head towards her, although she knew that he couldn't see her, and just for a second she glimpsed the little boy he had once been. The little boy for whom she would willingly have committed murder.

'Thanks, I'll look forward to that.' He bent his head to the heavy book in front of him and as his hands began to flow expertly across the page, Maddy scuttled away.

Oliver was here. Really here, within arm's reach of her, and she could scarcely take it in. It was as if all her birthdays and Christmases had come at once. She wanted to snatch him to her and tell him how very much she loved him and that she would never leave him again, but of course, she knew that would be totally inappropriate. He had said that he would be coming to the library again and she would somehow have to choose the right time to tell him who she really was.

Under Miss Miller's watchful eye she returned to work but her concentration was broken now. She had hoped to return to Oliver as soon as she could, but had no chance to do so as people approached her for help. It was almost lunchtime when Miss Miller leaned across her shoulder and snatched a book she had just placed there from the shelf.

'Really, Maddy. You seem to be off with the fairies today,' she scolded. 'It isn't like you at all. You are usually so efficient. This is a romance and you've put it back into the crime section.'

'Sorry, Miss Miller.'

'Look, why don't you get off for your lunch now? Perhaps you'll be able to concentrate better when you've had a break.'

Maddy flashed the woman a grateful smile and, almost tripping in her haste to catch a sight of Oliver again, she sped down the aisles in a most uncharacteristic manner. But she was sadly disappointed when she rounded a bend to see that the table he had been sitting at was empty. Nearly running again now, she raced towards the exit and once on the steps outside, her eyes flitted up and down the length of the busy street. There was no sign of him and she bit down hard on her lip to stop her tears from flowing. She had so wanted to have just one more glimpse of him.

'What's going on here then? You've got a face on you like a wet weekend.'

Spinning about, Maddy saw Emma standing with her hands on her hips.

'Oh, I just thought I saw s-someone I used to know,' Maddy stammered as disappointment stabbed her like a knife. 'But I must have been mistaken.'

'Well, go and get your coat then,' Emma said, pulling her own coat collar up. 'We've got some serious shopping to do, if I remember rightly, and it's freezing out here. Go on – get your skates on else it'll be time to come back to work before we've even started.'

Maddy went back inside to get her coat although she didn't feel at all like shopping now. Somehow all the fun had gone out of it. Even so, she didn't want to let Emma down, so they headed for the shops where Emma was in her element as she pulled one gaudy creation after another off the rails.

'Now this would look lovely on you,' she sighed as she held a particularly short little number up for Maddy's approval.

Maddy eyed the low-cut neckline and the tiny skirt. 'It's not really me,' she declared.

Emma sighed. 'All right then. You show me something you *do* like.'

Maddy spent a few moments flicking through the clothes before lifting out a plain black shift dress.

'Lord love us!' Emma snorted, then giggled. 'That would look better on Miss Miller than on you. Get with it, girl, and choose something a bit fashionable for a change. This is for your eighteenth birthday party, you know?'

The girls trudged from one shop to another but in each one Maddy turned her nose up at everything Emma suggested until eventually her friend got fed up.

'You're really not in the mood for this, are you? Why don't we try again another day when you're feeling more the ticket? We certainly aren't getting anywhere today and it's time to go back, anyway.'

'OK,' Maddy agreed, relieved that she was being let off the hook.

'Come on then. Let's grab ourselves a bag of chips before we go back. We might just have time to eat them if we get a move on.' And so the shopping trip was abandoned and the girls made their way back to work with Maddy in a very pensive mood indeed.

Andy picked up on it the second he set foot through the door that evening as Maddy made them both a much-needed cup of tea. She had only just arrived home and had barely had time to take her coat off.

'Is everything all right?' he asked after a while as they prepared the evening meal together in the kitchen. 'You seem to be miles away.'

'What? Oh, sorry, Andy. I was, to tell the truth.'

He waited for her to go on as he peeled the carrots and after a while she suddenly blurted out, 'I saw Oliver today – he came into the library.'

'Phew!' Andy watched her closely, trying to judge how it had affected her. 'And how was he?'

'He looked wonderful.' Maddy's hands became still as she gazed out of the window onto the dark garden. 'He's grown, of course. In fact, he's a head taller than me now and very handsome. He's going to break some hearts when he gets older.'

'And did he seem happy?'

'Very.'

Turning from the sink, she looked at Andy as he asked gently, 'And did you tell him who you were?'

'No.' Her voice trembled. 'I wanted to so much, but I didn't think it was right to go in like a bull in a china shop. It might have been too much of a shock for him. After ... the fire he was very traumatised and I didn't want to set him back.'

Andy looked at her sympathetically. He knew full well how much Oliver meant to her and could imagine how hard it must have been for her, to be so close to him today and yet to have said nothing. 'For what my opinion's worth I think you did the right thing,' he said. 'And the chances are, if he came in once he'll come in again and you could see how things go next time.'

She nodded in agreement before turning back to the potatoes she was peeling, but all the time a picture of Oliver floated in front of her eyes and she could think of nothing else.

Chapter Thirty-Seven

On Saturday morning as Andy got ready to go out, Maddy watched him gloomily. He had taken to leaving the house on her Saturdays off to give her some time alone with Nick while he helped his mother with some decorating. As it happened, Nick wasn't coming this week as it was his parents' ruby wedding anniversary and they were having a family party. He had begged her to come along to it but Maddy had shyly declined.

'Don't worry about the shopping. I'll do it later this afternoon,' Andy told her as he snatched up his car keys and headed for the door. Once there he turned to ask, 'Shouldn't you be getting ready? Nick will be here in a minute.'

'I'm just going to get changed now,' Maddy told him as she pulled her comfortable towelling dressing gown more tightly about her. She hadn't bothered to inform Andy that she had no plans for the day, reasoning that it wouldn't much affect him.

'See you later then.' Once the door had closed behind him she felt strangely restless as the long day stretched ahead of her. What was she going to do with herself? It was then that a thought occurred to her. She could go shopping for her party outfit. There was a greater chance of finding something she liked if Emma wasn't in tow. Bless her, she had a heart as big as a bucket but their tastes in clothes were very far apart.

Cheerful now that she had made the decision, Maddy nipped upstairs and got changed, and in no time at all was heading for the city centre. It was quite nice to browse at her leisure but the first three shops she went into had nothing at all that appealed to her.

Becoming despondent, she wandered into the back streets and it was there that she spotted a small boutique that she hadn't seen before. The clothes in the window were fashionable but classy, and deciding that there was no harm in looking she went inside where a smart woman who looked to be in her thirties addressed her.

'Were you looking for anything in particular or just browsing?' she asked.

'Actually, I'm trying to find something to wear for my eighteenth birthday party, but I don't want anything too fussy,' Maddy admitted.

'Hm.' The woman tapped her chin as she looked Maddy up and down. She then went to a rail and started to lift down a number of dresses. 'No, not that one,' she muttered, as she then held them at arm's length. 'That's too old for you. And this one won't do either. The colour is all wrong for your hair.' Quickly replacing them on the rail she

411

started to hunt through again until suddenly she said triumphantly, 'Now *this* might be just perfect. And it looks your size. Why don't you try it on?'

'I'm not sure,' Maddy said doubtfully as she eyed the dress the woman was holding.

'Well, my dear, this colour will complement your lovely dark hair, and whilst it's trendy it's also very elegant. Go on, just try it on. I usually get it right otherwise my customers wouldn't keep coming back to me, would they?'

Maddy headed to the fitting room, supposing there was no harm in trying it on. There was no one holding a gun to her head and if the dress wasn't right for her she was more than capable of saying so.

Minutes later, when she surveyed herself in the full-length mirror in the fitting room, she gasped with surprise. It might have been someone else staring back at her. The dress was a soft green jersey material that clung to her curves. It sat just above the knee, and the cowl neck was cut quite low, although not so low that Maddy felt uncomfortable in it. It had short capped sleeves and the design of it was very simple, but the way it was cut made it utterly stunning.

'How are you getting on? May I come in?' The curtain swished aside and the woman grinned with satisfaction. 'There now. Didn't I say that colour would suit you? It might have been made for you.' Peering at Maddy she asked, 'Would you mind very much if I made a suggestion? You have lovely hair, but ... well, if you were to have it cut to about here, I think it would make you look more fashionable.' She held her hand to a point just below Maddy's shoulders and Maddy had to grudgingly admit that she was right.

'And boots. Boots would look wonderful with that...' the woman went on. 'Let me get you a pair to try on with the dress so that you can see for yourself.' She hurried away and returned minutes later with a shiny black high-heeled pair. 'Slip those on,' she ordered, and Maddy, who was strangely enough beginning to enjoy herself, did as she was told. They instantly gave her height and she felt very grown up.

'They're perfect with that dress,' the woman said briskly. 'What do you think?'

Maddy nodded, and before she could change her mind she told the sales lady, 'I'll take them – and the dress.'

She left the shop shortly afterwards swinging her shopping bags and feeling on top of the world. But she wasn't finished yet. Now she wanted to find a hairdresser while she was in the mood. Luckily there was one in the very next street who assured her that she didn't need an appointment, so after telling the woman what she wanted, Maddy sat down and closed her eyes as the woman first washed her hair, then began to snip away.

An hour later, the girl could scarcely believe the transformation in herself. Her hair now reached to just below her shoulders in a long bob and looked thick and healthy. Maddy couldn't even remember the last time she had had it cut, and couldn't believe how bouncy and shiny it looked. The style seemed to enhance her heart-shaped face and her eyes sparkled with pleasure. Andy would hardly recognise her, she told herself as she hurried home. For the first time in her life, Madeleine Donovan was making an effort over her appearance – and it felt good.

When Andy walked through the door early that evening, he stopped dead in his tracks.' *Wow!*'he said appreciatively. 'You look all sort of...' he floundered for the right words '...grown up!'

'That was the general idea,' Maddy answered happily.

Andy couldn't help but stare at her. He had always looked on Maddy as the very young girl he and Kirsty had once fostered, but now he was seeing her as the attractive young woman she really was and he had mixed feelings about the change. It was good to see her taking an interest in herself, but at the same time it brought home the fact that she might not be with him for much longer. The thought was strangely unnerving. Over the last months they had fallen into an easy relationship and it was nice to come home from work to find somebody there again. Maddy had suggested on more than a few occasions recently that she should start to look around for some-where of her own to live. Up to now, Andy had managed to persuade her that she was better off for the time being staying where she was. But now... He pushed the thought of her leaving aside. There would be time to cross that bridge when they came to it.

'I got my outfit today for the party too,' she told him, her dark eyes flashing with excitement.

'Great. Are you going to show it to me?'

She shook her head coyly. 'No, not until the

day. I want it to be a surprise.'

'Fair enough.' He chuckled as he followed her into the kitchen and the smell of bacon sizzling under the grill wafted towards him. 'Mm, something smells nice.'

'Good. Supper is almost ready, so would you like to set the table?'

It suddenly struck Andy that they sounded like an old married couple and once again he tried to imagine how it would feel to come home to an empty house again once she had gone.

It was three weeks later when Maddy saw Oliver again. The streets of Plymouth were shrouded in fog and it was dark and dismal when she heard the distinctive tap-tapping sound coming towards her down one of the aisles in the library. The bad weather had kept most people tucked up warm and cosy beside their firesides, so Maddy hoped that she would have more time to speak to him this time.

'Hello,' she greeted him, before bending to stroke Zoop, his beautiful golden Labrador. The dog looked up at her from soulful brown eyes with his tail wagging furiously. 'It's nice to see you again. I spoke to you the last time you came to the library, if you remember.'

'Of course I remember.' He smiled broadly. 'I may be nearly blind but there's nothing wrong with my hearing. In fact, there's something about your voice that is strangely familiar.' He put his head to one side as if he was trying to remember as Maddy's heart began to beat a wild tattoo in her chest.

'The weather is appalling, isn't it?' she asked, hoping to distract him, and it worked.

'Yes, it is. That's why Mum brought me here. I was feeling a little bored. Of course, she had a hidden motive. She and my sister have used it as an excuse for another shopping trip. We're all going to Tenerife for Christmas this year and despite the fact that their wardrobes are bulging with clothes, they're both insisting that they have nothing to wear.'

They had reached the section where the Braille books were now and Maddy said tentatively, 'Your mum sounds lovely.'

He nodded. 'Oh, she is.' He found this young woman remarkably easy to talk to. 'She isn't my real mum,' he confided. 'She and Dad adopted me some years ago, but I couldn't have wished for a better family.'

'That's good.' Maddy was choked with emotion. It felt strange to hear Oliver talking about them that way.

He was sitting down now, and because the library was so quiet she decided to join him for a few minutes. Miss Miller was off sick with a bad dose of flu, so the staff were making the most of it and getting away with murder at present, especially Emma, who was taking two-hour lunch-breaks.

'I intend to make hay while the sun shines,' she'd told Maddy the day before, and as always Maddy found her highly amusing.

There was so much that she longed to ask Oliver but for now she was afraid that he would recognise who she was, so instead she kept the conversation centred on the sort of books he

416

liked as she sat there drinking in the sight of him. He was so different from the little boy she had held in her memory all those long lonely years.

'So, do you have a girlfriend?' she asked after a time.

He grinned self-consciously. 'I do actually. Her name is Madeleine and we go to the same school. Funnily enough, I used to have a sister called Madeleine before I was adopted, but I always called her Maddy. What's your name?'

Maddy was rendered temporarily speechless but then she told him, 'I'm Miss Tranter.' She had no idea at all why she had used Andy's surname. It had just been the first one to spring to mind, and she could hardly tell Oliver that it was really Donovan. He would certainly recognise who she was then.

'I ought to get some work done now,' she told him abruptly as she scraped her chair back from the table. He remembered her and the knowledge brought a choking lump to her throat.

'I'll perhaps see you again before you go. Enjoy the book.'

She scuttled away as Oliver frowned and once more held his head to the side, trying to think what it was about the young woman that sounded so familiar. After a while he shrugged and turned his attention to the book in front of him, and as his fingers flew across the page he forgot all about her for now and became immersed in the story of Robinson Crusoe, one of his all-time favourites.

In no time at all the day before the party rolled around and despite the fact that Maddy had not been initially thrilled with the idea she found herself looking forward to it now.

The lovely green dress was hanging ready in the wardrobe and she was longing to wear it. The party was to be held on Sunday night at the Anchor Hotel, a smart place near to the city centre, and Andy had spared no expense, insisting that it was his birthday present to her. There was to be a disco and a buffet with approximately forty people attending. Mary Law and Nick Preston, along with most of the people that Maddy worked with at the library would be coming, as well as some of Andy's workmates, many of whom Maddy had now met.

Nick seemed to be looking forward to it almost as much as she was, and had arranged to stay the night at the hotel when the party was over so that he wouldn't have to drive home. Andy had offered him the spare room at his house but Nick didn't like to impose.

And so on this particular Saturday, Maddy almost floated to work, her head full of the next day.

She was shocked after taking her coat to the staff room to emerge and see Oliver sitting at the table he had adopted on his visits there. Zoop was lying at his heels and as Maddy appeared his tail began to wag.

'Miss Tranter, is that you?' Oliver held his head to the side as Maddy approached.

'Yes, it's me. You're an early bird, aren't you?' She was quick to note that he didn't seem his usual cheerful self today and wondered what was wrong.

418

'Actually, I came to see you,' he told her without preamble. 'I need to talk to you.'

'Oh.' Thankfully, Miss Miller was on a course that morning so Maddy took a seat at the side of him and looked at him expectantly.

He seemed flustered and was constantly running his hand through his hair.

'The thing is,' he began, 'and I know this will probably sound mad, but the very first time I ever heard your voice it reminded me of someone.' He smiled apologetically. 'When you go blind, your other senses are heightened and my hearing and my memory are pretty sharp. I racked my brains to try and think where I might have heard your voice before, and then earlier on this week it came to me. You sound like my sister Maddy, the one I told you about. I used to live with her before I was adopted. She went into a home when I was a little boy and I haven't heard from her since.'

Maddy gasped as shock coursed through her, but she sat as still as a statue as she wondered how to respond. Outside, the traffic flowed past; inside, people went about their business as if this was any other day, but Maddy knew that everything might change, depending on her response, in the blink of an eye.

Tears began to pour down her cheeks but she was unable to speak. Since seeing him and knowing how happy and well-adjusted he was, she had found a measure of peace. But now, should she lie to him, or should she tell him the truth? The decision was taken out of her hands when he suddenly leaned forward in his seat and began to trace the outline of her face with his fingers. And now his eyes welled with tears too as he muttered, *Is* it you, Maddy?'

'Y ... yes, it is.'

And then their arms were tightly wrapped about each other as their tears joined and flowed together.

'But why didn't you tell me who you were? Didn't you recognise me?' he asked after a time.

'Of course I recognised you. The very instant I saw you, I knew who you were. But you seemed so happy... I didn't want to upset you by bringing the past back. You seemed to have moved forward so well and I had no wish to rake up old memories that might be painful for you.'

'I have moved forward,' he told her softly as he thumbed the tears from her cheeks, 'and I *am* happy. But that doesn't mean to say that I ever forgot about you, Maddy. Have you been OK?'

'I've been fine,' Maddy lied glibly. She could not bear to tell him what she had endured. It could only hurt him. 'After I came out of River House, the boarding-school where I was sent when we were split up, earlier this year, I came back to live with my former foster-carer here and that's about it.'

'That's a relief then. I ... I never forgot what you did for me, you know. I was worried about how it might have affected you.'

'Ssh, there's no need to think about that now,' she whispered lovingly. 'It's all in the past now and best forgotten.' But she swallowed as terrible memories of that faraway night flooded back.

His muscular shoulders rippled beneath his shirt as a shudder ran through him at the same time. 'I used to think that the Donovans were going to suffocate me, with all the attention they lavished on me,' he recalled. 'And even though I was only young I knew that they treated you differently, and I knew how unfair it was. I used to sit there with them in the lounge while you were slaving away in the kitchen or, worse, locked away under the stairs and I began to hate them for it. And then...'

'Please,' she interrupted him and placed a finger across his lips. 'Like I said, there's no need to rake it all up again.'

They sat for a time enjoying the closeness of each other until he went on, 'It wasn't until after the fire that I realised what you had done for me, and I was so afraid that they would punish you for it. And then when it was all over and I found out that you had gone into a home because you were too old to go for adoption again, I felt so guilty.'

'It was a long time ago,' she said quietly. 'And what's done is done. You have to put it behind you now and make the best of your life. I've been absolutely fine and I'm so proud of you, Oliver.'

'And I'm proud of you too and I'm so glad I found you again, Maddy. But what do we do now?'

'We go on just as we did before,' she told him, as a sense of peace crept into her heart. 'And then when you're eighteen we can spend as much time together as we like. In the meantime, we can see each other here.'

'But why do we have to wait until then?'

'Because you have a wonderful family who treat

421

you as their real son and I wouldn't want to spoil that,' Maddy answered truthfully. 'Let's not upset them for now by knowing that I've turned up like a bad penny. We'll have our whole lives to enjoy each other's company, once you come of age. So let's just be happy that we've found each other and keep it our little secret for now, eh? In the meantime, tell me all about them.'

And so Oliver began to do just that, and the next hour simply flew by as brother and sister chatted as if they had never been apart.

Eventually he rested his head on her shoulder, feeling as if he had finally come home after a very long journey, and in that moment they both knew that they would never lose each other again.

Chapter Thirty-Eight

'Good God! Is that *really* you?' Andy teased as Maddy stood before him in her new outfit the following evening.

Maddy blushed. She had used a little make-up for the first time this evening and brushed her hair until it shone like polished copper, and now standing there in her new outfit she looked every inch the fine young woman that she had become.

'You look incredible!' he grinned as he pecked her on the cheek. 'Nick won't be able to keep his eyes off you tonight.'

The smile slid from her face as she shrugged her arms into her coat. She wasn't really bothered what Nick thought of her – although she classed him as a very good friend, of course.

'Shall we be going?' she suggested and Andy nodded. She was quite right. The party could hardly begin without the birthday girl and they were due at the hotel in less than fifteen minutes. But first there was something he had to do.

'I ... er ... got you a little something,' he said shyly.

'What?' Maddy looked horrified. 'But Andy, you've already spent so much on the party!'

'Well, it's only a little keepsake. I hope you like it.' Crossing to the sideboard, he picked up a small leather box and pressed it into her hand. 'Sorry it's not gift-wrapped,' he mumbled. 'I'm not much good at that sort of stuff.'

Intrigued, Maddy opened the lid and found herself staring down at a heart-shaped locket on a slender golden chain. 'Oh Andy, it's lovely!' she gasped with genuine delight. 'But you really shouldn't have.'

'Why not?' He grinned. 'I wanted to give you something to remember me by when you go off into the great wide world. Though I hope that won't be for a long, long time. Here, let me fasten it for you.'

As she turned, he fastened the chain about her slender neck, and as excited as a child she ran to the nearest mirror to admire it.

'Oh, it's just perfect with this dress, it just finishes it off,' she cried.

'Looking like you do, you don't need anything else to enhance you tonight.'

Running back to him, she planted a soft kiss on

his cheek and he jumped away from her as if he had been burned. 'Come on then.' Holding his arm out, he bowed with a flourish and with a giggle Maddy slipped hers through it.

Many of the guests were already at the hotel when Maddy and Andy arrived and they instantly descended on her, pressing cards and gifts into her hands and wishing her a happy birthday. Nick's eyes almost popped out of his head when she took her coat off, and he stuck to her side possessively. 'You look absolutely beautiful,' he whispered in her ear.

She smiled with pleasure, dropping a little curtsy. 'Thank you, kind sir, I'm glad you approve.'

'I more than approve,' he answered, as he eyed her hungrily.

Feeling slightly uncomfortable, Maddy went to mingle with her guests, noting that Andy was talking to Mary Law who looked very pretty in a blue dress that exactly matched the colour of her eyes.

Soon the disco was in full swing and people poured onto the dance floor as the party got under way. In no time at all, Maddy was enjoying herself and wishing that the night would never end as one person after another dragged her onto the dance floor. At nine o'clock the music was stopped and the buffet opened, and then Maddy cut her cake and blew the eighteen pink candles out as everyone sang 'Happy Birthday' to her. She could never remember feeling so happy in her life, although she supposed that some of that was down to the fact that she'd had a few glasses of wine.

When the music started up again, Nick took her elbow and pressed her towards the door, asking, 'Can I steal you away from your guests for a moment? I have something I want to ask you.' In actual fact he had been waiting his chance all evening and was glad to escape from Emma, who had been glued to his side all night. It was past ten o'clock by then and Maddy was longing to cool off, so she followed him willingly. He led her through the foyer to the back of the hotel and soon she found herself in the gardens. They looked magical with the frost sparkling on the grass from the lights shining through the windows.

'So, what did you want me for?' she asked pleasantly.

Nick tugged at the collar of his shirt as he plucked up his courage. 'Actually, I have something for you.' Fumbling in his pocket he withdrew something and for the second time that night Maddy found herself staring down at a small leather box.

'I've had it for weeks but I wanted to save it until you were eighteen,' he explained. 'That is if you'll say yes?'

'Yes to what?'

As Nick snapped open the lid she stared down at a beautiful gold ring boasting three perfectly matched diamonds.

'I ... I don't understand,' she whispered as her hand flew to the locket Andy had given her earlier.

Nick lifted the ring from the box and reached

425

for her hand. 'Oh Maddy, you must know how I feel about you! It's been hell waiting for you to come of age but now that you have I'm asking you to be my wife. I love you, Maddy. Please will you marry me?'

For a moment Maddy was speechless but then she snatched her hand away. 'Oh, Nick.' She reached up to stroke his cheek as he stared at her bemused. 'I'm very honoured but I can't marry you. I don't love you, you see. Only as a friend.'

Nick's face fell and he looked as if someone had slapped him. 'But I thought you felt the same way that I do?'

'Then if I gave that impression I'm very sorry.' Maddy hated to hurt him but could do nothing else. 'I *do* care about you deeply, Nick,' she rushed on. 'But not in the way you want. I'm *so* sorry. I wouldn't hurt you for the world.'

Even as she uttered the words she wondered if she was doing the right thing. Nick would have made a wonderful husband. He was kind and generous and handsome, and had stood by her through her worst nightmare. If she married him she would finally have someone of her very own to care for. But it couldn't be him. Deep down she knew it.

'Oh well, we can't always get it right,' he shrugged as he hastily stuffed the ring back into his pocket. But his casual words did nothing to mask the hurt in his eyes and Maddy felt terrible.

'Shall we go back in then?' he asked now. 'It's a bit nippy out here, isn't it?'

Catching his arm, she asked softly, 'I owe you so much, Nick. Can we still be friends?'

'Of course.' He strode away and she watched him go with tears in her eyes.

Once back inside, Nick disappeared, no doubt up to the hotel room he had booked for the night, and Maddy went and got herself yet another very large glass of wine. Somehow the night had lost some of its magic now. Glancing around the room she saw Andy still deep in conversation with Mary, who was laughing at something he had said. Maddy frowned. Mary had commandeered him since the moment he'd set foot in the room and it was beginning to annoy her.

Draining her glass she joined Emma on the dance floor and soon she was enjoying herself again, or at least she appeared to be.

By the end of the night both Maddy and Andy were more than a little tipsy.

'I think you two ought to get a taxi home,' Mary suggested with a grin. 'You could leave the car in the hotel car park. The presents should be safe in the boot where you've put them.'

'That's a good idea.' Andy leaned heavily against the nearest chair as he smiled lopsidedly at her.

'Right, then I'll go and order one for you,' Mary offered. 'By the look of the pair of you, the sooner you're home and tucked into bed the better.'

Ten minutes later, they waved at her as the taxi pulled away and when they arrived home, they lurched up the path, giving a sigh of relief when they were inside.

'I reckon I'll put the kettle on,' Maddy said. 'A good strong coffee might do us both good.'

'Yesh, it might,' Andy slurred as he collapsed

into a giggling heap on the sofa.

Drink had dulled the guilt Maddy felt for turning down Nick's proposal earlier that evening, and she was smiling broadly as she carried two steaming mugs into the lounge some minutes later and put them on the coffee-table.

'Here we are. Just what the doctor ordered.' Gently elbowing the dogs out of the way, she dropped onto the sofa next to him and Andy picked his drink up gratefully.

'Ooh, I think Mary might have been right. We're both going to suffer for this in the morning.' Seeing Maddy tense at the mention of Mary's name, he asked with concern, 'Is everything all right? You have enjoyed the night, haven't you?'

'Oh yes,' Maddy told him hurriedly. 'It was wonderful. I can't believe how much trouble you went to for me.'

'I'd do anything to make you happy,' Andy replied, suddenly solemn, and as Maddy turned towards him and their eyes met, her stomach did a somersault.

'Thank you.' Putting her coffee down on the table, she leaned across intending to kiss him on the cheek, but somehow the kiss landed on his lips and before either of them knew what was happening, they were kissing passionately.

'Oh, Maddy, I was so proud of you tonight,' Andy muttered huskily as his lips roved around her neck. 'You looked so lovely and so grown up.'

'I am grown up now,' Maddy replied, as a million fireworks exploded behind her eyes. Emotions she had never known she possessed were bursting to life inside her, and for the first time she found

428

herself enjoying the feel of a man's hands on her. This was nothing like the rape and degradation to which Dumbarr had subjected her. This was two people coming together of their own free will and it felt right.

Afterwards she could not even remember going upstairs, but before she knew it, she and Andy were lying side by side in his large double bed, and he was taking her to heaven. For the first time she knew what it was to be loved as Andy kissed her tenderly and she responded with all her heart. And then he was on top of her and they were moving together as one and the whole world faded away as she gave herself up to pure pleasure.

When it was over she lay nestling against his naked chest as he held her possessively.

'Nick asked me to marry him tonight,' she murmured, and just for a second she felt Andy tense up. And then she turned and placed her lips on his once more, and before they knew it they were making love again and Maddy wished that it could go on for ever.

Sometime in the early hours of Monday morning they fell asleep with their arms entwined and contented smiles on their faces.

The sound of traffic in the road outside woke Maddy the next morning, and when she opened her eyes she blinked, disorientated. Then suddenly as the events of the night before came flooding back she turned to look at Andy's slumbering face on the pillow beside her. Sighing happily, she leaned on one elbow and toyed with the thatch of hair on his chest before sliding silently from the bed and heading naked towards the door. I'll make him breakfast in bed, she thought to herself as she went to her room to fetch her dressing gown. Down in the kitchen she slipped some bread into the toaster and put the kettle on as the dogs danced about her feet.

'Good morning,' she chirped brightly as she bent to stroke them. And it *was* a good morning. In fact, as Maddy stood there with her thick dark hair tumbling about her shoulders in all its glory she knew that she had never been so happy in her life. Everything suddenly made sense now. Her jealousy whenever she saw Andy and Mary together; her keeping Nick at arm's length. She had loved Andy for a long time but until last night she had never consciously realised it. But that didn't matter now. They had a whole lifetime stretching before them, and she intended to make the most of every minute.

Humming merrily, she tipped the boiling water into the teapot and placed it on a tray, then hurrying to the toaster she took the toast out and added that to the tray too. She was still humming, putting butter and honey and milk on the tray, when she became aware of someone behind her, and whirling about she saw Andy standing in the doorway watching her. He had thrown his old jeans and a creased T-shirt on, but to her he was the most handsome man in the world.

'Oh,' she groaned disappointedly, 'I was going to surprise you with breakfast in bed and you've spoiled it now. Never mind, we'll have it together down here.'

Seeing the look on his face, she fell silent, then asked, 'Is anything wrong, Andy?'

'Oh, Maddy.' Swiping a lock of hair from his forehead he avoided her eyes. 'About what happened last night – I can't even begin to apologise enough. It should never have happened, but I take all the blame for it. I'd had too much to drink and I took advantage of you. I shall never be able to forgive myself.'

'But–'

He held up his hand to silence her. 'It was sheer and utter madness. I'm years older than you, for God's sake. What would people say if they ever found out? They'd accuse me of being a cradle-snatcher.'

Maddy looked as if she was about to burst into tears but she remained silent as he ranted on.

'You've been through so much, which is why I wanted you to come here so I could look out for you, and instead *I* take advantage of you too!'

'From what I remember of it, I can't recall putting up much of a fight,' she said haughtily, her pride in tatters. She had truly thought that Andy loved her, but now she saw that she had just been the only available woman to satisfy a drunken man's needs, and the pain went deep. How could she have been so stupid and got it so wrong?

'Perhaps it is time you got yourself a place of your own, after all – just until you and Nick get married.'

She opened her mouth to tell him that she had no intention of marrying Nick, but then pride made her clamp it shut again. If this was the

431

excuse Andy was going to use to get rid of her, then so be it.

He looked at her standing there so proud with her head held high and a defiant glint in her eye, and his heart ached with shame. But it was too late to mend things now. What was done was done and there was no going back.

'I'm so, so sorry,' he muttered sheepishly. Then: 'Look, Maddy, I'd better go and collect the car, eh?' And looking utterly wretched, he turned and shuffled from the room.

Maddy had more spirit in her little finger than most women double her age. It had kept her going before through very dark times and she was determined it would keep her going again.

She stood there for what seemed an eternity until she heard the front door quietly open and close, and only then did she allow her tears to fall. Bitter tears of pain and regret. And then she slowly made her way to her room and began to pack her things. Andy had said that it was time to move on and she intended to do just that.

The suitcase that Maddy was carrying became heavier by the minute as she tugged it along Saltash Road but soon she turned into Glen Park Avenue and the station loomed ahead of her. A huge imposing building, it had an air of old-fashioned grandeur. Maddy wondered if this would be her last sight of it. She had emailed Oliver, who had a special screen adaptor to be able to read, to explain briefly about her decision to leave Plymouth, and she had promised to always let him know where she was.

Maddy headed towards the ticket office. She had come this far and there would be no going back now, although her heart was aching and tears were only a sigh away.

'When is the next train to Coventry, please?' she asked politely as the elderly ticket officer peered at her beneath the brim of his hat through a glass panel.

'About twenty minutes, love,' he replied good-naturedly. 'Though you'll have to make two changes on the way.'

Maddy nodded and slid the money towards him, then once she had her ticket she headed for platform two where she sank onto a bench with her suitcase tucked tight into the side of her leg. After leaving the house she had headed for the library where she had spoken to Miss Miller, explaining that due to a family emergency, she had to travel north, and as she might be away for a long time, it was best if she gave in her notice now.

Miss Miller had been sad to see her go, but had not questioned her too closely on her reasons for leaving because she could see that Maddy was deeply upset. Instead she had hugged her and wished her well, promising her a good reference, and that she'd post on her documents, before Maddy slipped away.

At that time, Maddy had had no idea whatsoever of where she was going. She had nowhere to call home as such, after all. But then it had come to her. Her life had begun in the Midlands, so why not go back there?

Once the idea had occurred to her it seemed the

obvious place to head for, and now all she had to do was wait for the train to Coventry, where she'd change for Nuneaton. She glanced around at the other people loitering on the platform. Most of them were chatting and laughing. There was a young family, a mum and dad and two small children, and it was taking the adults all their time to control the children as they skipped about in their excitement. Envy shot through Maddy as she watched – and loneliness closed around her like a cloak. Now, once more, she truly had no one. But she was a fighter – she had had to be to survive this far – and she would survive again.

Chapter Thirty-Nine

January 1996
'I estimate that you are about three months pregnant, Miss Donovan,' the doctor told Maddy as she came from behind the screens where he had just examined her.

She fiddled clumsily with the buttons on her skirt as she sank down onto the hard-backed chair in front of his desk, trying to ignore the note of disapproval she had heard in his voice. The doctor was of the old school and to his mind there were far too many young unmarried mothers about nowadays.

His words didn't come as complete surprise to her as she had already bought a pregnancy test from Boots and had a positive result – and yet having it confirmed by a doctor seemed to make it real. A mixture of emotions flowed through her as she struggled to think of something to say.

'I'll get you an appointment with the midwifery team at the George Eliot Hospital and you can do your ante-natal classes there,' he went on. 'In the meantime, if you have any concerns at all, don't hesitate to come and see me.'

'Th ... thank you, Doctor,' Maddy mumbled as she struggled into her coat. For some reason she had become all fingers and thumbs and she just wanted to escape, to digest what he had told her.

As she emerged onto Riversley Road she took a great gulp of cold air. People were coming and going, and everything appeared to be just as it had been when she entered the surgery, and yet she knew that from now on nothing would ever be quite the same again. In a few months' time she would be responsible for a little person. Andy's child. The apprehension was suddenly swept away by a wave of pure joy. Oh, she was more than aware that being a single mother wasn't going to be all a bed of roses. But for the first time in her life she would have someone of her very own, and she was determined to manage. She stroked her flat stomach as awe glued her feet to the pavement. Inside was a tiny human being that would soon become her whole life. This child would be loved as she herself had never been, she was determined on that. In the lonely weeks since she had left Plymouth she had missed Andy more than she could say, but now she would have a part of him for ever.

Joy sent her tripping along and soon she was

435

back in the little flat further along Riversley Road that she had rented when she first arrived in Nuneaton. It hadn't been much to shout about then but it was the best she could afford on her limited savings. If truth be told, it had been downright shabby, but over the last few weeks, with the landlord's permission, Maddy had emulsioned the walls and furnished the place with pieces she had picked up from secondhand shops, and now it was warm and cosy and Maddy had made it into a real home.

As her mind raced ahead, she looked about the compact sitting room. It wouldn't be ideal, having a baby in a first-floor flat, especially one without a lift, but if she bought a lightweight pram she could manage it up the stairs and the bedroom was more than big enough to house a cot. The smile temporarily left her face as she thought of her job. Miss Miller had given her an excellent reference, so now Maddy was happily working at the library in Nuneaton. She had received two emails from Oliver which she had read so often that she knew them off by heart. Fortunately, there was what they called 'an internet café' in Nuneaton, and once she had got herself an email address, Maddy had written to Oliver, simply saying that she'd been forced to return to the Midlands, and telling him her new whereabouts.

She had been desperately lonely since leaving Andy's home but doubted that Andy gave her so much as a second thought. He had made it more than clear that what had happened between them had been a dreadful mistake, and she would never forgive him for that.

Now she pushed the niggling fears about her pregnancy to the back of her mind. Other single mums managed and so would she. She would go on maternity leave and then find a recommended childminder to care for the baby when she returned to work. Already the thought of leaving the child was sobering, but she decided she would worry about that when the time came. For now she would keep this wonderful secret to herself and begin to prepare for the baby's arrival.

As the year progressed, Maddy's stomach began to swell and she spent most of her days off scouring secondhand shops for baby clothes and equipment ready for its arrival. Early June was scorchingly hot and Maddy was waddling like a duck now as she looked forward to the birth of her child. They had assured her at the hospital that everything was as it should be, until one morning when the midwife called in at the flat to give her a routine examination.

'Good God,' she chuckled as Maddy opened the door and waddled ahead of her back up the stairs. 'You look as if you're about to burst. I have a feeling that this is going to be a big baby.'

'Aw well, if it is, it is,' Maddy replied. She was so uncomfortable now that she just wanted to get the birth over with. She felt like a beached whale.

'Hop up onto the bed,' the midwife told her some minutes later. 'Let's have a little feel round and see how you're doing, eh?'

As her hands expertly roved around Maddy's stomach, she asked, 'Have you been having any backache?'

'Yes, I have, to be honest – but I thought that was normal. I've still got a few weeks to go yet, according to the doctor.' Her face became solemn. 'Everything is all right, isn't it?' she asked.

'Yes, pet. Now I know you missed your second scan because of a work crisis, so I think we'll get you off to the hospital for a scan now. But it's nothing for you to get worried about. I just want to be on the safe side.'

Maddy suddenly felt sick with fear. She had looked forward to this baby so much that she didn't know how she would bear it if anything were to go wrong now. 'There must be something you're concerned about,' she said tearfully. 'Please – tell me what it is. I need to know.'

'Well, I can't be sure but I thought I detected two heartbeats,' the woman said frankly. 'Twins, eh? But I need this to be verified, and the sooner the better.'

Maddy's mouth gaped open with shock. 'What? Do you think there might be twins in there? How can there be? Surely it would have shown up on the first scan!'

'Not necessarily,' Nurse Platt informed her. 'I know of two undiagnosed sets of twins. The first set didn't show up on the scan because one baby was tucked away behind the other. I'm not saying that's the case with you though, love, so don't get panicking. But it's important to check it out. Better to be safe than sorry, eh? I'm surprised I haven't picked up on it when I've examined you before. Right, I've got my car outside and I could run you to the hospital now if you like?'

'Thanks.' All of a fluster, Maddy straightened

her clothes before snatching her bag up and following the nurse from the flat.

At the hospital Maddy lay on a trolley whilst the doctor rubbed cold gel across her abdomen, and then the scan began.

'Well, Miss Donovan,' the doctor said with a smile, 'it seems that your midwife was right. Say hello to your son and daughter.'

'What?' Maddy stared in amazement at the two tiny bodies intertwined on the screen. 'So there *are* twins there then?' She could scarcely take it in.

'There certainly are, and if I'm any judge it won't be long before they make an appearance.'

'But ... I still have some weeks to go yet,' Maddy pointed out fearfully.

'I shouldn't worry too much about that. Twins have a habit of popping out early and so for that reason I think I'm going to bring you in to the ante-natal ward. Your blood pressure is a little high – not too bad at all at the minute,' he hastened to add, 'but I'd like to keep an eye on you.'

'I can't come in yet,' she protested. 'If there are going to be two babies I have to do some more shopping.'

'Very well. How about you come in on Saturday morning then? That will give you time to prepare. Meantime, I don't want you overdoing it.'

Maddy was helped off the bed and then waddled from the room. Life, it seemed, was full of surprises.

The rest of the day and the next were spent in shopping for the unexpected baby and as Maddy finally stood back and surveyed all her purchases she sighed with relief. She had managed to find a secondhand twin pushchair advertised in the local paper, and after going to view it she had declared that it was just what she needed and almost snatched the seller's hand off. The young woman was only asking forty pounds for it, which would stretch Maddy's dwindling savings, but it was worth every penny as it had scarcely been used. As Maddy pushed it all the way back to the flat she was beaming. Soon, hopefully, she would have two little faces smiling up at her from it, and now after the initial shock of discovering that she was having twins she could hardly wait to meet them. As far as she was concerned it was a bonus. She would have a ready-made family all in one go, and that would be enough for her.

Her joy was tinged with sadness as her thoughts returned to Andy. What would he think if he knew that he was about to become the father to a little boy and girl, she wondered. But then she pushed the thought away. Andy was an honourable man, and despite the fact that he had made it clear he didn't want *her*, should he discover that he was about to become a father he would want to support the children and do right by them. Maddy had no intention of becoming a financial burden on anyone and knew that it would be better if Andy never found out. These were *her* babies and she would fight tooth and nail if need be to see to it that they never wanted for anything, least of all love. That came free, and she had bucketfuls of it just waiting to pour into someone.

Late on Friday night, Maddy was woken by a

440

niggling pain in the small of her back. Dragging herself out of bed, she pottered away to the small kitchenette reasoning that a good strong cup of tea might settle her down. The babies had been unnaturally still all day, which was one relief at least. Over the last couple of weeks she had sometimes felt as if the twins were dancing a jig inside her.

As she was crossing to the sink she suddenly felt warmth on her inner thighs and gazing down was appalled to see a puddle of water on the tiles beneath her. Taking a deep breath she forced herself to remain calm. It seemed that there would be no need for her to be admitted to the maternity ward tomorrow. She needed to get to the hospital tonight.

Lumbering down into the hall below she lifted the pay phone and hastily dialled the hospital to inform them that she was coming in before ringing for a taxi. It was as she attempted to get back up the stairs to collect the bag that she had all ready and waiting to go that the first pain ripped through her. Gasping for breath she hung over the banister until it passed before quickly hurrying on. She was in the entrance hall waiting for the taxi to arrive when the next pain came and although she was afraid, she was exhilarated too. It wouldn't be long now before she met her little girl and boy.

'Come on, Maddy, you're nearly there,' the midwife encouraged her in the early hours of the morning. 'One more good push should do it.'

As the next pain tore though her, Maddy

441

gritted her teeth and pushed with all her might. And then suddenly the room was full of a newborn baby's cry, and Maddy stared in wonder at the tiny soul in the midwife's arms.

'Meet your daughter, and a fine little girl she is,' the woman grinned as she held her out for Maddy's inspection. 'And she looks to be a good weight too, for a twin.'

Maddy wanted to hold the child, who had a thatch of dark hair exactly the same colour as her own, but just then another pain brought her almost double. Hastily handing the baby to a waiting nurse, the midwife turned her attention to Maddy.

'Here we go again,' she smiled as she bent to her, and seven minutes later a lovely fair-haired little boy with a remarkably fine pair of lungs on him slithered into the world.

'Another little beauty,' the midwife announced as she cut the cord and held him aloft. 'Though I have to say, seeing as they're twins they're absolutely nothing alike.'

Maddy dropped back against the pillows exhausted, and feasted her eyes on the baby boy. He was like a tiny fair-haired copy of his father, and it almost broke her heart.

'Do we have a name for them?' the nurse asked cheerily as she handed the baby to another nurse.

'Yes, their names are Andrew and Holly Tranter.' Maddy sighed with contentment. Holly had been the best friend she had ever had, and now she would live on through this beautiful little girl, whilst Andrew would bear his father's name. It seemed fitting somehow, and as if Maddy had waited her whole life for this minute.

'Here you are then, Mum.' The midwife placed the babies in Maddy's arms and as she gazed down at the two little faces she was lost for words. They were both so perfect and she could hardly believe that they were really hers.

'Just a quick cuddle, mind,' the nurse warned with a smile. 'We need to get them washed and tidied up. They're actually very good weights for twins. Andrew is four pounds three ounces and Holly is four pounds and six ounces. No wonder you were so big.'

Maddy sighed with contentment. She could bear being separated from them for a short time because she knew that once she took them home, no one would ever be able to part her from them again.

Chapter Forty

May 1997

'Oh, you little monkey, come here,' Maddy laughed as Andrew toddled across the kitchen. The twins were now eleven months old and had taken their first tentative steps within a week of each other, which meant they could now get up to even more mischief. Maddy sometimes thought that she could do with eyes in the back of her head, although in truth she wouldn't have had it any other way. She had taken to being a mum as if she had been born for it and had loved every

443

minute since the twins had been born. In fact, her earlier life now seemed so far away that sometimes she wondered if she had imagined it. The nightmares had stopped and for the first time in her life, Maddy felt whole, or at least she would have if the twins' father had been with her. She still missed Andy every single day but she only had to look at little Andrew to feel close to him.

Maddy wrote regularly to Oliver, who was tickled pink to be the uncle to two babies. She had begged him to keep her whereabouts secret and Oliver had been happy to oblige. The bond between them was still strong even though they had been apart for a long time, and she knew that she could trust him. She had worried about how he would feel when she first wrote to tell him that she was expecting, but he had not asked a single question and she was grateful for that. One day she would tell him everything, and somehow she knew that he would understand. She heard from Emma occasionally too, and her emails always made her giggle. If what she wrote in them was anything to go by, her pal hadn't changed at all.

Now she snatched Andrew up and pushed his chubby little arms into his coat sleeves whilst Holly looked on. The twins were as different as chalk from cheese in both looks and character. Holly was a quiet little girl with a ready smile while Andrew was into all sorts of mischief and much louder than his sister.

'You're going to Mamma Brin today,' she told him as she planted a kiss on his cheek.

She had been fortunate enough to be allocated a two-bedroom council house in Hill Top, and

Mrs Brindley, her next-door neighbour, had turned out to be a registered childminder, which was ideal. She now had the twins for Maddy whilst she was at work, although she had only gone back to the library part time. That was enough, as she could hardly bear for the children to be out of her sight. Mrs Brindley was a great Amazon of a woman with a gentle nature that belied her enormous frame. She was greatly loved by all the children she cared for, who had christened her Mamma Brin, and Maddy thanked God for her every single day. She knew that she could go off to work leaving her children in safe hands and that meant the world to her.

Not that she would be leaving them to go to work today. Today she would be on a very special errand. Lifting Holly in one arm and the bag containing the things they would need while she was gone in the other, Maddy shepherded Andrew ahead of her towards the door.

'Come on,' she told him. 'Let's get you to Mamma Brin, eh?'

Andrew toddled unsteadily ahead of her and soon they were in her neighbour's homely kitchen.

'Ah, here you are,' the woman said affectionately as she lifted Andrew into the air and kissed him resoundingly.

As Maddy placed Holly on the floor to play with some brightly coloured wooden bricks the woman stood Andrew down and looked at Maddy with concern.

'Are you quite sure that yer want to do this, love?' she asked.

Maddy nodded. It had taken her a while to

pluck up the courage, but now she felt ready. Today she was going to the home that her mother had been placed in, to try and find out what had become of her. She had told her neighbour very little, just that her mother had been an alcoholic and placed in a home whilst she and her siblings had been adopted out to different parts of the country.

Mrs Brindley would have loved to have asked more, but something about the defensive look that came over Maddy's face whenever she mentioned her past prevented her from doing so. She had a feeling that there was a lot that Maddy hadn't told her about; the identity of her twins' father for a start-off. She never even mentioned him, which Mrs Brindley found strange, not that it was any of her business, of course. The funny thing was, Maddy didn't seem like the type of girl to be a single mum and at such a young age too. During the time she had lived next door, Glenda Brindley had never so much as seen her even look at a man. Maddy devoted every single minute of her time to her children when she wasn't working, and seemed fiercely protective of them. Not that this was a bad thing. Her neighbour just wished that a few other girls she could think of were the same. When all was said and done, she knew very little at all about Maddy, who kept herself very much to herself. But she knew that today would be a challenge for her; she could see the pain in the girl's eyes whenever she spoke of the mother from whom she had been torn away at a young age.

'You get yourself off,' she told Maddy now,

446

keeping a watchful eye on Andrew who was stalking the cat. 'These two will be fine. And good luck, love.'

'Thanks, Mrs Brindley. I shouldn't be too long.' Maddy stooped to kiss the children and then she was gone, her bright flowered skirt swinging about her slender legs.

'It's a bloody shame,' Glenda Brindley muttered to herself as she watched Maddy stride towards the front gate. 'She's little more than a girl herself.'

An indignant howl from the cat brought her attention back to the kitchen and she hurried towards Andrew, who was doing his best to pull her pet along by its tail. In no time at all she forgot about everything else as she concentrated on the lively little twosome.

At the door to Halfway House, Maddy paused to swipe the sweat from her forehead with the back of her hand. Now that she was finally here she wondered if this was such a good idea, after all. It had been so long since she had last seen her mother that she wasn't even sure if she would recognise her now. The home was situated between Bedworth and Nuneaton, and the grounds it was set in reminded Maddy of the grounds of River House, which made her break out in a cold sweat again. Drawing herself up to her full height, she quickly rang the bell before she could lose her nerve.

'Good morning,' she said brightly when she was confronted by a kindly-faced nurse. 'I was wondering if you might be able to help me?

Many years ago, my mother was placed here and my siblings and I were adopted.' She quickly launched into the speech that she had been practising and after a moment the nurse held the door wide and Maddy stepped inside.

Twenty minutes later, she left with tears glistening on her lashes. But at least she had discovered where her mother was, and now she had one more stop to make before returning home to her children.

An hour later she stepped into Chilvers Coton churchyard, shielding her eyes from the sun as she searched the neat rows of plots. The nurse had told her where her mother's grave was located and now Maddy slowly moved towards it. In the shadow of the church she looked down on a plain wooden cross with the name Anna Barnes carved into it and tears coursed down her cheeks.

'So you never made it, Mum, eh?' she whispered as she bent to place the flowers she had brought on the grass. 'The bottle got the better of you, didn't it?'

Strangely, although she was sad, she also felt a sense of peace. At least now she knew what had become of her mother and could forgive her for not coming to find her. The poor woman had never recovered from her addiction. When the doctor at the home had first informed her that her mother was dead, Maddy had been so distressed that she could barely answer him. Why hadn't Sue Maddox informed her that her mother had passed away? This was her first reaction. But then when the doctor went on to tell her that the death had occurred only months ago, the anger was replaced by guilt. Her mother had still been alive when Maddy had returned to Nuneaton, and if only she had plucked up the courage to visit her before, they could have been reunited, if only for a short while. But at least she knew that Oliver was happy now, and if she could only find Molly and Ryan, she could get on with the rest of her life.

'Sleep tight, Mum.' Blowing a kiss onto the grave she walked away for the very last time. For years she had hated her mother for all she and her siblings had been forced to endure, wondering why the woman had never bothered to try and find her. But now at last she could forgive her and lay her to rest.

Maddy was struggling through the library in the town centre with an armful of books the following month when her eye was drawn to the desk where a fair-haired man was talking to one of the librarians. He had his back to her but there was something so familiar about the way he was standing that it made her pause … and then the books she was carrying clattered to the ground as the colour drained from her face. It was Andy. But what was he doing here? And how had he managed to find her?

Hurriedly bending to retrieve the books, she glanced up into Andy's face as he stood over her.

'Hello, Maddy. You're looking very well.'

Snatching up the last of the books, she stood up awkwardly before striding towards the shelf where they belonged. He kept close on her heels and now she told him primly, 'Yes, I'm fine, thanks. How are you?'

'Very well, but I was worried about you after you did that disappearing act.'

'Really?' She could not keep the sarcasm from her voice as she glanced at him coldly. 'But wasn't it *your* idea that I should leave?'

'Well, yes, it was ... but I didn't mean you to go haring off like that,' he said lamely. 'I couldn't believe it when I got home later that day to find that you'd gone. I've been looking for you ever since.'

'And just how did you manage to find me?'

'Well, until a couple of days ago I couldn't. But then purely by chance I bumped into Emma in the town centre and she told me that you were working in the library here.'

Maddy made a mental note to give Emma a severe ticking-off the next time she wrote to her. Things would have been better left as they were, as far as she was concerned. Seeing Andy had dragged up all the old heartache.

'And just what else did Emma tell you?' she asked him, praying that her friend hadn't mentioned the twins.

'Nothing much. Just that you were here.'

'Oh.' Maddy sighed with relief, willing him to leave before she broke down and made an utter fool of herself.

'Look, isn't there somewhere we could go to talk?' he asked now, and after a moment of hesitation Maddy relented and nodded.

'I'm due for my tea break and there's a café over the road.'

Side by side they left the library and once

Maddy was seated at the window, Andy hurried away to get them some tea. She watched him, thinking how handsome he was. Seeing him again had reawakened all the feelings she had for him, not that anything could come of it. She had the twins to think about now.

In no time at all he was back, and sitting opposite her he said, 'So tell me what you've been up to then. I've missed you.'

Maddy took a great gulp of her tea, almost choking herself, before rejoining, 'I'd rather hear how Mary and Nick are. I haven't got that much to tell.'

'Right, well, the last I heard of Nick he was courting a young social worker from his office. But why didn't you tell me that you'd turned down his proposal on the night of your party, Maddy? I couldn't believe it when he told me the next time I saw him that you'd said no. He was worried sick about you for a long time. We *all* were. You could at least have let us know where you'd gone and that you were OK.'

Choosing to ignore his remarks, Maddy changed the subject and asked, 'And Mary?'

'Oh, Mary is busy getting ready for the wedding. It's only three weeks away now.'

'Oh!' Maddy's heart dropped into her shoes. So Mary and Andy were finally going to take the plunge? She wasn't really surprised; she had seen it coming for a long time.

'Then I hope everything will go well,' she muttered, keeping her eyes downcast. Despite all the promises she had made to herself, she longed to tell him all about his son and daughter, but how could she now on the eve of his marriage to someone else? It wouldn't be fair on any of them.

Suddenly scraping her chair back from the table she looked down at him. 'Look, Andy, I really don't think there's any point in this. We've both moved on and whilst I think it's lovely that you've taken the time to check up on me, I don't think we've anything else to say. As you can see, I'm fine, and I'll always be grateful for the way you stood by me, but that's in the past now. Goodbye.'

Andy's mouth hung slackly open as she turned on her heel and strode away. She had changed since he had last seen her. She'd grown up and seemed mature beyond her years, but he wasn't prepared to give up on her just yet. He had the strangest feeling that she wasn't telling him everything, and he was prepared to hang about until he found out what it was, even though she had made it brutally clear that he wasn't welcome.

As Maddy sat on the bus on her way home that evening, her heart was heavy. Seeing Andy again had reopened wounds that she had thought were healed, but now she knew without a shadow of a doubt that she loved him and always would.

When the bus stopped at the top of Coventry Road she got off and wearily walked down Donnithorne Avenue towards her little two-bedroomed house. Although it was small, it felt enormous after the confines of the flat she had lived in when she had first returned to Nuneaton, and she loved it. There was a little garden at the back for the children to play in and she had worked the same magic on the interior as she had on the flat. Now she was saving up for a dog. She believed in children having pets but would not buy one until she could afford a shih-tzu. As she thought of Andy's two she wanted to cry. Why had he had to turn up like that?

When she entered the kitchen at Mrs Brindley's the children toddled towards her ecstatically and the older woman chuckled. 'You'd think they hadn't seen you for a year at least,' she said, as she began to collect their things together. 'Same time tomorrow, is it?'

'Yes, please.'

'No problem. Now, how about I put the kettle on an' make you a cuppa before you go home? You look all in today.'

'No, I won't stay if you don't mind,' Maddy told her, eager to get away. 'To tell the truth I've got a bit of a headache and I'm looking forward to putting my feet up when I've got these two little terrors off to bed.'

'Hm, you should be goin' out enjoyin' yerself,' her kindly neighbour snorted. 'Yer don't give yerself any time fer fun. Most girls o' your age are off out flyin' their kites!'

'*Most* girls my age aren't the mother to twins,' Maddy pointed out with a rueful grin. 'Bye, Mrs Brindley, and thanks.'

As Maddy popped the children in their buggy to take them next door, Mrs Brindley headed for the kettle. Maddy might not want a cuppa but after looking after that pair of little terrors, she could kill for one herself.

453

Once the twins had had their tea, Maddy glanced at the clock and decided that there was time to allow them ten minutes playing in the garden before their baths.

'Come on, you two.' Taking them by the hand she led them out into the garden and settled on an old blanket under the weeping willow tree so that she could keep an eye on them.

It was as she was sitting there that she heard the back gate open and she looked up expecting to see Mrs Brindley, who would probably be returning something one of the twins had left behind. However, it wasn't Mrs Brindley she was confronted with, but Andy.

'Are you making a habit of following me?' she snapped as colour flooded into her cheeks.

Ignoring her jibe he looked towards the two infants toddling across the lawn before saying, 'In actual fact, I am. I followed you on the bus. I had the strangest feeling that there was something you weren't telling me and I wanted to check that all really was well with you before I returned to Plymouth. But whose are these babies, Maddy?'

In an agony of indecision she stood there, her hands clenching and unclenching into fists, before suddenly blurting out, 'If you must know, they're mine!' At the sound of the unaccustomed harshness in their mother's voice, the twins toddled towards Maddy and clung to her skirts as her hands came to rest protectively on their heads.

'Yours!' Andy stared at her in disbelief. 'You're telling me that these babies are yours? But ... how? And where is their father?'

'That is none of your business and I would be

454

very grateful if you would just go now, please,' Maddy told him coldly.

Andy just stood there staring at the children in stunned disbelief until asking suddenly, 'How old are they, Maddy?'

'That is none of your business either. Now just *go*, can't you? We have nothing more to say to each other.'

'Oh, I think you're wrong there. From where I'm standing it seems we have a lot to talk about – and I'm going nowhere until we do!' His temper had now risen to match hers and they glared at each other like two opponents in a boxing ring until Maddy's shoulders suddenly sagged. Knowing Andy as she did, she was aware that he meant every word he said, but now was not the time or the place for a confrontation. The children were becoming anxious and Maddy couldn't bear that.

'Look, why don't you come back tonight at about eight o'clock? The children will be in bed by then and we'll be able to talk in peace.'

His face set in a grim line, Andy turned and walked away, slamming the gate behind him as Maddy stood there as if she had been rooted to the spot.

'Are you all right, love?'

As Maddy's head snapped around she saw Mrs Brindley, who had been in the process of fetching her washing in off the line, watching her across the fence. It was clear that she had heard every word that had been said and Maddy felt tears of humiliation sting the back of her eyes.

'Why don't I come round and help yer get the little ones bathed? Yer lookin' a little peaky,' the

455

kindly woman volunteered. Maddy opened her mouth to refuse her offer of help but then closed it again. Perhaps just this once wouldn't hurt? She was usually so fiercely independent that it went against the grain though.

Taking her silence as acceptance, Mrs Brindley rolled towards her kitchen door, telling her, 'I'll be round in ten minutes. My Jim is just off to the pub so nothin's spoilin' round here.'

True to her word, she was on Maddy's doorstep in no time and soon the little ones were bathed, tucked into their cots and sleeping like angels.

'Right, now they're sorted out let's see what we can do for you, eh?' she said as she bustled back into the kitchen and put the kettle on. It seemed that Mrs Brindley, like many of her era, believed that a good strong cup of tea could cure all ills.

'So,' she said innocently when she joined Maddy at the table with two steaming mugs, 'what did yer friend want?'

'He's *not* my friend,' Maddy growled.

'Hm, well, all I can say is if he ain't now he must have been at one time, if the way he was lookin' at yer was anythin' to go by.'

When Maddy remained obstinately silent, her well-meaning neighbour leaned towards her and said, 'That bloke was the twins' dad, weren't he?'

Maddy stared at her miserably before nodding slowly.

'And do I take it he didn't know about 'em till today?'

Again Maddy nodded as the woman watched her thoughtfully.

'Then happen when he comes back tonight yer

456

should tell him.'

'I can't do that. He's about to be married,' Maddy shot back.

The woman shrugged. 'Whether he's to be married or not they're still his kids an' he deserves to know the truth.'

'But if I tell him now he'll think that I just want him to know so that he'll help to support them financially – and I don't want that,' Maddy declared hotly. 'I've managed perfectly well up until now on my own and I can go on managing.'

'I've no doubt yer could, but what about them two little 'uns – don't yer think they deserve to know who their dad is? There'll come a day when they won't thank yer for not bein' honest wi' 'em. You believe me. An' as fer managin'... Well, yer know the sayin', pride comes before a fall. We all need someone, Maddy, an' from where I was standin' he looked like a decent sort o' bloke.'

'I *don't* need anyone,' the girl shot back with her chin in the air. 'I've got my babies and they're all I need.'

'So yer say, but if I was you I'd think carefully on what I've said, love. An' now I'm goin' to leave yer in peace. If yer should need me I'm just on the other side o' the wall.' The woman slipped away, closing the door quietly behind her as Maddy sat there watching the hands of the clock ticking away the minutes until eight o'clock.

Chapter Forty-One

Andy arrived punctually with spears of colour staining his cheeks and his back as rigid as a sergeant-major's.

'Sit down,' Maddy told him and he perched on one of the hard-backed kitchen chairs, his eyes never leaving her face.

'So ... I think it's time we had a good talk, don't you?' he asked, as an uncomfortable silence stretched between them. 'How about we start with the babies?'

'Why would you want to know about them?' Her eyes flashed fire. 'They're *my* children and that's an end to it.'

'I have no doubt about that, but I'm sure they weren't an immaculate conception,' he said acidly. 'So why don't you tell me who the father is? Does Nick even *know* about them?'

'Why should I have told Nick about them?'

'Well, he did ask you to marry him – and then you go off and the next thing, you're the mother of twins.'

Maddy snorted with disgust. 'The twins have absolutely nothing to do with Nick,' she told him firmly. 'Until the night of my party I had never regarded him as anything other than a friend. Looking back, I suppose I was rather naive – I should have realised how he felt. But nothing happened between us, *ever.*'

'So if Nick isn't the father, then who is?'

Maddy sat there in an agony of indecision until suddenly her shoulders sagged. It seemed that she'd had to do battle all her life just to survive, and suddenly she was tired of fighting.

'Why should it matter to you?' she said wearily. 'You're about to be married.'

Shock registered on his face. *'Married?* Me? Whoever told you that?'

'You did when I saw you in the library,' she said indignantly.

'I certainly did not,' Andy denied hotly. 'I told you that *Mary* was about to be married – but it's not to me. She's marrying a doctor from Plymouth Hospital. He's a lovely chap, as it goes. It's been something of a whirlwind romance, from what I can make of it, but I hope it goes well for her. She deserves a bit of happiness.'

The wind was knocked well and truly out of Maddy's sails now as she stared at him blankly, but Andy hadn't come to talk about Mary Law.

'So, let's get back to you, eh? Are you going to tell me who the father of your twins is?'

When Maddy hung her head and began to cry softly he gasped as realisation hit him like a smack in the face. 'It … it's *me,* isn't it? They're *my* babies. But why didn't you tell me? And why did you run away as you did?'

'I didn't run away,' Maddy sobbed. 'You told me to go, or have you conveniently forgotten that?'

'I told you to find a place of your own because you said that Nick had asked you to marry him,' Andy explained. 'I didn't want to ruin things for you, and I was so ashamed of what I'd done to you that I couldn't look you in the eye. After all you'd been through I ended up behaving as badly as the perverts who had abused you.'

'No, you didn't. I came to you willingly, and for what it's worth you were the only man I ever slept with through choice.'

Andy scratched his head in bewilderment. 'So you didn't think I was taking advantage of you then, even with the age difference between us?'

'Andy, you're hardly in your dotage.' She smiled through her tears. 'I'm almost twenty now and you're in your early thirties. Is that such a huge difference? We could have been good together.'

'B ... but I used to be your foster-carer. What would people say?'

'"Used to be" being the operative words. Would it have really mattered? In case you hadn't noticed, I'm all grown up now and able to make my own decisions. No doubt we would have been a nine-day wonder before the gossips moved on to some other poor soul, but you weren't ready to risk your reputation, were you? I obviously wasn't worth it.'

'That's not true.' Leaping from his seat, he rounded the table before asking, 'May I see the babies?'

'I suppose so, but don't get any silly notions into your head about trying to get custody of them,' Maddy warned him.

Once upstairs, she paused on the landing to raise her finger to her lips. 'Don't get disturbing them, they're fast asleep,' she whispered.

He followed her into the small room that she

had painted so lovingly in bright colours, and stared in awe at the two sleeping infants in their cots. They both had their thumbs jammed into their mouths and with their long eyelashes curled on their cheeks they looked like little cherubs.

'What are their names?' he breathed.

'Holly and Andrew,' she whispered back.

'Holly looks just like you.'

'And Andrew looks just like you.' She was shocked to see the tears that were coursing down his cheeks and her heart melted a little. It must have come as a great shock to him to discover that he was the father of twins, the way he had. But then if he had kept away he could have lived in blissful ignorance.

They stood there for some time until Maddy gently ushered him from the room. She had the feeling that he would have stayed there all night if she had allowed him to.

Once back downstairs, Andy dropped heavily onto a chair as Maddy wrung her hands. Suddenly they didn't seem to know what to say to each other, and she was at a complete loss as to what might happen next.

'Oh, Maddy,' he muttered finally, 'what have I done to you? And after all you've been through. It must have been so hard for you, all on your own.'

'I'm used to being on my own now,' Maddy pointed out stoically. 'And despite what you seem to think, the twins are the best things that have ever happened to me. Before we were taken away from our mother I looked after Molly and Ryan as best I could. My mother certainly wasn't capable of doing it; she was drunk half the time. And then when we were adopted by the Donovans I tried to look after Oliver, and make sure that he felt loved. Olly hated them, as they smothered him with attention but never had any time for me and treated me as their servant. He just couldn't handle that, my little brother.'

Maddy squared her shoulders. It was time to say the thing she had never said, to share the secret she had never shared. She only hoped – Maddy never prayed, as she knew that God did not exist for lost souls like herself – that Andy could be trusted, for now she was putting *all* her trust in him.

'You thought it was me who set the house alight, didn't you?' she said. 'Everyone thought it was me, and I let them. That's why I got sent to River House, because there was always a question mark over whether I was dangerous or not. But do you know what, Andy,' she took a deep breath, 'it was *Oliver* who started the fire. He thought he was helping me, because he saw the way our so-called parents treated me and thought that if he burned the house down, we wouldn't have to live with them any more. The poor boy never intended to kill them when he started the fire – I know he didn't – he was just trying to help me.'

Shock registered on Andy's face. 'But ... but why didn't you tell someone that Oliver had set the fire?' he gasped. 'You could have avoided all the awful things that have happened to you.'

'I didn't tell anyone because I was afraid of what would happen to Oliver if they knew he had done it,' she said passionately. 'When you really love someone, you would do anything to protect them – and that's why I never told anyone. I'm sorry if you don't approve, but you know what? I don't have a single regret. I would do it all over again, to keep him safe.'

Andy remained silent, and eventually Maddy went on, slowly, 'Over the years, everyone I ever cared about got taken away from me, one way or another. Then when you and I spent that night together I thought I'd finally come home – but once again I found myself out in the cold. And then I discovered I was pregnant. I didn't know that it was twins until just before the birth. But since the day they were born they've given me a reason for living. They're mine. *Mine*, do you hear me?' Her voice rose – strong and calm and utterly determined. 'And neither you nor anyone else is ever going to take them away from me, unless it's over my dead body.'

Andy stared at her, and now he saw her for the woman that she had become. She might not be quite twenty years old yet, but she had matured.

'Could we try again?' he asked, with all his heart.

Maddy looked at him steadily as she considered his question. Was it her or his children that he wanted, she wondered. There was no doubt in her mind that she still loved him. Had it been just herself she had to consider, she would have gone to him in a sigh, but now she had her babies to think of, and they were the most important people in her life, even more important than Andy. He was an adult well capable of taking care of himself, but they were vulnerable and she was resolved that nothing was ever going to hurt them as she had been hurt.

'I don't know,' she said at last, and it was the truth.

'I want us to make a go of it,' he told her now as he took her hands in his. 'I admit that I'm thrilled to discover that I'm a dad, but it's *you* I came looking for. I love you, Maddy. Please give me a second chance.'

Maddy shook her head. 'My home is here now,' she told him, but even as the words left her lips she knew that a small part of her would always remain in Plymouth with Oliver. 'And I still have to find Molly and Ryan.'

'What about Oliver?' he asked gently.

'I've been writing to him,' she told Andy. 'He's still living not all that far from you.'

Andy shook his head in wonderment. It seemed that tonight was the night for revelations.

'So why didn't you tell me you'd told him who you were?' he asked.

'I didn't tell you because Sue Maddox explained that his adoptive parents wanted him to wait until he was eighteen before he decided if he wanted to see me again. Oliver and I didn't want to upset anyone so we kept our meetings a secret.'

'I see. Well, at least you know where he is then, but I could help you find Molly and Ryan if you're still set on it.' There was a note of desperation in Andy's voice. 'Just come back home with me and we'll search for them together. We could be a family – a *real* family.'

The offer was tempting but still she refused. 'I have the children to think about now. I can't just up sticks and move them miles away.'

'Then I'll come to *you*,'he told her. 'I'll do whatever it takes to prove to you how much I want us to be together.'

'But the children don't even know you,' she told him sadly. 'It would be too confusing for them to suddenly have a stranger in the house.'

'Then we'll take it slowly. I could come here every weekend after work.'

Maddy felt her resolve weakening.

'I suppose we could try it,' she said. 'But I warn you, Andy, I'm not going to go packing my bags and haring back to Plymouth with you. I want to see how it goes, first.'

'If that's what you want, then that's how it will be,' he agreed. 'We'll do this on your terms. Any way you want it.'

He would have liked to kiss her, but sensed that she wasn't ready for that yet. Instead he smiled and gently squeezed her hand, and suddenly Maddy saw light at the end of a very dark tunnel.

Epilogue

November 1997

'What's that for?' Maddy asked as she stared at the pile of ten-pound notes Andy had placed on the table.

Smiling, he hoisted Andrew up into one arm and Holly into the other as he told her, 'It's money for the fares for you to go and look for

Molly and Ryan. Seeing as I shall be here for the weekend, I thought you could get off and try to find them tomorrow. The twins will be fine with me. You've waited long enough, the way I see it, so why not take the bull by the horns and go for it?'

Maddy eyed the money warily. It was a tempting offer, she had to admit, but his suggestion had come as a surprise. She realised now that she hadn't given her brother and sister more than a fleeting thought for some time. It was unbelievable when months before thoughts of finding them had filled her every waking minute. But then she had been very busy recently. The twins were a real handful now and into everything, so what with them and her part-time job, she seemed to spend her whole life rushing about. Admittedly, Andy had been a godsend over the last six months. True to his word, he had arrived late after work every Friday night and stayed through until late Sunday afternoon when he would set off for his home in Plymouth again. He had taken to bringing his two little dogs with him some time ago, and the twins absolutely loved them, so much so that he now left them with Maddy rather than leave them alone in his house in Plymouth whilst he was at work during the week.

The twins were now seventeen months old and Andy adored them. His feelings were recipro-cated, if the welcome they gave him each time he turned up with treats in his pockets was anything to go by. They would squeal with delight and run to him on their sturdy little legs to be swung into the air and kissed soundly. Tonight looked set to be no different. Maddy always allowed the twins to stay up each Friday until Andy arrived, and then he would tuck them into the two little beds he had recently bought for them and tell them a story while Maddy prepared their supper. She was still fiercely independent and refused any offer of financial support, although she had reluctantly agreed to let him buy them clothes and the new beds. The twins were growing like weeds now and needed new clothes when they had scarcely had time to wear the old ones.

Now he herded the children towards the stairs as he told Maddy, 'Have a look in those bags by the door and see what you think. I'll just get these two little monkeys settled and then I have a proposition to put to you over supper.'

Intrigued despite herself, Maddy listened to the giggles as he shepherded them up the stairs ahead of him before crossing to the bags he had mentioned. She smiled as she took out two little pairs of denim dungarees and two warm jumpers, one in pink and one in blue. They were lovely and she knew that the twins would look great in them. Being as she only worked part time she had to make every penny count – not that she would ever tell Andy that. Her pride would not allow her to. Now her eyes settled on another bag and curiously she pulled it towards her. Inside was a gorgeous dress in a warm red jersey, very similar to the one she had worn for her eighteenth birthday party, a lifetime ago now. She stuffed it angrily back into the bag. Buying clothes for the twins was one thing – they were his children, after all – but buying clothes for her was a different matter entirely, and as soon as he came downstairs she intended to tell him so in no uncertain terms. She wasn't quite a charity case just yet, and he could just take the dress back to wherever he had bought it from.

When he came downstairs half an hour later, the smile was wiped from Andy's face as he saw Maddy slamming about the kitchen with her mouth set in a grim line.

'Is everything OK?' he asked tentatively.

'Not really, no.' She turned to face him. 'The clothes you bought for the twins are lovely. But why do you think I need you to buy *my* clothes?'

Stricken, he lowered his eyes and mumbled, 'Sorry, I didn't mean to offend you. I just thought with Christmas coming up you might fancy a new outfit. Mrs Brindley next door offered to babysit for the twins one night so I could take you out and I just thought–'

'Then you thought wrong!' Maddy's eyes were flashing fire. 'When and *if* I ever need your charity, I'll ask for it, thank you very much, but I think you'll find it will be a cold day in hell before that happens. I can manage perfectly well on my own.'

'Oh, Maddy.' Andy sank down at the table. 'Why do you have to hold me at arm's length all the time? Haven't I proved to you over the last months how much you and the children mean to me? Every Sunday when I drive away I feel as if I'm leaving a part of me behind. When are you going to stop being stubborn and marry me?'

Flustered, Maddy drained a saucepan full of cauliflower before taking a homemade lasagne

from the oven.

'I told you, I want to do this at *my* pace, and you agreed to it,' she reminded him.

Torn between despair, frustration and the deep love he felt for the feisty young woman standing in front of him, Andy said, 'I know I did, but I ... well, I love you all so much. If it's leaving here that's the problem, then it needn't be. I'll sell the house and come to you. I can find building work anywhere so that isn't a consideration. Mum would probably move here too. She wouldn't have anything left to stay in Plymouth for if I moved, would she? And she's longing to meet her grandchildren.'

Maddy joined him at the table. 'I'm not ready to make a big decision like that just yet,' she told him eventually, and with that they began their meals, although neither of them had much appetite.

Later that night, as Maddy lay in bed, she listened to the sound of Andy's gentle snores through the thin wall that divided them, where he slept on a put-you-up bed in the children's room, and her heart ached. Her mind was in turmoil over so many things. Firstly, now that she actually had the money and the opportunity to go and seek for Molly and Ryan, she was shocked to discover that she wasn't even sure if she wanted to any more. They were a part of her past, and she wondered if it would be fair to descend on them and open up old wounds. As for Andy ... with every week that passed she realised how much she loved him, but she was afraid of being hurt again – and more importantly still, afraid of the twins being hurt. Sighing deeply, she turned

on her side and shut her eyes tight. It had been a long day and for now she wanted to leave her concerns behind and sleep.

It was mid-morning the next day when there was a tap on the door and Mrs Brindley appeared with a rack of jam tarts fresh from the oven.

'I thought the twins might like a few o' these each after their lunch,' she told Maddy as she flashed a friendly smile at Andy. She had got to know him a little over the months he had been staying and thought he was a thoroughly good chap. It was just a pity she couldn't convince Maddy as much. The bloke obviously loved her but Maddy was such an independent little sod she couldn't see further than the end of her nose.

'Why don't you two get yerselves off an' do a bit o' Christmas shopping?' she offered. 'December will be on us afore you know it, an' it's never too early to start.'

'Mamma Brin!' The twins hurtled towards her at the sound of her voice, and they had almost reached her when Holly went flying and landed heavily on her knees. All three adults instantly hurried towards her. Maddy and Andy reached her at the same time and as they bent to her, their eyes locked.

Deeply embarrassed, Maddy turned about and began to fill the kettle at the sink as Glenda Brindley beat a hasty retreat towards the back door. If the look that had passed between them didn't give Maddy something to think about then nothing ever would, she thought as she quietly let herself out. But then, as her old mother had

always told her, there's none so blind as them that don't want to see.

It was now late Sunday afternoon and Andy was preparing to leave, the twins protesting wildly as they always did when they sensed that he was about to go.

'Don't forget to take that dress with you,' Maddy told him primly. 'I'm sure the shop you bought it from will refund the money.'

Masking his hurt, Andy stuffed the rest of the clothes into his bag before leaning down to the children and kissing them both soundly. 'You two be good for Mummy and I'll see you both again on Friday, eh?' It was getting harder to leave them each week but he was beginning to despair of them ever becoming a proper family now. Maddy was as stubborn as a mule when she wanted to be.

'Safe journey,' she told him as she took the twins by the hand. He hesitated as he drew level with her but then moved on.

'If you need me for anything, just ring.'

'I will' she told him, although he knew that she was lying through her teeth. And then the children ran to him and they had their arms wrapped about his legs and it almost broke his heart.

Long after he had gone and Maddy had dried their tears she sat at the kitchen table staring off into space as the mug of tea in front of her was left to go cold. She was still sitting there when Glenda Brindley bustled in.

'Gone again then, has he?' she asked after a cursory glance around the room.

'Yes, he has.' Maddy rose to get her neighbour

a drink as the woman eyed her warily.

'Andy gave me some money to go and find my brother and sister,' Maddy confided when she joined her again. The pair had become quite close and Maddy had confided the fact that her birth family had been split up and she and her siblings adopted. 'But the funny thing is that now that I have the opportunity, I'm not so sure that it would be wise to go ahead. What do you think?'

'Do you really want my honest opinion?'

Maddy nodded solemnly. 'Yes, I do.'

'All right then. From where I'm sitting, I reckon some things are better left alone. I know you've had a rough time of it from what little you've told me, but chances are your brother and sister are happy with their new families. If they ever want to find you they will, but I'd say leave it until they're old enough to make the decision themselves.'

The woman sighed before going on. 'Let me tell you a little story.' The memories she was about to recall were obviously painful for her, but she went gamely on. 'When I was just fifteen years old I met my old man, Jim. He was kind and reliable and everything I wanted in a bloke. But then a family moved onto the estate with a son who was seventeen. His name was Jason and the first time I ever laid eyes on him they near on popped out of me head I was that smitten. So I dumped my Jim and started going out with him instead. Little did I know that I were just one of many he had on the go,' she said ruefully. 'Anyway, next thing I know, I finds out I'm in the family way. Me dad hit the roof and stormed off round to Jason's and told his dad in no uncertain terms that when I

472

were sixteen, Jason was to marry me else he'd take a shotgun to him. Next thing we hear, Jason's upped and joined the army, just like that – and that were the last I ever saw of him.' Mrs Brindley swallowed, and Maddy averted her eyes. She could see how difficult this was for the kindly woman.

'Of course, in them days it were a great disgrace to have a child out of wedlock,' Mrs Brindley eventually went on as Maddy kept a watchful eye on the twins. 'So me mam and dad packed me off to an aunt in Manchester till after the baby were born. It were a little girl, and it nearly broke my heart when I had to give her up for adoption. Soon after I got home, my Jim comes round to see me. He knew what had happened but he still loved me and wanted me, can you believe that? So I married him and I ain't never regretted it. But all through the years I couldn't rest for thinking of the little 'un I'd given away, so in the end I set out to try and find her.' Tears were streaming down her face now and Maddy's heart went out to her.

'I knew she'd gone to a couple in Liverpool and eventually I tracked her down, although I didn't approach her. She were happy, see? It was written all over her pretty face. She were at college and doing well, and it suddenly hit me like a ton o' bricks, what it might do to her if I were to introduce myself. Her parents were very well-to-do, and here was me, a kid from a council house. So I came home and I ain't tried to find her since – not that I don't still think about her, o'course. But like I say, some things are best left alone and you have to take your happiness where yer can.

473

And these little 'uns here,' she thumbed towards the twins who were happily playing with their toys, 'have you given them a thought? I know you think you're enough, but do they *really* deserve to grow up not knowing their dad? He loves them – a blind man on a gallopin' donkey could see that. But more importantly, he loves *you* an' all. Don't let your chance of happiness slip away, love. Andy is a lovely bloke but he's only flesh and blood, and one o' these days he might just give up trying to prove how much he cares. How would you feel then, eh? But there, I've said enough and happen you've got some serious thinkin' to do, so I'll leave you to it. Ta-ra, love.'

With that she waddled away, letting a blast of cold air in as she left. Maddy sat there thoughtfully, and as her eyes settled on the bag containing the lovely red dress that Andy had bought her, she smiled. He hadn't taken it back to the shop, after all, and in that moment she knew what she should do. Just as Mrs Brindley had said, she could do nothing about the past. What was done was done – but perhaps it was time to look to the future before it was too late?

Two days later, a letter arrived bearing a Plymouth postmark and Maddy tore it open curiously. She withdrew the sheet of paper and began to read the unfamiliar handwriting.

My dear Maddy, it began, and as she read on, her eyes were soon awash with tears. The letter was from Oliver's mother, Mrs Drewer. It seemed that she had found out about their emails, and when she confronted Oliver, he had told her the truth about his long-lost sister, and had also confessed about the fire, and explained about the sacrifice she had made for him. He had also admitted that they had been keeping in touch for some time. When she had seen how much Maddy still meant to him, his adoptive mother realised how selfish she had been in keeping them apart, and now she was giving her permission for brother and sister to see each other whenever they wished. In fact, she even said how much she would like to meet Maddy herself.

Please tell us when you are next coming to Plymouth and we shall look forward to meeting you. After all, you are family too, Mrs Drewer had finished.

As Maddy sat there, a face swam before her eyes and suddenly she knew what she had to do.

'Come on, littlies,' she told the children. 'We're going on a long train-ride. I want us to be at home in Plymouth when your daddy gets back from work this evening.'

The journey was not an easy one with two young-sters in tow, but nothing could have prevented Maddy from making it now. She had finally rea-lised where she belonged. She left Andy's dogs with Mrs Brindley, promising that she and Andy would be back to fetch them the following week-end. The woman was only too happy to oblige. She was just thankful that Maddy was seeing sense at last.

And so, late in the afternoon, Maddy fumbled under the plant pot beside the front door where Andy had always kept his spare key and sighed with relief when she found it was still there.

The twins were worn out after their exciting train ride, so after making them a warm drink she tucked them into their father's bed for a nap and hurried back downstairs to prepare a meal.

It was almost six o'clock before she heard Andy enter the hallway, and she held her breath as he walked into the lounge. The gas fire was on, the curtains were drawn against the cold evening outside, and everywhere looked cosy and warm.

'Maddy ... this is a surprise,' he said, hardly daring to believe that she was really there. 'You didn't tell me you were coming. Is everything all right?'

'Everything is fine,' she assured him. 'In fact, it couldn't be better.'

'Oh.' He stood there uncertain of what to say as she slowly advanced on him, and then she laughed as she looked up into his handsome face and wrapped her arms tightly around him.

'I was wondering how long it might take before you can make an honest woman of me.'

'What ... you mean you...'

'I mean, Mr Tranter, I want to be your wife. Will you marry me?'

Andy didn't even bother to answer, he was too busy kissing her – but Maddy took that as a yes.

'It now gives me great pleasure to declare that you are husband and wife,' the registrar told them on a snowy Saturday the week before Christmas in the register office in Plymouth. 'Congratulations! You may now kiss the bride.'

Andy laughed as his lips settled on Maddy's and then they both bent down to lift up the twins.

476

'Thank you so much for coming in to be our witnesses,' Andy told Oliver's parents. Maddy had met them twice since coming back to Plymouth and they had made her feel so welcome in their home that Maddy knew they were all going to get along. Funnily enough, they reminded Maddy a little of her natural mother and father in the good old days so she could understand why Oliver loved them so much. Barbara, Andy's mother, was there too, fussing over her grandchildren and beaming like a Cheshire cat.

Now they all shook Andy's hand warmly. 'It was our pleasure – and many congratulations,' they chorused.

Oliver meantime stood there smiling widely, with Zoop furiously wagging his tail at the side of him. He had walked Maddy into the register office and it had been the proudest moment of his life.

Andy was dressed in a smart suit and tie and Maddy looked lovely in the red dress and the gold locket he had bought her for her eighteenth birthday. Mr and Mrs Drewer had very kindly offered to take them all for a meal following the wedding as their treat, but Maddy had politely refused. She had wanted the least amount of fuss possible and they had respected her wishes.

'Well, I think we ought to be getting along now, dears.' Oliver's mother addressed her husband and son tactfully. 'We'll leave the newlyweds to their own devices, but you won't forget to come to us for dinner on Boxing Day, will you?'

'We wouldn't miss it for the world,' the happy couple assured her, and then Maddy hugged

477

Oliver before his parents steered him and Barbara away, and at last she and her handsome husband were alone.

'So, Mrs Tranter,' he grinned, looking for all the world like he had just won the lottery. 'What would you like to do now? Are you sure there isn't somewhere you'd like to go or something you'd like to do?'

Maddy shook her head, her face glowing with happiness. 'No,' she whispered as she glanced down at her shiny new wedding ring. 'I think I'd just like us all to go home.'

Andy smiled at her tenderly and was only too happy to oblige. This was a whole new beginning for them all, and the future looked bright.

The publishers hope that this book has given you enjoyable reading. Large Print Books are especially designed to be as easy to see and hold as possible. If you wish a complete list of our books please ask at your local library or write directly to:

Magna Large Print Books
Magna House, Long Preston,
Skipton, North Yorkshire.
BD23 4ND

This Large Print Book for the partially sighted, who cannot read normal print, is published under the auspices of

THE ULVERSCROFT FOUNDATION